Seen

Seen

By

Julie G. Delegal

LE GLADE

Although this book was inspired by a real story – and informed by all too many similar stories, this is a work of fiction. The characters, incidents, and conversations are products of the author's imagination and are not to be construed as real. Any resemblance to actual persons, living or dead, is entirely coincidental.

Cover credit: Hope McMath
Book design by: Brad Kuhn & Associates, LLC

ISBN-13: 978-0-578-96291-7

www.juliedelegal.com

For my children

SEEN

CONTENTS

SEEN

SEEN

PART ONE

"We may not have chosen the time,
but the time has chosen us."
#goodtrouble

— Representative John Lewis
Twitter
July 11, 2016

SEEN

CHAPTER 1

Skipping Church

Jason Royals smiled the smile of a fifteen-year-old boy who was winning his mother's trust. He didn't divulge every detail of his plan, of course. A man's personal life was a private matter. Mothers, nonetheless, were known for testing boundaries.

"Who is Kim?" she asked.

"You don't know her, Mama. She's just a friend."

"Is that right?" Clarice Royals sipped her coffee.

He'd met Kim only five days before, so "friend" it was—for the moment, anyway. Jason held his breath, fearing his mother would quash the idea. She didn't.

"I imagine Mount Carmel can do without you for one Sunday morning."

He grinned at her, resisting the urge to dance in the proverbial end zone. Permission to skip church was his ticket through the well-guarded gates to adulthood.

Clarice reached over to smooth her older son's shirt collar. "You look nice." Her eyes gleamed as they met his. "Good luck."

For a moment, Jason allowed her approval to wash over him. "Thank you, Mama."

As he headed to the door, she spoke again. "If you need anything, call Dad on his cell phone. I'll remind him to turn it on before he heads to the hardware store."

"Will do." Jason patted his back pocket, checked for his wallet, and reached for the doorknob.

Just as he was stepping through the doorway, she said, "Remember..." He stopped in his tracks.

"Never mind. I'll see you after lunch."

"Yes, ma'am." He took a breath and turned just enough to deliver an actor's smile. "Bye, Mama."

Before she could say anything else, he shut the door behind him.

Finally! Jason spiked his elbows in silent victory.

The air-bounce in his sneakers propelled him toward College Boulevard. Standing straight, pulling his shoulders back, he felt taller. By mid-June, he would be walking in Florida's great, outdoor sauna, but on that last Sunday morning in April, 2001, the mild spring air was perfect.

Get the job, he reasoned, *and I can get a decent bike*. Later—much later, but eventually—he would be able to afford a car.

The thought of having his own car made his step a little lighter, a little quicker. The long running disagreement with his dad, the one about who should purchase said automobile, no longer bothered him. He was one step closer to supporting himself, and he was keeping his "eyes on the prize."

Jason laughed to himself, figuring his father, the history teacher, would disapprove of him using the phrase for anything other than describing the civil rights movement. Alvin Royals had a habit of wearing his teacher "hat" everywhere—in the classroom, at home, out in public.

Jason rolled his eyes. *The man sure can lecture.*

Within minutes, College Boulevard appeared in Jason's sight. The thoroughfare was a concrete strip of fast-food chains, gas stations, and auto-parts stores. The parking lot of each business seemed to join in a vast pavement plain, which broadened into a six-lane swath of asphalt. Though smaller than its northern neighbor, Jacksonville, Beau Rêve was overdeveloped, blighted, and abandoned by businesses sprawling outward to the suburbs.

Too many cars. Not enough trees. No wonder the world is heating up.

Not famous for its foresight in urban planning, Jason's hometown was well known for something else: mispronouncing its own name.

Only an out-of-towner would pronounce it correctly in French, "Boh *Rev*," meaning "lovely dream." For the locals, it was "Boh *Reeve*." The malapropism drove Jason's dad to distraction, sending him into tirades about the French feminine versus the French masculine.

"They're conflating the word for dream with the one for shore," Alvin explained. A native of Louisiana, Alvin took seriously his role as guardian of the French language, but then, he took *everything* seriously.

Jason didn't share his father's concern that their fellow townspeople were destroying "*la plus belle langue du monde,*" the most beautiful language in the world. He pushed away thoughts about global warming and the mostly treeless landscape before him. He focused on his meeting with Kim.

Wellstein's, where she worked, was a mere two-mile walk from home.

❖

"Come by on Sunday," she told him on Tuesday, when he'd popped in at the pharmacy.

He recognized her instantly from the open-air sidewalks of their school. Kim's short, black hair flipped out a little behind her ears, framing her pale, freckled face. *She's pretty cute.*

"Hey, don't you go to Oakwood?" he asked her, smiling behind the question.

"Yeah. You go to Oakwood, too?"

"Yeah. I'm in ninth."

She raised her eyebrows at him, tilting her chin upward. "A freshman, huh?"

"Yeah, but I'm almost sixteen." A blush warmed his cheek. "And I'm looking for a job." Kim was pushing a cartful of boxes to the back of the store. Jason walked alongside her.

As they talked, a speck of refracted light caught Jason's eye. It was a tiny diamond, adorning her left nostril. Mesmerized, Jason's mouth fell slightly open before he knew it was happening.

She smiled at him and his heart pounded. He had never dated any girl before, Black or white, and the fact Kim was white didn't faze him.

Somewhere amidst the thrilling, ten-minute conversation that had passed between them, she'd agreed to walk him through the store sections on Sunday to prep him for an interview.

"Sundays are slow," she said, wheeling the cart to the hair care aisle. "One of the kids who works here is leaving for college this summer. Some art school in Savannah. My manager will want to train someone to take his place."

"So, I have a shot?" Jason grinned at her, cocking his head.

Kim took in the sight of him, blushing. She nodded. "I think you do."

Jason's mouth dropped open again as self-consciousness flushed his face once more.

She laughed softly, and then she stopped the cart to open the cases of hair care products.

He allowed himself to notice the curve of her arm, surreptitiously following the length of it all the way up to her—Jason stopped himself. Shifting his eyes to her face once again, smiling politely, he tried to focus on what she was saying.

"So, what time do you get off on Sunday?" he asked her.

She was lining up boxes of L'Oreal True Brunette. "Why don't you ask me on Sunday?" Kim turned her head just enough for him to see she was smiling.

"Oh, I'll be here Sunday. Any chance we can talk before then?"

"I don't know." She fiddled with the products on the shelf. "Maybe." She turned around to face him.

For a brief, eternal moment, her eyes met his.

CHAPTER 2

Beautiful Sunday

Detective Sergeant John Marshall sat sipping coffee at his girlfriend's kitchen table. His open bathrobe revealed the muscular, long legs of a former wide receiver. He wasn't home to answer his parents' phone call, or to hear them pester him—again—to introduce them to Veronica.

Every Sunday of his adult life, John's mother had called him bright and early to invite him out to lunch.

She'd given up trying to get him to church.

"Don't worry," Veronica had once joked. "I aim to get you back in the habit one of these days, if we ever *legitimize* this thing."

John smiled at the memory of her slip of the tongue. They both knew *she* was more hesitant than he was about the prospects of getting married.

He was happy to give her the time she wanted, given what was happening at work. The best thing about being on the job, by far, was meeting the prosecutor whose coffee cup he held in his hands that morning. He and Veronica had started dating seven months before, after they met at a Labor Day barbeque.

September 4, 2000, he thought. *The first day of the rest of my life.*

At age thirty-three, Detective Sergeant John Marshall was about to finish his tenth year in service to the Beau Rêve Police Department. He figured it was as good a time as any to move out of Homicide.

Running a homicide squad was supposed to have given him a coveted vantage point in the department. Delving into the inner workings of the most complex, challenging aspects of police work would position him for his next upward move in the BRPD.

Little did he know what the view would be from Homicide. He knew he'd see dead bodies; he knew he'd be dealing with murderers. Nothing could have prepared him, however, for the nightmares.

He didn't dream about bad guys. His nightmares were about things left undone. He dreamed of documents, paperwork filled in by a third-grader's cursive—*his* handwriting from years gone by. There were blank spaces on the page, too, presented to him while testifying in court by some faceless defense attorney during a thundering cross-examination.

"Answer the question, Sergeant!" The lawyer's roar never failed to wake him.

Or was the accuser a professor of some sort? John could never quite picture it in the light of morning, the mockery of his work that so terrified him at night.

Some of the old-timers were beginning to talk about how the murder rate was creeping up, how it reminded them of the crack wars of the late 1980s. He didn't want to stay in Homicide—not with another crime wave looming. Since the Pruitt case, he wasn't altogether sure he still wanted to be on the force. John shuddered at the mere thought of Anton Pruitt's name.

◈

"Who started it?"

Newly minted Robbery Detective Sergeant John Marshall had flashed his badge and stared into each middle schooler's face, one by one. A former patrol sergeant, he'd spotted the bus stop brawl on his way to work that morning. The answer he received, from the half-dozen witnesses, was unanimous.

"*I didn't see nothin'.*"

As the yellow bus approached, he managed to get both fighters' names. He promised to revisit them, which he did. Once.

Anton Pruitt had been thirteen years old on the day of the fistfight.

I should have arrested them both, on the spot.

Two years later, Pruitt shot a woman through the driver's side window of her car, in front of her four-year-old child. The gunman hadn't noticed the backseat when he singled out his carjacking victim.

Pruitt then left the car, left the mother and the child, and left his fingerprints all over the door handle.

After apprehending him, it took only an hour for John to trap Pruitt into confessing.

"We have a witness," the detective declared.

Pruitt had stared at John until the detective's meaning dawned on him. "You mean the baby in back? Lord, that boy prob'ly can't even—." Pruitt realized his mistake. His eventual admission, however, hardly amounted to a come-to-Jesus repentance.

"How was I s'posed to know there was a kid in the back?" the killer whined. "That white lady just kept screaming and screaming at me. I just wanted her to stop screaming."

With the help of ballistics, prints, and a confession, Homicide Detective Sergeant John Marshall sent the teenager to adult prison for attempted first-degree murder.

The young mother had needed emergency surgery, weeks of hospitalization, and months of physical therapy—but she lived.

❖

John shook away the memory. Nearly half of his suspects were kids, teenagers who could have been outside playing football or riding bikes or washing cars, like he did when he was young. Instead, they were busy committing violence against other human beings, triggering homicide investigations in cases of death or near death.

On top of all of it, lying to the police came as easily to them as breathing.

Marshall looked up as Veronica, freshly showered and dressed, walked into the kitchen.

"What's wrong?" She read the stress in his eyes.

"Nothing that seeing you doesn't completely erase."

"I'll believe that," she said, hugging him from behind, "when you leave that godforsaken job. I don't know why you stay."

"Sure you do."

"Oh, yes." She sighed, squeezing his shoulders. "I know all about you upstanding Black men and your need to 'give back.' But if you're not careful, John, you're going to give yourself back to an early grave."

"Am I going to get the whole sermon this morning?"

"No, I'll spare you," she said, "just for today—only because I'd like get to Shimmer Springs in time for lunch. It's beautiful outside."

"It's beautiful right here, too." He turned, allowing his eyes to linger as he took in the vision of her. *I am so going to marry this woman*, he thought as he picked up his beeper, kissed Veronica gently on the lips and headed for the shower.

CHAPTER 3

Presentable

As Jason made his way down College Boulevard, thoughts of Kim quickened his pace. He finally got her phone number on Friday when he saw her at Oakwood. He was heading to the cafeteria; she was returning to class from the senior patio.

An older woman. Yeah. A man's got to keep his options open.

Job or no job, he'd definitely be talking to Kim. Meanwhile, connecting with her at the pharmacy made him think of something his father always said.

"It's not *what* you know, it's *who* you know."

Although Jason had heard it all his life, he finally understood it wasn't merely a complaint about the white, "old boy" network. Knowing people like Kim could work for him, too.

Strolling past a stand of trees and then crossing under the overpass, he noticed a church bus careening down the interstate off-ramp. A few blocks ahead on College, Burger King beckoned him.

He debated whether to stop and buy a Coke, ultimately deciding yes. Even though he was dressed to impress, he wouldn't take the time to ask Burger King for a job application.

Kim was waiting.

Jason smiled when he pictured her in her Wellstein's uniform, remembering her navy blue, logo-embellished golf shirt. He dressed, accordingly, in khaki pants and a polo shirt, tucked in, with a belt. "Presentable," his mother called it.

He and his brother had other words for it: "Dad proof."

Their dad liked to enforce his own dress code, both inside and outside of his classroom. He had often walked up to other boys Jason's age—in public—and said, "Young man, your pants are falling down," or "your drawers are showing."

Each time it happened Jason felt his blood run cold. He wished he could disappear whenever his dad embarrassed him in public, but all he could do was turn and walk a few steps away, pretending he hadn't heard what his father said.

Wherever they went—the doctor's office, the mall—Alvin pointed out to his boys the difference between "respectable" people and those he called "the rest." "The rest" were audible from a mile away—kids goofing off in packs like the whole world revolved around them—because, their father surmised, they had too much time on their hands.

"Respect is not a currency that grows on trees, boys. And as young Black men, it will be twice as hard for you to earn it." If their dad had given the speech once, he'd given it a hundred times. "Your thoughts beget your words and actions. Enfranchisement begins in your mind."

Enfranchisement. Jason almost uttered the word aloud as the rhythm of each syllable carried him down College Boulevard: En – fran – chise – ment. En – fran – chise – ment.

Enfranchised was his father's shorthand for a productive, hardworking, law-abiding citizen.

"If you're not enfranchised," Alvin always said, "then you're hanging out in the margins." His sons knew their father had no patience for people who were hanging out in the margins.

Alvin had grown up in a different time: before the resurgence of hip-hop music, before cable TV, before the Internet. He grew up in a time when people fantasized about the year 2000—but he was slow to embrace the brand-new century accompanying it. While Alvin still bought his music in stores, Joey Sullivan next door was careening into the Age of the Internet, using Napster to download whatever music he and his friends wanted to hear. Alvin warned the boys he thought the practice of burning music onto compact discs was illegal, but they paid him no heed. The man still read the newspaper, in print, every morning, and only two years before, in 1999, he began carrying a cell phone. He rarely remembered to turn it on.

Jason borrowed his dad's cell phone sometimes, but what he really wanted was to get one of his own, on his own, so he wouldn't have to account for minutes spent.

Cell! (Two, three, four.) Phone! (Two, three, four.) Jason marched to the cadence in his head. His pace slowed when a flash of movement caught his eye.

A block ahead, in front of the Burger King, a great egret was traversing the ditch. Its spindly, black legs stepped gingerly across the dry culvert.

Mama would love you. You're a beauty.

Puzzled, Jason stopped and looked around, wondering where the nearest pond or creek might be—where the fisher-bird might have come from. He spotted the patch of woods, blocks behind him, near the interstate. *Maybe there*, he reasoned.

Looking at the bird again, he said, "You won't find any fish here."

The egret paused and eyed Jason, as if it had heard and understood him. Unfolding its giant wings, it launched into flight. Two long, white flags undulated against the sapphire sky.

Shading his eyes as he looked up, Jason watched the egret fade out of sight.

You are my beloved...

Jason tried to remember the words his mother always said when she caught sight of a glorious winged creature. He would ask her later.

Eyes on the prize, man. He reminded himself as he walked. *Eyes! (Two, three, four.) Prize! (Two, three, four.) Eyes! (Two, three, four.) Prize! (Two, three, four).*

CHAPTER 4

Vacation Station

Morning callously reminded Gerald Patterson that morning was not what it used to be. The trip to the coffeemaker was, by far, the creakiest journey of the day. Coffee promised to lubricate the joints and ignite the brain cells. Sadly, the miniature brew machine in the motel bathroom looked like something from a child's kitchen playset.

The words "El Dorado Colombian Gold" were printed on the rather small filter packet. He and Betty would stop for breakfast— and for decent coffee—on the way down to their daughter's house in Fort Lauderdale.

Gerald looked back at his wife, who was still asleep in the king-sized bed. She'd had a terrible night—tossing and turning with every groan of the air-conditioning unit. The room was dank, so they opted to keep the thermostat low, even though the April heat was far from intolerable. They certainly couldn't open the windows there at night. Gerald didn't realize the full extent of the motel's seediness until after he'd checked in. By that time, they were too tired to look for another one.

"It's for one night," she'd said.

As impatient as he was to leave, he decided to let Betty sleep late while he showered. He would rest well enough when they finally got to Emily's.

Betty hated to be rushed when they were traveling, but Gerald was her opposite. He couldn't help but want to *arrive* already. He disliked the idea of forking over good money to any place merely on the way to his destination. Saturday night, they ended their drive in a rundown area of Beau Rêve, a mid-sized Florida city with a population about equal to that of the state capital, Tallahassee. They checked into the Vacation Station Inn, the motel closest to the interstate.

I should have skipped the car wash, he thought. *We'd have made it as far down as Daytona, if I had.*

Gerald trusted the band director and the boosters to run things back home in Georgia, but he genuinely loved being around his students. He relished every opportunity to show them how proud he was of them.

They're good kids.

He looked down at the residue on the bathroom floor, which only a dirty mop could bestow. Fifteen years as a school principal had taught him the difference between good janitorial work and bad.

He closed the bathroom door and turned on the shower as the tiny coffeemaker began its gurgle.

CHAPTER 5

Sirens

Jason heard the siren before he saw the police car up ahead, rounding the corner from Broward Highway onto College Boulevard. He had never seen one tear down the road quite so fast. He followed the flashing lights with his eyes and then rotated his body around to face I-95. The car turned near the interstate overpass, which he had walked under several minutes earlier. He couldn't tell exactly where the squad car pulled in. It might have been the auto parts store or the Vacation Station Inn.

A robbery? he thought. *Is the auto parts store even open today?*

He drained the rest of his Coke, ditched it into Burger King's outdoor trash can, and picked up the pace, walking fast toward Wellstein's Pharmacy. Two more police cars screamed past him. Walking briskly, he caught the eye of one of the drivers. In the next instant, Jason noticed the traffic light at Broward Highway had changed.

He broke stride and jogged across the northbound lane to the median, stopped to check for cars, and then picked up his pace to beat the southbound traffic and get across Broward.

He heard yet another police siren whiz by.

Man, something really bad must have happened.

Jason pivoted to look. To his surprise and puzzlement, he saw the same police officer he had glimpsed a moment prior, turning his cruiser around. Not only was he heading in the opposite direction from everyone else, he was heading toward Jason, pointing at him, directing him to the parking lot of the adult entertainment establishment on the corner.

Jason stopped and pointed to himself as if to say, "Who, me?"

The officer nodded and jerked his pointer finger toward the parking lot. "Yeah, you," he mouthed as plain as day.

Jason stood with his hands out by his sides as the policeman approached him. He was curious as to why he was being stopped. He figured he'd be asked whether he saw or heard anything back where the first police car turned. His parents had always taught him that if the police ever stopped him, he was to be as courteous and polite as possible: *"Always keep your hands in sight,"* he remembered, *"and answer 'yes sir' or 'no sir' when you're spoken to. And if you ever get arrested, it's 'I would like to call my parents, please, sir.'"*

His parents taught him something else, too, something Jason forgot when he crossed Broward Highway. *"Don't run."*

"Where're *you* runnin' to?" the policeman demanded loudly, exiting his car and walking toward Jason.

Jason froze. The way the officer said "you"—as if he hated him, or as if he were mistaking him for someone *else* whom he hated—set off a warning through every cell in Jason's body.

He was an officer with a homegrown accent, his skin a sunburned pink, his cheeks puffy under his eyes. The blond hair on his skin curled over his muscular forearms, which were also pink.

Careful, he thinks I am someone else, Jason thought, mouth frozen shut. The seconds that passed seemed like hours before the impatient officer roared his question again.

"Where in the hell have you been this morning?"

"I—I—Officer," Jason stammered. He took a breath. "I've just been walking, sir. I'm walking. I've got a few more blocks to the uh, to Wellstein's pharmacy." Jason tried hard to sound calm, pointing toward the drugstore.

"You're out walking on a Sunday morning to Wellstein's pharmacy," the officer said. "I don't suppose, then, you have any idea what happened back there?" He spoke with the same disgust and hatred Jason had detected before. As he spoke, the officer thumbed back to where all those police cars had turned, toward the scene of the serious crime.

Jason knew he'd better cooperate, better figure out what the policeman wanted and help as much as he could. "Back over there by the Vacation Station Inn?" he offered.

The officer's eyes narrowed as they homed in on Jason. "What do you know about the Vacation Station Inn?" he asked—but he didn't wait for an answer. "You're coming with me." He reached for the handcuffs on his belt.

Jason's heart pounded. Reflexively, he took a side step as if to run. The policeman lunged onto him, undercutting Jason's footing with a swift kick to his shins. Jason was on the ground, facing down. The sharp weight of a knee on his back forced the air out of his lungs.

I can't breathe. He gasped for oxygen, trying to get the words out. "I can't breathe!" he sputtered. The knee relented. The shock did not.

For some reason, the officer was arresting *him*, twisting *his* arms back, and clamping metal onto *his* wrists. An electrical current coursed through Jason's biceps and shoulders. He focused on the unnatural position of his arms and wrists, turning them within their shackles to find relief, but the cuffs did not yield.

The world seemed to tilt and whirl as cars whizzed by on Broward Highway.

This can't be happening. I'm not...this can't...

In a clichéd scene he had seen a thousand times before on television, Jason was center stage. He retreated to numbness. A surreal, otherworldly sensation fogged his mind as if he were witnessing the experience happening to someone else.

The policeman's hands slapped and grabbed up and down Jason's body while he was face down on the ground, tasting the dirt on the pavement.

He thinks I have a weapon? Me?

The officer frisked him underneath his hips, between his legs, and down his legs to his shoes.

"Get up, damn it." The officer grabbed a fistful of Jason's shirt collar as he might have grabbed a disobedient dog. He slapped both sides of Jason's chest from behind him, finishing the pat down before dragging him to his patrol car.

Dazed, Jason felt pressure on the top of his head as the uniformed man forced him onto the back seat. The officer, breathless, chanted the Miranda warning like a child reciting his times tables.

"This is a mistake," Jason said, gathering his breath. "I didn't do anything. Why are you doing this to me?" His voice pitched upward, insistent. "I don't know *anything* about what happened down there. I'm just trying to get a job. Why are you doing this?"

The door slammed shut, caging him in.

The officer, breathing hard from their tussle and the Miranda liturgy, snorted as he got into the driver's seat. "I don't know *anything*," he mimicked. Venomously, he added, "Well, if you don't know *anything*, then you don't mind coming down there and clearing everything up for us, do you?"

A flood of terror iced through Jason's veins. Shaking, he could hear the blood pulsating in his temples.

Get me out of here. How do I get out of here?

Jason looked at the cage barrier in front of him and then at the car doors. There were no door handles on the inside!

Jason grunted in frustration, digging his heels onto the floorboards. *I'm trapped.*

Pain reverberated through his shin where he'd been kicked, throbbing up through his knee, which had hit the pavement hard when the policeman took him down. Jason sucked air through his teeth as his mind registered his injuries. He'd been too stunned to feel it as it was happening.

A visceral groan erupted as his entire body exhaled. *Sweet Jesus.*

Jason did not speak to the officer—he did not waste his breath. He breathed through his excruciation, trying to re-govern his body. His eyes focused on a blond-haired arm, filling out forms on a clipboard.

After what seemed an eternity, the man barked. "Name?"

Jason stared forward.

"Look here now," the officer admonished, "you can give me your name and date of birth and address now, or we can sit here 'til you do."

Jason complied. He figured he would be out of the car soon enough, at the motel—assuming that's where the officer was taking him.

There will be other cops there. One of them will have a brain and will see that I'm no criminal. Jason remembered the stories his father told about being stopped by police, while standing outdoors eating a hotdog, while shopping at Dillard's, and for "driving while Black."

This must be what they call "running while Black."

He noticed his shirt had come un-tucked in the scuffle with the officer. When he made a motion to try to tuck it back in, the hard metal of the handcuffs caught and stifled his wrists. He held his breath, held his anger at the sharp pain of it, and then exhaled. He slid his feet forward and rested his head back onto the seat, trying to believe everything would be all right—once he was in the presence of other people. Then he looked down and noticed how dirty both knees of his pants had become when they had hit the asphalt.

Is that blood?

Jason stiffened, and then, defeated, he sighed. He was no longer passing as presentable.

CHAPTER 6

The Messenger

From the crime scene in room seven of the Vacation Station Inn, Detective Sergeant John Marshall sighed as he looked at the packed luggage on the dresser. Just a few more minutes, and the tourists would have been gone. The wife would still be alive, and Marshall would be on a day trip with Veronica instead of working a homicide. His beeper had sounded, skidding across Veronica's kitchen counter, just as she was packing the car with sandwiches and thermoses.

Closing his eyes for a moment, Marshall steeled himself for the work before him.

He retrieved the murder victim's cell phone and, removing the paper covers from his shoes, brought it with him when he exited the motel room to interview the victim's husband.

The man was still in shock.

Marshall had understood from the motel manager that Mr. Patterson was in the process of checking out when it happened, and that the couple had been traveling to see their daughter downstate. After piecing together the sequence of events, Marshall could see the husband was in no shape to make the call.

"Is Emily your daughter?" Marshall held up the cell phone, displaying the last call. Mr. Patterson stared at the tiny screen and then shifted his face into a question.

"Emily," Marshall said, pointing to the phone. "Is Emily your daughter's name?" he asked.

The man nodded.

Marshall nodded back. He pulled the paper shoes from his pocket, opting to go back into the motel room to make the call. As the medical examiner wrote notes on her clipboard, Marshall dialed the daughter's number on his own cell and delivered the unspeakable news, as gently as he could but with no ambivalence—no room for question.

"I'm afraid, Emily, your mother, Elizabeth, has been shot. She did not survive it. She was killed, Emily, I'm so sorry."

This is one part of the job I will not miss, he thought. *The disbelief. The cries of grief.*

Emily Patterson was as inconsolable as her father. Marshall spoke to the son-in-law, who promised he'd drive Emily to Beau Rêve immediately.

Marshall wondered how many more death notices he'd have to give, how many more families, how many more visits, before he could get out of Homicide. Usually, Marshall would go along with Chaplain Ray to deliver the news to the victim's loved ones. Normally, Ray was the one who spoke the words. *This happened. Your mother/father/brother/sister didn't survive it. Your loved one is gone. I'm so sorry.*

Marshall hated the phone calls most of all. They were easier on the messenger, to be sure, but he couldn't imagine having to hear the news of a loved one's death over the telephone. He snapped his phone shut and put it in his pocket.

"Nine-millimeter," the medical examiner said, closing the door and drawing Marshall's attention to an evidence marker. It lay next to a bullet casing the ME found slightly under the perimeter of the mattress.

"She was shot from point blank range," she added, looking up and down at Marshall. "Pretty close to where you're standing."

CHAPTER 7

The Faint

Gerald Patterson sat in the back of a police cruiser, his hands trembling. Trembling with them was the plastic cup an officer had filled with water for him.

The policeman touched Gerald's shoulder, taking the drink from him. He told him it would be just a few more minutes at the scene. They were waiting for the police chaplain.

"You'll go with the chaplain once he arrives," the young officer told him. "You and your wife's possessions will stay here for now. They'll be brought to you later."

Gerald had heard the litany three or four times, and he'd overheard that another policeman had caught a suspect running away from the motel.

"I have to contact my daughter," he thought aloud for the fourth time, as he rose from the back seat of the squad car. A young officer kept telling him to wait just a few more minutes.

"Your daughter is on her way, remember?" The officer reminded Gerald.

The chaplain was on the way, Gerald heard once again. The chaplain would keep "the victim's husband" comfortable until his daughter and son-in-law arrived.

The victim. The woman he had been married to for twenty-seven years, the woman whose patience and kindness had guided him through his entire adult life—his gentle and precious wife—was reduced to being called *the victim.* Betty was no more.

Gerald was dazed. He wanted to go fetch the overnight bag out of the room, to continue what he started before he had left Betty alone. If only he hadn't been so impatient, if only he had waited in the room with her while she called Emily and then checked out with her instead of leaving her alone—she might still be alive.

Regret and self-hatred welled in him—welled in his eyes—as he walked an ellipse between the police cruiser and the motel room where Betty's body lay. She was surrounded by detectives and evidence people—all strangers. He wanted to complete the action he had begun, to check out, get his wife, and leave. He started toward the room again.

"Mr. Patterson," the young officer said. He grasped Gerald's upper arm, leading him back to the open door at the back of the squad car.

The young officer was no older than his son-in-law and merely a few years older than the kids at the high school where he was principal. He recognized the officer was a good kid. His parents had taught him well. The young man was trying to be helpful in the most god-awful, most horrific of situations.

Gerald could not absorb it.

The young officer and the other two at the scene turned their bodies to the street and watched as a fourth cruiser rounded into the motel parking lot and glided past them. They turned in unison as the car pulled into the spot, a few spaces down from the cruiser Gerald had been sitting in.

"Stay right here with me, sir." The young policeman held Gerald's elbow. They were facing the room where Betty's life had ended. The medical examiner had pushed the door closed, sparing Gerald any more views of his murdered wife.

A stocky, slightly sunburned policeman paraded past the motel door, guiding a disheveled, handcuffed, teenage boy.

Gerald took in the scene of the teenager who was being steered past him in handcuffs. His heart sank, and his eyes began to well again. It had happened so fast, when he heard the gunshot and saw a Black man in tan pants running toward the back of the motel. When he'd first spotted him, Gerald would not have guessed the suspect was the same age as his students. He knew kids that age, had taught kids that age. He began to turn, to walk in a circle again, but the earth gave way underneath his feet. He sank into the strong, young officer whose kind voice he heard once again.

"I gotcha, I gotcha." The officer pulled him up, inadvertently ripping Gerald's shirtsleeve, which had caught on the open car door when the older man fell. The young officer helped Gerald back into the car.

"I think we've got our man," Gerald heard another officer shout from the vicinity of the car to the cluster of officers. Someone had witnessed his collapse upon seeing the boy they caught running from the scene.

"Your *man?*" Gerald muttered, sighing and shaking his head, with incredulity. "He's a *child*. How could this child have murdered my Betty?"

CHAPTER 8

"Catch Anything?

"Yo, O'Donnell, did you catch anything?" another blond officer shouted as the arresting officer pushed Jason through the halls of the Beau Rêve Police Department.

Jason stiffened, hot with indignation, until he realized the two policemen were talking about fish.

"Nothing that meant anything at the weigh-in," O'Donnell replied, "but we pulled in some beautiful reds."

"It ain't all about the weigh-in," said the other officer, pausing.

"Nope, true that." O'Donnell stopped walking, holding Jason in front of him. "But I do love to win."

Two other officers walked up behind them. Jason, turning his head, recognized them as having been at the motel where O'Donnell took him, where the older white man fainted when he passed by him.

"What have we got here?" O'Donnell's fisherman friend grew curious about the small crowd beginning to form around Jason. It was apparent something sizable was underway.

"Gunshot homicide," O'Donnell said.

The word "homicide," uttered aloud, hit Jason like a kick to the back of his legs. His knees began to give way, but instead of taking a fall, his body decided to run.

O'Donnell lunged at him. He grabbed Jason's cuffed hands. He yanked him back hard, undermining Jason's balance. When he released his grasp, Jason stumbled backward into the other officers, who shoved him upward and off. Jason teetered but did not fall.

O'Donnell took hold of the cuffs. "I suggest you don't try that again." The officer repositioned his prisoner in front of him.

Jason felt the eyes of three uniformed officers boring into his back.

The motion of people walking in the halls of the police department had come to a complete stop. Movement resumed once again, as if in calliope cadence.

Jason's heart was pounding and he was sweating, feeling dizzy. He realized, as O'Donnell and his pack turned him past dozens of staring eyes, that he would not be able to find his way out of the building even if he could break away again. The halls were a maze of artless, off-white tableaus, with mottled brown carpet delineating the blandness.

And he knew he shouldn't have had the Coke—he was paying for it. How many times had his mother warned him about his blood sugar: what goes up must come down. The walls and floor were rocking a little.

When are these people going to let me sit down? When do I get to talk to a sane person who can see I didn't do this thing? I need to call my mom.

They entered a large office with polo-shirted men talking on telephones, and a woman, also on a phone, seated near the door. O'Donnell steered him over to a chair six desks away from the door.

"Sit here," he commanded, motioning with a swift jerk of his arm to one of the uniforms to guard Jason.

Yes, you. Jason remembered O'Donnell mouthing the words from his patrol car with the same authoritative point of the arm. *Meet me right over there, right now.*

If only I had pretended not to see, Jason thought. *If only I had just kept running. If only I hadn't turned to look to see where the sirens were going.*

A cop like O'Donnell, Jason realized, might have chased him down anyway.

O'Donnell joined the huddle of uniformed and plainclothes policemen, some sitting on desks, some standing, a few desks away. The huddle of white men bloomed open like a flower, petals loosening, as another, vaguely familiar man entered the room. He and Jason were the only African-Americans there.

Where do I know him from? Jason wondered from his chair.

Ah yes, Jason remembered. He was the car dealer's son. The dealership's owner was a rich businessman—a legend in Beau Rêve. He remembered the television commercials with the son clasping the football—*Catch YOUR best deal at Marshall Motors!* The detective had been a wide receiver for the Florida Gators. He and his dad were both famous in Beau Rêve.

Looks like he's assigned to this case, Jason deduced, excited. *He's got to see this is a mistake; he'll be the one who realizes I'm no criminal.*

Jason tried to stay calm as his heartbeat quickened in his chest. He watched the former Gator talking to O'Donnell at length. Finally, appearing exasperated, O'Donnell extended his arms in the air as if to say, "He's all yours now."

O'Donnell shoved some papers at Marshall and motioned to the other uniforms that they were done. The uniforms jumped at the signal to leave. The whole scene reminded Jason of a football coach disagreeing with a referee.

Here comes the referee, thought Jason, as Detective Sergeant John Marshall approached him.

CHAPTER 9

The Handshake

"Jason Royals?" Marshall asked.

Jason jumped up, nearly falling back onto the chair. He shuffled his feet just in time to compensate for his handcuffed lack of balance. Embarrassment flooded his face.

"Yes sir," Jason replied, forcing himself to look up at the man in front of him. He felt his face flush again. The metal on his wrists clamped against his urge to shake the famous John Marshall's hand.

"Sit back down, Mr. Royals. I'm going to need a minute before we get started."

Jason sat.

Marshall looked at him. "Did Officer O'Donnell read you your rights, Mr. Royals?"

Jason sighed and looked away. Perhaps no one in the building would be interested in knowing that he was no criminal. He held his tongue. There was no time for mistakes. He remembered hearing O'Donnell tell him his rights as he was being pushed into the squad car.

"Yes sir," he replied to the question, "but I didn't do anything, sir, and I would like to make a phone call."

"You'll get your phone call, son," Marshall said, "when I'm good and ready for you to have it." He shifted his attention to the shorter, white man walking toward him. "Detective Pershing, would you mind taking Mr. Royals here to the interrogation room and keeping him there until I get back?"

Detective Pershing opened the door to a small room with a verbal, "Yes sir." He told Jason to have a seat and stood outside of the room, pulling the door almost shut to talk to Marshall.

"Here, give him my cell phone." Marshall handed it to Pershing. "Chances are this kid doesn't know any attorneys, and none worth his salt is going to come over here on a Sunday. We'll have him back out to the scene before any lawyer can get here anyway. Let's get Herman in here to check for gunpowder residue first—would have been nice if O'Donnell had at least bagged his hands for us." The detective sighed and continued.

"I'm also going to need you to get his shoes. Got it?" he asked Pershing.

"Call, GSR, shoes—I got it."

"Hey, have a look at that knee, too, if you don't mind. Offer him a Band-Aid if he needs it."

"Call, GSR, shoes and Band-Aid. Okay."

"Oh, and Pershing," Marshall said. "Don't stay in there alone with him for long unless you have a secondary with you, understand? I'm going to take care of the kid's constitutional right to eat lunch."

CHAPTER 10

Leaving Church

Clarice Royals hung up the phone in the church's dining hall, shaking her head in frustration. No one was answering at home and, of course, Alvin had his cell phone turned off. She should have thought to give Alvin's phone to Jason so she could touch base with him.

Alvin was not much for church. He always took the opportunity, when the subject came up, to tell Clarice that church was part of the problem when it came to young people, instead of being a solution.

"Our young men are already disillusioned enough, suspicious of the system, suspicious of the middle class," he'd rant. "How do we honestly expect them to embrace such a literal approach to the Bible?"

Clarice smiled at the thought of her husband's academic approach to life. Her older son was beginning to pick up the habit, too. Jason was becoming as analytical as his father.

She shook away her worried-mother thoughts and told herself Jason was fine, and that he had safely arrived at the pharmacy. She imagined his day going as planned.

Her younger son, Lucas, and her parents were waiting for her. "No answer," she told them. "I'll borrow Mack's phone at the restaurant." She was referring to her brother, Clarence, Jr., who earned the nickname playing defensive tackle for Westside High School in Beau Rêve. Getting stopped by him, players said, was like being run over by a Mack truck. Although decades had passed since he'd played football, the name had stuck, and Mack liked it.

It was getting close to lunchtime. Clarice figured Jason should be arriving back at the house soon.

CHAPTER 11

"You Play Ball, Son?"

Marshall returned to the interrogation room where Jason sat. He brought the young suspect a pair of rain boots, a can of Coke, and a chicken salad sandwich from the vending machine in the cafeteria.

He traded the items for his cell phone and Jason's shoes. Pershing and Marshall stepped out, hovering around the interrogation-room door while Jason ate. Pershing told him the kid had tried at least two numbers but had been unable to reach anyone on the phone.

Marshall knew that whomever the kid called wouldn't be able to identify the number on his police-issue cell phone. He hit the redial button and got a voice mail message for "Mack."

"Who the hell's Mack?" he asked, shutting the interrogation-room door from the outside, with Jason inside.

"Probably some gangbanger," Pershing said. "Any kid who gets mixed up enough to shoot a tourist at a motel is probably not going to want to call his mama."

Marshall nodded, wincing and shaking his head. There was something about the kid that got under Marshall's skin. To look at him, you wouldn't figure him for a banger, with his hemmed-up pants and his off-brand sneakers. How was it, he wondered, that boys who looked as clean-cut as Jason Royals believed they had so little to lose?

Has it gotten that bad? *Surely, this kid had better things to do with his time.*

Marshall pushed those thoughts out of his mind and concentrated on the task at hand: getting a confession.

"Here's what we've got so far, Pershing. One, the kid was caught running from the scene, matching the description. Two, he tried to run again when O'Donnell arrested him. Three, the victim's husband passed out cold when he saw Royals at the scene again—even though O'Donnell shouldn't have taken him by there—and four, Royals tried to run yet again here at the station, in front of God and a half-a-dozen cops."

"So, you think the victim ID is going to get thrown out?" Pershing asked.

"No, I don't *think* it'll get thrown out, I *know* it will," Marshall said. "The defense will have a field day with it. O'Donnell should have had more sense. He should have just brought him in for a lineup. The man has no impulse control."

"You suppose he takes steroids? He always looks flushed to me."

"I don't know. Seems he's got more adrenaline than judgment." Marshall sighed. "As many times as this kid has tried to run, he's our shooter all right. But now we're going to have to find the gun, or get his confession. Or both."

He opened the door and followed Pershing into the room where Jason was sitting. The kid had taken a couple of bites from the very unappetizing sandwich.

"Taste good?" Marshall asked.

"Yes, thank you," Jason replied, but his face said otherwise. He pushed the sandwich away. "I'm not hungry right now." Jason gulped down the rest of the Coke and held the can in his free hand, looking around for the trashcan.

"I'll take that," Pershing said, walking out of the room with it. Jason could hear the opening and slamming of desk drawers in the large outer office.

"Who's 'Mack,' Jason?" asked Marshall.

Jason's eyes widened, and then Marshall brandished his cell phone.

"You mean who I called on your phone? My uncle. Uncle Mack."

Marshall nodded, waiting for the boy to say more.

"His real name is Clarence. We call him Mack because that's what they called him back when he played football for the Westside Eagles. Because he hits like a Mack truck. He played about six or eight years before you got to Florida, sir. But he never played any college ball."

Marshall's eyes widened. *The kid follows football from way back. Knows who I am. Has an uncle who played ball.*

"You play any ball yourself, son?" Marshall doubted such a skinny kid would ever go out for "that particular American obsession," as Veronica had phrased it.

Jason blushed and looked down. "No sir. I don't play football. Just YMCA basketball—used to, anyway." His face brightened, "But I do watch college games and I keep up with the SEC and all. And I follow some of the pro players from Florida like Emmitt Smith. Didn't you play a couple of games with him your first year at Florida?"

Marshall smiled when he thought about the Gator who made it big. *Emmitt Smith, indeed. This kid is unbelievable*, thought Marshall. *He's chatting up the homicide detective. Emmitt freakin' Smith—doesn't that beat all?*

Well, no one ever said lawbreakers were dumb. He knew that some of the deadliest were very smart—so smart they figured they could get away with whatever they wanted to do, because they believed they would not be caught. He figured half the country watched college football. In the past, he'd arrested perps who had recognized him from his dad's commercials, too.

"Mr. Royals, you are obviously not stupid. And, as you no doubt realize, we are not here to talk about football. You know why you're here. Right?"

"Because you think I shot that lady at the motel, but I did not shoot her."

Marshall froze. His decade of police experience led him to expect a Black suspect to say, "that white lady," but Royals did not. Royals had been taught, much like Marshall himself, not to refer to individuals by their race in conversation. It was a subtle thing, but there it was.

How did a kid like Jason Royals get mixed up with gang members? Marshall wondered. *And how does he know the victim is female?*

"What makes you think the victim was a woman?" Marshall asked.

Jason shrugged. "I guess the officer who brought me in told me." *I can't tell if this kid is lying.*

Marshall tried a different angle. "What school do you go to?"

"Oakwood," Jason replied, sitting taller in his chair. He covered his mouth and leaned over the table. He lowered his hand only to bring it up to his mouth again.

Marshall took it as a sign of stress, and pressed forward. "Oakwood. Off of College Boulevard."

A gang known as the College Lifers claimed the territory near Oakwood. Their name didn't have anything to do with college *life*. The word "lifers" was used in the sense of people sentenced to prison for life. Marshall still bristled at the irony of the gang name, but less and less each time he heard it.

"What do you know about the College Lifers there, Jason?"

"College Lifers? I don't know what you're talking about, sir."

For a brief second, Marshall couldn't tell whether Jason was being truthful, or whether he was being a smartass. As he sat at the table, turning his cell phone over in his hand, calmly, coolly flipping it open and closed again, he thought about Anton Pruitt. Something about Royals reminded him of Pruitt.

Marshall tilted up his chin in disbelief. He decided Royals was adept at being a smartass.

Pershing re-entered the room and tapped on his wristwatch for Marshall's benefit.

"Are you going to eat any more of that?" Pershing asked Jason.

Jason shook his head. "I'd like to use the phone again." He cleared his throat as his voice cracked. "Please?"

The boy swayed a little in his seat.

Marshall liked what he saw. The kid was nervous, and he was pleading with him.

CHAPTER 12

Chicken Salad, Revisited

Jason looked at the phone in Detective Sergeant Marshall's hand. Maybe his mom would be home from church, finally. Or maybe his dad would be home. He knew his dad would forget to check his cell phone.

The disgusting sandwich had made him queasy, and his stomach upset was made worse by Marshall's question about football. It was a sore spot for Jason.

Lucas got those genes. I'm built like a scholar, like Dad, he thought, recalling how his family made a joke of it.

Gulping the Coke after the bites of sandwich, which he thought would help, had only made things worse. He was having a hard time telling whether he was hungry, nauseous, or anxious. "Breathe," his mother used to tell him when he felt sick to his stomach.

Stay calm, he told himself. *You know you're innocent. They will, too.*

Jason believed he'd be able to clear up the misunderstanding because he hadn't done anything wrong. Apparently, though, everyone at the police station seemed to believe he was the shooter. The day was going sideways, and he didn't want to try to convince the police on his own anymore.

He asked again. "Can I please use the phone now?"

"Tell you what, Jason," Marshall said, leaning back in his chair, stretching his long legs in front of him. "You don't really want to burden your mama with the fact that you are down here on charges of murder right now, am I right?"

Jason froze, feeling the blood going cold in his veins. The mention of his mother in the same sentence as "murder" caught him off guard. The room began to tilt a little. *Oh, God.*

"I think," Marshall continued, "you want to get this straightened out before you call her, don't you?"

The room teetered into a full spin. Jason grasped the edge of the table with his un-cuffed hand for balance, but his movement sharpened the whirl of the walls around him. He could no longer stop the violent propulsion welling up in his gut.

Jason vomited forcefully onto the table in front of him, his torso unfurling.

"Jesus," shouted Pershing, jumping up and going for the door, barking instructions to the secretary to call the janitor.

"Bring me some paper towels!" Pershing yelled, holding his wet, bare forearm in the air.

Marshall stood in stunned silence, backing away from the table. Tiny, whitish, regurgitated chunks littered rivulets of diluted Coke. He set a trashcan near Jason's chair, close enough to him for his un-manacled hand to grab, and then he backed away again, staring.

Jason sat still and tried to calm the terror shaking every cell in his body. He focused on not vomiting again, casting his eyes downward. As his stomach churned, he repressed the urge: Once. Twice. Three times. The physical impulse became a distant echo in his body, shrinking and shrinking until it was gone.

"Son, you're going to have to get cleaned up before you use my phone again." Marshall dabbed a finger at his own cheek, and then he pointed to Jason's face.

Jason kept his eyes downcast as Marshall passed him a paper towel. "Let's get you and Detective Pershing here cleaned up. We're going to take a ride."

Jason looked up, panicked.

"I'll let you use the phone in the car on the way back to the scene." Marshall's voice was reassuring. "You're also going to need to take off those socks before you put our boots on," Marshall said, pointing out the vomit, which had dribbled from the table onto one of Jason's socks. Marshall retrieved the galoshes from nearby the interrogation room door.

Jason pulled off his socks with his free hand and slid on the black rubber boots, which were at least two sizes too big. He sat still as a blond-haired lady in a janitor's uniform cleaned up the table around him.

Pershing emerged from the adjoining bathroom drying his hands. He rolled his shirtsleeves down and buttoned them before detaching Jason from the table. He held Jason's cuffed hand at eye level as he led the suspect to the sink in the bathroom.

"I'm going to stand in here with you until you do what you need to do; clean yourself up," the detective said. "Don't even think about trying to run again. You know Florida's a fleeing felon state, and if you try to run, any of us would be within the law in shooting you."

Jason winced, and his shoulders dropped. "But I'm not a felon." His voice, scared and quivering, broke on the word "felon."

Pershing shook his head and released Jason's hand. "But you have been warned," he said, remaining in the doorway to the bathroom. Pershing nodded towards the sink, prompting Jason to wash. The empty handcuff clanked on the porcelain, jarring Jason.

I'm in a bathroom in a police station with detectives who think I shot somebody. No one even knows where I am.

Jason pushed away his fear, replacing it with the belief that he'd soon be on the phone to his mother. *She can get me a lawyer,* he thought, *in case I can't straighten this out myself.* Jason dried his face and hands, dried the wet metal handcuff, and held his hands up in a question to Detective Pershing, who cuffed them in front of him.

"We need you to be able to walk around. But remember my warning."

Jason began to say something, paused, and started again.

"Do I need a lawyer, sir?" he asked Pershing.

"Oh yes, by all means, please call one," Pershing scoffed. "That way we can throw your ass in jail for murder and call it a day. It would sure as hell make my life easier. But, for some strange reason, my sergeant's giving you a chance to help yourself out. You get a lawyer involved and the time for explaining is done, you understand me? You want a lawyer? You tell me."

"No sir," Jason replied.

I am not going to go to jail for something I did not do, he thought. Take me to the scene and I will find a way to prove it. You have the wrong guy.

The Ride

Marshall and Pershing believed they were dealing with a new initiate. Any self-respecting gang member with any experience would have lawyered up and would already be sitting in lockup.

"May I please use the phone now?" Jason asked Sergeant Marshall from the back seat of the unmarked police car.

"As soon as you tell us what went down at the Vacation Station Inn." It was Pershing's voice from the front driver's seat. Sergeant Marshall was documenting something on a clipboard as Pershing took Bethune Bridge across the St. Johns River.

"I told you I wasn't there," Jason whined, surprising himself. *Getting upset is not going to help me,* he thought, looking out the passenger's side window. This was the gleaming, steel bridge his dad always took on their Saturday morning trips back home from the downtown library.

Jason's dad had always pointed out the huge trees billowing like clouds on their driving descents from the top of Beau Rêve's highest bridge—leafy green treetops pierced by church steeples. Alvin always said he felt like he was landing an airplane as they approached the opposite shore. As they made their descent, his little brother was more interested in the baseball field rising up below them, on the grounds of the Catholic high school campus.

"It looks like a *model* or something from way up here. It looks like it's not even real!" Lucas would exclaim each time, as if for the first time.

Since the new, main library had been built downtown, the boys made a habit of going along more often. Jason would take Lucas to the cove-like, retro-decorated children's section, while his dad checked out books and CDs and videos for his classes. His dad's students liked movies. Sometimes he'd check one out for him and Lucas, too. And sometimes they found bargain movie-cassette videos at Wellstein's.

Jason suddenly remembered how he had started the day—walking to the drug store. He never planned to be stuck in the back seat of a detective cruiser, trying to explain his innocence.

Damn. I guess Kim's given up on me by now. At that moment, Jason thought of something.

"Hey," he said. "Sergeant Detective Mar—"

"Detective Sergeant. What?" Marshall tilted his head but did not turn around.

"I had told Officer—what's his name, the blond one, kind of hyperactive?"

"O'Donnell." Marshall and Pershing both answered at the same time, and then they looked at each other.

Jason saw the exchanged glance and registered that maybe Marshall didn't like the arresting officer. It might explain the near altercation Jason witnessed in the squad room.

"Anyway," Jason continued, "I had told Officer O'Donnell that I was walking to the Wellstein's Pharmacy to talk to a girl who works there about a job. I figure you can call her, and we can get this straightened out, and then you can let me go and go find the real guy who shot that lady."

"Are you telling me, Mr. Royals, you had a job interview today—on a Sunday morning?" Marshall asked.

"I'm telling you I was going to *talk* to her about *getting* a job there."

But the Sergeant had not caught his meaning. Marshall turned around and frowned quizzically at Jason.

"It was to practice for the real job interview," he continued. "Go ahead and call Wellstein's. My friend Kim will tell you what's what." In truth, Jason and Kim were not well acquainted, but *friend* it was. "You've got the wrong guy, Sergeant."

Pershing couldn't help himself. "You've got the wrong guy, Sergeant," he mimicked, in a fake southern accent. "I think you're gonna wanna give that Kim girl a call, there, Sarge."

"Besides calling your friend, Kim, at Weinstein's—" Marshall began.

"*Well*stein's," Jason interjected, correcting him.

"Wellstein's, okay, besides calling Wellstein's, was there anything else you wanted to tell us that you haven't told us already, Mr. Royals?"

"Yeah, actually," Jason continued without missing a beat, "you can check the trash can in front of the Burger King for a Coke cup with my fingerprints on it. I'll even give you my fingerprints to prove I was in the BK while that lady got shot," he offered respectfully.

The two policemen exchanged glances again. Marshall raised his eyebrows at Pershing before speaking.

"Jason, you can give us your fingerprints just as soon as you show us where you put the gun."

They still think I did this! Jason thought. *Unbelievable.*

"I don't know where any gun is."

"Yes, you do, Jason. You're the one who decided to come with us to the scene," Marshall said.

"I only came with you because *he* was going to put me in jail," Jason said, pointing at Pershing.

"You made a decision to cooperate instead of waiting on a lawyer, right?" Marshall turned around to look Jason in the eye.

Jason froze, speechless.

Marshall shook his head and turned back around.

As if someone had flipped a switch in his mind, Jason remembered the promise about being able to use Marshall's phone. "Can I at least call my mom?"

Marshall reached for his phone. Hesitating, he said, "Well. Look at that. My phone's dead, son." He made a show of plugging it into the car charger, adding before Jason could object, "I'm sorry about that."

CHAPTER 14

Sunday Brunch

There's nothing like brunch with the family to make you forget whatever it was you were worried about in the first place, Clarice thought.

Her family had always been partial to Shoney's and IHOP. Those places were tidy, polished, and brightly lit. They were also staffed by waiters and waitresses of all skin shades.

"Equal opportunity grease," Alvin had once quipped, on a rare occasion when he'd accompanied her.

Smiling, Clarice watched her brother dredge every last drop of pancake syrup from his plate. "Mack, will you let me use your phone?" She asked him. "Jason was going to walk to Wellstein's Pharmacy to see a girl about a job."

Mack laughed through his pancakes. "A girl?" he said, covering his mouth with his hand. "About a job?"

"Yeah." Clarice chuckled. "You remember being fifteen?"

She turned on Mack's phone, dialed home, and got no answer. Knowing the chances were slim that her husband would answer his cell phone, she dialed the number anyway. *Oh, Alvin, turn on your phone.*

Clarice's father bickered with her brother over whose turn it was to pay for Sunday brunch. After Mack lost the volley to pick up the tab, he put cash on the table for a tip. Clarice put her hand over his.

"No one's answering my calls. Oh, and Mack, it looks like you might have missed a call earlier—but the number is blocked." She handed him his phone.

"I am sure Jason's fine, Clarice," Mack said, ignoring the missed call. "You want me to run down to the store—Wellstein's—and check it out for you?"

"Yes," she told her brother, "but take me with you."

Brenda, her sister-in-law, agreed to take Lucas home to play with Cam.

"Yay!" the boys exclaimed in unison.

Margin People

"Detective," Marshall said to Pershing, "do me a favor and pull into the next convenience store so I can get something to settle this kid's stomach. We don't need him getting sick again." Marshall pointed to a Li'l Stop store.

"Um, Sergeant Detective?" Jason asked.

"Detective Sergeant," Marshall reminded him.

"Detective Sergeant. Okay. Well, if you do go in someplace, would you please get me a Diet Coke instead of a Coke?" Jason asked. "I'll pay you back. When you give me my wallet back."

As Pershing made the U-turn to get to the store, Marshall turned around. His eyes betrayed concern. "You diabetic?" he asked.

Jason shook his head. "No, sir. But sometimes I have problems with my blood sugar. I can't take any more real sugar after all my stomach's been through today."

"Diet it is, then," Marshall replied. "Pershing, you want coffee?" Pershing nodded.

They were in a low-rent section of Broward Highway—too much asphalt with trash strewn around, and too many adults appearing too unoccupied. Three greasy, flannel-shirted white men and one dirty-haired white woman in a tight t-shirt were smoking cigarettes in a huddle in front of the store. They recognized the unmarked Chevy Lumina for what it was, a police vehicle, and immediately fanned out when they saw Marshall get out of it.

"We ain't doin' nothin'," their body language announced to the plainclothes policeman.

Hangin' out in the margins, thought Jason. He peered at the scene from the back of the cruiser. *Margin people.*

Marshall disappeared into a store with windows that were papered with ads from the inside and barred in iron on the outside. A few minutes later, he emerged with bags hooked over his wrist, hot coffee in one hand, and sixteen ounces of Diet Coke in the other. After handing off the coffee and the Diet Coke, he pulled out a bottled water for himself, along with packs of potato chips, peanuts, and peanut butter crackers.

"Tell me what you want to eat, Jason."

Jason settled on the peanut butter crackers.

"Get something with some protein," his mom would always tell him. "To help steady your sugar levels."

CHAPTER 16

Looking for Jason

"Why don't you let me go in, Clarice?" Mack asked her as they pulled into the parking lot at Wellstein's. "It could be a complete coincidence that I was coming in to pick up allergy medicine for Cam. It would be less embarrassing for Jason, anyway."

She nodded. "I'll wait right here in the car."

Mack disappeared into the store for a few minutes before emerging with a shrug, motioning Clarice to come inside. She jumped out of the car to join him.

"The girl at the counter says she hasn't seen Jason all day," he said.

Clarice walked to the checkout counter to speak to her. "Kim," her nametag read. Clarice put on a calm, composed smile and introduced herself as Jason's mother. Trying not to lead on that she was worried, she asked, "Jason did not make his meeting with you this morning?"

"No ma'am," Kim replied. "I figured he must have had something come up because he seemed really interested in the job when he stopped by last week."

"And you haven't seen him or heard from him at all?" Clarice asked.

"No ma'am."

CHAPTER 17

Into the Woods

After cruising around the motel where the murder occurred, and after circling and re-circling several surrounding parking lots, Detective Pershing pulled up to the only stand of woods within a three-mile radius of the Vacation Station Inn. The wooded area was just south of College Boulevard, abutting the interstate.

As Sergeant Marshall helped Jason out of the back, Pershing remained in the driver's seat and signaled to his superior to wait with the suspect at the woods' edge. "Burger King," Pershing mouthed to Marshall.

Attaboy, Marshall thought. *He'll call in the information about the outdoor trashcan.* Marshall knew the man had his quirks but respected Pershing's job skills. They thought alike, most of the time.

Marshall reasoned if they had the right guy, then gunpowder residue could be sitting on a cup, which, in turn, could be sitting in a trash can. Suspects had a knack for telling partial truths: "I was at Burger King and not at the motel." Those half-truths were, in many instances, crucial to unlocking new evidence. Marshall's work was made harder—but not impossible—by careless cops like O'Donnell.

Marshall made a mental note to get back to the ETs about the residue test they'd done in the interrogation room. At least Pershing had acted quickly to print the Coke can once the kid was finished. O'Donnell could take a few lessons from the likes of Marshall's partner.

Back at the unmarked car, Pershing learned the evidence technicians had searched eleven dumpsters at and around the Vacation Station Inn, and at adjacent businesses on both sides of the busy thoroughfare. Though the ETs were expanding their search, so far, they'd found no gun, and they'd found no wallet with the victim's identifiers.

"You're looking for blood, hair, any DNA from the victim or our suspect." Pershing told the ET over the phone. "You're looking for the victim's wallet—Betty Patterson's. And there might be gunpowder residue on a cup, along with our suspect's fingerprints. We now have those prints entered for processing. Verify with the Burger King staff when the receptacles out front were last emptied— you may have to go through several bags. And you can talk to them about whether they saw the suspect. You might want to take the bags downtown."

◈

Jason was rocking slightly in the too-large rubber boots, trying to get his footing in the pine straw. Marshall braced him with one huge, strong hand to Jason's elbow.

This kid is such a lightweight.

Marshall gazed up and down at the boy, wondering if he was dizzy. He'd learned from the best how to extract confessions and gather evidence from murder suspects—without violating their constitutional rights.

"You can trick the hell out of 'em," an old homicide veteran had told him once, "as long as you don't starve 'em, beat 'em, or forget to Mirandize them." Marshall realized it was easier to get his suspect some crackers than to deal with some overexcited, underpaid public defender making life miserable because he says "you knew" he had low blood glucose.

"How's your sugar, Jason?" he asked.

"I'm okay now. I get a little hypoglycemic. I don't have diabetes but my mom keeps testing my blood sugar, anyway, because my Grandma's going blind from it. Runs in my family."

Marshall nodded, as Pershing slammed the car door and hustled to catch up with them in the pine trees.

CHAPTER 18

Trapped in the Woods

Jason stepped carefully through the pine straw, limbs, and litter as the detectives guided him into the woods.

"Let's see if you can help us find the gun, Jason," Marshall said.

"If I were you, I'd be checking dumpsters first," said Jason.

"Is that right?" Marshall shot a look over his shoulder to Detective Pershing. "Did you hear that? He says we ought to be checking dumpsters first."

"I'll bet he does, now, doesn't he?" Pershing replied, catching up to Jason and Marshall. "Something tells me it's in here, though. And it has your fingerprints all over it, Mr. Royals."

"Not gonna happen," answered Jason. At that moment, he stepped with his oversized boots into a soft spot in the underbrush and teetered forward. Hands cuffed at his waist in front of him, Jason lifted his arms and fought for his balance. Suddenly, Sergeant Marshall struck him in the gut, knocking the air out of him. The Sergeant's other hand grasped his upper arm, forcefully.

"Sorry, Jason," Marshall said.

But Jason was not sure what had just happened.

As he recovered his balance and his wind, he wondered whether Marshall had been trying to keep him from falling, or whether the punch in the gut was intentional. The three had stopped walking.

"Y'alright?" asked Pershing.

"Yeah." Jason worked to catch his breath, trying not to show the pain as he straightened and stood. Marshall's hand remained clasped tight on Jason's arm.

Pershing walked ahead, grabbing a long stick, from which he broke off the smaller twigs. He poked the ground with it as he proceeded through the branches and brush a few yards ahead of his partner and Jason. Pausing for them to catch up, Pershing pushed back a thin woody branch at head level as he walked, releasing it into Jason's face.

"Ow! My eye!" Jason screamed. His cuffed hands flew up to his face, as his body dropped into a squat.

Marshall let go his grasp.

Pressing his hands against his cheek and closed eye, Jason exhaled. As he opened his eye, he was relieved to find he could see. The branch had scraped only his face. Shaken, Jason was beginning to doubt the mishaps were accidental.

The two men stopped. Pulling Jason up, they tried to get a look at his eye.

"Looks alright to me. Grazed his cheek. He can still see to find that gun for us," Marshall said, gripping Jason's upper arm again.

Reality seized Jason.

I am alone in the forest with two cops who don't seem interested in the fact that I'm innocent.

No one else was near. Turning his head, he could no longer see the road where they parked.

His face still stung, and he could still feel the force of Marshall's swift arm to his gut. He was completely at the mercy of the two policemen.

If they decide to hurt me, no one else will see it; no one else will know. Jason tried not to let on that he was scared. "I don't know anything about any gun."

"But, Jason, you promised us some fingerprints." Pershing's baby-talk tone oozed sarcasm.

Jason shook his head, fighting angry tears. He steeled himself, channeling his fear into a façade of stony indifference. His body stiffened and, as he stared into the woods in front of him, his heart pounded.

Marshall tightened his squeeze on Jason's arm as they trudged farther away from the car.

Pershing asked, "Which way, Jason?" Receiving no reply, he added, "We can stay out here all day, son."

Oh, God.

Jason's body reacted before his brain could. He pulled away from Marshall's grasp, twisting with his whole body to escape it.

Marshall clamped harder into Jason's biceps and triceps, struggling to pull him upwards as Jason continued to try to pry himself loose.

"Give me a break!" Marshall sneered, releasing his grip on Jason's arm with a push—enough to send him crashing into the brush.

Marshall bent down, hand extended.

Jason flinched and turned away, covering his head. Curled in a ball on the ground, he was a near-spherical armadillo, but without the armor.

"Oh, please," Pershing whined. "Ain't no one gonna beat nobody here, son. But you do need to remember what we talked about back in the bathroom. About felons who run."

Jason, heart pounding, clenched his jaw and said nothing. He stared at the ground, not moving to get up.

"Where do you think you are, son? Fucking Vermont?" Pershing berated him. "You know how many people Florida sends to death row in any given year? You know how many of 'em are Black? You should—"

"Pershing." Marshall interrupted his partner's rant.

"It's a fact. It ain't racist to state a fact. More Blacks go to death row—"

"Yeah, okay." Marshall stopped him again, hands held up in concession to his partner. "Mr. Royals can read up on the death penalty on his own time. Now let's get back to what we came here for. Finding that gun."

"As long as he understands this is his chance to avoid a needle in his—"

"Pershing." Marshall was brusque. He extended his hand down to Jason again, who took it, albeit reluctantly, as the ex-football star pulled him to his feet.

Jason stayed quiet, following their lead through the woods, for what seemed like hours, until they gave up on him finding the gun. He stepped slowly, alert to uneven ground, ducking at eye-level branches. He cringed when he felt Marshall's huge, warm hand at his elbow, but he did not pull away again. He steeled his body, removing his mind to a place slightly above himself. He felt as if he were witness to a dream, watching a bizarre series of events: a young man being led through the forest by two policemen.

One had a strong grasp of his elbow; both of them wore guns.

Do not try to run.

CHAPTER 19

The Game Room

Clarice and Mack headed toward the strip mall near Jason's neighborhood. The Steer House Restaurant's game room was a popular destination for Jason and Lucas when they were with the Sullivan boys. Mack cruised the street leading back behind the interstate, where a largish, late-model, American-made car was parked in the grass strip next to the woods—a Chevy Lumina.

"Cop car," Mack quipped.

"How can you tell?" Clarice was doubtful.

"I can tell."

Clarice squinted back at the car once they'd passed it.

A minute later, they pulled into the parking lot at the Steer House strip mall. Both exited the car wordlessly, quickly. Their eyes, adjusting to the relative darkness inside, cased the restaurant and landed on the "Games" sign over a doorway in the back. They charged toward it.

A cacophony of bells filled the air as young teenagers played on, oblivious to the adults who had entered their cramped space. Immediately, Clarice and Mack saw that Jason was not among the kids who were there. Clarice walked the length of the room, as if Jason might be hiding between *Crazy Taxi* and *Galaga*. He wasn't.

Mack saw the worry plaguing his sister's face. "I'll check the bathroom," he said. "You stay here."

Clarice clenched her jaw and nodded. She spoke with the gamers in the dim room, who, while barely taking their eyes off their screens, told her they had not seen the boy she described.

Bring him back, Lord, she prayed, *so I can beat him senseless for going off like this without telling anyone where he went.*

Clarice and her brother left the tiny room and began to canvas the restaurant. They talked to the waiters and waitresses and the people at the front counter. Clarice insisted on going back to the car to get her purse so she could show them a picture of Jason. It was to no avail. No one had seen him.

"Alvin, he's not here." Clarice tried not to cry over the phone. "Mack is going door to door here at the strip mall. We're just going to look a little bit more. Then I'll come on home. I am going to wring his everlovin' neck when I see him," she growled.

"Not if I wring it first," he quipped.

"Lord, Alvin. He's got to be okay. Right?"

"Yes. It's going to be all right, Clarice. He must have gotten carried away with something and he's forgotten to call us."

"It's not like him, though. If we haven't heard from him by the time I get home, I think we should call the police."

CHAPTER 20

The Body Never Lies

Detective Sergeant John Marshall consulted his watch. The afternoon hours were drifting by, and their young suspect's endurance was waning. The emotional strain began to creep into the boy's face.

Unbelievable, Marshall thought, as he sat once again looking at Jason across the interrogation table. *Found running from the scene. Matching description and everything. Tried to run, three times now. Did he honestly think he'd actually get away with it?*

He shook his head.

He held out longer than some, I'll give him that.

Marshall saw the telltale signs of softening, of malleability. *Time is definitely on my side*, Jason Royals.

Slow and easy. You're almost there.

They were all tired—he, his partner, and the kid. Marshall sat silent, unmoving, as he watched the young suspect begin the transformation he'd witnessed a hundred times in his career.

Marshall and Pershing had been through it together before—with dozens of suspects. Patience, they had both learned, was a detective's best friend. They recognized the signs: How the suspects would give way, ever so slightly in their shoulders; how their faces would begin to draw downward in an unspoken yielding; a concession.

"You've got me," the body would say to them. And, in their experience, the body never lied.

We've got him. Marshall saw the worry as it crept into Jason's eyes. He read terror, followed by a silent plea for mercy. Jason's eyes beseeched his, and then his partner's.

Marshall could tell the suspect was looking for a way out. The eyes always ask.

Marshall believed Jason Royals, like many before him, was finally on the inevitable path to confessing. Marshall read the unuttered queries. *He's wondering if he can trust us, hoping we'll throw him a rope.*

Marshall did what he always did when one of his perpetrators began to relent. He slowed his own breathing and tried to slow his pulse.

Pershing and Marshall had learned to control the little adrenaline surge that came with knowing their suspect was preparing to spill his guts.

These are the moments that make me live for this job, he realized. The negativity with which he had begun his day and the doubts about his career were gone.

It all leads up to this. Lord Jesus, help me not screw it up.

With a flick of his hand, he motioned to Pershing, as he had done at least a dozen times before. Pershing rose to fulfill his partner's silent orders. He retrieved a pen, some paper, and the Miranda waiver form.

The detectives saw that their suspect had his head down. Jason looked defeated.

When Pershing came back in, Marshall broke the silence with a soft, fatherly voice.

"Jason, I know this is hard for you. You've made some mistakes today. Some pretty bad ones. But, son, if you don't come clean right now, you are going to have to answer for this by lethal injection. And then…" Marshall paused to gauge the effect of his lie before he finished his sentence. "And then…you won't have the chance for forgiveness."

CHAPTER 21

The Voice of God

Jason lifted his head as Marshall spoke. The room began to rock. He braced his arms and put his head down again, feeling chilled as his damp, sweaty forearms caught the room's air-conditioning. Sweat burned the scrape on his cheek, under his eye.

His wrists were sore, his skin tender from bruises, barely visible in the dim light. He was not connected to the table, but his hands were still cuffed in front of him.

A fog of confusion swirled around him. He remembered having been in the same room before, but he couldn't remember the details of leaving or coming back. *Was I in the woods?* he wondered. *Or did I dream the whole thing?*

Jason closed his eyes and breathed. He drifted off and yielded to his strange dream, perplexed by the turn it had taken.

Thoughts of protest arose in him, distant echoes. He could feel his feet sweating in boots that did not belong to him. *Where are my shoes again?* The dream kept cycling back to the interrogation room. He felt Marshall's big, warm hand on his arm. *Uncle Mack*, he dreamed, *Uncle Mack, thank God you're here.*

Marshall pulled his chair closer to Jason, speaking softly to him, turning his body to exclude Pershing.

"The lady you shot is a white woman from backwoods Georgia, Jason," the detective said. "You know what those kinds of people will want to do to a Black man, Jason, you know. I want you to search your conscience, Jason; I want you to think for a while, concentrate hard about what you are going to say to me. I want you to pray, and I am here to help you."

Jason's heart pounded. An electric panic coursed through his chest and arms. *This is my dream,* his mind said to him, *this is my life. Life is but a dream,* he drifted. *God gives us dreams, God grants us our prayers. Let us pray.*

His mother's voice whispered in the distance. *Hail Mary, mother of God,* he heard, or said, or dreamed. He had heard the beginning of the prayer so many times on TV; he wished he knew the rest of it—wished he were a Catholic instead of AME. Dreams were so strange, but it was his dream, he was in charge. He saw his mother's face. *Mama, you're here!*

Pray Jason, wherever you are, whatever you need to do, baby, you just stop and pray. God is always with you. He heard his mother's voice speaking to him, as she had done a thousand times before. It was more than a memory, it was her voice. Jason prayed. Amidst the strangest and scariest and most terrifyingly real nightmare he had ever had, he prayed.

He tilted as another voice pulled at him, it was the deep voice of Uncle Mack again, whose hand he felt on his arm, but Uncle Mack looked like a policeman.

"Jason, think of your mama and daddy," the policeman said to him, "and what you will put them through if you go to trial."

Jason groaned. *Had the policeman heard his mom, too? Oh God, what was he supposed to do? God help me. God help me.* Jason squeezed his eyes shut. *Please, Jesus, help me now.*

"*Greater love hath no man than this: that a man lay down his life for his friends.*"

The voice was as real as his mother's. What it said braced him, jolted him. Jason had prayed, and a phrase he had heard a thousand times before came to him as his answer.

That can't be right. He felt his heart beating harder. He felt the hand of the detective who was sometimes Uncle Mack.

"Think about your mama and daddy," the policeman-as-Uncle-Mack said. "You can spare them a lot of heartache, son."

Why is Uncle Mack working with the police?

Jason could not believe what was happening to him. The policeman was there in the room with his mother. His mother had told him to pray, and the answer had come. Clear as a bell was the voice in the room with him. It repeated:

Greater love hath no man than this: that a man lay down his life for his friends.

His father had always said God was a metaphor. But it was his mother he trusted. It was his mother he always looked to, even though he didn't understand why she believed so strongly. He closed his eyes again and saw her face. *God is always with you,* she promised him. *I would not tell you these things if they were not true,* she said. He'd heard those words his whole life. At last, he knew it was true in a way he could not have imagined before.

Mama?

When he prayed the Hail Mary, his mother's face had come into focus. When he prayed to Jesus, the words had come. His mother, Jason realized, was *literally* blessed among all women; and he knew who *he* was, too, and what he must do. The word was life. With certainty, he felt exactly what the phrase really meant. *He* was the word.

I have to hand over my life to these people who have asked me for it. To spare my mama and daddy. God is real. I know that now with all my heart and all my mind. And He has spoken. To me.

Could he do it? Could he confess to a murder? A momentary burst of adrenaline shot through his body—*I cannot do this,* he thought. He felt a deep heavy pull in his marrow—pure fear, pure panic—drawing him downwards.

The words he had heard a thousand times before struck him and echoed in his blood like flashes of electrical current: *Why have you forsaken me?*

Please don't make me do it, he silently begged his God, tears running down his cheeks.

It is written, came the answer, stored somewhere inside of him, yet speaking in the room with him.

But why me? he silently asked.

You, too, shall see the glory of God, was the answer.

It was all there—everything his mother had ever taught him about God, every word in the Bible—it was coming to life for him at that moment. It's real. *This is real, and now I know what I must do.*

Jason's tears burst forth. He could not control the torrent of confused joy and grief culminating inside of him. He understood everything. There in the interrogation room, the entire world had become crystal clear.

He was the Chosen One, and one day everyone would know. But he had to get through the hard part first. He gasped at the memory-thought of the pain of the cross, a pain heaving at his arms and making him feel weak. He lifted his eyes to the man sitting at the table with him, beseeching him for instructions as to the next thing his sacrifice entailed. He was ready.

"It is going to be all right," said the man who was Uncle Mack, and yet was not Uncle Mack. Jason sobbed once more, and then he sat up, staring at Marshall, helpless.

CHAPTER 22

On the Way "Home"

The cold vinyl of the squad car's back seat jolted Jason. He was less confused, a bit more alert, than when he'd been at the police station. The officer in the driver's seat was someone he hadn't seen before, an older white man.

I guess he's the one who's going to drive me home.

Trembling and hungry, Jason was thankful his Uncle Mack and his mom had somehow worked everything out with the police.

Why didn't one of them take me home when they were at the station? Oh, yeah, the paperwork. I had a lot to finish up with Marshall. That must have been it.

He felt as if he were awakening, slowly, from a bad dream—he couldn't remember the details. He knew only that the situation had somehow been resolved, and he felt a sense of relief.

Marshall was true to his word. I knew they'd figure out I wasn't their guy. I could feel it.

"Thank you for the ride home, sir," Jason said sheepishly. He felt weak as he feebly resisted his body's urge to relax into the seat. Although he was sweating, Jason felt a little chilled, too.

The silver-haired head tilted upwards in front of him, glancing into the rearview mirror. The older man's eyes momentarily met his prisoner's.

Jason was a tremulous, little bird floating on a sea of blue vinyl. The vulnerable child in the back seat was irreconcilable with the heinous crime for which he had been arrested. The car veered unconsciously to the left, tires thumping the reflectors on the centerline.

They both felt a sudden swerve as the officer righted the vehicle.

"Son," the officer began, not unkindly, glancing into the mirror again, "you do know," he said slowly, "you're not going home tonight?"

"But Detective Sergeant Marshall said—"

"You've confessed to murder," the officer interjected. "You're going to the juvenile detention facility. And they may move you later to the adult jail, depending on the state attorney."

"But the detectives told me," Jason started to say, squirming, feeling the sharp pull of metal on his wrists–again. He gasped audibly.

Oh my God! They still have handcuffs on me! What the fuck did I say? What have I done?

Jason jerked and twitched in vain, trying to wriggle out of the handcuffs. Thrusting himself sideways on the seat, he kicked at the car door. He braced his feet against the door as he tried to pull his cuffed hands, which were behind him, under his rump and underneath his legs. He yelped as his extended, twisted arms strained painfully. He cried out again as metal assaulted skin and bone.

"I think I've pulled my arm out of joint," he yelled to the officer. "Oh fuck, man," he sobbed, wet and sloppy. "I am innocent. Please don't lock me up. Please. Please."

Jason's loud sobs turned to coughs. He began to wretch. His body tried to vomit with all its might, but there was nothing left in his stomach. He lay on the back seat, sobbing, shivering, dry heaving, and gagging.

"Sit up, son," the officer said firmly. "Sit up!" he shouted. The officer pulled the car over and looked over his shoulder to see Jason shaking, as if he were having a seizure. He jumped out of the vehicle and ran around to the back-passenger's side, flinging the door open.

He felt Jason's neck for a pulse. A definite throb met his fingers and the officer exhaled.

"Do you have epilepsy?" the alarmed officer shouted excitedly, but Jason could not respond. The shivering stopped, and the officer watched Jason's eyes roll upward into his head. He felt for a pulse again. The boy had lost consciousness, but he was still alive.

"You better hold on for me, son," the officer said to the child in his back seat. "Don't do this to me today, you hear me? You hold on for your mama, kid. You hold on, you got it? You hold on."

The officer stepped swiftly to his trunk, grabbed a blanket, and tucked it over and around Jason's recumbent body. He clasped the boy's shoulders from the open car door and told his young, still unconscious prisoner—one more time—that he was to hold on.

He pushed Jason's head clear of the car door, shut it, and got back into the driver's seat. He flipped on his lights and sirens.

CHAPTER 23

A Child's Handwriting

John Marshall was sitting at his desk, shuffling a stack of reports. He was straightening them for the file folder when he experienced a strange sense of déjà vu. For a moment, he was breathless. The piece of paper at the top of the stack sent him reeling into his recurring nightmare.

He looked down at the page.

A child's handwritten scrawl. He recalled the dream memory. *But there's no scrawl here. There are only my handwritten sentences, with Jason Royals' initials, at every line.*

Marshall felt a strange electricity run through his being—from chest to toe and up again, outwards through every appendage.

I am not going to let this freak me out. If anything, the dream made me more cautious. I got him to sign each line just like they taught us. This one is by the book.

As he closed the folder and stood up, a secretary from another division entered the squad room. He'd met her but couldn't remember her name.

"Hi, Detective Sergeant," the young woman began, after nodding and smiling at his secretary, Lucy. "My division chief told me to walk this down to you. The suspect you arrested for murder today may also be a missing person."

Marshall looked at her, stunned. He looked over the file she brought and sat back down with it.

"He's been booked and is on his way to juvenile detention," the detective said. "What do you need from me?"

"You just told me what I needed," the girl replied. "My chief didn't want us to contact his parents until you were finished with him. Lucy told me a couple of hours ago y'all had him here."

"You knew he was missing two hours ago?" Marshall began, raising his voice as he rose to his feet again. "And you knew I had him? And you and Lucy didn't bother to tell me?" He was yelling—to the shock of the half-dozen people in the room. Lucy stiffened in her seat, with her back to him.

"Y'all either need to stop talking to each other or make sure you get the info up both chains of command, you understand?" Marshall was, to everyone's surprise, yelling at the women.

"Yes, sir," Lucy replied, quietly. She had turned to face him but couldn't make eye contact. The other, younger secretary stood mute, still near his desk.

"How's it going to look," his yell became an escalated whine, "when this kid's mom tells the media he was 'missing' and we had him all along and didn't tell them?" The room remained motionless. "Do you understand how serious this is?" The question demanded an answer. The younger secretary—whatever her name was—began to cry.

"Oh, Jesus," Marshall said, more quietly, still aggravated. He rubbed his temples with both hands, eyes closed.

"I'm sorry," he said in a calmer voice. "I shouldn't have yelled." The room thawed, ever so slightly, as a bit of activity resumed.

"I need a minute to think, okay?" He looked at the wet-faced young woman, motioning for her to sit in the vacant chair next to him, as he sat down again at his desk. "Please stop crying. I'm sorry."

She nodded, eyes downcast, as she sat. Raising her eyes again, she saw he was still looking at her. She smiled through wet eyes and nodded again. "Okay," she whispered.

The division chief should have told me, instead of wimping out and sending this poor girl down here. But just because this boy's mom is missing him doesn't mean the kid wasn't involved in a gang initiation. It doesn't mean he's not guilty of murder.

Marshall opened the other file folder and looked at the suspect's initials, duplicated at the end of each line of the detective's own handwriting.

"Okay, so I'm assuming you shared the information from Lucy with your boss, right?" he said.

The young woman nodded.

"It appears Lucy has not yet had the opportunity to share it with me, because I've been a little bit tied up. So, you are catching me a little off guard here. I apologize for losing my temper—you didn't deserve that."

"It's okay," she said. "I understand."

"What I need now," Marshall said slowly, looking her straight in the eye, "is for you to please go back and ask your sergeant to come in here so we can sort this out."

She nodded once, stood up, and did as he asked. As Marshall watched her walk out, he heard his call numbers on the radio, signaling him. He pulled the radio from his belt and responded, telling the officer to go ahead.

What now? He thought, as he listened to the signal numbers. *Suspect en route to St. Mary's Hospital. Unconscious person. Guard personnel requested for prisoner at the hospital.*

Unconscious? Being transported to the hospital? My suspect? What the hell happened?

"Lucy!" he roared. "Get St. Mary's on the phone. Now! The suspect passed out on the way to detention. He's got a history of hypoglycemia and they need to know that."

"He has what?"

"Hypoglycemia," Marshall pronounced the word slowly. "It's low blood sugar. He's not diabetic—he's the opposite."

"Yes, sir," she replied, flipping through her Rolodex. It was a number Homicide used often. "What's the kid's name again?" Lucy asked.

"Jason Royals."

CHAPTER 24

"Take Me to My Child"

"Thanks for bringing the boys over here, Brenda," Clarice said. "There's no way I could wait around in this house alone."

"I wouldn't be anywhere else."

Hours had passed since Clarice had called missing persons. Still in her church clothes, she paced the terrazzo floor in her kitchen.

"I'm not even sure the girl was paying attention," Clarice told her sister-in-law. "I spelled everything for her, Jason's name, our address, so I can only assume she was writing it down."

"It's routine for the police department," Brenda answered, "but it's anything but routine for us when we're missing someone. They forget how people feel, honey. I'm sure she wrote it down. She wasn't a very sensitive person. That's all."

Clarice nodded, still pacing. "I wish Alvin or Mack would check in."

"You know they're covering every inch between here and Wellstein's. Every backstreet, Clarice. Even the Nude Delhi." Brenda headed to the fridge and pulled out some sandwich meat.

"Jason had better not be in any gentlemen's club if he knows what's good for him."

"Well, if he's there, Mack and Alvin will pull him out," Brenda said, retrieving the mustard and mayo. "Sit down, honey. Let me get you something to eat."

"I can't eat." Clarice continued to pace, head down. All at once, she stopped and looked up. "Did you hear that?" She was frantic.

"Hear what? I didn't hear anything."

"Sounded like a car door slamming." Clarice ran out of the kitchen, toward the front door. She opened it at the precise moment the doorbell chimed.

"Ding dong!" Cam cried out as he skipped from the back of the house, Lucas trailing behind him. "It's the doorbell, Auntie Clarice!"

A man in a suit was standing on the front stoop. Brenda steered the boys back to Lucas's room.

The man introduced himself as Detective Philip Wesley from the police department's missing person's division. He asked for "Mrs. Royals."

"Finally!" Clarice opened the door and motioned for him to come inside. "We called you hours ago. Did you—" Clarice studied the man's face. "Have you found our son?"

"Could we sit down please?" Wesley asked.

"Why? He's not—" Clarice's voice pitched with fear.

"No, ma'am. No, ma'am. He's alive, ma'am."

"Let's sit down, Clarice," Brenda said.

Detective Wesley gazed around the room before sitting with them, taking in the furnishings. The vestiges of Easter—figurines of brightly colored bunnies bearing eggs—sat on the mantelpiece next to framed photographs of the family.

"He's alive," the detective repeated. "But he's been arrested."

"What?" the two women exclaimed at once.

"Jason?" Brenda continued. "There is no way Jason is in trouble. No way. What on earth could you have possibly—"

"Mrs. Royals. Mrs…?"

"Porter. I'm Jason's aunt."

"Mrs. Porter, Mrs. Royals, Jason was stopped in connection with a homicide scene this morning. He matched the assailant's description."

Clarice shot up, fire in her eyes. "My son was not involved with any *homicide*! He was going to see about a job. You tell me where you have him. *Right now!*"

"Ma'am," the detective replied, standing up to address her, "you need to understand. He's confessed."

Stunned, Clarice turned away. Her knees began to buckle. Wesley helped guide her, gently, back to the sofa.

"I need to tell you," he said quietly, as he helped her settle herself, "your son has been booked for murder and is on his way to juvenile detention as we speak. If the prosecutor decides to try him as an adult, he could be transferred to the county jail as early as tomorrow. I'm very sorry to have to tell you this."

Clarice, indignant, straightened her skirt and brushed off her elbow where the detective had touched her. Wesley backed away.

"Where is juvenile detention?" she asked without looking at him.

"I'm sorry," Wesley said, looking at his cell phone. "I have to get this." He walked toward the front door. The two women stood up again and heard him say, "You've got to be kidding me—I'm with his mother now."

"What?" Clarice demanded. "What has happened to my son?"

"Mrs. Royals, he's at the emergency room at St. Mary's," Wesley said. "He's had some sort of…collapse."

"Collapse? What in God's name have you done to my child?" she roared.

"Ma'am, I told you all—"

"Clarice, let's just go down there, right now. I'll drive you," Brenda offered. "Call Alvin and we'll go. Cam and Lucas can stay with me in the waiting room while you go in to see him."

"Ladies, he will be under police watch at the hospital," Wesley said. "He's still in our custody."

The two women stared at him, exasperated.

"Let me see what I can do about getting you in to see him," he added. "I can wait in the car until you're ready and you can follow me down there."

"Brenda, I'll drive myself—I really don't want the boys down there at all," Clarice said. "I'll be fine."

"You're welcome to ride with me, Mrs. Royals," Wesley offered.

"Do it, Clarice," Brenda said. "Go now. I'll call Alvin and Mack and send them down. The kids and I will be right here if you need anything."

Clarice nodded, found her purse, and said, "The kids don't need to know about the police part, Brenda." Jaw clenched, refusing to cry, she hugged her sister-in-law.

"Take me to my child," she said to the detective as she headed for the door.

CHAPTER 25

Hospital Inmate

Jason regained consciousness in a hospital bed situated within a curtained stall. As he moved to sit up, he felt a tug on his left arm. An intravenous needle had been inserted at the inside of his elbow. Crisscrossing opaque medical tape—lots of it—covered the insertion site securely, preventing his motion from ripping it out.

"Hold on there! Let's sit you up," a nurse said. She stopped writing and shuffled to show Jason the remote control for operating the bed. She pressed the up button a moment before she handed it off. "You're in St. Mary's Hospital. How are you feeling, Jason?"

Jason's eyes followed the intravenous tube up to where a bag of clear fluids was hanging. "I'm okay. What's that?"

"It's glucose, Jason. Tell me, have you ever been diagnosed with diabetes?"

"No, ma'am."

"Have you ever had insulin injections?"

"No. Never."

"And you don't take insulin tablets? Or any other diabetes medicine?"

"No, ma'am." Jason frowned. "I'm not diabetic. I get hypoglycemic, though."

"Good." The nurse blew out a sigh of relief. "That's what we wanted to hear. Please understand, the treatment for unconsciousness for *hyper*glycemia is far different from *hypo*. Good thing that detective called. This might have been a whole lot worse."

Jason groaned, pushing his head backwards in the pillow. "I passed out," he said, as if informing himself. "How did I get here?"

"Policeman brought you in. He was pretty worried about you."

Jason realized he was naked except for his undershorts. Eyeing his clothes piled on a chair in the corner, he pulled the sheets up over his shoulders.

"We had to cut them off of you," the nurse said, following his gaze. "We needed to check you for injection marks on your stomach, buttocks, thighs, and the backs of your arms. You can always get new clothes. You can't always get a new life."

Jason smiled a tightlipped smile and nodded.

"You're pretty bruised up, too. What happened to you?" she asked, pointing to her own cheek at the spot where Jason's was injured.

"The police had me out in the woods." Jason closed his eyes. He could remember snippets of the afternoon. "They were kind of rough. At first, I didn't know whether it was on purpose or an accident. But now I'm pretty sure it was on purpose."

Jason heard a chair scrape on the floor on the other side of the curtains. The nurse shot a glance in that direction and then back to her young patient. She looked at him with her lips pressed into a sympathetic half-smile before she asked him another question. "When is the last time you ate?"

"I had some peanut butter crackers and Diet Coke before they took me in the woods. What time is it now?"

"It's after eight."

"My parents are going to kill me. I need to call my parents." Jason looked around for a telephone.

"We had to take the phone out, honey. It's procedure with inmates."

Inmates? Jason sprang to a full sitting position in the bed. *Why did I think I was going home?* His mind's eye flashed—an older man's eyes in a rearview mirror were the last things he remembered before losing consciousness.

"I thought the last police officer was taking me home," he told the nurse, swinging his legs to the side of the bed.

"Don't get up!" the nurse snapped, loudly. "We got the officer to uncuff you, but they'll come strap you down if they think you're trying to leave."

The officer who had driven Jason to the hospital pulled the curtain open from the other side, where he'd been sitting. He stood and walked around into the stall toward Jason.

Jason laid back down, tugging the sheets over him. He turned his face away.

"You gave us a good scare," the officer said. "It's a good thing Sergeant Marshall called the hospital. The ER got the message right when they got you."

"So when can I go home?" Jason asked, still not looking at the man.

He didn't answer.

Jason turned his head to face him.

The officer shot a glance to the nurse. "Not quite yet," he said.

"The doctor wants you here for the night," the nurse said. "We'll take you upstairs as soon as we find you a bed. Are you warm enough?"

She began looking through cabinets for a blanket as if she already knew the answer. She held one up, in a question.

Jason nodded.

"I'll be right outside if you need anything," the policeman told the nurse as he walked out, pulling the curtain behind them.

"You're a lot more cooperative than most of the patients the police bring in here." The nurse patted Jason's hand. "Do you want to tell me what's going on?"

Jason's eyes welled with tears. He'd been waiting all day for someone to see him, to see who he was. As he turned away from her to wipe his tears, he wondered whether she treated all her patients—inmates and non-inmates—as she treated him.

He took a breath and blew it out. "They've mistaken me for someone else."

I need to call Mama and Daddy, he thought. He vaguely remembered seeing his mother and Uncle Mack down at the station. *Why didn't they bring me home then?* "I need to call my parents. Please!" Jason begged the nurse, looking her straight in the eye.

"Let me see what I can do. Can you sit tight here for me?"

Jason nodded.

"Here, why don't you write down your mom's phone number? We'll get her on the phone, if not here, then upstairs. We're working on admitting you."

CHAPTER 26

"He Looks Just Like You"

The emergency room nurse spotted Clarice and the plainclothes detective right when they walked in. She motioned to the uniformed policeman who had brought in Jason.

"You must be Jason's mother," the nurse began, walking toward Clarice. "He looks just like you."

Clarice was taken aback by the petite, blond woman whose eyes met and held her own. All she could manage to say was, "Where is he?"

"They moved him up to a room. The doctor wants to keep him overnight," the nurse said, reading Clarice's concern. "Don't worry. He's okay. He's had a hypoglycemic incident, and he's a little scraped up—"

"A little scraped up?" Clarice was alarmed.

Detective Wesley and the other officer shot glances at each other. The older, uniformed man spoke.

"Ma'am, your son has been in police custody for most of the day. He gave me a good scare when I was transporting him to the juvenile facility. He seemed confused and incoherent. He thought I was driving him home, and when he found out where I was taking him?" The officer shook his head. "Well, he got very upset and passed out."

"Passed out? He lost consciousness?" Clarice looked at the nurse.

"He's okay now, Mrs. Royals," the officer reassured her. "He was sitting up talking to nurse Jillian here, and me. He didn't seem to have any memory of what happened. I can't say much more," he paused, throwing a look toward Wesley, "but I'm going to give you my card, for future reference. Please don't hesitate to call me if I can help you."

Officer P.J. Howard, the card read. Clarice looked at the officer, confused.

"Ma'am," he said, "your son has the right to counsel. I want to reiterate that now. And I'm no lawyer, but he's a minor. In my mind, he ought to have the chance to see his parents." The uniformed officer folded Clarice's hand around his card. "Don't hesitate," he said again.

Detective Wesley cleared his throat. "Officer Howard, could I speak with you for a minute please?"

The two policemen walked away from Clarice, who stood stunned. She looked down at the business card, running her thumb over the embossed Beau Rêve Police Department badge. She felt the nurse touching her arm, guiding her toward the elevator.

"I've been taking care of your son," the nurse told Clarice. Looking around her, the nurse whispered, "I can only believe there's been a terrible mistake. And I'm pretty sure Officer Howard believes it, too."

"Jason's really okay?" Clarice asked.

"He's really okay. The doctor wants to rule out any growth disorders associated with reactive hypoglycemia—and diabetes, too, of course."

"Of course." Clarice nodded as the two women boarded the empty elevator. "We have a family history of it. Do you think it was hypoglycemic shock, Ms.—?"

"Jillian. Call me Jillian. Are you a nurse, Mrs. Royals?"

"Clarice. And yes. I'm an RN. I do home-based nursing."

"Then you have a pretty good understanding of what may have happened," Jillian said. "We know he lost consciousness right before Officer Howard brought him here. The doctor has ordered a neurological workup just to be on the safe side, but yes, he's thinking what you're thinking—low glucose. What we don't know is how much of his shock was dietary and how much of it was triggered by stress or trauma."

Jillian looked squarely at her young patient's mother. "Jason said something about the police being rough in the woods, Mrs.—um—Clarice. He didn't want to talk about it, but something happened to him today."

"The woods? Dear Jesus." Clarice grasped hold of the handrails along the elevator wall. "Dear Jesus," she said again, as much in prayer as in abject fear for her son. A cold current of adrenaline coursed through her body.

Is that why he confessed to something he didn't do? They took him to the woods and beat him?

The elevator doors opened, and Clarice saw a uniformed man sitting in a chair several doors down in the corridor. She began running to her son's room, her church heels clattering on the tile floor.

The large policeman rose to block the door, his palms held up in front of his protruding belly. "I'm sorry, ma'am, but inmates are not allowed to have any visitors."

"I'm told it's different for minors, young man," Clarice shot back. "I am his mother and I have the right to see my son. You all have had him all day long, without so much as a phone call to us, even after we called missing per—"

"Not me, ma'am. I got here an hour ago. And I have strict orders not to let visitors in to see inmates."

"He's a fifteen-year-old child," Jillian interjected, indignant. "Not an inmate." Looking up at the five-o'clock shadow dotting his acne-ridden chin, Jillian stood a full two feet shorter than the slovenly rookie. "Let me go in with her," Jillian offered, "and I'll call you if I need you."

The gargantuan officer shifted his weight to block the door and hitched his thumbs underneath his bulging belly fat. He said, with near-gleeful authority, "You, nurse, can go in to check on him. But this other lady here will have to stay outside."

Clarice clenched her fists and turned away, holding back angry, hot tears.

"This *other lady*," Jillian said, "is Mrs. Clarice Royals, and you will treat her with respect. I'd like to speak with your superior officer right—"

"No! Wait!" Clarice interjected. "I need for my son to know I'm here for him. Now. Go on in, Jillian, and tell him…tell him…"

The tears spilled onto Clarice's face as her voice cracked. She couldn't get the words out. She choked back the sobs, weeping silently.

"Oh, for Pete's sake," the guard muttered. His tone softened. "Come on. Sit down, Mrs. Royals." He offered her his chair.

"Here you go," Jillian said, pulling out a small pad of paper. She flipped it to a clean page and handed it to Clarice. "Here's a pen, too."

The uniformed man was indignant. "Now wait a—"

"You will not prevent me from delivering this mother's note to her child." Jillian was adamant. She waited for Clarice to finish before taking the note and entering Jason's hospital room.

The guard made no move to stop her.

Jillian's young patient turned to look at her when the door opened. He appeared to have been oblivious to the commotion in the hallway.

"Jason, they won't let you have any visitors, but your mother is right outside the—"

"Mama?"

"She's right outside. She said to give you this." Jillian put the folded note in his un-cuffed hand.

When he moved the other to unfold it, the metal around his wrist surprised him, as it had countless times before throughout the day.

"I'm sorry they had to put those back on you." Jillian nodded toward the handcuff linking him to the hospital bed.

His mind flashed to the first police car he rode in that morning— it felt like eons had passed in the interim. As he moved his hands together, the IV cord tugged at the inside of his elbow. He grimaced against the pain, but the pain won—with some help from utter frustration, embarrassment, trauma, and a child's simple longing to see his mother. Sobs wracked his entire body as he struggled not to cry out.

"It's alright, Jason. With what you've been through, you're entitled to let it out." Jillian unfolded the note for him. "You know your mom is out there arguing with the police officer right now. Giving him some what-for."

Jason chuckled a little through his sobs, and then he sobbed some more. Jillian moved to get a box of Kleenex.

"She's one tough lady, your mother. Thought I was going to have to pull her off of him."

Jason avoided eye contact. He smiled the lip-pressed smile of a hurt child, lovingly cajoled. Burying his head into his shoulder, he wiped his face onto his hospital gown, wincing when the fabric rubbed against the tear-salted wound under his eye. He stared at the note in his uncuffed, IV-side hand, breathing through the pain, trying to compose himself.

Jillian busied herself by shaking the half-full pitcher of water on the bedside table. She moved to check his IV supply.

Jason watched her, trying to get a look at her nametag. *Trust nurse Jillian*, his mom's note read. The woman with him was the same nurse who'd taken care of him in the ER, but was it Jillian? After everything that had happened to him, it wasn't worth taking a chance. Following her every move, he observed her as she lowered her arm from the IV bag and saw the words, "Jillian Powell, RN, BSN" emblazoned next to the hospital logo on her nametag. He exhaled in relief.

Jillian smoothed out her uniform, pretending not to have noticed Jason watching her.

"The police wouldn't let me call her," he said. "I tried to call my uncle, but I couldn't get him. They told me if I called a lawyer, they'd put me in jail right then. Then they took me out to the woods."

Jillian sat down on the edge of the bed, concern pinching her forehead. "You—" she began but stopped. "Do you remember telling me the police got rough with you in the woods?"

Jason nodded, eyes wide and emphatic.

"I know you probably don't want to go through it, but it's important for you to try to remember what happened, while it's still fresh in your mind. My bet is your mom will have an attorney here by morning. So, let's start with this." Jillian pointed to her own cheekbone, below her eye. "How's it feeling, first of all?"

"Pretty sore. You got a mirror?"

Jillian pulled the meal tray across the bed, pulled out the drawer and flipped up the miniature mirror.

Jason stared at himself, turning his head to assess the damage.

"Your eye is going to look even worse tomorrow," Jillian said. "Can you tell me more about how it happened?"

"Yeah, the detective, the…um…shorter one," Jason began, trying not to refer to Pershing as white. "He was walking in front of me and he pulled back a branch and let it fly in my face. I almost thought it was an accident, except, well, it happened right after the other detective, Marshall, punched me in the stomach. He also threw me down to the ground."

"Threw you down? Which one threw you down?" Jillian scribbled a couple words on her notepad.

"It was Marshall."

"So, the scratches on the backs of your arms and your neck, those are from being thrown down in the woods?"

"I guess so."

"What do you mean when you say *thrown down*, Jason? Were you fighting with—what's his—with Marshall?"

"No, ma'am. He had a real tight grip on my arm, and I was trying to get loose of it, and he threw me down. Hard."

"Marshall," Jillian repeated. She remembered the bruises on Jason's upper arm, and she remembered the name. "Marshall might have been the one who called in about your hypoglycemia. Did you talk to him about it?"

"Yeah, after he gave me some peanut butter crackers and Diet Coke. Because I threw up the disgusting chicken salad sandwich they tried to feed me."

"Hold on—you vomited while you were in police custody? *Before* they took you to the woods and roughed you up?"

"Yeah," Jason exhaled, relenting to the question. He decided not to be embarrassed about it anymore. "It was pretty bad. Pretty gross. It went everywhere. Got it on my socks. Had to take them off."

Jillian tilted her head in a question. "Your socks?"

"They took my shoes for evidence," Jason explained. "I still can't believe they think I did it."

"Me either."

"But I didn't. I didn't hurt anyone. They think I shot—" Jason shook the thought out of his head. "A lady got shot at a motel and they believe *I* did it." His voice rose in anger and frustration. "Like I even have a gun. Like I'm some street thug or a gangster or something. They took me out to find the gun, even though I told them it wasn't me. They didn't listen."

"They said you confessed, Jason." Jillian repeated what Officer Howard had told her.

Helpless, Jason's face fell. His eyes begged for a logical explanation but it wasn't forthcoming from Jillian. He looked around the room. His eyes settled on a large sign with the silhouette of a saint. "Compassionate Care," it read. "St. Mary's Hospital."

Did I confess?

"I don't remember confessing to anything," Jason said. "I kind of remember some paperwork. And I remember seeing my uncle and my mom there! Why didn't they take me home then?"

"You saw your mom where? At the police station?" Jillian asked. Jason detected the incredulity in her voice.

"Jason, are you *sure*?"

"I …" He looked down at his hand. At his mother's familiar handwriting.

Jason,
  Relieved you are alive. Getting you a lawyer. Trust us. Trust God. And trust nurse Jillian. I love you.
  Mom

"Your mom said," Jillian began, before Jason could say anything else, "they kept you all day without calling her or your dad. I'm pretty sure I heard her say she hadn't seen you since this morning."

Jason's eyes flashed with panic.

"Jason, you were pretty out of it when you came in. Sometimes people confuse imagination with reality when…well, you were in hypoglycemic shock."

"She wasn't there? Are you saying I—"

"I'm going to double-check that with your mom. But no, honey, I don't believe she was there. And there's nothing wrong with your mind. Whether she was there or not, you had a huge glucose drop— not to mention physical trauma. The stress would be quite a bit for anyone to handle, let alone someone who's only fifteen. Under those circumstances, any of us might have gone into shock of one sort or another."

The boy closed his eyes and turned his head away.

Jillian's voice grew soft. "You rest, sweetie. I'm not going to be long. I just want to look at this arm." She pulled the hospital gown up over his bicep to reveal finger marks, light—but discernible—bruises.

She smoothed the gown back over his arm and marked something in her notepad. Although she and another nurse had documented Jason's bruises and abrasions downstairs in the ER, she created her own set of notes to keep with her.

CHAPTER 27

Living the Dream

From his seat on the witness stand, Detective Sergeant John Marshall eyed the defense attorney with defiance.

Bring it on, man.

The courtroom felt unseasonably warm to him. No one else in the room was listening to the exchange between him and the lawyer. The judge, the court reporter—everyone seemed oblivious to the substance of the cross-examination. The others appeared distant, like backdrop scenery.

No one else was sweating, either, including the attorney pelting him with accusatory questions. Marshall stared at the paper in his hands.

"You tell *me* what's missing, Detective Sergeant."

Nothing. I did my job.

"Do you see it yet?" the dark-suited man asked. "Do you see it now? It's right there!" Dark-suit was growing impatient. "Right there, before your very eyes!" he yelled.

"What's happening?" Marshall cried out.

Oh, Jesus. What was that? Did the room just blow up? Marshall's eyes squinted open, and a greenish light burned his visual field. As his eyes adjusted to the darkness, the numbers on his clock clarified, and he realized he'd been dreaming.

It was after three a.m.

He shut his eyes against the neon glow and his dream-paper flashed in front of him again.

A child's handwriting.

Oh, fuck me.

The detective's mind shot back in double-barreled déjà vu. He remembered the previous day—the day he spent with a teenage murder suspect. The sequence of events tumbled through his head like rapids in a jagged river. The moment of doubt he'd felt, right after the confession, scraped him and tossed him. He sat up in his bed, in a panic.

Okay, get ahold of yourself. Breathe.

He inhaled.

He exhaled.

It's only a dream. More like a recurring nightmare—but still—it's not real. It's just stress. It's this damn job.

Marshall threw off the sweat-soaked top sheet and bunched his pillow beneath his neck as he lay down again. The bottom sheet felt damp and warm and wrinkled under his naked torso, as he tried to wriggle into relative comfort.

Wakefulness took root in his body, instead. The clock was an impassive witness. Its green digits shone "3:33." He stretched his arm outward, reaching for Veronica.

Damn. He sighed. *My clock. My bedroom. She's at her house.*

Marshall tried to remember what day it was. What day it would soon be. He tried to calculate when he would need to be at work.

I don't have to go in today. Good.

His tension loosened its nocturnal grip.

I don't have to go back in again, period.

He rose from his bed, threw on a robe, and padded into his kitchen. He poured cold milk into a tall, plastic Florida Gators game cup.

Marshall entertained the idea of the bottle of Scotch he'd closeted away after New Year's. His dad had brought it to him for Christmas, insisting he open it. He smiled at the memory of their shared indulgence.

Good stuff. Incredibly good. But no.

Sipping his milk, he ambled over to his kitchen table—another college remnant. He sat on the fiberboard chair he'd constructed himself, out of a box, more than a decade before.

When're you going to grow up? he asked himself. *When I go furniture shopping with Veronica,* he answered. *After I switch out of this godforsaken job. No more nightmares. No more panics. No more cold sweats in the middle of the night.*

The tiny glow-in-the-dark clock on the back of his two-burner stove read three-forty-seven.

A couple more hours and she'll be up.

CHAPTER 28

Monday Sunrise

"Jason Royals?" The question was asked in a sonorous baritone. Fluorescent lights flickered before flashing completely on, illuminating the hospital room.

Jason squinted his eyes open and then flinched. As the stranger walked toward his hospital bed, Jason remembered where he was, but he didn't recognize the intruder. The voice belonged to an imposingly large, ebony-skinned man, who was dressed in a navy blue, pinstripe suit.

"It's alright, Mr. Royals. I'm your attorney, Aaron Hampton."

Jason gave him a bleary-eyed stare. "What time is it?"

"About six thirty." The attorney walked to the window and opened the blinds. He smiled at the pre-dawn darkness covering the city. "We've got a lot to talk about before the rest of Beau Rêve gets moving."

With the bed's automatic controls, Jason used the fingers of his IV-armed hand to incline his head. His new habit of distrust made him ask, "Have you got an ID or something?"

Hampton turned to hand him his card.

"Thank God," Jason said. "How did you...?"

"Your parents hired me last night. Good God!" The lawyer motioned, raising his hand up to his own eye. "Did the police do that to you, Jason?" Without waiting for an answer, Hampton pulled out a cell phone and began dialing.

Jason nodded. His grogginess evaporated, leaving hyper-vigilance. Thinking about the events of the previous day pulled him down like weights, as did his body. He was sore all over.

"Have you left yet?" Hampton spoke into the phone. "You're going to need to bring a camera, even if you have to pick up a disposable one at the drugstore on the way over." He paused. "Jason Royals. Room 317," he said, before flipping the phone shut.

"How soon can you get me out of here?" Jason's voice was tired, but hopeful.

"Hold on, son. Let's take it one step at a time. You've been injured by the police. We've got to make sure you're medically sound, first and foremost, so it's up to your doctor. But I will tell you the longer you're in the hospital, the better it could be for you in the long run. And it's sure better than jail."

"Jail? But I didn't do anything!" Jason whined, kicking his legs in an effort to sit more upright.

Hampton held up his hands. "Take it easy, Jason. I know. I'm on *your* side. Your granddaddy knows my daddy from their railroad days, and from the church. Nobody in your family slept much last night. It was all I could do to get everyone off the phone so I could catch a few winks before coming here."

"So, you believe me?" Jason's eyes pleaded with Hampton.

Hampton opened his mouth to speak but, as he took in the sight of his helpless client, he hesitated. After a moment, he said, "Yes, as a matter of fact, I do believe you. And not only because of your bruises." He looked Jason in the eye. "But it doesn't matter if I believe you or not, you understand?"

Jason stared at the lawyer, confused.

Hampton explained. "Look. I usually tell my clients it doesn't matter what I believe. I tell them I don't want to know any more than I ask them. Criminal defense work is about how the system operates, more than anything else. I get paid to vigorously defend the accused, Jason, because that's the way the system works. I enforce their rights—just like I'm going to enforce your rights, under the law. And I'm very good at what I do."

"But you do believe me." Jason's voice was calmer.

The lawyer nodded. "We've got a lot of ground to cover."

"Who were you talking to on the phone?"

"My law clerk. She's bringing a camera to document your injuries." Hampton leaned over the bed to examine Jason's face. "Unbelievable." He shook his head. "I've seen the police get rough before, but this is truly unbelievable."

"They wouldn't listen to me," Jason said. "I thought I could straighten it out because I didn't do it."

Hampton straightened up, crossed his arms, and looked at Jason, listening intently.

"I don't even have a gun, and I wouldn't hurt anyone, anyway. Ever. Man, I don't even foul people on the basketball court. I got *best sportsmanship* on my team at the Y, two years in a row."

"Two years in a row, huh?" Hampton smiled.

"Yeah! You can even talk to my coach. I'm sure my mom can get his—"

Hampton put up his hand and redirected the conversation. "Tell me what happened. What were you doing when the police first stopped you?"

"I was going to see my friend Kim about applying for a job over at Wellstein's." Jason watched as the attorney opened his briefcase, got out a legal pad, and pulled a chair to his bedside. He waited for Hampton to look up from his note-taking. "They didn't believe me because it was Sunday, but Kim really was going to walk me through and prep me for an interview with her manager. All I wanted was to get a job. I'll be sixteen in August, and I've got a work permit. I'll also be getting my learner's permit this summer, and—"

"You were walking, from your house? To Wellstein's? When they stopped you?"

"Yeah." Jason exhaled his relief. At last, there was someone who could help him get the truth out. But while Hampton was writing, Jason realized he needed to correct himself. "I was walking, except when I crossed Broward Highway…at the corner of College. I ran. I was running to beat the light. That's when this cop named O'Donnell got me. He banged up my knee pretty good when he arrested me."

"O'Donnell, you say?" Hampton was writing furiously. "Let me take a look at your knee."

Jason obliged.

Hampton glanced at the dark bruise and the abrasion and shook his head, unsurprised. "Hmm," he grunted. "The officer who did this, did he read you your rights?"

"Yes, sir. After he handcuffed me while I was on the ground. Then he threw me in the back seat." Jason kept talking as the attorney kept nodding. "I was looking like a mess when he took me back to the motel where the lady got shot."

Hampton stopped writing. "Hold on a minute. He took you to the crime scene instead of downtown?" He was unable to hide his amazement.

"Yes, sir. He took me to the crime scene."

"Huh."

"Why? Was that bad?" Jason asked.

"It could be. Do you think it's bad, Jason?"

"If it is, it could be why the detective got pissed off at him—I mean *ticked* off. Excuse me."

"The detective got upset with the officer who arrested you?"

"Yeah." Jason nodded, slack-jawed. He sat up a little taller in the hospital bed, composing himself. "Yes, sir. When I was sitting in the office where the detectives were. I couldn't hear them, but I know what I saw."

"Okay, so after O'Donnell, who else did you come into contact with, from the police?"

"Detective Marshall. The one who got ticked off at O'Donnell. He's a sergeant or something, too. And his partner. Name begins with a 'P'; reminds me of a fish, his name. Then there was the guy who drove me here. He talked to me a little bit in the emergency room."

"Officer Howard," Hampton said. "I've got a meeting set up with him today."

Jason was shocked. "That's fast."

"I've learned that in my business the harder and the faster you work up front, the better off your client is. After him, I've got an appointment with the nurse. She's going to be golden for you, Jason, absolutely golden. You lucked out there."

"Miss Jillian? Yeah, she was nice." *So, Jillian and Mama talked, and Mama talked to Granddaddy Porter, and Granddaddy got his friend to get Hampton here.* "Did you talk to my parents?" Jason asked.

"Did I talk to your parents? Jason, they kept me up half the night! Your daddy's down the hall in the waiting room. Staying overnight was the only way he could get your mama to leave."

Jason's eyes widened.

"The waiting room down the hall has been command central for your case."

The door opened and a short-haired woman in a jogging suit

backed into the room, carrying a cup-holder with three coffees with one arm and a tote-bag with the other. She held the bag out for Hampton.

"Hello, Katrina!" Hampton jumped up to grab the bag. He peeped inside. "Ah, yes, a good old-fashioned Polaroid. Fantastic!" Hampton pulled out the camera and the instant film. "Jason, this is Katrina Westmore. She just finished her second year at Florida Law and she is top notch."

"Call me Katrina," she said to Jason, still tending the coffee from the counter by the sink. She took a sip as she turned around to greet their new client. Startled by what she saw, she held up the paper cup, reflexively, splashing coffee onto the floor.

"Look at that eye." She gasped. "Oh, my Lord."

CHAPTER 29

"You Don't Have to Worry Anymore"

Hampton walked Katrina to Jason's hospital room door, sending the Polaroid photos with her. He said a few words to the guard out in the hallway.

"The judge has postponed first appearance but gave us permission to let my client see his parents." Hampton motioned toward the waiting room. "So, I'd like to go get them now."

In Hampton, the guard faced a much bigger—and more muscular—potential adversary than he had the night before. The lawyer meant business and wouldn't be swayed. Nearing the end of his twelve-hour shift, the uniformed man nodded his assent to the attorney, but without moving away from the door. "You'll understand, sir, I will need to make a few phone calls to verify—"

"Please do." Hampton turned to fetch Alvin and Clarice Royals from their campsite down the hall. Returning, Hampton held the door for Jason's parents—a door that had separated them from him since Sunday evening. The uniformed officer made no move to stop them.

Neither parent had seen their son since he walked out of their kitchen the morning before. Jason's bruised face appeared tiny; his head was nestled in a large pillow, his arms frail and thin in an ocean of white bedclothes. He lifted his IV-tubed arm in a wave as he smiled sheepishly at his parents.

"Jason!" Clarice gasped and ran toward her child. "Oh, my...how are you feeling?" Her purse dropped to her elbow as she reached to embrace him. Disentangling herself, she threw the purse onto his bed and tried again, gingerly working around the IV connection. "Oh, honey, we were so worried." Her voice cracked and yielded to tears as she held her son.

Jason wanted to cry, too, as he relaxed into her embrace. Looking over her shoulder, he forced a smile at his father and Hampton. With his mother's arms around him, he closed his eyes for a moment. He felt the silky nylon fabric of her flowery dress, a dress he'd seen her wear a hundred times before. He inhaled the faint, familiar smell—a mixture of soap and his mother's perfume. *This is really you, Mama,* he thought. *You're really here this time.*

"I'm okay now, Mama," he said, still hugging her. "You don't have to worry anymore, see?"

Clarice, sitting on the edge of the bed, released him. Wiping away her tears, she laughed. "Easy for you to say!"

Hampton chuckled.

Alvin walked over and took his son's hands into both of his. "We're so relieved, son. This has been hard on your mama." Seeing the light leave his son's eyes, he edited himself. "It wasn't your fault, Jason. I didn't mean it that way, son. We know who's to blame here, right, Mr. Hampton?"

Hampton nodded. "If we're going to work together, you're going to need to call me *Hamp*, alright?"

"Hamp, we will definitely be working together," Alvin said.

"What happened there?" Clarice pointed to Jason's eye.

Jason touched the still-tender spot over his cheek. "It's a long story, Mama. Basically, a branch got flung in my face. In the woods. Over by the interstate near the house."

"It got flung?" she asked.

"Yeah, at first I thought it mighta been an accident but these little *accidents* kept happening, you know?"

Hampton interjected. "No *accident* about it. I've seen it before—too many times in this city. But we can't talk with your parents about what the police did, not when I'm in here, you understand, Jason?"

"Why not?" Jason asked.

"You understand everything you say to me is confidential, because of attorney-client privilege, right?"

"Yes, sir."

"But privilege can go away whenever there's anyone else in the room with us."

"What?" Alvin said, outraged. "You mean we have no privacy

as a family? He's supposed to make decisions about his defense, by himself?"

"The first part is true," Hampton confirmed. "There is no parent-child privilege, per se. I'll engage you and Mrs. Royals as much as I can, but my obligation is to Jason, and I have to protect him."

"Wait—we can't even talk about what the police did to him?" Alvin was incredulous. "I need to know how they made my son confess to something he didn't do."

"Not right now, you don't," the lawyer replied. "You want to avoid any knowledge whatsoever of the circumstance surrounding his so-called *confession*."

He's right, Daddy. You don't want to know. You don't want to know how I thought I was hearing God speak to me. Or how crazy that makes me.

"Was it a dark-blue Chevy Lumina?" Clarice's non-sequitur got everyone's attention.

"Dark-blue what? What are you talking about, Clarice?" Alvin asked.

"The car. The car the police drove him in," Clarice explained. "Mack and I saw a dark-blue Chevy on the side of the road—"

"Yeah, that was it. That was the detectives' car," Jason confirmed.

Hampton shook his head and shot a look toward Jason, silently warning, "No more."

"Mack called it a *cop car*." Agitated, Clarice spoke a little faster. "We passed right by it; it was empty, sitting on the edge of the road and he said *cop car* and I asked him how he knew. He said he *just knew*. Oh, dear God!" Her voice teetered on the edge of tears. "We were right there! We drove right past where they took you to...to..." Clarice couldn't stop the tears. "To beat up on you."

Alvin moved to comfort his wife. "Clarice, no. No. Honey, you couldn't have possibly known. This is not your fault."

Hampton shook his head at Jason, putting a finger to his lips.

"Why didn't we stop?" she cried out, angry.

The officer guarding the room cracked open the door and Hampton sped over to him. The guard whispered something under his breath and closed the door again.

"Listen to me, Clarice." Alvin looked into her eyes. "You and Mack didn't stop because you thought he was at the Steer House, remember? You thought he went to the game room. We had no idea he'd been arrested. It didn't occur to any of us." Alvin turned to his son as he continued. "We didn't know the police had you until the missing persons' detective came to the house yesterday evening."

"Missing persons' detective?" Hampton asked, as Jason, Clarice, and Alvin looked at him. Hampton grabbed his legal pad. "When did you make that report?"

"I believe it was about three in the afternoon," Alvin said. "Is that important?" He and Clarice looked at each other.

"If the police took a missing person call for somebody they had in their custody? It could be very important."

Alvin digested what Hampton was telling him. "We called them around three. After Clarice and Mack got back to the house. Before Mack and I went out looking again."

"Okay, who is Mack?" Hampton asked.

"My brother-in-law. Clarice's brother," Alvin said.

"It's a football nickname," Clarice added. "His given name is Clarence Porter, Junior."

I mighta been back at the station by three, Jason thought, as images of his cuffed hands and Marshall's muscled forearm flashed in his mind's eye.

"Mama?" he asked, sounding as vulnerable as a five-year-old. "Where else did you and Uncle Mack go looking for me?"

Say "police station," Mama. Say you were there. I saw you there. I heard your voice.

Clarice got a nod from Hampton before she answered. "Well, we left brunch with your grandma and granddaddy, and I sent your brother over to stay with your Aunt Brenda and Cam. And then we went over to Wellstein's, first of all.

"I met your friend, Kim. She was worried because you didn't show up like you two had planned. After that, we went over to the Steer House and the strip mall there."

"Jason, I'm going to need Kim's number if you've got it," Hampton said.

"Where else, Mama?" Jason asked, as if he had not heard Hampton. *It was so real. Please say you were there with me, Mama. Please tell me I'm not a crazy person.*

"Your uncle drove me home and he and Daddy went..." Clarice

motioned to Alvin to fill in the blanks.

"We combed the entire east side of Beau Rêve," his father said. "All up and down College and Broward. Three, four times. All around the strip mall, several times. We looked high and low for you, son. But we didn't think to look in the woods."

Jason absorbed his father's words, and then a thought crossed his mind—a thought that would explain it all. "Y'all came to the police station to report me missing?"

"No, son." Alvin frowned in confusion. "Remember, I said we called the police from the house, when Mack and your mama got there."

Jason looked at his mother, who assented to what his father said.

"Yeah, okay," Jason said, sheepishly. "Maybe my blood sugar is still not leveled out." He looked up at the IV bag. *Or maybe I'm going crazy. Maybe when you get really low blood sugar you go permanently crazy.*

"It's understandable, given what's happened," Clarice chimed in, patting him on his leg through the bed sheets. "You've been through a *lot*. But I believe the glucose problem is going to work itself out, honey. The doctor has ruled out diabetes, so that's good."

Jason sighed, partially relieved. He looked at his mother. *How does she do that? It's like she knows what I'm thinking.*

Clarice took Jason's free hand in hers. "The doctor told us it was postprandial hypoglycemia, Jason, and a little dehydration. You're having low glucose reactions a few hours after you eat, and stress makes it worse. But we can help manage it through diet, sweetheart. Good, protein snacks. And the other good news is there's no growth disorder, either. Your endocrine system is in perfect shape."

Right. Jason faked a grin. *I must be mental, then.*

"I expect you'll grow to be bigger than I am, any day now," Alvin said, eliciting a half-smile from Jason. "Your Uncle Mack better just look out," he continued with a quick wink, "pretty soon you'll be able to take him down."

"I've got to meet this Mack," Hampton said.

"Jason," Alvin addressed his son, "we've got a tough road ahead of us, but you've got the best in Mr.—in Hamp, here. He knows his way around a courtroom."

Courtroom. Jason felt his blood run cold. Pershing's taunts echoed in his head. *"Where do you think you are, fucking Vermont? We've still got the death penalty down here, boy."*

"You know I didn't do this, right?" Jason cried out. "You know I'm innocent, right? You can't let them give me the death penalty for something I didn't—"

"Oh, no, honey. We are not going to let that happen, are we Mr. Hampton?" Clarice bent over to hug her child. "Shh. It's going to be alright." Straightening up, she added, "Anyone can plainly see they forced you—"

"We're not going to talk about it, Mrs. Royals," Hampton interjected. He added, more quietly, "And no, I'm not about to let your son be railroaded by the system. I'll give him everything I've got, I promise you."

Hampton waited for Clarice to nod before continuing. "By the way, in this country, we don't execute people for crimes committed before age sixteen, no matter what the police might have told Jason. The police lie to their suspects all the time."

The room grew silent for a moment before Jason spoke again. "When can I get out of here?"

Hampton moved closer to the bed. "We are working on it. Your detention hearing is set for tomorrow morning."

Clarice stood, motioning for Hampton to sit in her spot. "The doctor wants you here, Jason," Clarice explained, "for x-rays and a few other tests."

Hampton nodded and looked at Jason. "And they won't do the hearing at the hospital. I've already asked. Your parents and I agreed I should appear in court on your behalf tomorrow, if it's all right with you."

Jason nodded. "And then they'll let me go home?"

"That's up to the judge," Hampton said, looking Jason in the eye. "I'll do everything I can in court, son, but the charge is serious, and it may take a little while for your case to get to trial. Trial is when we defend you against the charges; tomorrow's hearing is only about where you'll wait for that trial."

"So, I might have to go to jail until my trial?" Jason's voice rose in panic. "For how long?"

"It might be jail, yes. There's a chance it could be juvenile detention. Our job," Hampton spoke slowly and calmly, "is to try to get you home to your parents. Before tomorrow, though, you and I have some work to do, just the two of us. And then I'm off to meet, let's see," Hampton consulted his notes, "Officer P.J. Howard and Nurse Jillian Powell."

Jillian. I wonder how much she told Mama about my...about what I imagined.

"Mama, did Miss Jillian ever get the chance to talk to you after she brought in your note last night?"

"Only for a minute, honey. Wasn't she an angel?"

"Yeah, I liked her." Jason couldn't tell from his mother's reaction whether they'd discussed his hallucination or not.

An angel. At St. Mary's. Right after I imagined God was talking to me at the police station, with Mama and Uncle Mack.

❖

Jason watched through his hospital room window as the afterschool traffic began to thicken. He'd counted four yellow school buses crossing the river that afternoon, before Hampton's second visit.

"I can't believe it was all just yesterday," Jason said to his attorney. "It feels like it was days ago."

"I want to get as much as we can on paper while it's still fresh in your mind," Hampton said. "When you got to the police station, you told me earlier, you tried to run away again?"

Stupid. Stupid. Stupid. Jason sighed and looked down. "Yeah, pretty dumb, huh?"

"I don't know, son. I might have done the same myself. Sometimes the body acts before the mind can think. Fight or flight, right?"

"Yeah, well, trying to *fly* in a building full of cops was not a real smart move."

"I imagine you were scared. Give yourself a break."

Jason hung his head.

"Listen," Hampton said. "I'm not going to pretend that what you did makes this any easier. They're probably going to throw in resisting arrest charges on top of everything else. But from what you've told me, and from what I've seen, none of this is your fault."

Jason nodded without looking up.

"Let's have you walk me through what you told me before. They took your shoes and your shirt. They fed you—"

"A chicken salad sandwich. It was gross." Jason looked at his hands. "I lied and told them I liked it though. Right before I ralphed."

"Ralphed?" Hampton's confusion began to morph into a smile, but then he resumed his serious expression. "Did they let you get cleaned up, at least?"

"Yeah. There was this little bathroom off the room where the table was."

"The interrogation room?"

"I guess so." Jason shrugged. He was starting to make eye contact with Hampton.

"So, you went to the bathroom to wash up…and?"

"And I asked the detective if I needed a lawyer."

Hampton stopped writing. "Hold up. You said 'lawyer'?"

Jason nodded.

"*Before* that little trip to the woods? Who'd you talk to about getting a lawyer?"

"Pershing—the short one—the white guy. Before we went to those woods. He told me if I got a lawyer, they'd go ahead and arrest me and I'd have to wait at the jail for him—for you. For the lawyer—you know what I mean. But if I didn't call one and went with them, I figured I could prove I didn't do it."

"Jason, *you* don't have to prove anything."

The boy wrinkled his forehead.

"The state—the police and the prosecutor—they're the ones who have to prove everything," Hampton told him. "In law, we call it the 'burden of proof.' A person charged with a crime is innocent until proven guilty."

Jason nodded. He'd heard the "innocent until proven guilty" phrase before. *Seventh-grade civics class. And I aced that class, too.*

"I should've known that," he said, hitting the mattress with his fists, wincing when he felt the IV cord pinch. He squeezed his eyes shut. *Let this be a bad dream. Please.* Opening his eyes again, he saw Hampton, still sitting in front of him. Jason turned his head away and shut his eyes, to keep the tears at bay.

"You're not the first person they've deliberately tricked, not by a long shot," Hampton said. "Guys like Detective Pershing keep me in business. Their game is to buy time, to see if they can wear you down."

"Yeah, well, it worked on me, didn't it?" Jason looked at his attorney, no longer trying to hide his angry tears.

Hampton let the room go silent for a moment before answering, softly. "Like a lot of people do, you figured you could talk your way out of it. A lot of grownups make the same mistake, Jason. And the police are well aware of it. They don't care what you say; they'll twist whatever anyone says to fit some story or other about the crime. They take what you say and they develop their narrative from that. Did they leave you alone for a while?"

"Yeah. After we got back to the station."

"And when they finally came back, that's when the confession started?"

"I guess so. I was pretty out of it by then. I don't remember much that happened at that point." *That's only half a lie. I do remember praying. I do remember seeing my Mama and Mack—imagining them. Hallucinating. But I don't remember confessing. Why would I confess to something I didn't do?*

"Why," Jason asked, giving air to his thoughts, "would I confess to something I didn't do? It doesn't make sense. I was pretty much out of it. I guess I have to plead insanity."

"What are you talking about? Insanity pleas are for guilty people."

Jason stared at Hampton, confused. "Well, I didn't shoot anybody. I would never. Ever."

"That's my boy." Hampton smiled and grabbed Jason's arm, giving it a friendly shake. "You get that fight up, and you keep it where you can find it, because you're going to need it. They violated your constitutional right to counsel, they kept you way too long, and they caused your hypoglycemic shock. People sign their names to false confessions under less duress than that. We are going to get these charges dropped. That's my number one priority, starting right now."

A tingle of hope energized Jason. *They can't put me in jail for something I didn't do, no matter how stupid I was after they trapped me, not even if I was seeing things and hearing things that weren't there.*

The glimmer of hope Hampton had given him turned into a fiery adrenaline and surged through Jason's arms and down to his fingertips. When it subsided, he felt weak. He sank back into his bed, settling his head into the pillow like fog on a mountain.

"I've got what I need, Jason," Hampton said. "You get some rest and I'll see you tomorrow. After the hearing."

CHAPTER 30

Tuesday's Headline

Veronica let the newspaper slip from its bag onto the kitchen counter as she dried her face and chest with a towel. Standing on one sneakered foot, she grabbed the other behind her, pointing her knee downward to stretch her quadriceps.

A bleary-eyed John Marshall padded into the room, barefoot, his bathrobe hanging open over his pajama pants.

"Good morning, sleepyhead. You slept through our run."

He nodded and headed toward the coffee pot.

Veronica grinned at his non-responsiveness and alternated feet to stretch her other leg. Looking down at the paper, she noticed the headline—and the photo of John

Juvenile Confesses to Tourist Murder

Lawyer alleges police brutality

"Oh, boy. Front page. My boyfriend."

Boyfriend? Sounds horrible. Marshall wrinkled his forehead. *Fiancé sounds better.* He yawned, carrying his mug of coffee to the kitchen table.

"John?" Veronica's voice filled with worry. "Did you hear me? You're on the front page and…well." She plunked the newspaper in front of him as he sat down with the grace of an arthritic dog.

"Oh," he said, remembering. "The arrest. Yeah." Then he looked down and saw the headline she was talking about, the headline he'd worked to avoid throughout his entire career. And the pictures. *His* picture.

"Oh!" he shouted, finally awake. "No way."

Big and bold, above the fold, a row of square-tile photos stared back at him: headshots of him, Pershing, O'Donnell, and a bruised and battered-looking Jason Royals.

"Shit," he said, his irritation rising. "When a defense lawyer cries brutality, it's front page news, with pictures."

"Yeah. It's Aaron Hampton. I knew he was a fierce advocate," Veronica said, "but I never dreamed he'd stoop so low." She poured glasses of water for both of them before joining him at the table. "Who the hell is giving them your photograph, anyway? I'm pretty sure the department doesn't have to give them to the media."

Marshall didn't hear her. He was reading about the bruising on the kid's body—his knee, his ribs, his face. *No one ever died from minor bruises, right?*

He read on, transfixed and mortified, assimilating the journalistic gem about the suspect's "hypoglycemic shock."

"Yes, the police took him to the hospital—and we're glad they did," Hampton said, referring to his juvenile client, Jason Royals, who is expected to be charged as an adult. According to Royals' attorney, the parents consented to release their minor child's name to the media.

"He could have died or suffered irreparable harm from hypoglycemic shock. But my client wouldn't have needed hospitalization in the first place had the police not violated his constitutional rights, and had they not completely ignored his pre-existing medical condition," Hampton said.

"Instead, they put a medically

fragile fifteen-year-old child in a
very stressful situation—and then
they essentially starved him. Not
only have they coerced a false
confession from an innocent
child, they put his family through
hell with a medical event that
could have ended quite badly."

"Starved him? I stopped and bought the kid food!" Marshall
resisted the urge to throw the paper across the room. "Damn reporter
didn't even call me."

Marshall read further and saw the journalist did try to call—but
got no response from the Homicide Division. *Damn secretary! How
hard is it to give me a heads-up on my cell phone?*

"This guy is a piece of work," Marshall roared. "Medical *event*.
The little punk got low blood sugar and the uniform who was at the
hospital told me he was *fine*. I haven't even had a chance to go talk to
the state attorney about it and they're already accusing us—accusing
me—of fucking *brutality*!" He pushed back from the table with such
force that, as he stood, he sent his chair crashing to the tile.

"John." Veronica's voice was barely above a whisper.

He picked up the chair and pushed it back under the table. "I'm
sorry," he said.

It was the second time in three days he found himself apologizing
to a woman for losing his temper. *This fucking case!* He hung his head
with his hands at his temples. Unclenching his jaw, he tried to focus
on breathing.

"I'm so sorry, Vee."

"I'm okay. Are *you* okay?" She got up, walked over to him, and put
her hand on his shoulder. "Come on. Why don't you sit back down?"

He obliged, sliding the offending newspaper across the table.

"Have you called your union attorney like we talked about?" she
asked. "Or at least the steward?"

"I called yesterday. The lawyer's got me penciled in on his calendar
next week, right after Pershing."

"Oh, no he doesn't. No way." Veronica was animated. She marched
over to open the top drawer in the kitchen, near where the telephone

hung on the wall.

"Listen here, John. There's a conflict of interest, with that lawyer representing both of you, and he's going to go with the first one he sits down with. I know you and Pershing are on the same team, but your *legal* interests might not match up here. You cannot predict what someone will say or do when their ass is on the line. You need your own attorney," she said, rifling through the drawer.

"Philip Zeigenhertz. Call him today. He is the best in town and the union will have to cough up the money to pay for him, since their guy has a conflict." Her voice rose in frustration. "Where the hell did I put the white pages?" She tossed the yellow pages to the floor with a loud thump and slammed the drawer shut. Coins and keys jangled inside of it.

"I'll be right back." Veronica headed to the rear of the house. "You sit there—and breathe."

John nodded, exhaling his steam. He stared through the window at the grass, each blade standing erect, unburdened by the evaporated morning dew. He lowered his head into his hands, glaring at the paper across the table.

With a swift lunge across its surface, he grabbed the newspaper and ripped it up, tearing at his own likeness and the brazen headline.

Fucking defense attorney! Fucking reporter!

Once again, the sound of the wooden chair crashing onto the tile floor reverberated throughout the house.

◆

CHAPTER 31

"Where is Young Mr. Royals?"

Despite Hampton's advice, Clarice and Alvin Royals showed up in juvenile court half an hour before the judge took the bench. They watched as not one, but four members of the media filed into a section reserved for reporters.

Alert, the couple sat behind the railing on a worn, un-cushioned pew, watching as a dozen or so orange-clad young men—nine of them Black, all of them handcuffed—were paraded across the courtroom to a bench in front of them. "Judge Alexander Kirk, Presiding," along with the date, had been written on a dry-erase board, which rested on an easel in front of the dais.

"They're so *young*," Clarice whispered to her husband, as the first name was called. Hanging on every word spoken in the room, they squeezed hands when their son's name was finally called at nine forty-five.

"Jason Royals," the bailiff announced.

"Aaron J. Hampton representing Mr. Royals, Your Honor." Hampton stood, giving embodiment to the deep voice commanding everyone's attention.

The prosecutor, Fred Kirk, spoke. "Your Honor, the state requests the defendant be detained. As you can see by the department of corrections' calculation, the seriousness of the charge outweighs any possible mitigating circumstances. Mr. Royals cannot be permitted to go home. He'll need to be transported to the juvenile facility once his physician releases him from St. Mary's."

By sheer coincidence, Prosecutor Fred Kirk had landed in his uncle's courtroom for the dependency hearing.

"His physician?" Judge Kirk asked. "Where is um…," the judge wondered aloud as he thumbed through the file in front of him. "Where is young Mr. Royals?"

"He's at St. Mary's Hospital, Your Honor." Hampton's baritone voice resonated throughout the courtroom. "He's still recovering from the events of Sunday, when he suffered a very rough several hours in the custody of the Beau Rêve Police Department, which included a loss of consciousness."

Judge Kirk nodded, frowning. "How is he? Does your client's physician expect to discharge him soon?"

"He's improving, thank you, Your Honor. He should be released within the next several days," Hampton said.

"Your Honor," Fred Kirk intoned. "This juvenile is charged with the brutal gunshot murder of a fifty-seven-year-old woman from Fitzgerald, Georgia, Mrs. Betty Patterson."

"I realize that, Mr. Kirk," the judge said.

Clarice, alarmed at the mention of the prosecutor's last name, which matched the judge's, traded looks with her husband as Judge Kirk continued.

"I'm looking at the juvenile arrest report right now," Judge Kirk said. "Mr. Hampton?"

"You might also want to take a look at these, Your Honor." Hampton carried the Polaroid photos to the clerk, who started to hand them to the judge.

"Not until you tell me what they are," the judge said, skeptical, holding up his hands in refusal.

Prosecutor Kirk whined once again. "Your Honor, defense counsel has not provided—"

"They're photographs of my client's face, Judge," Hampton proclaimed, ignoring the other attorney, "and they belie any notion of a *voluntary* confes—"

"That'll be enough, Mr. Hampton." The judge was terse. "Nice try, but you know better. The issue here is to detain or not to detain. The rest will have to wait for trial."

The clerk handed the Polaroids back to Hampton.

"On the matter of detention, Your Honor, I move Jason Royals be released to his parents. It is obvious," Hampton said, holding up the photos, "my client was beaten and coerced into a making a false confession. He had nothing to do with this horrible crime."

"Counselor." The judge's tone rose in admonishment.

"Your Honor," Hampton said, "the child's condition is directly probative to the question surrounding his eligibility for release—his potential danger to society. He simply doesn't pose one. He's fifteen years old; he's on the A-B honor roll at Oakwood High School; he lives with both of his parents, Alvin and Clarice Royals."

On cue, the couple, dressed as if for church and holding hands, stood up.

"The boy can't even drive a car yet," Hampton said. "He weighs in at a whopping one hundred and twenty pounds."

"Ma'am, sir, you may sit back down now," the judge said, respectfully nodding at Jason's parents. "Mr. Hampton, let me be perfectly clear, one last time. This court will not hear evidence regarding the validity of Mr. Royals' confession or any other evidentiary matter. As for release, your motion is denied. Mr. Royals will not be going home. He will be committed to the Satsuma County Juvenile Corrections Facility, pending his release from the hospital. Any further business, counselors?"

Clarice leaned on Alvin who hugged her and whispered, "It's okay. It's going to be okay."

"Your Honor," Hampton said. "I move you recuse yourself from this case on the basis of your familial relationship with counsel for the state of Florida, Fred Kirk."

His Honor, caught off guard, was silent for a moment before speaking again.

"Mr. Hampton," the judge said, leaning back in his chair, settling in. "You might have saved us some time had you made your motion for recusal *before* we got started. I might have obliged you, as judges often do. But at this point, in my opinion, you're grandstanding."

The judge took off his glasses and rubbed the bridge of his nose before continuing. "Mr. Hampton, my name came up in the rotation this morning for juvenile dependency hearings, a fact I regret more with each passing moment."

Light laughter punctuated the tension that had taken hold of the air in the room.

"Do you honestly believe," the judge asked, "my judgment is impaired on this simple question, because State Attorney Kirk and I have the same last name?"

Hampton opened his mouth to speak, but the judge didn't pause long enough for the lawyer to have his say.

"Your motion for recusal is denied."

Hampton nodded. "Something else, Your Honor. Yesterday's judge granted permission for Jason's parents to consult with him privately and with me, under guard, while Jason is in the hospital. I move to extend the previous judge's order until he is discharged, after which the detention facility rules will apply."

"That one I'll grant you, Mr. Hampton. Anything else, gentlemen?"

"No, sir," Kirk said.

"No, Your Honor. Thank you," Hampton said. He turned around to face Jason's parents and tilted his head to indicate they'd talk outside. Walking with purpose past the courtroom's bar, Hampton headed toward the double doors.

Clarice and Alvin filed into the trickle of reporters and other observers who were leaving the courtroom. Hampton was way ahead of them.

CHAPTER 32

TV News

The May sun had already warmed the clear, cloudless air by the time Marshall entered BRPD headquarters. He exchanged a few "good mornings" with the other officers and civil servants in the building and headed down the broad, main hallway.

Pershing and two other detectives were hovering in the doorway of the lieutenant's office when Marshall got to Homicide Division. Curious, he walked toward them, looking over their shoulders at the TV set mounted high in the corner of the absent lieutenant's quarters.

Feeling Marshall behind them, the other detectives looked back, shuffling to make way for him to enter. He and Pershing took the two empty chairs inside.

Marshall's eyes widened as he heard the female reporter's voice. "...detained under guard under suspicion of first degree—"

"I take it you haven't seen—" Pershing began, as Marshall raised his palm to hush him.

"Attorneys say the boy was in police custody for the entire day on Sunday and was not permitted to call his family or a lawyer," the reporter said. "Officials at St. Mary's Hospital confirmed the fifteen-year-old suspect, Jason Royals, has not been discharged from his doctor's care as of this morning, but they refused to comment further on his medical condition."

The anchorman spoke. "Michelle, is there any indication the suspect's hospital stay is related to allegations of police brutality?"

Marshall sighed. *Well, thanks for putting it out there, you asshole.*

The collective groan in the lieutenant's office echoed his thoughts.

"Jim, we don't know at this time whether Jason Royals'

hospitalization is due to mistreatment, other injuries, or some other reason altogether."

"Stop there," Marshall whispered, standing, as the reporter paused to take a breath.

"What we do know is he sustained bruises to his face, and his lawyers contend those bruises were inflicted by the police. All eyes in the Beau Rêve community will be on this case, as charges are filed. And we will be watching it, too, keeping our viewers informed every step of the way. Back to you, Jim."

"Yeah, who's watching you, huh?" Pershing muttered. The roomful of men reverberated with disgruntled dismay.

"Bullshit," one of them said.

Marshall grabbed the remote and turned up the volume.

"...she's live, outside St. Mary's Hospital in downtown Beau Rêve. News Voice 8 has photographs of the suspect's injuries and will bring them to you right after this break."

"Photographs?" Marshall asked, remembering the morning newspaper. "Damn lawyer."

"The kid is scraped up and bruised under his eye. Remember how he walked right into that branch out in the woods?" Pershing said.

Marshall looked at his partner before addressing the other two detectives in the room. "Will you please excuse us?"

"We've got your back, Sergeant," one said as they walked away, closing the door behind them.

"I remember," Marshall told Pershing. "I remember him having a scrape—nothing more." Marshall's eyes darted from Pershing to the TV and back again. "Damn commercials. You saw the photos on TV?"

"They didn't look so bad to me, Sergeant. Apparently, his knee is banged up, too. Bad bruise. He did trip while we were out there, but…" Pershing shrugged.

"Better go talk to O'Donnell," Marshall said. "We know the kid tried to run when O'Donnell stopped him, so we can pretty much bet he was tackled. Find out about it—but don't offer him any other information. Or anyone else, for that matter."

"Oh, joy." Pershing rolled his eyes. "O-fucking-Donnell."

"Yeah, well, he's not my favorite person either, but we need to get this nailed down, right now."

"Remember, Sergeant: We know he fit the description, and he tried to run upon arrest." Pershing held up two fingers, before counting off his other points. "We know he tried to run here, too. He scraped his eye on a branch—so what? He also broke loose from you again, in the woods," he said, holding up four fingers, "and that made him fall out there. And we know, when he got back here, he confessed." Pershing waved five fingers at Marshall.

"Right, good," Marshall said, still distracted by the TV. "Two escape tries, three if you count the woods. Plus, he was stopped while running away from the scene."

The TV noises changed as the commercials ended, and the two detectives turned their attention back to the newscast.

"News Voice 8 is the first to show you these photographs taken of Jason Royals, a juvenile who is expected to be charged with first degree murder as an adult. As you can see, this fifteen-year-old suspect has sustained bruises to his face and, here in the second photo, his knee appears to be badly injured. Michelle Green, are you still there?"

"Yes, Jim."

"Michelle, what do the police say about these injuries, which allegedly occurred while this young suspect was in their custody?"

"Well, Jim, they haven't said anything yet. Calls to Sergeant John Marshall at the Beau Rêve Police Department have not been returned. Attorneys say Marshall was the detective who took the suspect's confession. We also tried the public information officer at the BRPD, but he has not issued a statement as of this morning. We'll stay on top of the story and update you when we get further information."

Shit.

"Go, Pershing. Let me know what O'Donnell says, pronto. I'm going to call my buddy in public info, and we both need to talk to the union rep."

Aaron Hampton. So, this is what you had up your sleeve.

Marshall headed back to the hallway. He needed to visit the public information guy in person. Maybe they could get the homicide lieutenant on the phone from there. He wanted to get on the record with his lieutenant and his union rep. He had nothing to hide.

He entered the public information suite and began chatting with the secretary. "I need to speak with the chief," he said.

"The chief is tied up with the mayor at an event," she replied. "And the sergeant is out sick today. May I leave a message for them, Sergeant Marshall?"

"When will Chief Higgins return?"

"I don't expect him until after lunch," she said. "But I can beep him if you need him sooner."

Marshall thought a minute. *Hampton has already fired his first shot. What more could happen before lunch?*

"Would you please beep him to call my cell, about the time you expect the event to end? Let me write down the number for you."

The secretary handed over her steno pad and Marshall wrote the number, but he hesitated before giving it back. "Would you also make a note, please, that we need to schedule a meeting between him, me, and Fred Kirk from the state attorney's office as soon as possible?"

"Yes, sir." She gazed at the calendar lining her desk. "If you don't mind my asking, sir, is this about the juvenile who was just arrested for murder?"

"Yes. The suspect's lawyer is creating a press circus already, and we haven't even filed the murder arrest warrant yet."

"I'll make sure he understands this is priority number one," she said. She looked down and started scribbling notes intently. Marshall waited for her to look up.

"I've got it, Sergeant. I will beep him at twelve o'clock sharp."

He felt confident she would.

Leaving the Public Information Office, Marshall wracked his brain to figure out what else he could be doing to handle the matter. He concluded, again, that he'd dotted his i's and crossed his t's. He'd gotten a solid confession from a kid who matched the suspect's description, ran away from the scene, ran from the uniforms twice, and broke away from his grip in the woods. He had plenty for countering what the kid's lawyer was alleging.

The evidence is there, Marshall reasoned. *We'll push this one across the goal line.*

CHAPTER 33

The Comfort Room

The "comfort room," which was a gentler name than "murder victim's family lounge," was nestled off of the entry foyer of the chaplain's office. In it sat a pullout couch and two comfortable reclining chairs. A kitchenette equipped with a sink lined the back wall. There, a coffeemaker gurgled to a full pot.

Marshall grabbed a chair from the table in the kitchen area and moved it near one of the recliners. He was ready to speak to the murder victim's husband. Barely forty-eight hours had passed since she was shot dead.

Shrunken. Marshall remembered his impression of Mr. Patterson from the scene.

Deflated.

Back at the motel, the husband had confirmed the manager's account of the loud noise: they'd hoped it wasn't a gunshot. Marshall was satisfied Mr. Patterson was with the manager when the shooting occurred.

Later, Marshall worked the scene inside the motel room with the medical examiner. He was still in the room when O'Donnell showed up with the suspect, parading past the closed door and past Mr. Patterson.

What in hell were you thinking, O'Donnell? Marshall opened the file to the arresting officer's report, reading again the "resisting arrest" charge.

The kid tried to run. At least O'Donnell did the paperwork.

When he heard a woman's voice outside the comfort room, Marshall rose and left the folder on a chair. The victim's daughter had brought Mr. Patterson. Marshall greeted them both.

"I'll be right out here with Father Ray, Daddy," the man's daughter said.

Gerald Patterson looked even smaller in the room than he did at the scene. His eyes were sunken, and his pallor, gray.

He's sick with grief.

Marshall blinked away the memory of blood puddling around Mrs. Patterson's head; he pushed away the image of the dresser mirror, shattered and spattered, as if with crimson paint.

"Mr. Patterson," Marshall said, extending his hand, "I'm so sorry for your loss."

The older man held the handshake a beat longer than necessary, nodding at Marshall, who motioned for him to sit.

"Sir?" Marshall asked. "May I get you a cup of coffee?"

"I believe I'll take you up on that," he replied. "I drink it black."

After the two men sat for a moment, knee to knee, hunched over their coffees, Marshall set his on the low table in front of them. "Are you up to talking about that day, Mr. Patterson?"

The older man nodded, resigned.

"We haven't buried my Betty, yet." His words were numb. Flat. "It'll be a closed casket when we do. I'd like to finish up with you here and get her on home."

"Of course. I can't imagine, Mr. Patterson." Marshall the detective melted into Marshall the human being. His parents were a little older than Betty and Gerald Patterson. He let the man's grief hang in the air.

Marshall didn't move his pen. He left the folder closed. After a moment, he adjusted his chair ever so slightly, which prompted Mr. Patterson to sit farther back in the recliner.

"I understand," Marshall said, "you and Mrs. Patterson were on your way to see your daughter when you decided to stop in Beau Rêve."

"Yes. We can't drive more than six or eight hours anymore. I mean," Mr. Patterson looked down, "we *couldn't.*"

Marshall flinched. How many times had he sat in the same chair and heard family members make the same gut-wrenching correction in verb tense?

"I'm not much for long car trips, either, sir. I'd have done the same thing myself." Marshall looked down a moment before asking,

"About what time did you two check into the Vacation Station?"

"It was already dark," Mr. Patterson said. "So, it had to be at least eight or nine o'clock. I probably wouldn't have stopped there had I seen it in the light of day. Figured we'd check out early enough." The victim's husband looked down at his feet.

"I'm so sorry, sir."

"Thank you, Detective."

"Do you feel up to continuing, sir?"

"Yes. Thank you for asking."

"Okay, so the next morning—tell me about what happened, if you can, starting with when you woke up." Marshall grabbed the folder from the table and began taking notes.

Mr. Patterson recounted rising, showering, drinking bad coffee, and letting his wife sleep until nine. "She's a light sleeper and the noise of the air conditioner woke her up the night before."

"She told you about it before she went back to sleep?"

"No. I woke up with her once, during the night. Said she couldn't catch one wink because of the noise." The husband's eyes welled with tears. "That morning, after she showered, she asked me to wait five minutes for her to finish packing. She said I could load up those last few items and we could drive up to the motel office together.

"Then she looked at me and laughed because I was antsy to get going. As usual. And she told me," he said, his voice breaking, "to go ahead without her."

Marshall leaned forward and touched Mr. Patterson's shoulder. Standing up, Marshall gathered both coffee mugs. After topping them off, he came back and Mr. Patterson restarted their painstaking, pain-inflicting work of remembering his wife's brutal death.

"So, you went to the motel office. Did you talk to the clerk?" Marshall asked.

"Yes, when I turned in the key. It was metal, not one of those plastic cards. They run a small operation. The man behind the counter, an Arabic man, I believe, chatted a little bit about how warm it was getting so early in the season. I told him the AC in our room was on its last legs and he chuckled and said he was well aware. The motel belonged to his parents, he told me. They were trying to decide whether to renovate or sell the property for the land. He had me sign the credit card slip, and that's when we heard something that sounded like a firecracker.

"So, he comes out from behind the counter," Mr. Patterson continued, "and we both walk outside. And that's when I see someone running away from the area where our room was." Gerald dragged a trail with his finger on the armrest of the recliner, as he traced the layout of the motel and the path of the perpetrator. "He ran toward the end of the sidewalk and around the end, here, to the back of the motel. And that's when I ran to our—"

"Before or after you saw the man, Mr. Patterson? When did you start running?"

"The exact moment I saw him—I ran to our room that exact moment."

"Okay, stay outside the room a minute for me. Can you describe the man you saw running away?"

"He was Black. Not terribly tall. Skinny. And he wore tan khaki pants."

"Was he sort of medium-dark like me, or lighter or darker skinned?" Marshall asked.

"I guess about medium."

"Did you see his face?"

"No, Detective," Mr. Patterson said. "I did not."

"How about his shoes?"

The victim's husband shook his head. "I honestly don't remember."

"It's okay," Marshall said. "How about his shirt? Did you see what color shirt he was wearing?"

"It was light colored. But I couldn't tell you what color it was, no, sir."

"Could you see his arms, Mr. Patterson?"

"I don't know. He was a blur. Well, at least until the policeman brought him back."

"Officer O'Donnell."

"I couldn't believe how young the boy was," Mr. Patterson said. "Handcuffed like that. I couldn't imagine someone so young could have so much hatred inside of him. I'm a high school principal, Detective, and in all my years..." Mr. Patterson shook his head.

Marshall paused before asking his next question. "Do you remember losing consciousness at the motel?"

"No. But I remember coming to," the older man said. He took

a quick breath and searched his mind's eye. "I remember I ripped my shirt on the car door when I fell. And I remember the other uniformed policeman who helped me back into his car. He was quite kind to me."

"Why did you faint, sir?"

"I don't know. Shock, I guess."

"Okay, we're almost finished," Marshall said. "Can you be certain the suspect who walked past you when O'Donnell brought him to the motel was the same person you saw running from your motel room earlier?"

Mr. Patterson frowned. "It looked like he was."

"Looked like he was?" Marshall asked.

"He was wearing tan pants, I did see that. It had to be him, right?" Mr. Patterson looked at Marshall with worry in his eyes.

"We believe it was, yes." Marshall smiled reassuringly at the murder victim's husband and then reached into his folder and pulled out a photo array, two rows, each comprising photos of young Black men. "Mr. Patterson, do you think you could identify the perpetrator now?"

The victim's husband scanned the photographs carefully. "Isn't that him?" He pointed to Jason Royals' photo.

"Thank you, sir. We'll just have you sign a statement before you leave." Inwardly, Marshall knew the man's identification of the suspect was fraught. It was one more reason to meet with the prosecutor right away. The state would be relying on the kid's confession—and the confession was on him. He wanted to walk Kirk through it while it was still fresh in his mind. The kid took a tumble in the woods—yes. But the confession was in no way coerced.

Damn O'Donnell.

CHAPTER 34

A Matter of Time

Katrina delivered the news as gently as she could.

"I have to tell you, Jason, we weren't able to get you released before you go to trial."

His eyes teared up as he nodded, stoically. The IV had been disconnected, and he was sitting up in the hospital bed. Jason pushed away the tray holding his breakfast, which he'd hardly touched. His doctors had decided to keep him yet another day, to run a few more medical tests.

"Once the doctors discharge you, you'll be going to the juvenile detention facility. Hamp is meeting with your parents now, to discuss what's next."

Jason kept nodding, as tears streamed down his face. *I've got to pull myself together.*

Katrina reached for her briefcase on the floor, retrieving some tissues. Jason took them and turned toward the window, hiding his face. Outside, the azure sky shone bright over the darker, sapphire river. Beau Rêve sparkled in the sun. The city was going on about its business, uninterrupted by the events that had turned his life upside down. The world would keep turning, he realized, whether his life was falling apart or not.

"I was hoping you had good news." His voice cracked as he tried hard to hold back his sobs. "I want to go home," he said, kicking his feet under the hospital sheets. "I can't stand this. It feels like a nightmare."

Fuck this, he screamed in silence.

"I'm sorry," Katrina paused to give him a moment to vent his frustration. "You've got a right to be angry." She was looking past him, gazing through the window.

"It's only a matter of time," she said. "You will get out. You know that, right?"

Jason nodded and turned away from her. He pulled an arm over his head to hide his face.

"I'm afraid I have to tell you something else, Jason."

"Oh, God," he mumbled. He turned toward her, baring his tear-stained cheeks. "What now?"

"Hamp and I want you to be prepared for the worst. There's a good chance the lawyer who represents the state against you, the state attorney, is going to do a direct file in this case."

"A direct file?"

"Yes. What it means is because of the nature of the crime, the state attorney—the prosecutor—can bypass what we call a certification hearing, and he can go ahead and treat you as if you were an adult."

"The nature of the crime? But I didn't do it." His voice rose in frustration.

"I know, I know. We are on your side, but we want you to be prepared. This is likely what's going to happen. The state's going to charge you as an adult."

Jason slumped and hung his head.

"And that means," Katrina said, resting her hand on his shoulder, "once they make the filing decision, you'll be placed in the adult jail."

"Oh my God!" he shouted. "For how long?" He gasped. "How long am I going to have to stay in…with all those…"

He started thrashing, gasping for air.

"Breathe, Jason." Katrina sat on the edge of his bed and took his hands. "Slow it down, now…there," she said, as Jason did his best to calm himself. "Nice and easy. It's just until trial. If not before. We're trying to get your case dismissed in the pretrial stage."

Jason nodded faster. *Getting the case dismissed before trial.* "How long will it take?"

"I don't know. It could be weeks. Or longer."

He half screamed, half grunted, in his anger and frustration.

"I'd be angry, too," she said, giving him a minute to kick and thrash again. "I want you to know Hamp and I are working as hard as we can to make it sooner, not later. We are doing everything we can to prepare for your pretrial motions. For starters, we're aiming to get the confession thrown out of court."

"Good. What are our chances on *that*?"

"Not bad. Not bad at all. And if the confession goes, there's not much left in the way of evidence."

Jason nodded, his eyes brightening. "What do we need to do to get ready?"

"We need to revisit that evening." Katrina retrieved her briefcase. With her other hand and her knee, she pushed the side chair closer to Jason's bed, making a sharp scraping noise. "Can you remember anything about what was happening when you signed the confession?"

"I wasn't thinking right that day. The day they made me sign those papers. Those detectives had me all messed up, and you know, my blood sugar…"

"I know." Katrina got out a legal pad and wrote something on it. "And the fact it was done in the detective's handwriting speaks volumes." She reached down again and pulled out a copy of the confession Jason had signed. A messy, loopy "JR" punctuated each sentence in the text. Katrina pointed to one of them. "Are these your initials?"

"Yeah."

"What was going on when you were initialing the detective's sentences?"

Jason put his head in his hands for a moment. *How much do I tell her?* "My blood sugar was pretty whacked out."

"Yes, and we have the medical evidence to prove it."

"You mean the doctors?"

"Yes. And also the officer who took you to the hospital when you lost consciousness. He's agreed to testify on your behalf."

"He was sorta nice. I think he knows I'm innocent."

"I think he does, too." Katrina put down her pen and looked at him. "Now, can you tell me anything about the room you were in when Detective Marshall wrote the confession? Who else was there?"

"I'm pretty sure it was only Marshall, but Pershing was in and out…maybe. I don't remember. It was like the lights were dim or something."

"Do you think the lights were turned down in the room?" Katrina asked.

"I don't know. It might have been what was going on in my brain, needing to eat and everything." *Should I tell her about hallucinating Mama and Uncle Mack? Will she think I'm nuts?*

"The reason I ask is because I have a friend with diabetes who has the sensation of her surroundings going dim when she gets hypoglycemic from too much insulin and not enough food. She calls it 'the twilight zone.'"

"Yeah. That's kind of what it felt like. Like the world was slipping away a little." *It feels like I can trust her.* "Miss Katrina, if I tell you something about that day, will you promise to not think I'm crazy?"

"I know you're not crazy."

"Well, I don't want Hamp to think I am, either. But I was so out of it that day, when I was initialing the papers. I'm pretty sure I cried like a baby. I don't remember it all. I was so messed up, for a minute I thought I saw my mama and Uncle Mack in the room with me. But now I know I dreamed them up. They weren't really there."

"Jason, so much was going on with you. The stress, your medical condition. You're not crazy."

"That's what the nurse said. Jillian. About the stress and all."

"There you go, then. The circumstances were pretty extreme."

"Well, I don't know whether to tell Hamp or not. Seeing Mama and Uncle Mack was kind of the reason I thought I was going to go home."

I don't need to tell her about the prayer part. Keep the blood sugar part, leave out the God part.

"I must've thought I should hurry up and sign everything so I could go home with Mama and Mack," he said. "But they weren't there."

"Did the detective tell you that once you got the paperwork done, you could go home?"

"Yeah." Jason nodded. "I don't remember his exact words but I remember that was the idea. It's kind of like a dark swirl in my mind."

"That's helpful. *Not* remembering may reinforce the idea you were dealing with something medical. And they didn't care. They needed you to sign off on each line, since they have absolutely no physical evidence tying you to the shooting."

"Of course, they don't. I didn't do it!" He relished the words she had just spoken. *Absolutely no physical evidence. I like hearing those words out loud.* He asked, "Should I tell Hamp about dreaming up my mother and my uncle?"

"You should tell him. Just because you tell him doesn't mean he'll bring it up in court. Everything you say to either of us is confidential. Your medical condition will probably be enough to keep out the confession. And the part about them telling you they were going to let you go home. I'm going to write that down, if you don't mind."

"No, it's good." Jason felt more and more confident in his legal team, and more and more sure that what happened to him was because his *body* betrayed him—not his mind. Well, his body betrayed him and his mind followed, because his brain lived in his body, after all.

I'll figure out the God part later. Just because I imagined Him answering my prayer, doesn't mean He's only imaginary.

"Miss Katrina?" Jason asked, as she finished writing her thought. She looked up at him.

"Do you believe in God?" he asked.

Katrina raised her eyebrows. Resting her pen, the law clerk leaned back in her chair and thought for a moment. "Well…I believe in *something*. I don't know whether I'd call that something *God* though. Maybe spirit. Or love. Something."

Jason nodded. "My dad says kind of the same thing." *I can go with that.* A slight grin pulled at Jason's mouth and found its way to his eyes.

"Well?" Katrina asked. "What do you say? Do you believe in God?"

"I don't know. I can't figure out why He'd put me through this."

"Well, I'm pretty sure God's not the one who did it to you, Jason."

"Yeah," he said, frowning. "But He *let* it happen, didn't He? And He let that lady get shot, too. And He lets people get sick."

"I hear you. And I don't know what to tell you. It's above my pay grade." Katrina smiled.

Jason smiled back. *I like this lady.*

"Keep asking questions, though. My aunt always says it's our doubts that make us stronger in our faith. Do you have a composition book or something you can write in?"

"Nope."

"I'm going to talk to the guard at the door about letting you have one in your room, so you can write down your thoughts about...about whatever you want. But don't write anything specific down about your case."

"Yeah, they'll twist whatever I write against me."

"Now you're starting to think like a lawyer."

For a fraction of a second, Jason's face beamed at the compliment. "But I can write about other stuff, right? Like if God exists."

Katrina smiled. "Absolutely. You might have to check out the pens for a couple of hours at time, though."

Jason frowned his confusion.

"You wouldn't misuse a pen, Jason, but it's not something they allow for most...um...most people being held over for trial."

"I guess they expect bad people to act bad." He sighed. "It'd be cool, though, if you could get me something to write in, Miss Katrina, thank you."

"You're welcome. Hang in there, okay? It's a matter of time. We'll let you know when we get the suppression hearing scheduled."

CHAPTER 35

The Statement

Detective Sergeant John Marshall had picked a time when his own attorney, Ziggy Zeigenhertz, could join the meeting about Marshall's public statement. When they arrived at the public information office inside police headquarters, prosecutor Fred Kirk was already in the room chatting with Chief Higgins and Lieutenant Cornelius.

The five men greeted each other with waves and handshakes.

"John." Lieutenant Cornelius nodded at Marshall, without getting up.

"Lieutenant," Marshall replied. "Thank you all for meeting so late in the day. I wanted to catch you before the next news cycle. Jason Royals' attorney, Aaron Hampton, obviously has a friend at Channel 8."

"We've got friends of our own down there, Sergeant. Don't you worry," Higgins said, motioning for everyone to sit down, "but we've got to proceed in a manner that protects everyone's rights, including yours."

"My client appreciates that," Zeigenhertz said. "I've explained to Sergeant Marshall he does not have to make a statement unless he's given a direct order to do so. And, if he is ordered to make a statement," the attorney said, directing his gaze to each face in the room, "anything he discloses under those orders cannot be used against him in any potential criminal proceeding."

Marshall winced at hearing the words "criminal proceeding." Zeigenertz had explained it over the phone, but it sounded different in a room full of police professionals. It was extremely unlikely he would ever face criminal charges, but Marshall's lawyer wasn't taking any chances.

"I want to make it clear, right now," Kirk chimed in, "that we don't have any reason to suspect police error or misconduct, much less anything *criminal* on the part of the police." The prosecutor looked Marshall in the eye and then shifted his gaze around the room. "That's not even remotely on our radar, gentlemen. From my view, at this moment, all I see is a homicide suspect with a medical condition and a few bruises."

"And as your superior," Cornelius said, "I see the same, John. We know you're good police."

"I appreciate the vote of confidence, LT." Marshall yielded the floor to his attorney.

"What my client has opted to do is to proffer a statement," Zeigenhertz said.

"He won't go into detail, but it's important to him to get his side of the story out there, so the defendant's lawyer doesn't dictate the media's version of events."

"And it's important to us," Chief Higgins said, "to have as much transparency as possible. It's what the public wants, too."

Marshall said, "I want the public to know—"

"Hold on there, John," his lawyer said. "Let's slow down a min—"

"No, Ziggy—let me finish. I want the public to know something about that so-called *child*." Marshall was insistent. "Just because he's in a hospital bed doesn't make him a saint. That *child* shot a woman in cold blood. And he confessed to it—with no coercion whatsoever."

Marshall's words hung in the air a moment. The PR chief broke the silence.

"I hear you, Sergeant," Higgins said. "All of us here know that *child* and *thug* are not mutually exclusive terms. And I believe everyone in this room respects your reputation for getting clean confessions."

All heads in the room nodded in agreement.

Higgins addressed Zeigenhertz. "We're going to take each fact one at a time, before I write them down, so everyone in this room is clear on what gets released. But before I touch pen to paper," he said, placing his pen and legal pad in front of him, "let's talk a minute. What are your opinions on whether to explain the kid's bruises, the ones in the photos on the TV news?"

"He tried to escape." Marshall's answer was matter-of-fact. He looked at his attorney, who nodded for him to go on.

"He was stopped while running away from the scene, and when

Officer O'Donnell questioned him, he tried to run away from him. He tried to run again when they got him here inside headquarters, and again when my partner and I took him out to look for the gun."

Higgins asked, "Did you ever find it?"

"No, we have not found the gun yet. The suspect did not cooperate. Well...not until he confessed," Marshall said.

Kirk chortled, exchanging glances with the lieutenant.

"Okay. Well. We're going to leave the details regarding the gun for trial," Higgins said. "So, we've covered the escape attempts. I'm going to note them for our statement. Any chance he was charged with resisting arrest?" he asked Marshall.

"Yes," Marshall answered. "He absolutely was. With violence."

"Okay," Higgins said, writing as he spoke. "How does this sound to you gentlemen? 'The defendant is being charged with resisting arrest with violence. He also tried to escape police custody multiple times.'"

"Can we say *multiple* for three?" Marshall asked.

"Absolutely," Higgins replied. "I'd rather not use a specific number. I don't want it to come back at you."

"And I don't want this case to be tried in the press," Kirk interjected. "We don't need to give any more details than what you just said, Chief."

Higgins nodded. "Agreed. Now, was there probable cause for the arrest?" he asked Marshall.

"Yes, he matched the descript—"

"It's a yes or no question, Detective," Kirk said, interrupting him. "We in this room might like to hear it for our personal edification, but beyond having probable cause—the press doesn't need to have the details."

"I agree," Chief Higgins told Marshall, "depending on the details. Sometimes less is better."

Marshall looked at his attorney who nodded for him to go on. "Okay, for the benefit of the people in this room, Royals matched the description of the shooter, given by the victim's husband, who observed him running from the scene. And Officer O'Donnell caught the defendant while he was still running away."

"So, O'Donnell had PC to stop him," Higgins said, making another note.

"Yes, sir. And I need to talk to you about that, Mr. Kirk," Marshall said.

"About the arrest?"

"No. About O'Donnell. He's not in the room, but it's not anything I haven't told him to his face," Marshall said.

"Go ahead and say it, Sergeant," Higgins said, putting down his pen.

"Okay. There will likely be a problem with the husband's identification of Royals," Marshall said. "O'Donnell basically walked the suspect—in handcuffs—right past the victim's husband."

"He did what?" Kirk asked, stunned.

"You heard me right. He contaminated the husband's ID of Royals at the motel," Marshall said.

"Great. Can't wait to meet Officer…"

"O'Donnell," Marshall said.

"O'Donnell. And just so we're clear, not for the press, when the suspect resisted arrest, it was O'Donnell doing the arresting?" Kirk asked.

"Yes, sir," Marshall said.

"Great again," Kirk said.

"Wait," Higgins said. "Is it possible the suspect's bruises may have all come from his struggle with O'Donnell?"

Marshall looked at Zeigenhertz, who shook his head, admonishing Marshall not to answer.

"My client and I have discussed at length the events of April 29," Zeigenhertz said. "And I would like to say while it's entirely possible— your hypothesis that the defendant was injured solely while in the custody of Officer O'Donnell—my client is choosing not to address that question at this time."

Lieutenant Cornelius looked at Zeigenhertz and then at Kirk.

Kirk nodded, speaking slowly. "I don't want you to worry, Sergeant Marshall. I don't think there's any reason that any state witness will need to take the fifth when I try Royals for first-degree murder." He looked at Cornelius. "We need to trust Mr. Zeigenhertz is only being cautious with his client," Kirk said. "If you'll trust me," he continued, turning to address Marshall again, "I believe we can work together on this before trial."

"So long as we're clear I didn't coerce the suspect—not in any way, shape, or form," Marshall said, looking at Kirk. "That much we all need to be clear on."

"We know that, John," Cornelius said.

"Of course, we know that," Higgins said.

Kirk nodded in agreement and said, "I'm pretty sure 'multiple escape attempts' covers the gamut, here. He could have been injured in any number of ways."

"Exactly," Zeigenhertz said.

Marshall frowned. He'd decided before the meeting to trust his attorney's advice by not talking about each of the ways in which the suspect might have sustained injuries that day—walking into a branch, falling down in the woods. He wanted to tell them every bit of everything that had happened, but Zeigenhertz didn't want to hear it.

I don't have anything to hide. And I hate looking like I might.

Marshall deferred to his attorney. He knew he had to trust him.

"So," Higgins said, "here we go: The Beau Rêve Police Department arrested the suspect on probable cause for first-degree murder. The suspect resisted arrest and tried to escape multiple times while in police custody."

"Sounds good to me," Zeigenhertz said.

"Me, too," Kirk concurred.

"Okay, now we need to attend to the whole medical, blood-sugar issue," Higgins said. "In broad terms. We need to address how the suspect's rights were protected."

Zeigenhertz said, "My client followed all procedures relevant to holding suspects in custody through meal-times."

"He means I fed him," Marshall said. The room erupted in laughter, and a layer of tension evaporated.

"You fed him." Higgins chuckled. "Perfect. How about this?" he asked, looking at what he'd been writing. "The Beau Rêve Police Department has firmly established policies regarding caring for suspects in custody, and those policies and procedures were followed here."

"Beautiful," Zeigenhertz said.

Marshall nodded, avoiding eye contact with his attorney. *Policies* and *procedures* were important buzzwords, Zeigenhertz had told him. So long as Marshall could show he followed the BRPD rules, Royals' attorney couldn't sue him *personally*. If, by some off chance, the homicide trial went haywire and Royals went free, any lawsuit would have to be directed at the department and not him.

Hopefully, I'll be out of Homicide long before that ever happens, if *it happens,* Marshall thought.

When he'd brought the subject up with Zeigenhertz, the attorney advised him to wait a few months before making any departmental transfers, giving time for the media coverage in the Royals' case to die down a little. Marshall could start the process behind the scenes, but he needed to wait to change divisions in order to avoid public speculation about why he was transferring. Although he'd been thinking about switching out of Homicide for months, he could be patient a little longer. He wanted to make his next career move quietly.

Marshall allowed himself a momentary sigh of relief. For the first time since he'd seen the newspaper headline, he finally felt like he was getting out his side of the story. Even though the press wouldn't have all the details, the department was backing him up. So was the state attorney. And that was good enough for him.

Plus, he'd insulated himself from being sued personally.

On the way out of the meeting, Marshall saw Pershing walking toward him with the union attorney.

Well of course, he realized. *They have to talk to my partner, too.*

Marshall projected as much calm self-assurance as he could to his fellow detective. "Hey, man," he said, reaching out his hand.

"Sergeant," Pershing said, shaking hands.

The lawyers exchanged cards while Marshall leaned in and whispered to Pershing, "It's all good, partner. There's good police in there."

"Good to know," Pershing whispered back. "Thanks."

As Marshall and Zeigenhertz left Pershing and his attorney, Marshall realized Veronica had been exactly right. *I've got the right representation.*

He hoped Pershing's younger lawyer, the union's counsel of record, would listen equally as carefully to the seasoned professionals in the room.

CHAPTER 36

The Re-Arrest

"Fred Kirk, line one," Hampton's secretary said, as her boss carried his coffee mug back to his office.

"Thanks, Sandy." Hampton nudged his door closed, set down his coffee, and punched the speakerphone button. "Good morning, Mr. Kirk," he said, sitting. "What can I do for you today?"

"Mr. Hampton, good morning. Tell me, is your client still in the hospital?"

"Yes, sir. They've had to run a number of tests this week. Took a little longer than we thought. Not only does he have a complex medical condition, but he was also in pretty bad shape once your officers got finished with him."

Kirk did not respond to his colleague's baiting. "When is he expected to be discharged?"

"I'd say by the beginning of next week," Hampton replied.

"Well, I'm about ready to file an arrest warrant on him for first degree murder, and I wanted to let you know."

"Thank you, Mr. Kirk. You're direct-filing?"

"Yes, sir. Call me Fred, please."

"Only if you call me Hamp."

"Alright, Hamp. I have to tell you; this kind of heinous crime is exactly why those statutes were written."

"Too bad you've got the wrong guy," Hampton said. "But I'm going to enjoy seeing your case fall apart in pretrial hearings."

Kirk laughed. "Not with our evidence, you won't."

"We'll see about that. When can we expect the arrest warrant to be served?"

"Well, that's why I'm calling—as a courtesy to you. I can have the police come get him at the hospital or at the juvenile shelter. It doesn't matter to me, one way or the other, but I thought you might have a preference."

"How about a third option?" Hampton asked.

"Like what? A white Bronco?" Kirk asked, chuckling.

"Funny, Fred. But unlike Los Angeles, Beau Rêve doesn't have enough highways. Or enough helicopters with TV cameras. And unlike Nicole Simpson's killer, my client didn't drop any gloves. Or anything else for that matter, for the simple reason he was not there."

Kirk bypassed the baiting again. "We're past the point of letting him turn himself in, Hamp. We're not going to let him out of police custody, sorry."

"I had to ask. When should we expect the police to pick him up?"

"Monday. Barring any unforeseen medical complications, of course."

"Of course. I'll stay in touch with the family, and with Jason's doctors, and with you. I'm thinking we'll do it at the hospital, Fred. Let's touch base Monday morning to firm up."

"Will do. We'll get him to adult jail, where he belongs."

"Where he'll await dismissal of his case," Hampton retorted.

"See you in court, Hamp," Kirk said and hung up.

Hampton sat back and smiled, taking a long draw from his coffee mug. It would probably be easier for Jason to go straight to jail instead of making a stop at the juvenile detention center. The optics could work in Jason's favor, either way, but the teenager had been through enough. Minimizing his trauma was the way to go.

That is, unless Kirk was planning something.

Hampton thought through the contingencies. If Kirk were planning something, he would definitely have press there. It would be a chance for the police to respond to the brutality allegations.

Hampton pressed the intercom button on his phone. "Sandy?"

"Yes, sir?"

"Would you please put in a call to Michelle Green at News Voice 8?"

"Sure thing."

"Tell her it's not earth shattering—I'd like to share a little information before day's end."

＊

Jason had dressed as if for church, in a light-blue oxford shirt and fresh-pressed khakis. Tucked in, with a belt, he told himself, as it was on the previous Sunday morning when he left the house—before the unimaginable happened.

He'd held his composure as much as he could all week long, with Hampton, with his parents, even with the officer guarding his door, especially with the officer guarding his door. But when Katrina told him the police were coming for him—and where they'd be taking him—he lost it. That moment, he had to face that they'd be taking him to adult jail, and not juvenile hall.

He sat on his hospital bed, next to Katrina, crying into her shoulder.

"It's okay to let it out," she said. "It's going to be all right. We're going to make sure you're safe. Hamp's working on getting you your own…um, your own room, without a roommate. And we're going to get you out as soon as we can, okay?"

Jason nodded and pulled himself upright, grabbing the Kleenex box.

"This is hard. I can't imagine how hard it is for you. But Jason, you're a strong young man. You've got to remember how strong you are, okay?"

"Okay." He quieted his sobs.

"Okay. Hey, I wrote something down for you, but it's a little mushy so you have to promise not to laugh."

Jason's eyes widened. "Okay. I promise. I won't laugh."

She pulled out the composition book she had pledged to bring to him.

"Thank you," he said.

"It's inscribed, there on the first page. Take a look."

He opened it. "It's in cursive."

She laughed softly. "Yeah. Can you read it?"

He tried, nodding. Her neat and tidy script was easier to decipher than he thought it would be, a little like his mother's.

Dear Jason,

Between your family and our law office, you have a whole team of people who love you and care for you very much. We are working as hard as we can for your freedom. You are very important to us.

Please remember that even when we're not with you in the flesh, we're still right there with you.

And, Jason, as hard as it will be, I hope you will try to find something to be grateful for every day.

Best regards,

Katrina

Jason beamed at Katrina and reached out to hug her. "I'm grateful for you," he whispered. "Thank you."

"You're welcome. I'll make sure you get this when you're all settled in." Katrina inhaled and blew out her breath before speaking. "Now, I want to tell you something important, okay?"

"Okay."

She braced her hands on his shoulders and looked him in the eye. "Don't make any facial expressions or aggressive motions when the police walk you out, in case there are any cameras arou—"

"Cameras? News cameras?" Jason was crestfallen. The last image he wanted anyone to see was of him being escorted out of the hospital in handcuffs.

"Just in case, Jason. I want you to be prepared. Keep your hands down, and keep your head up, but don't smile or frown. Look at something in the distance. Focus on a clock, or a painting— something on the wall would be good."

Jason adjusted his clothes. He smoothed down his shirt and judged himself presentable. He never got his sneakers back, but his mom had sent his church shoes.

As he took a breath to steel himself, the guard opened the door to let his parents into the room.

"Well," Clarice said, pausing to take him in, "don't you look handsome?"

Jason could feel the tears welling up but he resisted them. She'd said the same to him that Sunday morning. He wanted to be strong for his mother. He stood to hug her.

"Remember, Mama," he whispered. "I'm still with you even though I won't be with you, you know?"

Clarice took a sharp breath, fighting her own battle to hold her emotions intact. "And I'll always be with you, son. Always. Promise me you won't give up hope, okay? Promise me you'll keep your faith."

Faith. In God?

Jason had decided he would be putting his faith in Hamp and Katrina. He'd be putting his faith in the fact he was innocent. But he said, simply, "I promise, Mama."

"Jason," his father said, "I'm going to arrange for you to keep up with your classes while you're...while you're away from school. It will give you some positive tasks to focus on, when you're ready. No pressure."

Jason nodded, smiled a tight-lipped smile, and then hugged his dad. *Here they are getting ready to put me in jail, and he's worried about my schoolwork.*

"We love you, son," his father said. "We're going to get through this together. Set your mind on it and keep it there. Can you do that for me?"

"Yes, sir."

"We'll be down to see you as soon as they'll let us."

A uniformed policeman, who Jason had not seen before, walked into his room. His skin was the color of iced tea, like Jason's own, though the officer was an inch or two taller. He was slightly heftier than Jason, too—fit and muscular.

"Jason Royals?" the uniformed man said.

"Yes, I'm him," Jason replied.

"You understand what I'm here for?"

"Yes, sir."

"I have a warrant for your arrest. Could the rest of you step away from Jason, please?"

Katrina, Clarice, and Alvin stepped aside as the officer approached.

"We're right here, son. It's going to be okay," Alvin said.

"Keep your head up, Jason," Katrina reminded him.

"Jason Royals, you're under arrest for the murder of Betty Patterson. You have the right to remain silent...."

Jason stood mute as the officer read him his rights and handcuffed him. Unlike the first time it happened, Jason was prepared. He'd already cried his tears, and he'd already hugged his parents goodbye. He didn't fight, and he didn't try to run.

Numb, he looked out the window as a few cars trickled across the concrete bridge. He saw the even blue tone of the river below, mirroring its sky.

The water looked calm and still, but Jason knew it was flowing, as rivers do, toward the ocean.

PART TWO

"You don't become what you want,
you become what you believe."

— Oprah Winfrey

CHAPTER 37

"Why Are You Here?"

When the jail alarm sounded at seven a.m., Jason was already sitting up on his bunk, awake. He waited for the inevitable shipyard whistle that followed—it blew at seven and eight in the morning, noon and one p.m. to delineate lunchtime and, finally, at five o'clock in the afternoon. Ralph, one of the nicer correctional officers, had explained that Old Jack had blown for generations in Beau Rêve, signaling workers when to start and finish work. It was a downtown phenomenon, Jason figured. He'd never heard it at home on the Eastside.

He rose to get ready for his twice-a-week shower. Soon, Ralph, who worked weekdays, paraded down to his door with huge, lumbering Octavius.

Octavius walked with slumped shoulders, his head down, reminding Jason of a stray dog. When a dog walked around in such a manner, Jason thought, it usually meant it had been beaten.

Another guard stood behind them with Clyde, a nonviolent offender who had permission to mingle with Octavius and Jason, the only two juveniles in the B wing of the adult facility.

Jason breathed in through his nose, as he did each time he left his solitary cell. He smelled urine, bleach, vomit, and body odor—especially the suffocating body odor. The mixture was still discernible even though he'd been there for more than a week. He never wanted to get accustomed to the god-awful smell of jail.

While Hampton could not get the judge to agree to bail, he had been successful in keeping Jason segregated from the other inmates. He had attended the jail classroom a few times with Octavius, but Jason ate his meals alone in his cell.

Octavius didn't say much, and from what Jason had observed, didn't *do* much during their classroom stints.

Octavius's cellmate, Clyde, on the other hand, was talkative. He was serving a year for taking money from his company's Christmas charity fund when he needed to have his car fixed.

"I thought of it as *borrowing*," Clyde had explained. "And my boss didn't want to press charges. But, to the state, it was grand theft. So, my lawyer pled it down to a misdemeanor, and here I am. I got a year here, which I'll take instead of Raiford, any day."

Talking to Clyde, Jason learned the difference between jail and prison. The local jail was where people usually waited for trial. However, it was also used as a lesser sentence for people who could plead their way down from a felony to a misdemeanor. Prison, on the other hand, was a state-run ordeal, which was to be avoided at all costs.

The guards led the trio to an open, tile room with showerheads jutting out of the walls. It was another feature of incarceration Jason did not want to get accustomed to—the lack of privacy, the guards watching them. Those indignities strained his patience. Jason waited a full two minutes for the water to heat to lukewarm. The prison-issue block of soap yielded only a weak, gray lather. He turned his back to the others, soaped himself quickly, and rinsed.

He then walked back to the dressing bench and patted himself with a minuscule, threadbare towel. The towels were small and thin for good reasons: so no one could use them as weapons or as ropes for committing suicide by hanging. It was the same reason they couldn't have belts, or drawstrings, or shoelaces.

It's only a matter of time. Jason's mind echoed a phrase soon to become his mantra. *It's only a matter of time. I'm innocent. They won't be able to convict me. It's a matter of time until I'm home showering with hot water, drying off with real towels.*

The CO, Ralph, tilted his chin upward, actively averting his eyes to afford the men a momentary measure of privacy. He handed Jason a fresh jumpsuit. The boys' uniforms were a washed-out green, signifying juvenile inmates, while Clyde wore a bright orange jumpsuit, giving his white skin a yellowish pallor.

Jason got dressed. "Why're you here?" he finally asked Octavius.

"'Cause my stepdad hate me," Octavius said.

Jason looked at him quizzically.

"Grand theft auto, 'cause I borrowed my mama's car." The large man-child towered over Jason.

"C'mon, gentlemen," Ralph said, leading the three inmates and the other guard out of the shower and back to the floor. "Let's get you back now."

"*What?*" Jason said to Octavius, confused, as the five of them walked toward the cells.

"I didn't know the car was registered in the asshole's name. He hate me. Mama let me borrow her car all the time. 'Specially since she got her license 'spended."

"You got a good lawyer?" Jason asked him.

"Yeah. She just slow. She say goin' slow is good, though. She hopin' I get time served when it finally come up."

"How old are you?"

"Seventeen."

"So, you're a junior in high school?"

"Naw. I dropped out last year. Miss Holden tryin' to get me to do my GED." When Octavius mentioned their jailhouse teacher, his head sank lower and sadness crept into his eyes. "But I ain't cut out for school."

"Ah, man, you've got to stay in, okay?" Jason said, as Ralph opened the first cell.

"Last coming out, first going in, Jason," the CO said, as the other guard held the other inmates' arms, one in each hand. "We'll make sure Octavius meets you in class, don't worry."

"Yeah, don't let me be the *only* one in there, alright, man?" Jason said to Octavius from inside as the barred door slammed securely shut.

The guards and Clyde looked at the hulking boy. "Ah-ight," Octavius said. "Ain't right you havin' to go by yourself."

Three days later, Jason would learn from Octavius's cellmate that the boy could not read. "He's embarrassed," Clyde whispered to Jason on the way to the shower room. "He won't talk to me about it."

How Octavius earned his driver's license remained a mystery.

CHAPTER 38

The Visitor

Jason glanced up from his writing to see Ralph was still working in the makeshift office across from his cell.

When he saw the other correctional officer approaching him, Jason closed the composition book. His list, *What to Do When I Get Released*, could wait.

"Someone's here to see you." The guard unlocked the door and slid open the bars.

"Who?" Jason asked.

"Kim Callahan. Says she's a friend of yours."

Kim Callahan? Oh, yeah, Kim!

Jason dashed over to peer into the dull metal slab, bolted to the wall over the lavatory. It was a poor substitute for a mirror.

"Don't worry." The CO chuckled. "You're beautiful. Not as cute as she is, though. Your mama know you're seeing a white girl?"

Jason suppressed the grin he felt overtaking his entire body. *Kim. I can't believe she came to see me.*

He walked through the open door and waited for the guard to shut it. Jason had gone out of his way to be polite and respectful to the COs, and he felt like it was paying off. Maybe it was because of his age, or maybe they sensed his innocence. He noticed a difference between how they addressed him and Octavius compared to the other inmates. Even so, he vowed not to be fooled again by people in authority.

They may like me better than the others, but they are not my friends.

Following the guard to the visitors' area, Jason spotted Kim on the other side of the Plexiglas, before she saw him.

She, on the other hand, is definitely my friend.

The two sat down and picked up the phones.

"Hey," he announced, nonchalantly.

"Hey," she replied, taking a couple of warm and lilting syllables to do so. Her eyes, shimmering blue kaleidoscopes, smiled along with the rest of her freckled face. The two looked at each other, awkwardly. She eyed his green outfit and her smile faded for an instant before she brought her gaze back up. A warmer, softer smile beamed at Jason, as if to say, "You're still the same guy I know."

Jason took a breath before breaking the silence. "I'm sorry I stood you up."

Kim frowned in confusion before laughing loudly. "Yeah, looks like something came up!"

"That's one way to put it," he said. "How come you're not in school today?"

"I'm done." She shrugged. "Last day for seniors was Friday. I graduate tomorrow."

"Aw, wow. Congratulations." He gave a thumbs-up from his side of the window. "Wait—you mean you're graduating tomorrow and you're sitting here talking to me *today*?"

"I figured you probably haven't had many friends from school visit, you know? Plus, I wanted to bring you this." Kim reached down to her feet and lifted a large piece of orange construction paper. It had been folded in half to create a giant greeting card. Jason's name was spelled vertically down the front, in big block crayon letters, with words spelled out to the right.

Jason is…

Awesome,

Superb,

Our friend, and

N. O. Cent.

She held it up to the Plexiglas so he could get a good look. Then she opened it to reveal dozens of messages and signatures.

"We support you all the way, Jason," wrote Carleen Jones. "We've got your back, man," appeared in C.J. Bradford's barely legible scrawl. "You have lots of friends pulling for you, including me," Kim had penned, leaving her phone number. Their messages resembled the inside cover of a yearbook.

The tiny, mathematically precise cursive in the lower right-hand corner caught his eye: "Jason, you're strong enough to overcome this outrage, and I know you will. Hang in there, man. See you back on the court soon." It was signed, "your friend, Brendan Taylor."

Brendan signed my card?

He and Jason had been friends when they played for the Blue Gators at the YMCA when they were in grade school, but they lost touch in middle school. Though they'd started to reconnect in high school, Brendan had always seemed a notch or two above Jason on the "cool" scale, so Jason didn't push the friendship beyond the occasional "hi" or "what's up." Jason had always intended to get back into basketball—besides playing in the driveway or at the church—but hadn't been able to make it happen yet. To see the words, "You're strong," connected with Brendan's name, caught him off guard. He looked away and looked back again and started to speak but didn't.

"What is it?" Kim asked.

"All these people took the time to sign this for me. Even Brendan."

"Are you kidding?" Kim lowered the card. "*Especially* Brendan. He took what happened to you pretty hard, Jason. It was all he could do to hold his temper when the police came to interview every—"

"The police came out to the *school?*"

She nodded.

"To ask about *me?*" Jason slammed back in his chair and slumped.

"They wanted to know about some gang. The College Lifers. Strange name for a gang, if you ask me."

Jason closed his eyes and shook his head.

"Hey," she said, as she watched his chin hit his chest. He was still holding the phone receiver. "Hey," she repeated, louder. "Look here. Don't worry about any of that. Your friends know you didn't do what they're saying, Jason. We know you're innocent, see?" She held up the front of the card and pointed to the "N" in his name.

He nodded and forced a smile, but the magic of her visit had evaporated. Somewhere inside himself, for a few minutes, he'd forgotten he was in jail, wearing a green jumpsuit, sitting behind a partition. For a brief moment in time, he'd allowed himself to become a kid again, the same kid who first met Kim back at Wellstein's while she was stocking shelves. He looked up at her again, wishing they were somewhere—anywhere—else. A tiny glint caught his eye, and he drifted back to the day he met her.

"What *is* that? A diamond?" he asked, pointing to the base of his own nose.

"Yeah, a little one." She blushed. "It's my birthstone. I bought it for myself when I turned eighteen, a year ago. My mom actually cried when she first noticed it, but my dad? He constantly annoys me over it. He calls me *Diamond Girl* now and sings some song from the seventies. Drives me nuts."

Jason's face broke into a broad grin.

"I'm so glad it amuses you," she said.

"Your dad sounds a lot like my dad, Diamond Girl."

She rolled her eyes. "This is what I get for coming all the way down here?"

"So, you're nineteen now?" he asked. "You said you turned eighteen a year ago?"

"Yeah. I'm behind a year in school. Long story."

"I've got time." His words hung in the air, heavily, between them. Neither of them knew how much time he would be spending in the county jail. "C'mon. Tell me the short version."

"Okay. I was in a really bad car accident when I was seven. Drunk driver. Took me a long time to recover. Bones in both of my legs were basically shattered, so I had to have lots of surgeries and physical therapy." She looked down, remembering. "I had to learn to walk all over again."

Jason stared at her, his eyes wide, horrified.

"I'm okay now," she said. "I'm really, really okay. It was a long time ago."

He wrinkled his forehead, trying to picture a child of seven struggling to walk. "You must have missed a lot of school."

"Yes. Surgeries, medicines—there was no sense even trying. I was in the hospital for the better part of a year."

"A year? Did anyone come visit you?"

"Yes, but mainly grownups. I didn't see my friends for a long, long time."

She knows what it's like—to have your whole life turned upside down in one day. "Well, if you can get through *that*," he said, "me getting through *this* should be a cinch, DG."

Kim blushed again. "It's only a matter of time," she said,

unknowingly echoing the exact words his lawyer, the law clerk, and his parents had each said to him. Somehow, hearing it from Kim, Jason believed it more.

"Some of us put our phone numbers in there," she explained, "so you can call us when you need us, like when you go to court, and when you get out of here." She held up the card, waving it. "They said you could keep it and take it back to your...um...back to your room. I already asked."

CHAPTER 39

A Girl Named April

As the suffocating heat of Beau Rêve's summer days dripped past, Detective Sergeant John Marshall longed for October. He could set his watch by the daily, four o'clock thunderstorms. Drier, crisper days were still months away. He headed to the men's room at BRPD to blot the sweat already soaking his face and neck. It was eight a.m.

When he reached his desk, Marshall grabbed a pencil and lifted the sheets of his calendar to write in several depositions and court dates. The bit of graphite at the point had fallen out.

Walking toward the division secretary's desk, he wondered how long it would be before he was using another electric sharpener, in another department, with different coworkers.

He smiled and nodded at Lucy as he inserted the Ticonderoga number two.

"I like your shirt," she said to him. "Very sharp. Even though it's hot as Hades, I like seeing you guys in dress shirts as opposed to golf shirts all the time. Especially on weekdays."

"Thank you."

Marshall was eager to transfer out of Homicide, but he had chosen not to share his plans with his current division, at least not until something solid was on the horizon.

Even after the transfer, he'd be keeping up with his batch of homicide cases for months to come, maybe even years. There would be numerous court appearances and depositions to attend, and countless loose ends to tie up before he could pass the torch—especially on death penalty cases. They could go on for decades.

"John," Lucy said, as the detective was walking back to his desk, blowing the shavings off of his pencil.

"Yeah?" He turned.

"I hate to hit you with this first thing in the morning, but the lieutenant asked for you and Pershing to please take this one." She held out the file. "It was a special request."

He read the file name aloud. "April Meadows." He opened it and, in a low voice, said, "Oh, sweet Jesus. Ten years old?"

Lucy nodded at him, tight-lipped, eyes watering. She took a breath before speaking. "Pershing's not in yet, but if you want to head to the hospital, I'll have him stay here until you call."

"Call his cell and make sure he's on his way here. I'll be at St. Mary's. Don't wake up the officer who took the report. Not yet. Let her sleep while I see what I can come up with."

Homicide, as a matter of practice, got called in on cases where the victim's life was in peril. A little girl named April was fighting for hers in the intensive care unit.

Goddamn monster. There's a special place in hell for child rapists.

After parking in a space reserved for law enforcement, Marshall navigated the clean, brightly lit halls of St. Mary's. Passing two cafes and an enormous gift shop, he felt as if he were in a shopping mall instead of a hospital. The building's cheerfulness belied the tragedies occurring behind hundreds of hospital room doors.

"I'm so glad you're here," a nurse said, spotting the badge at his belt as she moved toward him in the corridor. She walked him through the double doors of the ICU entrance, which automatically closed behind them. He handed her his card.

"Sergeant Marshall," she read. "Thank you. My shift is finished, but I wanted to see this one through before I left."

Marshall was not prepared for what he saw. Through the opened blinds of her intensive care room, he watched as April's frail, bruised body heaved in rhythm to the respirator. The apparatus and tape holding the breathing tube in place obscured the child's face, along with the bandages wrapped around her forehead. A huge temporary cast on her right arm made her left arm seem that much tinier, that much more delicate.

"That animal beat the hell out of her," Marshall said.

The nurse, exhaling an angry sigh, nodded. She gestured to the woman curled in the chair next to April's bed. "Her mom was delirious, hardly able to speak, when she came in."

As he watched the tiny girl shudder with each mechanical breath, Marshall wondered whether surviving the horror—and the years of recovery the child faced—would be better than dying.

Don't let your mind go there. Focus on getting the bastard who did it.

"We didn't get much from Mom before we had to sedate her," the nurse said, dropping the bombshell. "It was April's uncle who did it. Her dad's half-brother."

Marshall felt the anger—the heat of ten thousand suns—well up through his body. "Where was her father?"

"In the Army, on active duty. Apparently, the mom needed the uncle's girlfriend to babysit. When the girlfriend had to go somewhere else, she left the child with…"

"Have you got an address?"

The nurse nodded. "Yeah, and I'm pretty sure the information fits under the exceptions to HIPAA. For the record, do you fear for the safety of individuals or the public, Detective?"

"Yes, ma'am, I do."

The nurse went to her station to retrieve the information.

Marshall filled in Pershing over the phone and dispatched him to the family's apartment. He'd have the office get Fort Orange on the phone to try to reach the father. He would command the investigation from the hospital until April's mom woke up. Snapping his cell phone shut, he walked to the nurse's desk to resume their conversation.

"Tell me the extent of her injuries. Broken bones? Concussion?"

"All of the above. Spiral fracture of the radius and a dislocated shoulder. Most likely concussed. She also has two broken ribs and her spleen is ruptured, but not to the extent that the doctors want to do immediate surgery. And then there are the injuries from the rape." The nurse turned her head, willing her tears away. "She's so tiny," she said, her voice giving way. "He brutalized her."

Marshall looked at his feet. "You performed a rape kit?"

"Yes. We had a physician from the U of F child protection team here. I'll get you her contact information." Steeling herself, the nurse delivered the rest of the bad news. "Her lungs are pretty badly bruised. The docs thought the respirator would make her breathing easier."

"Easier?" It looked anything but easy to Marshall. "Dear God. Is she going to make it?"

"Maybe. We hope so. We're trying to keep her quiet enough to heal."

"Any idea when she'll be able to talk?"

"No. We're not even sure *if* she'll be able to talk. The blow to her head was severe. They pulled out the larger glass pieces in the ER. He may have hit her with a drinking glass or a bottle."

Marshall winced, and made a note about the glass for Pershing. "So, you think there might be brain damage?"

"Yeah. We won't know for a few days, at least. She's on heavy-duty pain meds. We may have to keep her medicated to keep her pain manageable—to keep her breathing."

CHAPTER 40

Harry Morning, Noon, and Night

Jason's optimism was fading. He couldn't keep up the adrenaline that had seen him through the first several weeks of jail.

He'd worked to keep his mind on the future and tried, like Katrina had advised, to find something to be thankful for every day. He took the time, and he had plenty of time, to write them down. Topping his list were her weekly, legal-update visits—though he didn't understand why depositions stretched over weeks and months.

Why does justice move so slowly?

He was also grateful for the surprise visit from Kim.

As for his mother's visits, it was always emotional for him when she came, less so with his dad. And he never, ever wanted Lucas to see him in a green suit, behind Plexiglas. He missed his little brother, but he was adamant about it. His dad understood, and sent Lucas to play with Cam during their Sunday-afternoon visits.

Jason put his big-brother energy into being friends with Octavius, even though O, as he called him, was older. He got to see Octavius in the jail classroom two hours a day, twice a week during summer school at the jail. Never mind that it made the rest of the time lonelier than ever. Octavius, whose mother was always drinking, drugging, or drying out, had less than nothing, not even a home—not with his stepfather looming there.

33. I'm thankful my parents are still married.

Hampton had the judge sign off on basketball games and movies with O, Clyde, and three other adult inmates who were in jail for economic crimes, like bouncing checks to the electric company or the grocery store. Jason couldn't say he knew what a bounced check was before one of the guys explained it to him, along with a game he had not heard of: "Beat the Bank."

"Being poor ain't a crime," Christmas-fund Clyde had told him. "But trying to survive sure might be."

"You couldn't find someone in your family to borrow it from?" Jason had asked. He vowed not to let himself or anyone he loved become so poor.

"That would've been a better idea," Clyde had said, nodding. "But I was too embarrassed at the time. And I thought I could pay it back before anyone noticed it missing. Don't ever be as stupid as I was, Jason."

Jason nodded. *Too late*, he thought. *I was so stupid I got arrested for something I didn't even do.*

He'd promised Katrina he wouldn't write or talk about his case, and he didn't. Whenever someone asked, he'd say only, "False arrest."

Jason assumed the other inmates knew his arrest was for first-degree murder. Every now and then, he'd catch someone peering at him from a distance, frowning, as if to ascertain whether Jason was capable of shooting a person in cold blood. But none of the "good-behavior crew," as Ralph called them, ever treated him as if they believed he were a murderer.

34. I'm thankful Ralph is a decent human being.

Jason grew tired of his many lists. It was no longer enough to imagine the friends he would call when he got out, the basketball games he'd be playing with Joey and Jimmy Sullivan from next door, the new bike he'd be buying, the learner's permit he'd be getting, the video games he'd be playing, the movies he wanted to rent.

He'd imagined the dozens of conversations he'd have with Brendan, with C.J., with Kim. He'd imagined a group of friends going to prom. The limo they'd rent. The photographs they'd take. The colleges everyone would apply to. The car he would eventually drive. That reminded him.

He flipped back in his composition book and wrote "Honda Civic" on his *Possible Cars* list, scratching out the current numbering system to rank it somewhere above Toyota Corolla.

Both of those were far, far below Ford Mustang.

He'd already imagined everything he possibly could.

Jason's focus on keeping his mind strong succumbed, eventually, to numbness. At times, he wanted to scream at the top of his lungs, *Get me out of here! I don't belong in here!* But he pushed the urge away until the icy pins and needles of fear and anxiety melted, washing over him like cool water.

His demeanor was important, he told himself. He'd do nothing to indicate he was anything less than an upstanding citizen.

Sometimes he thought he heard someone crying, softly, in the distance. The cries, buried and muffled somewhere deep in his consciousness, were his own.

A psychic veil fell between him and the realities of incarceration: the indignity of being watched every moment, the lack of privacy, being herded from place to place like an animal, and the chill of the godforsaken metal surrounding him.

He was there, yet not there. During a few, surreal instances, he felt as if he were watching himself from a distance, as if from outside his own body.

◆

The annoying voice of the new inmate was ruining Jason's newfound numbness.

"Roo-oo-oo-oom service!" the twangy voice rang out several times a day, followed by the low, echoing, metal thuds of a jail-room door being kicked.

It was the inmate Jason had secretly named "Harry," and his voice never failed to stir a distinct mix of disgust, fear, and nausea in Jason. The man was charged with raping his own ten-year-old niece.

A scraggly-looking white guy in his late twenties or early thirties, Harry apparently got a kick out of the fact Jason did not eat with the other inmates. His meals were brought to him on a tray, instead.

The prisoner, like Jason, had been housed alone, but unlike Jason's lawyer, Harry's attorney had not needed to make a special request. Harry's cell was located across the wide hall and down one door, where the COs could easily get to him.

Jason learned the scraggly man's real name was Varken; his own, secret appellation was a tribute to the man's frizzy, dishwater-blond hair and his wild, unkempt beard.

He hadn't looked at the prisoner long enough to comprehend which scaled animals were tattooed on his forearms. Fish? Or snakes? Whatever they were, the bluish creatures began on the man's hands, wrapped around his wrists, then his arms, and crept upward underneath the sleeves of the orange, prison-issue jumpsuit. The thought of those slithering scales sent Jason's skin crawling.

He was careful not to let himself stare, or worse, to get caught staring.

That morning, Jason cut his eyes to the cell directly across from his own, which Ralph and the other COs used as a makeshift office. Large, stacked file boxes lined the far wall. Taped to the ends of the boxes were the first letters of last names, written in black marker and crossed out and rewritten as the contents shifted or expanded. An ample, worn, metal desk with duct-taped feet sat in front of the boxes and was often occupied by Ralph or another guard. Filing duty occurred in short stints, but Ralph was spending more time at the desk since the new inmate arrived.

Jason sometimes chatted with whichever CO was engaged in clerical work. It wasn't much more than "Hi, how are you?" but it was worth the trouble of getting up and walking toward the front of the cell before retreating to his preferred perch on the top bunk, where he did most of his schoolwork and wrote most of his lists.

He couldn't see any other inmates besides Varken, and because of the position of their catty-cornered cells, he couldn't see him unless he deliberately tried. He'd made eye contact with Harry only once, aiming a nod of acknowledgement in his direction.

Remembering that moment made him shudder.

The scaly, mystery animals had lunged forward. Tattooed hands grasped the cage and rattled it. Harry growled, "What are you looking at, nigger?"

Jason had darted back to his bunk, where he couldn't see Harry and where Harry couldn't see him. His blood turned cold and his heart tilted, pounding.

Jason knew the word. He'd been raised never to repeat it. He'd heard it occasionally, from peers caught unaware, around blind hallway corners at his school. But until that moment, over the course of his entire life in

Beau Rêve, Florida, no one had ever directed it at *him*—to his face.

"Yeah, that's what I thought," Varken had crowed. "Stay outta my sight. Better yet, go back to Africa, you stupid nigger."

"Enough!" the CO roared, banging his billy club on the metal desk. "Cut the crap, Varken, or you'll be back in the hole."

"Your mama's hole!" Varken retorted.

A chorus of "Ooohs" echoed through the previously calm corridor, followed by Harry's bizarre cackle. The ill-timed chortle inspired chuckles and laughs, which reverberated down the row, but which ceased when the CO spoke again. No one wanted to miss a word.

"Call that strike one." The guard spoke without yelling and without rising from his desk. "Solitary's waiting for you. And I'd love nothing more than to put you in there and forget about you. Now shut the fuck up."

Varken had, indeed, shut the fuck up on the CO's order. But it didn't stop his ritual of yelling "Room service" every time he caught a glimpse of Jason.

Jesus, where'd this guy come from? As Jason surveyed the paint deficiencies in the ceiling, his father's words tumbled to the forefront of his thoughts. *Margin people.*

It must take work to be so disgusting, to get so far away from decent living, Jason thought. *So far away from* covenant *living*, his father would say. For a man who professed his general dislike for church, Jason's dad had a good grasp of religious vocabulary.

Jason sat up, opened his composition book, and doodled the words "Harry Reptile Varken." Then he laughed out loud when he imagined hairy reptiles, summoning the image of a furry iguana. He flipped to a page in the back of his book to experiment with herpetological drawings.

I'll get Mama to bring the How to Draw Animals *book we have at home. May as well. What else am I going to do around here?*

On his third try, Jason nailed the essence of the iguana's image and turned back to the front of his book to draw a bigger version, one with long, flowing hair emanating from the lizard's head. He framed his hairy reptile with the words "Harry Reptile Varken" written over and over again around the scaly creature. The name, quite naturally, circled the page's margins.

CHAPTER 41

Keep Santa Alive

The visit from his mother had not been easy.

Jason regretted how he'd responded to her nagging about Pastor Junior. Part of him regretted it, anyway. Another part of him felt liberated by his act of defiance.

I'm the one incarcerated—not her. I'm the one using the toilet with only a newspaper for privacy—not her. I'm the one eating mystery meat every day—alone—while the racist across the hall yells "room service."

He was the one enduring it all, but he kept reading, kept writing, kept working ahead on his school assignments because there was nothing—*nothing*—to do in jail. It was Hampton and Katrina who'd get him out, not God, certainly not the same God who allowed him to get locked up. Pastor Junior was not going to get the chance to hijack Jason's arrest—or his incarceration, or his court battle—for some sermon on the triumph of Christian suffering.

He'd be just fine without some fool talking to him about God's will.

What kind of God would will *an innocent person to be put in jail?*

When his mother raised the subject of the young reverend, Jason had accidentally raised his voice.

"No way, Mom. No way! Keep him away from me!"

"Alright, Jason," she said, exasperated. "But I really wish you'd tell me what it is you have against Pastor Junior. Why don't you like him?"

"I just *don't*, okay?"

"Well, you never reacted this way to Pastor Lawrence. Should I see if he could come instead?"

"No, Mama!" Jason was shouting again. "Please don't!"

His mother looked down.

"I'm sorry, Mama. I didn't mean to yell. I don't want to see *anybody* from the church. If I change my mind, I'll let you know. But stop asking me, okay?"

◈

Pastor Lawrence R. Rodman earned the nickname "Senior" only after Pastor Barnaby Elliott, Jr. was assigned to Mt. Carmel AME Church as his assistant. Pastor Lawrence, aka, "Pastor Senior," was perfectly wonderful. Lawrence was a quiet, studied man not prone to the emotional urgency Jason reviled in "Junior." Jason had disliked Junior ever since the church lock-in in sixth grade when the young and unseasoned theologian was fulfilling his first pastoral assignment as youth leader.

An older, seventh-grade boy had made the mistake of sneaking over to the girls' building to kiss his girlfriend. Junior berated the boy in front of everyone before lapsing into a diatribe about the "sins of the flesh" and "purity" and not permitting "Jezebels" to derail young men from their righteous paths.

Jezebels!

Pastor Junior didn't quit there. He launched into a rant about hellfire and damnation.

He went on and on for what seemed like hours to Jason.

As soon as he could manage it without calling attention to himself, Jason quietly faked a stomachache to one of the peer counselors, a high school boy. The boy helped him get to a phone so he could call his mom to come pick him up. To his relief, his mom had been appropriately concerned. She took him straight home, cooing over him, trying to determine whether it was a ginger ale stomachache, a Pepto-Bismol stomachache, or a Phillips' Milk of Magnesia stomachache. He hadn't needed to explain why he couldn't stay another minute in the same room with Junior, and he wasn't going to go into it during her jail visit.

He'd rather forget the whole episode.

◈

"What *can* I do for you, Jason?" his mother asked him. "What about your birthday? What would you like for your birthday?"

He had expected the question. He knew his mother would be thinking about his upcoming birthday. He didn't want to upset her again, but he'd already thought through his answer. Taking a breath, he said, "I don't want any celebrations until I get out, Mama. It's just—it's too emotional right now."

She looked at him, but did not speak.

He knew he'd hurt her, but he also knew he didn't want his mom and dad to try to pretend they were happy, or to pretend *he* was happy, simply because the calendar was going to flip to the next year of his life.

"There must be *something* I can do for you, Jason." His mother's voice shifted an octave lower, as she—thankfully—avoided crying.

Damn. Look what I've gone and done. There's got to be something she can get for me...

"Yeah, actually, there is something, Mama. You remember those Matt Christopher books I used to read in elementary school?"

"The sports stories?"

"Yeah. If you could bring me two or three of those, I'd appreciate it. There's a kid in here who has trouble reading, but I might be able to help him out with the right books."

"I imagine you *will* help him, Jason." Clarice beamed at her son, her eyes glassy but tearless. "What a nice thought. I'll bring them."

Clarice thought for a moment. "Better yet, I'll get them to Mr. Hampton and have him or Katrina bring them, since they're technically educational materials. That way they won't get lost sitting in some corner waiting to be searched. Hey," she asked Jason, "what's your friend's name?"

My friend? He's not exactly...well, in here, maybe he is my friend. "Octavius."

"Octavius," Clarice repeated, smiling. "Well, I'm glad you have someone to talk to, son. I'll get you those books."

❖

If nothing else, Jason figured, he could read aloud to Octavius. He planned to talk it over with Mrs. Holden first. He couldn't imagine not being able to read or write.

I'd go crazy in here! Damn, it's boring enough as it is. Damn.

Back in his cell, Jason whipped down on his pillow with the rolled-up newspaper. The guard, working in the makeshift file room in the cell across the hall, glanced up.

"Sorry," Jason said.

The CO nodded without looking up again. Jason felt like the guards *knew*. He wondered whether he could be misreading them. Maybe it was only his young age, relative to the other inmates; or, it could be because he was polite—a lot better mannered than most of the people in the Satsuma County Jail. His gut told him most of the COs realized his arrest was a mistake, and they knew he wasn't capable of hurting anybody. After all, he'd apologized for thumping a pillow!

The clock behind the CO at the duty desk read a quarter to three. There'd be another couple of hours to fill before dinner. Jason resisted the urge to slam the pillow again, and instead opened the paper to look for the crossword puzzle. Not a baseball fan, he set the sports section aside.

Summer is such a dead time for sports.

As he laid out the local news section, a headline caught his eye: "Local man shot, killed by police."

A shudder ran down Jason's spine as he realized his own predicament could have been much worse than jail. He, too, could have had a fatal encounter with the police. He knew too well, how one wrong moment could forever alter a life.

Thank God they didn't kill me.

As he read further, Jason learned the man had been "agitated" and spoke of delivering "the righteous wrath of the Lord." It was right before he'd lunged for one police officer's gun. The officer's partner didn't give God's messenger a second lunge.

As Jason read and reread the article, he felt slightly nauseous. There was a guy who believed he was hearing the voice of God.

He was crazy. Does that mean I'm crazy, too?

Jason ripped the article out of the newspaper and reached for his composition book, which had found a permanent home on his bunk. Katrina's idea to write down his thoughts had been a good one. While Jason hoped his mother would never read what he'd been writing, he wished one day *somebody* would. Then, maybe *somebody* would tell him the truth.

Had Jason been lied to his whole life? He remembered when he told his mother, years before, he no longer believed in Santa Claus. She told him, for Lucas' sake, he needed to keep Santa alive.

Keep Santa alive!

Jason had laughed out loud when his mom said it, because he knew it was a reference to the video his parents had made him and Lucas watch when they were little. A Black civil rights activist who had run for President kept saying, "Keep hope alive! Keep hope alive!" Over and over again he said it. "Keep hope alive!"

Jesse Jackson. That was his name.

Keep Santa alive. What was that supposed to mean? Help his parents lie to his little brother? Be part of a conspiracy of liars? Was God another trick—another lie—like Santa Claus? Was his mom in on it, or did she truly believe everything she said about God? Did his dad say he believed in something "bigger than himself" just to keep the peace with his mom? Jason understood why his dad didn't really like to go to church, but he was not sure about an invisible force in the sky who was "bigger than himself." Not anymore. Furious, he wrote as fast as his hands could get the words out.

> Okay, here's this guy the cops shot dead. I don't know why they couldn't have shot him somewhere that wouldn't have been fatal, like in the leg or something, but they killed him.
>
> Here's the problem, though. He said he heard God talking to him, so of course he was crazy. And I guess crazy is dangerous.
>
> Apparently, anyone who has full-on, two-way conversations with God is mentally ill. It'd be like a grown person saying they'd talked to Santa Claus. Which, of course, they say all the time in front of their kids around Christmastime.

But if anyone walked into a restaurant if it wasn't Christmas and claimed they were talking to Santa Claus, well, it'd be a little weird, wouldn't it?

Actually, it's not the talking so much as the listening that gets you into trouble. Praying seems fine and good. But hearing God's actual voice? That's not okay.

Once this guy said out loud that God was giving him specific directions, then everybody knew he was crazy. Then they had to go get him some mental help. Except they never got that far.

What if he really did hear God's voice? Does everyone who hears God talking have a permanent mental problem? That's a scary thought. Don't mention that one to the ladies at my church. Correction, Mama's church. I'm not going there anymore.

I wonder what the guy—the one who got killed—had to eat that day. I wonder what it was made him so stressed out.

Are there people who are allowed to get messages from God while others aren't allowed? Like maybe if you go to church long enough you can tune into the God frequency, like it's on a radio? God radio! Ha ha! Gotta remember that one. Could make a lot of money off of it.

Maybe if you get your degree as preacher, it gives you some free, all—

access pass to actually hear His voice. It doesn't make any sense. Do they teach you some special chant or magic word or something? Ridiculous! How can people believe this stuff? Getting to be a preacher is just a way for people to use their own brains to say what they want God to say, isn't it?

Like, when you sit in church on a Sunday morning and someone gets up during the peace and gives a testimony about what God told them to do. And everything worked out hunky-dory for that person so everybody says, "Amen." "Praise the Lord." "Praise God."

No one ever gives a testimony and says, "I thought I heard the voice of God but I was way, way off and now my life totally sucks."

No, the only people who get up in church to talk are people who have something bad happen, and then something good happens to them and they thank God for the something good. Maybe something bad just happened and then something good just happened. If there's a God, then he's the one who let the bad thing happen in the first place, right?

CHAPTER 42

"Happy Birthday, Jason"

"What's this?" Jason pointed to the box on the table as he entered the lawyer-client conference room.

Katrina smiled. "Don't you have a birthday coming up?"

"Yeah." Jason caught himself. "I mean—yes, ma'am. This coming Saturday. I'll be sixteen."

"Good," she said as she opened the box to reveal a giant cookie. "I got the number right!"

The one and the six took up the center of the cookie in thick, swirly white icing, with "Happy Birthday, Jason" rounding out the top and bottom. Katrina used a plastic knife to cut a generous wedge for Jason and handed it to him on a napkin.

After slicing it like a pizza, she took the piece of plasticware to the door and knocked. "Thank you," she said, handing it over to the guard. Turning her attention back to Jason, she said, "I hope you like chocolate chip."

Jason couldn't help but smile. "I *love* chocolate chip. How'd you get this in here? They don't ever let my mom bring any food in."

"They're a little more liberal with the law offices—at least here at the county facility."

"Thank you, Miss Katrina."

"You're welcome, Jason. And you don't have to call me *Miss*. Katrina is fine. I'm not much older than you are, you know."

"How old *are* you?"

"Twenty-five. Twenty-six in December." She wiped a bit of icing off her lip with her finger and kissed it clean. "I'm about old enough to have been your babysitter, back in the day."

Jason laughed through his cookie. "Back in the day. Huh." He absentmindedly talked and chewed at the same time. "I bet you were a fun babysitter. You would've let us stay up late and order pizza, right?"

"You know it!" Katrina thought for a moment. "I forgot—you have a little brother. What's his name again?"

"Lucas. He started middle school a couple weeks ago."

Jason's mood shifted. *And I'm now doing my sophomore year* here, *in jail.* He looked at Katrina, and decided Lucas was a good way to keep the conversation going. "He's four years younger than I am."

"So, if he's starting sixth grade, you'd be starting tenth?" she asked.

"Yes, ma'am. But…you know. In *here*."

"I'm sorry, Jason. Not being with your friends—it's got to be… well, it's got to suck."

Jason gave her a sly smile.

"What?" she said.

"You're definitely closer to my age than my parents' age, for sure. They'd jump on me if I said that word."

"Yeah, well, sometimes only one word will do." Katrina winked at him. "Go ahead. Say it if you want to. What happens in the conference room stays in the conference room."

Jason swallowed the last bite of his cookie wedge. Then he sat up straight and stretched out his arms, as if he were preparing to lift weights. "Okay. I will!"

"Go ahead."

"Are you sure you're ready?" he asked. "Now?"

She nodded.

"This," he said, gesturing to the room. "This!" he said louder, indicating the entire jailhouse and the situation in which he found himself. "This s-u-u-u-cks!" he exclaimed, laughing. "It sucks so bad!" He started yelling, trumpeting the word. "It s-u-u-u-cks!"

Amidst his guffaws, he slammed his hands down on the table, triggering the attention of the young, female correctional officer who had not been bothered by the yelling. She peered in through the window, frowning at Jason. At the sight of the paralegal laughing with the inmate, the guard rolled her eyes, shook her head, and turned back around.

"All righty then!" Katrina said.

"I know some worse words." Jason grinned.

"I'll bet you do," she retorted, holding up her hands. "We're good, though. Save those for your journal. Are you writing?"

"Yeah, I am." Jason relaxed in his chair. "It helps, too. You were right, Miss—you were right, Katrina."

"I'm glad. I hope it helps you pass the time, along with your books. Oh—" She reached down into her satchel. "I almost forgot why I came here. Aside from your birthday, of course." Katrina winked at him. "Your mom sent these for you. She said you might be teaching someone how to read?"

"Yeah, his name is Octavius. I may end up reading the books to him. I don't know yet." Jason picked up the Matt Christopher novels. Holding them in his hands, he felt as if he were revisiting old friends.

"Reading to him sounds like a good start. And you can see if Mrs.…." Katrina waved her hand as if to summon her name. "Your teacher. She might have some ideas, too."

"Mrs. Holden," Jason said. "Yeah, now that we're back in school every day, maybe she'll give me some time to work with him." He thought about Octavius and Octavius's strung-out mother, and how his no-good stepfather had him arrested. "He's had a pretty hard time."

"How old is Octavius?"

"He's seventeen."

"I'm glad he has you."

"I'm glad I have *him*. It's pretty lonely in here. Not to mention boring."

"Oh! Speaking of not being bored…" She reached into her bag once again. "This one's from me. Happy birthday!"

Jason unwrapped the present—undoubtedly a book, given its size and weight. "Oh my gosh." His eyes widened. "How did you know?"

"Your mom told me you finished the third one last Christmas. You know the movie for the first book is coming out in November."

"*Harry Potter and the Goblet of Fire*." Jason read the title out loud. "Have you read it?"

"No. I'm just now getting started. I borrowed the first one. My niece is a huge fan. She says number four here is her favorite—so far."

"Cool!" Jason held up the book. "Thank you so much for this."

"You're welcome."

"Hey, Katrina?"

"Hmm?"

"Hey, any chance I'll be out in time to see the Harry Potter movie?"

Katrina went silent.

"Never mind," he said, shaking his head. "Don't even—"

"I don't know, Jason. I won't lie to you, okay? Not ever. But I just don't…given where we are, in the middle of depositions…" She looked past him. "I don't think the chances are too great at the moment."

"Well," he said, "that sucks."

CHAPTER 43

Not Unwarranted

Laughing, Detective Sergeant John Marshall shook his head as he hung up the phone. He stretched his legs and pushed his chair back from his new desk—in the Fugitives and Warrants division.

"What's so funny?" his new partner asked.

"My last name."

Detective Ken Bateh absorbed what his partner was saying, then chuckled. "Not to be confused with the U.S. Marshals Service. Ha!"

"I can't believe it never even occurred to me before I transferred in."

"You can always change your last name. To something like 'Agent.' Or wait—wait—how about 'Sergeant?' Sergeant John Sergeant."

"Yeah. Keep it up, funny man." Marshall grinned. He closed the file he was working on and tossed it into his out basket. "I sure hope our other colleagues across the country are brighter than the bulb I just got off the phone with."

"Where'd you call?"

"Oklahoma."

"You must have gotten an Okie from Muskogee."

"A *what?*"

"I guess you're not a Merle Haggard fan. I'll have to put it on a CD for you."

"Can't wait."

Bateh laughed. Marshall smiled, nodding. He and his new partner were going to get along fine.

Father Ray had been right—Fugitives and Warrants was a more relaxed, congenial place to work. The biggest part of his new job was logistics and planning, centered on how to get bad guys from one jurisdiction to another. Other people's felons landed in Beau Rêve often enough, and Beau Rêve's criminals, likewise, invaded other people's states and cities.

He didn't mind the travel. Even when they had to drive instead of fly, he would never be more than two or three days away from the love of his life.

Veronica.

The thought of her quickened his pulse.

"You are set on keeping that old monster, aren't you?" she'd said about the infamous chair on the day he moved in.

"At least until we can find it a good home. It reminds me of my football days."

"You know something that would remind you even more of your football days?"

Marshall gave her a puzzled look.

"C'mon, John. We've talked about you volunteering a million times. You know you're a natural coach. There's a bunch of little boys out there who'd give up their Nintendos—even their PlayStations— to play football with *you*. You have so much to *give*."

His shoulders fell, and he sighed. "It's going to take some time, baby. It might not be *this* year. I need to keep a low profile for a little bit longer."

"Why? My God, it's been months since—"

"Don't say it." He knew she was about to mention one of the two cases he tried to forget when he left Homicide. The problem was those two cases wouldn't forget *him*.

The warrants gig was temporary—a parking spot—until the publicity in the Patterson murder case died down. Veronica was right. He *would* be a great teacher—maybe. Eventually. He might go back to school, get his master's, get into education, and move up the ladder as a principal or dean somewhere. He wondered whether he could tie his city tenure to the state pension system if he went the teaching route.

The first step was to wait out the false allegations of police brutality. With the accusations the defense attorney was spreading around, Marshall didn't want to apply to *volunteer* for the Police Athletic League, much less transfer into PAL as an employee. Plus, if he did decide to seek teacher certification, he wanted the case well behind him.

So, warrants it was. Warrants it would be, for however long it took. As he was mapping his upcoming trip to Augusta, Georgia, his cell phone rang.

"Marshall here."

"Hey, John. It's Rick Pershing back in Homicide. I've got some bad news."

Marshall sighed, remembering the girl in the hospital bed. "Is it April Meadows?"

"Yeah. She took a turn for the worse and they couldn't put off surgery any longer. She didn't make it through. She's gone."

Marshall's blood ran cold, down the back of his neck, into his shoulders.

"You there?"

"Yeah, I'm here, Rick." He fixed his eyes on the bulletin board covering the far wall, to contain the rush of emotion. "What a damn shame."

"Well, I didn't know if you wanted to come with me on the arrest. The son of a bitch we caught for rape is now going to be charged with murder."

"I appreciate you asking me, but you're the one who found the bottle. You found his prints, and shoot, you found *him*. How about if I pop in when they get the needle ready for his arm?"

"I hear you. No one's going to be sorry to see Donald Varken leave this earth. I just wanted to check with you before I went to see Kirk."

"Thanks, man." Marshall dug a coffee mug out of his desk drawer. "Hey, give my regards to Kirk, will you?"

"You bet. Catch you later, Sergeant."

"Catch you later," Marshall replied, and both men hung up.

Bateh had overheard most of the conversation.

Marshall raised his cup, signaling to his partner he was going out to find some coffee and would be back soon. Then he quickly walked out of the office, resisting the urge to throw the ceramic against the wall, resisting the need to see it explode—as he wanted to explode.

◆

CHAPTER 44

Satsuma County Reading Lessons

Jason smiled as he walked into the classroom, remembering the word Mrs. Holden had used the previous week.

Splendid.

It was a *splendid* idea, she'd told him, referring to his offer to help Octavius with his reading. Jason wondered if anyone besides teachers ever said the word out loud.

"I'll need to speak with Octavius about it first, though," Mrs. Holden explained. "I don't want him to be embarrassed—or worse, resentful. He likes you a lot, and I think I can get him to go for it. But it's got to be his choice."

He said yes!

Before class began, Mrs. Holden met Jason in the jail classroom with a list of sight words and a handful of blank index cards.

"I wouldn't overwhelm him," she said, looking around for the older boy who had not yet arrived. "One or two sight words per week should be enough. I'd also pull a few words from the book when you read aloud to him."

"Done! I've already found some I think he'll like. From a couple of books."

Mrs. Holden smiled. "Good job! Remember—concentrate on the fun of the story, Jason. Keep it light. Your time reading together should be something you both enjoy."

Makes sense. Maybe O never got a chance to like books.

Jason thought about the times his mom and dad read to him when he was little—every night at least. Anytime he wanted, really. He'd done the same for Lucas, on nights when his younger brother couldn't get to sleep—even though it drove him nuts sometimes.

From what Jason had gleaned about Octavius's mom and family life, there was a good chance *no one* ever bothered to read to him.

Mrs. Holden had arranged to give the boys the last twenty minutes of their three-hour block in her classroom, provided they keep up with their other work. Jason had worked ahead in most of his subjects.

The slump-shouldered teenager finally lumbered into the classroom.

Mrs. Holden said, "Good morning, Octavius."

"Mornin'," he replied.

"Hey, O," Jason said.

"Hey." The older, larger boy looked from Jason, to their teacher, and back again. "I guess I'm late. Ralph had to help the other guards tie down Varken. I don't know what he done."

"They restrained him, then?" Mrs. Holden asked.

"Yes, ma'am. Restrained. But it took a minute. Sorry."

"It's quite all right."

"Oh, God." Jason's voice was as hard as gravel.

"What?" Mrs. Holden and Octavius asked at once.

"I heard Ralph and another CO talking about a murder arrest going down in the jail…maybe it was the little girl that Varken attacked…oh, God. I think maybe she died. His own niece."

The weight of the news plummeted before them, and each of them looked at their feet.

"Boys," Mrs. Holden said. "Shall we have a moment of silence before we get started?"

Both students nodded. She held out her hands, and they formed a tiny circle.

"It's for you to remember the soul of the girl who died, however you feel comfortable. Let's remember her and her loved ones, and let's also envision you two remaining totally clear and separate from Mr. Varken."

"Amen," Octavius said.

Jason winced at the word "amen." *It was supposed to be a moment of silence, not a prayer.* He felt Mrs. Holden and Octavius squeezing his hands on either side. After letting go, the trio stood in place another moment before dispersing.

Poor girl.

Mrs. Holden then got Octavius started on some handwriting exercises before administering a History test to Jason.

With a half-hour to go in their morning block, Jason eyed Mrs. Holden. She nodded for him to go ahead.

"Hey man," Jason said, walking toward Octavius's desk. "I brought some sports stories I thought you might like. I thought I could read them out loud. Mrs. Holden already said it was okay."

"Sports stories?" Octavius squinted his curiosity.

Jason pulled a desk close to where his friend was sitting. "Yeah. I've got one about soccer and one about football." He showed him the paperbacks from his childhood. "You up for one of these?"

"Maybe." Octavius frowned. "But not soccer. I don't know nothin' about soccer."

"Me, either, really, but we could read it to learn more. If you want to."

Octavius raised his eyebrows, considering the possibility. Then he shook his head. "I rather be reading the football one, okay?"

"Okay with me, man." Jason tossed the book to Octavius. "It's called *Catch that Pass*."

Octavius grinned at the joke and nodded his approval, turning the book over in his hands as if to inspect it. "Looks good to me."

"The main guy is Jim and he plays on a team called the Vulcans."

"Did you already read it?"

"Yeah, but it's a good one. Definitely worth reading again."

Jason wrote "Jim" on one of the index cards and set it down on the desk in front of Octavius.

"It says 'Jim.'" Jason pointed, spelling. "J—I—M."

Octavius nodded. "Jim," he repeated, putting a finger on the card.

Jason couldn't tell if Octavius was really reading the card or not. For the moment, he decided, it didn't matter.

"Okay if I start reading?" Jason asked.

"Yeah, man. I'm waitin' on you."

CHAPTER 45

Twin Towers

Jason knew why his father had come to visit him that Tuesday afternoon.

"Do you get any TV in here?" Alvin said through the phone, looking at his son from the other side of the Plexiglas partition.

"Yeah. We saw the news about New York, Dad," Jason said. "I can't believe it."

"What exactly did you see?"

"About the planes crashing into the World Trade Center. And another one hitting part of the Pentagon in DC."

Alvin nodded. "And a passenger plane crashed in Pennsylvania. Everyone died."

"Oh my God," Jason said. The shock of the morning news had worn off, but the other event shook him all over again. "Are we going to have a war?"

"No!" Alvin looked around the jailhouse and then back at his son, watching Jason's youth slip away. "I don't think so, son. I really hope not. Truth is, we don't know. It's kind of moment by moment right now."

The world's going to war and I'm...here. If they bomb Beau Rêve, I'm trapped. I can't get out!

Terror washed over Jason, then receded into detachment, flattening the gleam in his eyes. He retreated to a place just beyond himself, beyond the here and now, as if he were watching his uninhabited form. *Is this a dream? This can't be real.*

"Jason? Jason? Hey, can you hear me, son?" Alvin had just witnessed the light leaving his son's eyes. It was as if Jason were looking *through* him, instead of at him. "Jason?"

Jason refocused on his father, a glimmer of recognition returning.

"Look, son. You can't shut down like that, okay? Do you hear me?"

Jason nodded.

"You've got to keep your mind strong. Getting you out of here is still our first priority. Got it?"

"Yeah."

"Look at me," Alvin said. "That's why I came. So you know you're not alone. There's nothing more important to us than getting you out of here. Got it?"

"Got it." Jason sighed. "I…"

"What?" Alvin asked. "Say it."

Jason sat mute.

"Say it!"

"I hate this, okay?" he yelled. "I fucking hate it." Jason's belligerent look dared his father to scold him for using the F-word. "I fucking *hate* having to be trapped here while all this is happening."

"I'd hate it too." Alvin spoke firmly, and then he looked down for a moment. "Truth be told, you'd hate it if you were anywhere else, too. There's not a lot any of us can do right now. Your mama went and got Lucas from school and they're at home. But for the most part we're doing what you're doing—trying to get information."

"What about the Navy bases up in Jacksonville, Dad? We're pretty close by. Wouldn't those be targets?"

Alvin looked at his son for a moment, frowning. "Could be. Or, maybe, the people behind this don't have any real power. Otherwise, why send hijackers?" His voice pitched up as he shrugged. "Why not bombs? Why not warships? Their plan to destroy the Pentagon backfired. It might have been their big play. But they missed."

"I hope you're right about it being their big play."

"Me, too. But even if it was, they killed a lot of innocent people. Civilians. We'll still probably have to respond—somehow."

"I still can't believe someone attacked our country. I remember when I was a little kid I watched a war on TV. But it was in someone else's country."

"You couldn't have been but five. You remember the Persian Gulf war?"

"Yeah, Mama got mad at you for letting me watch."

"Yes, she did," Alvin said, smiling. "She was right."

"How is she?"

"She's hanging in there, son. Trying to stay positive about you. I had to convince her to limit her calls to Hampton's office to twice a week, unless something comes up. They've been good over there—trying to explain the process, every step of the way."

"Yeah, Katrina's great. I don't hear much from Hamp, but Katrina says they've been going to depositions. People are testifying with a court reporter and all. She says once those get typed up, we'll have something to work with."

"Hamp knows what he's doing, Jason. He's the best in town. Your Grandpa Clarence wouldn't have it any other way."

"Is Grandpa the one paying Hamp?"

"Don't you worry about it. We've got it worked out. We'll get a second mortgage if we need to."

"What's that?"

"It's a loan on the house. Thank God we have some equity we can borrow against. Your grandpa has already got the bankers lined up for us, you know. He's got a bunch of friends in the Black bourgeoisie. The Black Boulé."

Jason nodded. For all his dad's talk about education, "enfranchisement of the mind" as he called it, Jason could feel Alvin's deep respect for his grandfather's social circle—a club Alvin himself was not a part of.

"We may not be upper-class Blacks," Alvin said, "but—"

"But we have graciously been granted *access*." Jason finished his father's sentence, which he'd heard a thousand times before.

Alvin's face lit up in surprise. "Lo and behold. The boy has been listening after all."

"You still have Grandpa Clarence come to your classes to talk?" Jason asked, smiling.

"You bet. I try to do it in the spring—give my AP American History students a break before the test. Got a pretty good group this year. You keeping up with your reading?"

"Yes, sir. The textbook and the Zinn book. Especially the Zinn book."

"Always remember: history doesn't belong only to the dominant culture. Zinn is college-level material, but you've been reading at college level for a while now."

Jason was taken aback, but played it cool, nodding in response to his dad's compliment. Alvin had never been effusive with praise. If anything, he was reliably critical, always holding him and Lucas to a higher standard, always nitpicking.

"How's Lucas?" he asked. "How's sixth grade going?"

"Pretty good, when the child gets enough exercise." Alvin grinned. "So long as we limit the video games."

"I remember." Jason smiled. "He turns into a monster if he plays too long."

"Yes, he does. Too much adrenaline, not enough movement." Alvin looked down before asking, "You sure you don't want him to visit? He asks. Every week."

"No, sir. No way."

"All right, all right. We'll keep it to me and your mama then, since you don't want anyone else."

"I don't want Lucas or Grandpa or anybody to have a mental picture of me in here. You and Mama, well…"

"There's not a person in the world who could keep your mama away, son—including me."

"I know." Jason smiled. "She did better this last Sunday. Only mentioned Pastor Junior once. She actually seemed to hear me this time, when I told her I didn't want him to visit. I can't handle it, Dad."

"I understand. Junior is to be taken in small doses, and preferably never one-on-one."

"*That's* for sure. I don't even know what I believe in, anyway." Jason shook his head, allowing his anger to rise. "How could any all-powerful God let me end up here?" He flung himself back in his chair. "How could God let hijackers kill all those people today?"

Alvin shook his head. "God didn't have a part in it. Evil people did. But we *will* find a way to move through it—the planes, your arrest—all of it. Believe it. You've got to set your mind on it and look for opportunities to affirm your faith."

"My faith? Faith in *what*?" Jason heard himself yelling.

But his father was unfazed. "If nothing else, faith in faith. Believe and you will see. Isn't that in the Bible somewhere?"

Jason shrugged. "You're talking about not giving up. That's different from God."

"Is it?" Alvin asked.

Jason squinted his eyes in skepticism. "How do you *know*, Dad? How do you know everything's going to be all right?"

"I believe it, son. Listen, I'm not some Pollyanna going around saying everything is rosy. It's not ro—"

"Who's Pollyan—"

"Don't interrupt me." Alvin gave his son a serious look. "I know that things are not rosy. They're pretty damn terrible at the moment. But we can choose how we respond, and it's our choices that make us, Jason."

"I'm sure not here by choice."

"Of course not. But you can choose to believe that you will overcome this. Like your ancestors did. Hell, like Grandpa Clarence did with Asa Philip Randolph and Hampton's daddy."

"I guess," Jason said. "I thought all that was *history*."

Alvin's shoulders slumped downward as he lowered his head. He took a breath and closed his eyes to compose himself.

Then he spoke quietly. "History's still happening, son. In my mind, history is just stories of the fight. The struggle to survive. The struggle for equality. Justice. None of it comes automatically, you know—Dr. King told us. History is full of Davids going up against Goliaths. Colonies and kingdoms. Wars and warriors. You come from a long line of fighters, Jason."

"Yes, sir."

"I'm sorry this happened to you. So sorry."

"It's not your fault, Dad."

"I know it isn't." Alvin rubbed his temples, as if he were in pain. "But I'm still sorry it happened. I hate that you have to endure it."

Jason nodded. "I'm getting through it. But today sucks."

"Yes, it does," Alvin said. "But you've got to keep your eyes on the prize, son."

Eyes-two-three-four. Prize-two-three-four.

As he remembered his walk to Wellstein's four months before, a bolt of emotion struck Jason. He couldn't stop the tears.

"That's what I…that's…" Jason's words turned into air. Then, his whole body shook with sobs, against his best efforts to keep them inside. Dropping his head into his hands, he succumbed.

"It's all right. Let it out, son. God knows you've been through

Hell." Alvin's eyes glistened.

Yielding to his dad's words for a few, long seconds, Jason remembered the boy he had been a few months earlier, the carefree child who walked toward a job and a girl on a mild spring morning— before everything changed.

If only I could go back in time.

But I can't. Jason wiped his face and sat up straight, swallowing back what was left of his childhood.

His dad waited a moment before asking, "You all right?"

Jason bumped a closed fist onto the Plexiglass. "I'm all right."

The two held their fists against the glass for a few seconds, Jason's face still wet, and his eyes still watery. He took a few deep breaths and calmed himself as their hands receded.

Alvin looked at Jason with un-cried tears in his eyes. "Well," he said, in a voice on the cusp of breaking. He took a breath to recover it. "Your mama is going to kill me if I take up all the time for this week, you know."

Jason nodded. "Give her and Lucas a hug for me, okay? Tell them I love them."

Alvin looked down, nodding fast. He raised a hand to wave goodbye as he hung up the phone, and the two of them stood at the same time.

"Bye, Dad," Jason said, waving.

As his father backed away, Jason could see the wet streaks forming on the older man's face. Alvin, standing tall, waved to his son in a silent salute, as he allowed the tears to roll down.

It was the first time Jason had ever seen his father cry.

CHAPTER 46

By the Book

Marshall padded out the front door in his bathrobe, noticing the absence of summer's suffocating humidity. Most of Veronica's neighbors had already realized he'd moved in. Many were young families who didn't give a hoot about unmarried people living together.

The old church lady across the street, however, had found a way to lodge her protest. She spoke to Veronica, but not to him, even if the two were out together. It was a novel feeling.

I can pretend to be invisible.

As he uncurled the newspaper from its wrapper, he frowned at the irony of his thoughts. *So much for invisibility.*

He walked into the kitchen where Veronica stood watching as the coffeemaker sputtered to a finish.

"What's wrong with this picture?" he roared, as he slammed the door behind him and flattened the paper onto the kitchen table.

"Uh, nothing some strong black coffee can't cure?"

He took a cup and took his cue. *I don't want to lose my temper here, not with her.* "Speaking of Black," he said, "why do you suppose these photos are laid out like they are? My face next to this accused murderer's?"

"'Parents reported child missing before murder arrest,'" she read aloud. "Wow. I thought you said the deposition went well yesterday."

"I thought it *did*!" He joined her in sitting down at the kitchen table. "Aaron Hampton is smooth. He's as nice and polite as can be. Factual. Methodical. But so was Ziggy. I felt pretty positive about it all."

"Well, the journalist did his homework." She glanced over the news piece. "He got copies of the missing persons report with the time stamp."

"I should have expected this." He sighed. "I yelled at the secretary for not telling me about it the moment she knew."

"Wait—you already knew the suspect had been reported missing?"

"Yeah, the night of the arrest. *After* he confessed. The fact someone reported him missing had nothing to do with him being the shooter. Bad guys go missing all the time. But time passed, and I didn't think…"

Her eyes widened.

"What?" He looked puzzled.

"If *you* knew," she said, "then Aaron Hampton surely knew—long before you ever walked into his depo."

He sneered. "Oh my God. You're right." Marshall shook his head, incredulous. "Hampton glossed over it yesterday like it was no big deal. He had two, maybe three quick questions on the missing persons issue. He already *knew*!"

She nodded. "He was holding out this little gem for the press. Looks like he spoon-fed it to them."

"He's implying that I *intentionally* didn't inform the parents we had the kid until *after* he spilled his guts. But he knows damn good and well I didn't hear about the report until after Royals confessed."

"That's not in *this* story." Veronica tapped her finger on the newspaper.

"I told him in the depo it was a clerical error, but who cares? It's still on us—the whole department. It makes us *all* look incompetent, which takes the focus off what his client did." Marshall pointed at the newspaper. "And the press happened to use my face on the front page. Not the Missing Persons chief, not Pershing, not O'Donnell. Why me, do you imagine?"

"Can't imagine." Veronica rolled her eyes. "I'd be angry, too, if I were you. I'm not you and it still pisses me off."

"Now, if I call this so-called reporter and tell him my colleagues didn't inform me about the mis-per report until after the kid confessed, it's going to look like I'm trying to shift the blame."

"Says here, you couldn't be reached for comment."

"Yeah, what do you want to bet there's a note on my desk today from the night shift? I know their game. Maybe I'll call them and make sure they have my goddamn cell phone number."

"It's low, even for a criminal defense attorney." With that, she got a half-smile out of Marshall.

"Especially a Black defense attorney. Making me into some sort of Willie Horton. He's not above using racial stereotypes to gin up a story for his future police brutality lawsuit."

"That's true, John. But you're also in a leadership position. You outrank the other guys who worked on this case, and rank is also at play here, not just race. You took this kid's confession." She planted her fingertips on the full-color image of Jason Royals. "You know you did it by the book."

"Yes, I did. It was all by the book. How is it you can do everything right and still, somehow, it goes all to shit?"

"Ah, honey." She got up, walked behind him, and hugged his shoulders. "The truth will come out. You know you've done nothing wrong. You've got to trust the system."

"The system broke down at BRPD."

"So, make sure your colleagues know exactly what happened."

"You're right. I will. I'm not taking the heat for the screw up down at Missing Persons."

CHAPTER 47

Warm Bunk

The bell blared at eight, jolting Jason as always. From his perch behind the open newspaper, he could feel someone lurking outside his cell.

"Jason," Ralph said, "have you got *today's* paper?"

"No. Why?" he asked, without moving his makeshift privacy barrier. He heard the alarm's reprise, Old Jack's eight o'clock whistle, from outside of the jail.

"When you…um…*finish*," the CO said, "I've got today's for you. You're going to want to see it."

A few moments later, Jason flushed. Turning his bare backside toward the front of his cell, he pulled up his pants, and then washed his hands. The damp, acrid warmth of bad air conditioning had transformed, with the season's change, into a dry, autumnal chill.

The nip in the air was especially shocking in the Satsuma County Jail, where all the metal surfaces—the bars, the commode, the bunk frame, the sink—conspired to make his surroundings feel even colder. Jason surveyed the care package his mother had brought: Ten pairs of tube socks, sweatpants, hand lotion, and a warm, if cut-up, hoodie. Sweatshirts were fine, the guards had told his mom, but hoods were not allowed because they could camouflage an inmate's identity. Rather than taking it back home and bringing in another one later, risking a cold night for Jason, she'd asked a guard for a pair of scissors, and opted to simply cut off the hood.

"Here you go," Ralph held out the morning's edition. Looking from the photo in the paper to his charge, the CO said, "You look a whole lot better now."

"Oh, wow." Jason looked at the photo of his bruised and swollen face, next to some police sergeant he had not seen before. He read the headline:

BRPD Knew Arrestee was Missing; Sergeant Disciplined

Jason sat on the bottom bunk, frowning in concentration, as he continued to read the article. He hadn't expected to be reading about his case, but there it was, with all the details his parents had told him months back, while he was in the hospital. They'd called Missing Persons and made a report the afternoon he was arrested, but Missing Persons held the report for several hours, until after he confessed.

> Contrary to what we reported last week, Homicide Detective Sergeant John Marshall had no knowledge that then-fifteen-year-old Jason Royals had been reported missing by his parents. Marshall was informed only after he secured Royals' confession, some hours after the report was taken.

Jason's blood ran cold. He didn't want to think about the confession—or the hallucinations leading him to it. Katrina had told him they'd get the confession suppressed because it was forced, but the thought of that night still unnerved him.

He took a deep breath and reread the paragraph. *Last week? How did I miss the other article?* He read on about the other sergeant's written reprimand and clenched his jaw at what came next.

> After Royals confessed to murdering a Georgia woman at the Vacation Station Inn last April, he collapsed en route to the Juvenile Detention Center, and was taken to St. Mary's Hospital, instead. BRPD

officials say they credit Marshall
with saving the boy's life, because he
called the hospital to report a medical
condition he had become aware of
during his earlier conversations with
Royals.

*You've got to be kidding me—after the way they threw me around
in the woods? He gets to say he saved my life?* Jason read on, and felt
somewhat vindicated.

"My client would not have had to
visit the hospital in the first place,"
attorney Aaron J. Hampton said,
"but for the actions of the BRPD. It's
clear he sustained severe injuries at
the hands of the Beau Rêve Police,
and it's clear his confession was
coerced."

Thank you, Hamp.
Jason felt tired. He climbed to the top bunk and snuggled under
the blanket of his yet-to-be-made bed. Pulling the covers up to
his ears, he curled up on his side, facing the wall. The warmth was
welcome. He heard the breakfast tray slide into his room, but he
ignored it.
I'll sleep until it's time to go to Mrs. Holden's room.

CHAPTER 48

Satsuma County Basketball

Like most Floridians, Jason had a hard time discerning how hot or cold any given day would be during the last few months of the year. He'd overdress on basketball afternoons, only to peel off layers and tie them to the chain-link fence during games.

"Why you do that?" Octavius asked.

"To keep it up off the ground. Keep it clean," Jason said. "Just because we're in jail doesn't make us dirty."

Octavius plucked his jacket from the filthy court, shook it out, and tied its sleeves next to Jason's. The puffy winter coat dwarfed Jason's thinner athletic jacket. The two stared at the garments for a moment, before something in the sky caught Octavius's attention.

"Look!" the bigger boy said.

Jason smiled. "Yeah, how about that? It's a great egret. I saw one of those on the day…" Jason's face clouded over.

"What? You saw one of those on the day, what?"

"The day I got arrested. It was before I even got stopped. He was walking in the ditch and then he took off flying. He couldn't have been more than ten yards from me. His wings were huge."

"Well, I'll take it as a good sign, then."

"You sound like my mama." Jason grinned and shook his head. "She's always seeing good omens, especially when it comes to birds. Like they're angels or something."

"Well, I'm serious. The day you first saw him was the day you fell into the ditch, and this-here egurt …"

"Egret." Jason pronounced it for his friend.

"And this-here E-*gret*, he's flying away from this place. Just like you gonna fly outta here."

"You're gonna fly out of here with me, O, right?"

Octavius looked to the sky. "Yeah. Watch for my bird. He comin'. You'll see."

Jason laughed. "I'll be watching for him then."

"You ready to catch what I throw you today?" Octavius grinned.

"If you can bounce it under to me," Jason said. Everyone on the court, including Octavius, was twice his size, but Jason was developing speed.

The boys joined Clyde and three non-violent detainees, Ralph's "good behavior crew," on the court. Jason was ready for the challenge. The vigor of the games in the Satsuma County Jail far surpassed any game he'd played as a kid at the Y.

◈

December's bright cerulean skies belied the gloomy specter of spending Christmas in jail. Jason kept to his rule about not wanting Lucas or his grandparents to visit him. He asked for more reading material and more writing material for Christmas. He'd already used up the composition book Katrina gave him as well as most of the two legal pads she'd brought.

On one of the pads, he took notes on the depositions she wanted him to review. With the other, he wrote letters to Kim, Brendan, and Lucas, being careful not to discuss his case with any of them. Jason didn't send everything he wrote to his friends. Instead, he learned to wait for their much shorter, much more sporadic replies, and then he edited his epistles, sending back briefer versions. The last thing he wanted was to scare them off by overwhelming them with his long ramblings. He knew he had a lot more time on his hands than they did, and he tried not to imagine the fun they were having without him.

As long as his parents sent the books, paper, and pencils through his lawyers, the COs seemed okay with him having them. Ralph explained lawyers were "officers of the court." Jason surmised it was some sort of honor code, and it meant the lawyers would take the heat if any contraband was smuggled in—it would mean serious trouble for them. Hampton and Katrina were willing to stick their necks out for him because they trusted him and his family.

CHAPTER 49

Deposed

Katrina instructed Jason to underline any passages he had questions about in the depositions she brought him to read. If he wanted, she said, he could write down the questions he would like for Hampton to ask during the pretrial hearings—but no other notes.

"Pretend you're on Jeopardy and you're talking to Alex Trebek. Put everything in the form of a question."

"Okay," he said.

"What is...'okay'?" she corrected him, winking.

"What is...gotcha?" he replied, grinning back at her.

"Technically, your notes are protected by privilege," she explained, "but in practice, we've learned it's best you don't hold out any expectations of privacy at all while you're incarcerated—not with these depos, not with your letters or journals, not with anything. Better safe than sorry."

Reading Detective Sergeant John Marshall's deposition infuriated Jason, and he marked up nearly every page. It was as if the detective denied the violence in the woods had ever occurred.

You're such a liar! Jason's mind screamed. He responded by busying his hand.

"How did JR get that scratch by his eye?" Jason wrote for his lawyer. "What about the bruises on his ribs and on his arm?" Then, "Didn't you see your partner flick that branch into JR's face?" "Don't you remember punching JR in the gut?" "Why didn't you let him call his parents?" "How many times did he ask?"

When the deposition moved on to the subject of his alleged confession, Jason's blood ran cold.

"The suspect was in an obvious state of distress, and wanted to talk," the detective testified.

Oh my God, what was I thinking? I don't even remember what I said to him. Anything he wanted me to say, I guess. All I remember was I was crying like a big, fat baby—oh yeah, and imagining Mama and Uncle Mack were there. Not the best time in the world to lose my freaking mind.

"We wrote down what he said, and he initialed each line," the detective testified. "Mr. Royals said he intended to rob Mrs. Patterson, that he shot her in the head with a nine-millimeter Beretta, grabbed her wallet, and ran away."

I don't even know what a Beretta is! I've heard of a Glock, and a nine-millimeter, but I've never heard of a Beretta. And I never touched that lady's wallet. I wasn't there!

"Did he say why he would want to rob and kill a tourist from Georgia?" Hampton had asked Marshall.

"He did not," the detective had replied.

That's because I didn't have any reason! Because I didn't do it! You got the wrong guy!

"You've got the wrong man, Sarge." Pershing's taunts from the driver's seat of the unmarked car stung Jason's memory, thrusting him back to the afternoon of his arrest. He winced as if he'd been struck in the back of the head.

He slammed the thick, spiral-bound deposition closed and tossed it to the foot of his bunk with his pencil, which fell to the floor.

Son of a bitch! Jason fought off a wave of nausea. *I can't read any more of this shit right now.*

CHAPTER 50

The Skeleton Man

The corridor was black when Jason awoke to the shrieks of a man in pain—or was it a man terrified? Was someone having a nightmare?

"Please...please," were the only words Jason could decipher, punctuated by unearthly, shrill screams. Jason felt the hairs stand up on the back of his neck.

He slid down from his bunk and walked to the barred doors of his cell. As the unintelligible pleading and terrified cries assaulted his ears, Jason's eyes adjusted to the darkness.

Choruses of "shut up!" erupted among his fellow prisoners.

Jason tried to make out the numbers on the clock across the hall, but it was too dark.

The lights in the corridor flashed on. The screaming and the "shut ups" were joined by groans of interrupted sleep and angry profanities—as if a volume knob had been turned up full force with the switch of the lights. It was a quarter after three a.m., and the whole wing was awake.

The steel door next to Jason's cell heaved open.

"Quiet!" The guards were angry as they entered, nightsticks drawn. Their commands, too, were full of obscenities accentuated by the loud bangs of batons hitting bars. As the inmates began to settle, the original offender's shrieks intensified.

"No! No! No! No—"

One crack of the baton ended the plea.

Wailing—the most plaintive and pain-filled sound Jason had ever heard—replaced the screaming. The wailing yielded to whimpering but then escalated again.

Two guards half-carried, half-dragged a wild-eyed man through the hall and toward Jason. "Jesus help me," the prisoner whined. "Get 'im out, get 'im out. He's inside of me."

Jason stepped backward and froze, unable to stop staring at the inmate. The guards were lifting him by his elbows, and his bony wrists and fingers dangled as he glided down the hall. "Help me," he whimpered as he passed, his desperate eyes piercing Jason's.

When he saw the man's emaciated face, Jason couldn't help but gasp. *You're a skeleton!*

❖

Jason lay awake on his bunk. Burrowing deeper under his blanket, he pulled his arms inside his sweatshirt to warm his hands.

He turned to face the wall. Drawing up his knees, he squeezed his eyes shut in an attempt to block out what he'd seen a couple hours before. The image had kept him tossing and turning for the rest of the night.

Never in his life had Jason seen any adult person so emaciated. He remembered seeing photographs of children in Somalia on TV when he was little. He remembered asking his mother about their big, swollen bellies.

"Lack of protein," she'd told him. "Lack of everything. They're starving, honey." Her voice had broken, and her eyes had filled with tears. "There isn't enough food in their country to feed them."

Jason ran to his mother and threw his seven-year-old arms around her. "It's okay, Mama," he told her. "Don't cry. Maybe we can send them some of our food. We have a lot."

She smiled down at him, through her tears, nodding. "We *will* find a way to help. Our country will find a way to help theirs."

Jason had always figured his mother had a tender heart and was reacting with empathy to what she'd seen on TV. He wondered if she had ever seen real, live people starving, maybe when she was in nursing school. He wondered if they, too, cried out loud.

How could he possibly be so thin? Did drugs make him so skinny?

Jason couldn't imagine the pain that would make a grown man scream the way the inmate had done.

Is it the hunger or the drugs that make him feel like there's a monster inside of him? At least I wasn't that crazy when my blood sugar dropped that night.

Was I?

The skeleton-man was the worst thing Jason had ever seen—or heard.

CHAPTER 51

The Tree Exhibit

The transparent tape holding up Lucas' Christmas card was losing its stickiness, a casualty born from Jason's habit of removing it from the wall to hold in his hands. The stifling, institutional heat hadn't helped. Even on warm, Florida days in February, there seemed to be no adjustments to the jail's thermostat: The heat was blowing full blast. He took down the card and read it, as he had several times since receiving it.

I'll never let him see me here. Jail is no place for a kid.

He re-taped the card, scratching the tape so it would adhere to the cinderblock once again. Backing up, he admired what he had come to call The Tree Exhibit. He smiled at the postcard with Santa and his sleigh, from Brendan and his school friends, but he didn't take it down.

Recalling their short note by heart, he didn't need to read it. The guys were looking to get together in the event he got out in time for winter break. *What a joke.*

Brendan's postscript had meant a lot to him, though. "Can't wait to get you back out on the basketball court, J." Jason stared at the wobbly Christmas tree teetering out of Santa's bag perched in the sleigh on a rooftop.

The Christmas card from his neighbors, Jimmy and Joey Sullivan, didn't feature a tree, but he fit it, nonetheless, into the larger pattern of one he was creating on the wall. It was nestled between one he received from his church youth group and another from the congregation. Jason had kept it up even though Pastor Junior had signed it. Next to the manger with Mary, Joseph, and the baby Jesus stood a Christmas tree. Jason had heard from his dad, a thousand times, the festive tradition of decorating trees was a holdover from pagan solstice celebrations and had nothing to do with the birth of Jesus.

I bet that kind of tree doesn't even grow in the Middle East. Continually aggravated by the very thought of Junior, Jason shook his head in disgust before moving his eyes toward the top of his collage.

It was the postcard from Kim. Tan, granite-mountain crags cradled thick drifts of white in the background. In the foreground, spruce trees, their branches laden with snow, stood sentry. She had spent Christmas vacation in Aspen with her parents.

Jason remembered her face, her freckles, and the twinkle in her eye when they spoke to one another at the store. He yielded, for a second, to the tilt of his blood and the sway of his heart, stopping himself before…

I'm pretty sure she knows I like her. I'm pretty sure she likes me, too.

Instead of peeling it off the wall, he scratched down the tape holding Kim's card, ensuring its adhesion. "Snow for Jason!" the back of it read, signed by "D.G.," for "Diamond Girl," which, after her visit, had become his secret appellation for Kim.

Enno, short for the word "N. O. Cent," from the card featuring his name, had become her secret name for him.

Kim sent the postcard in an envelope with a "K" emblazoned on the back. He kept the "K" envelopes, and the letters from Kim they contained, tucked into the older composition books under his mattress. The two corresponded about her college classes and his History report. He wrote to her about his homesickness. She wrote to him about her roommate from Pennsylvania. Kim also mentioned her publication in *The Independent Florida Alligator*, which she clipped and sent to him. The piece was about students' thoughts and reactions to September 11 and whether it affected their plans for the New Year.

"The article was very well done," he'd written back. "You're a great writer, DG. You sure do shine."

His favorite part of their correspondence by far, however, lay centered in the middle of the Tree Exhibit. It was the Valentine she'd sent him: a drawing of Yoda, with a note from Kim in the bottom righthand corner.

Hey, Enno!

Yoda says, "MTFBWY!"
Happy Valentine's Day. This is about as close as I could get to those Star Wars Valentines you loved as a kid. Remember, I'm a writer, not an artist!

MTFBWY,

D.G.

Ah, you're a pretty good artist, D.G. You even got the little hairs on his head right. And I like the folds in his Jedi robe. He isn't a tree, but he sure is green, so he's perfect for the Tree Exhibit.

And I don't care if it's February. I'm keeping my tree up.

The Pledge

Mother Earth tilted her eyes up toward the sun, and spring began again in Beau Rêve. In the Satsuma County Jail, the clocks reset themselves, swirling their minute hands forward in their mechanical rites of spring.

Even though "Hairy Reptile" Varken was no longer there, Jason cringed each time he walked to the front of his cell. His body still anticipated the inmate's verbal assaults: Room service!

He tried to forget the other words Varken had spat at him. The tattooed human horror had pled guilty to a homicide charge and moved to state prison in Raiford. He would be serving a life sentence, with no possibility of parole. Newspapers reported Varken pled guilty to avoid lethal injection.

He deserved it for what he did to his poor little victim. His own niece. If anyone ever deserved a needle in his arm, it's him.

A memory flashed in Jason's mind. *"Needle in your arm."* He heard Pershing's words from the day of his arrest, when the detectives dragged him through the woods. *"Where do you think you are? Fucking Vermont?"*

Jason grasped the bars of his jail-room door and closed his eyes. He shook away the image of his younger, weaker self and of the two detectives who'd pinned him like a panicked little bird.

How could I have been so stupid?

He tried to push away any thoughts about the death penalty. Despite Pershing's deceitful taunts, Hampton had assured and reassured Jason the United States Supreme Court had already removed the option. Since Jason was fifteen at the time of his arrest, prosecutors would not be able to seek capital punishment in his case. The cutoff in early twenty-first century America, it turned out, was age sixteen.

Missed it by four months.

The thought of being merely four months older coursed through him like an electrical current, whooshing out of him in an audible sigh of relief. *If it had been Octavius running across Broward Highway instead of me...*

Jason shook his head, refusing the thought. He involuntarily moved as if to rattle his cell's door, but it didn't give. Ralph, working in the makeshift office across from him, registered Jason's movement with a frown but did not look up.

The defense bar was working to exempt people younger than eighteen—*all* minors—from the death penalty, according to Hampton.

Maybe everyone *should be exempt, since we know how wrong the system can be.*

"My goal is to get your case dismissed *before* trial," Hampton had told him. "Prosecutors can't win a trial without evidence—and the little bit they have? I aim to get it thrown out. Judges don't allow coerced statements." His lawyer turned his hands outward, offering a question. "Otherwise, why not return to the days of medieval torture chambers?"

Jason trusted in two things: the knowledge of his innocence and the reassurance of his experienced attorney. He also knew time was on his side. Hampton couldn't guarantee results, of course, but his confidence was infectious. Whenever he listed the litany of reasons the judge would throw out the confession, Jason felt as if a heavy burden were being lifted off his back, a few pounds at a time.

"The statement was coerced no matter how you cut it, Jason. Because of your age, first." Hampton counted off the reasons, from his thumb to his pinky. "Because neither your parents nor a lawyer were there, because of your medical condition, because they starved you, because they beat you."

The lawyer held up his entire hand, trilling his fingers. "Without this evidence, all the state has is a very weak, very circumstantial case. And a contaminated witness identification."

Jason released his grip and examined his own hand, bending each finger in silent recitation of Hampton's articles of faith. He hoped and wished for the truth to prevail; he hoped and wished for Hampton's unabashed skill and confidence to win in court—when they finally got there.

Maybe prayer is nothing but hoping and wishing. Consider this a prayer, God. If you're there at all.

❖

Spring soon tumbled into the first anniversary of Jason's arrest. The day marking one year was as monotonous as any other: Old Jack whistled its first call to the city's workers at seven a.m., and the lights blinked on thereafter. Old Jack blew again at eight, right after the jail bell sounded. Breakfast arrived at his room a few minutes later. The cold, undignified ritual of showering occurred before nine a.m.—on shower days. There was school on the weekdays, with reading on the weekends.

At one p.m., Old Jack's lunch-ending whistle signaled lunch's beginning for Jason, in his cell, after the other inmates had eaten in the cafeteria. Often, there was an afternoon hour outdoors for him and the others, but usually, Jason stuck to his reading and writing.

❖

Only Katrina bothered to mention the anniversary milestone.

"I know it's easy for me to say," she'd told him, "while you're the one suffering through it. But it is better when cases drag out. Hamp says your chances for a better resolution increase with time."

"Resolution?" Jason asked. "You mean getting me out of here and clearing my record?"

"That's precisely what I mean. That's the resolution we're looking for."

❖

As if nothing extraordinary had happened, Mother Earth continued her revolution, steady on her passage around the sun. Jason finished tenth grade in jail. A new math tutor, Mrs. Macy, was coming each week to help him with Algebra II. He reread the fourth Harry Potter book and started *The Autobiography of Malcolm X.* To the delight of his father, he began learning Latin. *Agricola* was his first word in the ancient language. It meant "farmer."

"Keep reading, thinking, and writing," Katrina had told him. "It's the bulk of what lawyers do, Jason, and you'd make a good one."

The shortened classroom hours of Jason's second summer in jail sped by, and Octavius became a more fluent reader. Jason's mom had brought in a handful of early-reading books to help build the older boy's confidence.

Watching Octavius's face as he read aloud, from *Go, Dog, Go* and *The Cat in the Hat*, gave Jason a feeling of pride he had not experienced before. It was only a matter of time before Octavius would be reading the Matt Christopher sports books—and any other book his curiosity desired—without Jason's help.

On some Fridays, Mrs. Holden brought in music for them. It was usually light and innocuous like the soundtrack from the new movie, *Shrek*. Even though he knew it was a kids' movie, "see *Shrek*" soon appeared on Jason's "List of Things to Do When I Get Released."

Mrs. Holden also had her radical moments. Jason would always remember when she brought in Tupac's greatest hits remix album so she could introduce the concept of "internal rhyme" to him and Octavius.

Before playing the rapper, though, she played an old eighties hit by Bruce Hornsby and the Range. Then she played Tupac's "Changes."

Jason's favorite between the two was no contest. Tupac blew his mind. He immediately identified a line in Hornsby that was different—missing—from the rapper's sampling of "The Way It Is."

Hornsby's got to be a white guy. It's easy for a white guy to tell us not to believe it. But Black people know: Some things don't change. Not for some people. Not for cops like O'Donnell.

With Mrs. Holden's blessing, Jason wrote six pages comparing the two songs. Without going into detail, after deconstructing a few lyrical stereotypes, he used his own arrest to illustrate how stereotypes enable abuses of power.

❖

Jason commenced his junior year of high school in the fall and read a play called *The Crucible* by Arthur Miller. At the same time, he helped

Octavius sound out words like "linebacker." The first anniversary of September 11 came and went without fanfare.

In accordance with a memo from the county, Mrs. Holden asked them to stand for a ritual with which she had never before bothered— The Pledge of Allegiance.

Jason, hand over his heart, rolled his eyes when they uttered the words "One nation, under God." After they recited "with liberty and justice," he stopped speaking altogether, leaving Mrs. Holden and Octavius to enunciate "for all."

"The pledge is optional, you know," she told Jason, "but I'm curious as to why you would leave out the last two words."

"Because it's not true. We don't have liberty and justice for all. Not by a long shot. Not in this country. And pretending that we do is a bunch of fascist bullsh—uh, a bunch of fascist bull."

Mrs. Holden nodded. "I see." She shuffled some papers on her desk while the boys took their seats. "The way I see it, that's what makes it a *pledge*."

Jason scrunched his face. "Huh?"

"A pledge, in this sense of the word, is the same as a promise. I pledge to do something, I promise to do something."

"So, you're promising allegiance to a flag?"

"Well, yes, but also to the ideals the flag stands for. The pledge isn't *descriptive*, Jason. It's *prescriptive*. When we say it, we're not describing some perfect, imaginary country where all these goals magically happen. We're promising to do what we can to make them happen, bring them into being. We're pledging to create liberty and justice for all."

Jason nodded, speaking aloud his father's words, Dr. King's words. "They're not automatic."

Mrs. Holden looked at him. "No. Things like liberty and justice are not automatic at all." She breathed out a deep sigh. "If they were, you surely would not be here."

Her validation caught him off guard, summoning tears. He wanted to cry, but he didn't. "No, ma'am," he said, clearing his throat. "I would not."

It would be a matter of weeks before Jason would find out whether he and his lawyer could pull off "liberty and justice" for *him*.

CHAPTER 53

"Don't Speak. *Write.*"

The late-October sun slanted its beams into Judge Sandra Drake's courtroom. The hush of rustling of papers surrounded the defense table. It was the day Jason had been waiting for, the day his lawyers would begin representing him in the first of two hearings, either of which could set him free.

Nervous, Jason sat between Katrina, a newly minted member of the bar, and Hampton. His eyes darted around the courtroom and then back to his legal team, until something familiar caught his eye. The paper had come from the file Hampton was thumbing through. Jason motioned for Hampton to pass it to him.

"This?" Hampton held up a copy of Jason's composition book entries from jail.

"No. That one." Jason pointed to Kim's drawing of Yoda.

Jason was stunned. The unexpected sight of Kim's hand-drawn valentine had blown his concentration on what was supposed to be the first day of the rest of his life.

Why would anyone want to copy Yoda?

Before he could say a word, Katrina, sitting to his left, put her hand on his arm. "Don't worry about it. There's nothing sensitive to your case in there. We get copies of everything they could possibly use as evidence. You knew they'd be monitoring your correspondence, right?"

Jason didn't answer.

"It's okay," she said.

"It's not okay," he whispered, as if through gravel. "It's *private.*"

Katrina exhaled. "You're right. I'm sorry." She held his eyes for a moment. "You okay?" she asked.

Jason blew out a sigh and then leaned in to listen to the man who held his future in his hands.

"I need you to know some things before we get started," Hampton whispered. "This is your hearing. The prosecutor and the police are going to be talking about you. A *lot*. And you're not going to like what you hear. But you *must*—and I mean absolutely *must*—stay silent. We will have our turn to speak, do you understand?"

Jason nodded.

"And no making faces, either. Got it?"

A single, slight nod told Hampton Jason understood.

"You know how much we've gone over every little detail of what happened, over and over again. Right?" The lawyer's tone took a more conversational volume as the courtroom began to bustle.

"Yes, sir," Jason said.

"So, you *know* I'm not going to let them get away with *their* version of the facts, right?"

"Yes, sir. I mean yes, I know—no, sir, you won't."

Hampton smiled and Jason looked up at him with more trust than he'd ever mustered, or was ever required to muster, in his entire life. He then felt his lawyer's warm, reassuring hand on his shoulder.

A memory from when he was six years old flashed in his mind. Lucas was only two, and he had just toppled over into the pool at the YMCA. Although his whole family had been there, Jason was the only one who saw it happen. Terrified his baby brother would die, he jumped in and grabbed him, pulling him to the side, saving his life. His mother had half-screamed, half-wailed when, finally, she saw what was happening.

Jason quickly stole a glance over his shoulder, where his parents sat. The guards wouldn't let them touch him, but they'd said their hellos, each of them holding Jason's eyes long enough to calm him, long enough to slow down his galloping heart. As he looked back at her that moment, his mom's eyes, steely and resolved, met his.

She didn't see Lucas fall in. It happened so fast.

The day with Lucas at the Y had been his first experience of ice-in-the-veins terror, matched only by a few shrill moments of fear-driven adrenaline on the day of his arrest. He was feeling it again in the Beau Rêve County Courthouse.

Hamp has got me. Jason exhaled. *He and the truth are strong enough to pull me out of the water.*

The older attorney placed a brand-new legal pad in front of Jason, along with a pen.

"Don't speak. *Write*. And don't hesitate to let Katrina or me know if something urgent comes up. Use your pen."

"Okay."

The hearing began with everyone standing up, and then sitting down, as the judge entered the room. She asked the attorneys to approach the bench, with their calendars, to straighten out a few scheduling details.

Detective Pershing was the state's first witness. His suit didn't fit him well.

The sleeves were too long and the shoulders, slightly baggy. Pershing's suit collar poked up around the back of the neck in a manner that reminded Jason of Dracula.

The vampire is not quite as pasty as Pershing, though.

Initially, the questions asked by State Attorney Fred Kirk were standard: How long had Pershing been with the department? How many years as a detective? How many of those in Homicide Division?

The word *homicide* struck Jason in the gut. He felt as if his suit jacket were grabbing him, as if his tie were shrinking tighter around his neck. Katrina, sensing his tension, patted him on the back. Her light touch calmed him, and as he relaxed, his clothes loosened their chokehold. He didn't see that behind him, his parents had likewise stiffened, intuiting his distress. Clarice and Alvin Royals resisted the urge to reach out to their son, and held each other's hands instead.

Trembling and sweating, Jason remembered something his father had told him about the judge being able to see who he was. He closed his eyes and slowed his breathing, enduring the testimony about Pershing's job history.

As Kirk walked the detective through the events of that infamous Sunday morning, Jason's clothes resumed their oppressive shrink-wrapping. Katrina touched his back again and handed him the pen.

Jason fidgeted with the cheap blue Bic, staring at it as he twirled it through his fingers, over and over again. Judge Drake, a dark-haired woman with intense, black eyes, looked at him as he twirled. Glancing up, Jason saw her and froze. Mortified, he put down the pen immediately and stared at the table before him.

Here I am with my life in her hands, and I've annoyed her.

Jason straightened himself in his chair and put his hands in his lap. When he finally looked up again, and the judge glanced at him for the second time, he thought he might have caught a hint of warmth—at least in her eyes, if not in the remainder of her stern-looking face. He blushed.

He sat motionless for several minutes of dry testimony before he heard Detective Pershing say, "Yes. I advised Mr. Royals of his right to have an attorney."

The words from the witness box hit him like a punch to his stomach. Shaking his head, eyes wide with panic, Jason abided Hampton's advice to remain silent. He scribbled away on the legal pad in front of him at the defense table. The pen was new and the ink, spotty. Frustrated, he ripped the page on which he was trying to pen his outrage.

Jason struggled to hold back his tears.

Katrina put her hand on his and leaned in to hear his complaint. The disruption had caught the judge's attention. Katrina nodded in response to Jason's plaintive whispers, shushing him more than once.

Kirk, standing at the podium, puffed out his chest and turned to look at the defense table in mock astonishment. Silent, he waited for the commotion to die down before addressing the judge. "Your Honor, I request the witness repeat his last statement."

"Mr. Kirk, there's no jury here," Judge Drake intoned. "I heard the detective say he advised the defendant of his Fifth Amendment right to counsel." Shifting her gaze to the defense table, she asked, "Is everything okay? Do you need to take a break?"

Kirk's eyes widened.

"No. Thank you, Your Honor." Hampton took the opportunity to stand up to address the judge. His commanding voice turned the heads of the handful of reporters in the room. Hampton's appearance was striking. Sporting a custom-made, dark-blue pinstripe suit and a red tie, he took his place as the visual center of the courtroom.

Jason, eyes glued to the vibrancy that was Aaron Hampton, relaxed a little.

Kirk, an older, white attorney who looked faded by comparison, paused to let Hampton's moment pass before speaking. "May it please the Court, Your Honor. May I proceed with my direct examination?"

"By all means," the judge said.

"Thank you. Detective Pershing, when you advised the defendant of his right to counsel, how did he reply?"

"He declined to call an attorney." Pershing's neck stretched forward when he spoke, which, combined with the too-big suit collar, elicited the impression of a turtle.

"Was this the first time he'd been advised of his right to have an attorney present?"

"No sir." Pershing said the two words as if they were one.

"So, he'd previously been advised by police of his right to counsel?"

"Yessir."

"And how do you know this?"

"Because Officer O'Donnell included in his report that he had advised the suspect of his Miranda rights when he arrested him."

Hampton looked up but did not object.

"Is this the police report to which you're referring?" Kirk stepped away from the podium to proffer the evidence to the defense table.

Katrina flipped to a tab in the case file, revealing the same document. Kirk then approached the witness with the report.

Pershing looked at it. "Yessir."

"Was there any other way that you confirmed the defendant had, indeed, been advised of his rights, at least once, prior to your reminder?" Kirk asked him.

"Well, my partner, Sergeant Marshall, questioned him when—"

"Objection, Your Honor." Hampton's voice dominated the courtroom again. "Hearsay."

The judge wrinkled her forehead in a manner that made her long, serious nose look even longer and more serious. Her tiny, dark eyes bored first into Hampton's and then darted to Kirk's before she looked at the witness.

"Detective," Judge Drake asked, "were you present when the other detective asked the defendant whether he'd been advised of his rights?"

"No, ma'am."

"Your objection is sustained, Mr. Hampton. Next question please, Mr. Kirk."

"But, to be clear, you did speak to the defendant about his right to counsel?" Kirk asked.

"Objection, Your Honor." Hampton rose to his feet. "Asked and answered."

"Let me rephrase Mr. Kirk's question, if you will, counselor," the judge said, turning toward the witness. "Detective, did you ask the defendant outright whether he wanted an attorney?"

Pershing retreated into his turtle-shell of a suit, composing his answer. "I *reminded* the suspect he could have an attorney, yes ma'am."

"And what was his response?" she asked.

"He said 'no,' Your Honor."

Pausing a moment to make sure the judge was satisfied, the prosecutor spoke. "Thank you, Your Honor. I'd say that's a good stopping point. The state has no further questions for this witness at the moment, but we reserve the right to redirect."

"Your witness, Mr. Hampton," she said.

Hampton stood, waiting for the prosecutor to return to his table— and for all eyes to be on him—before he began.

"Detective." Hampton enunciated every consonant in the word. "You didn't advise my client of anything, did you?"

Pershing blushed, retorting in a voice two octaves higher than before, "I told him he had the right to—"

"Yes or no?" Hampton interjected.

The judge held up her hand, stopping the questioner and the witness. "Mr. Hampton, as I explained to the state, there is no jury here," she said, turning toward Pershing again, "what exactly did you say to the defendant about his right to counsel?"

"I told him he had a right to counsel," Pershing said. The judge nodded and motioned for Hampton to continue.

Hampton acknowledged the answer. "Hmm. Yes. You've said that. Several times, in fact. Let's start again, shall we? Where were you, Detective Pershing, when you *told* my client he had a right to counsel?"

"I believe it was in the bathroom off the interrogation room, before we took the defendant back to the scene to find the gun."

"In the *bathroom*?" Hampton acted surprised, as if that were new information to him. "Why, may I ask, were you in the bathroom with my client?"

"It's standard operating procedure not to leave suspects alone.

Ever."

"I understand that. Let me ask it this way: For what purpose did my client enter the bathroom?"

Detective Pershing couldn't hide his smirk. "Are you asking me why he had to go to the bathroom?"

A few chuckles littered the courtroom.

"I object, Your Honor," Kirk said, smiling. "It seems to me this question has been asked and answered."

The judge, wrinkling her forehead, looked at Hampton. "I don't know what you're trying to get at here, but give it one last try and then let's move on."

"Yes, Your Honor." Turning to the witness again, Hampton said, "Had my client vomited moments before you entered the bathroom together?"

Pershing looked at Kirk, who squirmed in his seat but did not object. The witness went silent. His neck shrank toward his body. The judge nodded to Hampton to repeat his question.

"Right before you went into the bathroom, where you say you advised my client of the right to counsel, what happened?"

"The defendant threw up. It went all over the table and he got some on himself."

"And by *it* you mean, the vomit?"

"Yes. He got vomit on himself."

"Detective Pershing, after my client vomited, why did you accompany him into the bathroom?"

"He needed to clean himself up. I did un-cuff him, so he—"

"How long had my fifteen-year-old client been in police custody before he vomited, Detective?"

"About two hours."

"Two hours," Hampton repeated. "And after he threw up, when he was washing up, is that when you *voluntarily* offered the information about how my client could get an attorney?"

"I told him he had the right to—"

"Your Honor." Hampton shook his head as he addressed the judge.

"Objection, Your Honor," Kirk said. "We've been over this already. The fact that the defendant got sick right before Detective Pershing reminded him of his rights does not negate the fact that the detective did, indeed, *remind* him."

The judge heard out Kirk's argument but didn't bite. "It seems to me counsel asked a yes or no question, but the witness didn't give a yes or no answer. The vomiting is news to me, counselor. It's the defendant's state of mind I'm interested in at this moment, Mr. Kirk, along with his ability to evaluate his need for an attorney. I'm overruling. The witness will answer the question."

"Thank you, Your Honor." Hampton turned to Pershing. "Now, isn't it true it was my client who asked *you* about an attorney, and not the other way around?"

"Yes. He—"

Hampton held up his hand. "When you responded to my client, isn't it true you gave him the choice of having an attorney and going to jail right then, or not having an attorney and cooperating with police."

Pershing shook his head. "That's not—"

"Did you or did you not tell my client…" Hampton walked back to the table to retrieve his notes and, after glancing at them, held the yellow tablet high in the air before he continued, "he could either have an attorney and go to jail right that minute, or that he could take advantage of your sergeant's generous mood and cooperate with the police?"

"That isn't—"

"You didn't?" Hampton interjected, cocking his head. "You didn't tell my client he'd go to jail right that moment unless he waived his right to counsel?"

"I…"

"Your Honor?" Hampton looked at the judge.

"Detective?" she asked, addressing the witness once more. "Did you suggest to the defendant, in any manner whatsoever, that if he called a lawyer he'd be put in jail?"

Pershing's face turned red. "Yes, ma'am."

The judge narrowed her eyes and then nodded to Hampton to continue.

"After you made it clear that you would put my client in jail if he asked for an attorney, did you suggest that *waiving* his right to counsel would *prevent* him from going to jail right then?"

"Yes, I did."

"Thank you, Detective Pershing. Couple more questions, if you'll bear with me. Did you at any point in the afternoon threaten to shoot my client?"

"I—"

"Yes or no, sir."

"No. I didn't *threaten* to shoot him."

"Did you talk at all about using your gun?"

"Yes."

Hampton stared at the witness for a beat, hoping he'd continue. Pershing sat mute, not taking the bait.

"Thank you, Detective. Last issue. Did you at any point in the day discuss the death penalty with my client?"

"Yes, I may have mentioned it."

"Do you recall at what point, during the nine-plus hours you had my client in custody, that this discussion took place?"

"I do not."

"Detective Pershing, isn't it true your discussion of the death penalty came during the time you and your partner had my client out in the woods, alone?"

"It's possible, yes."

"Okay. Are you aware the U.S. Supreme Court has outlawed the death penalty for defendants under sixteen at the time of their alleged crimes?"

"Yes."

Hampton looked at Pershing again, but the police officer was not planning to elaborate. Hampton asked, "Would you characterize your statements about the death penalty as designed to trick my client?"

"Yes. We're permitted to—"

"Thank you, Detective Pershing." Hampton gave him a slight bow before turning to face Judge Drake. "Your Honor, we're finished with this witness. We believe his testimony alone establishes that my client declined counsel under extreme physical and psychological duress during the bathroom incident, and therefore he did not freely or voluntarily decline his right to an attorney at all."

"Your Honor." Kirk stood up. "It is a well-established principle of criminal law that the police may deceive or trick inmates in order to gain their cooperation."

"That's true, Mr. Kirk, for purposes of interrogation. But we're talking about a fifteen-year-old suspect, and we're talking about the Miranda warning—and in this court's opinion, that's different from an interrogation technique. The question here is whether the defendant felt threatened to the point of coercion. Did he make his decision based solely on the fear induced by adult policemen, or did he make a fully informed and considered decision?"

Kirk shook his head. "Your Honor, being afraid of the police in and of itself doesn't let any defendant off the hook for failing to invoke his Fifth Amendment rights. May I please redirect the witness?" Kirk asked.

Judge Drake assented.

"Detective Pershing, was this the first time any suspect had ever vomited in an interrogation room?"

"No, sir. It was not."

"And why does a defendant vomit during interrogations?"

"Objection!" Hampton said. "The question calls for the witness to speculate. It also presumes everyone vomits for the same reason."

A reporter hooted loudly, followed by a few snickers around the courtroom. The judge scanned the gallery, and silence resumed.

"I'll rephrase, Your Honor," Kirk offered.

She nodded.

"Detective," Kirk said, "in your extensive experience interviewing suspects, what are some of the reasons a defendant might become physically ill?"

"Objection, Your Honor," Hampton interjected.

"Mr. Kirk," the judge said, "I'm sustaining defense's objection. I see your point, and I see what you're trying to establish, but you're still assuming facts not in evidence about various unknown defendants' motivations. Do you have any other questions for this witness?"

"No, ma'am."

"Then the witness is excused."

After Pershing left the courtroom, Hampton said, "At this time, Judge, the defense moves to exclude the confession the police extracted from my client, because he'd vomited moments before the discussion of his Fifth Amendment right to counsel. And then when my client did ask about calling an attorney, invoking his right, he was essentially threatened with jail for doing so. The custodial confession was made without benefit of counsel, and my client waived his rights without fully understanding the consequences. He was under extraordinary duress, Your Honor."

Frowning, the judge looked at the prosecutor. "Mr. Kirk?"

"Your Honor, first of all, the defendant waived his right to counsel in writing, prior to confessing to Sergeant Marshall, who is on our witness list."

"Your Honor," Hampton retorted, "the time written on the alleged confession indicates it was completed approximately a half hour before my client was rushed to the emergency room for hypoglycemic shock." Hampton glanced over his shoulder at Katrina, who was already thumbing through a box of papers to find the documents—the confession, and the hospital admissions record.

"Judge Drake," Kirk said, "we all know the defendant got sick the night of his arrest. But the state has evidence that the detective who took his confession acted in good faith, and that he had no reason to believe the defendant was in any way impaired at the time. Sergeant John Marshall will testify the defendant freely and willingly confessed to first-degree murder, and the confession makes ultimate sense in light of the facts of the case."

"We're not here to try the case, counselors—only to determine whether the defendant's confession should be admitted. I need to understand the totality of the circumstances. I will hear from Sergeant Marshall. I need to hear more about the defendant's state of mind."

"Your Honor," Hampton argued. "Is the defendant's state of mind, many hours later, relevant at all if his rights were found to be violated hours earlier? We don't know how benefit of counsel might have completely changed the events of the afternoon or evening. The first violation of his rights is sufficient to throw out any statement by my client for the rest of the day, as fruit of the poisonous tree."

"Interesting." The judge considered Hampton's argument. "Your position is if the police violated his right to counsel at an early point in custody, then the violation taints anything they find later the same day, even with an ostensible waiver?"

"Yes, Your Honor. That's the gist of it," Hampton said.

"So, in your opinion, getting a waiver in writing later in the day doesn't cure the alleged rights violation issue from earlier in the day?"

"That's right, Your Honor," Hampton agreed, "because the day might have gone quite differently with benefit of counsel. My client may have stopped cooperating under the advice of an attorney—he almost certainly *would* have stopped cooperating. He may have refused to go back to the scene. He might have done any combination of things differently *but for* the police coercion in getting him to waive his right."

"Hmm." The judge paused. "Well. If you have case law on that point, I'll take it. We can wait for your briefs first, or we can proceed to hear from Sergeant Marshall and consider briefs after."

Hampton nodded, and then he looked over his shoulder at Jason. "I think your second idea is best, Judge. Let's proceed with Sergeant Marshall first, with briefs coming sometime after."

Kirk rolled his eyes.

It was to Hampton's advantage to hear from Marshall before having the judge rule on the case, because a civil trial for damages would be inevitable. The more evidence Hampton could elicit to prove coercion, the better the civil case would be for Jason.

Even if Hampton could get the confession excluded based on the first time Jason asked for an attorney, mining for more violations during the pre-trial criminal hearings could be worthwhile for the upcoming lawsuit. Hampton had covered his bases, alluding to not one but two instances of civil rights violations, not only to the court, but also to the press.

The hearing was set to resume the following week.

"One last item, Judge," Hampton said.

"Yes?"

"The defense reserves the right to call its rebuttal witnesses following Sergeant Marshall's testimony. The state has our list."

"Mr. Kirk?" she asked.

"The state has no objection."

CHAPTER 54

The Art of War

The following Tuesday morning, Detective Sergeant John Marshall entered the courtroom and greeted the prosecutor. Checking his watch, he sat behind Kirk and waited for the judge. Marshall was ready to defend the confession he took from then-fifteen-year-old Jason Royals.

Unlike most police officers, Marshall didn't dread testifying. Even as a rookie, his calm demeanor, unfazed by defense attorneys, had distinguished him. Lawyers like Kirk had written letters of commendation on Marshall's behalf, praising him for respecting suspects' rights, which always made the prosecution's job easier. Marshall had never had any of his confessions excluded from evidence—and he didn't expect that fact to change during the Royals hearings. At the beginning of his career, he promised himself the suspects he confronted would not escape on technicalities, at least not any technicalities based on *his* mistakes.

Marshall straightened his tie. *The reputation I have, I've earned. This confession is as clean as any I've taken.*

The menacing world of night, of darkness and dreams, was rendered impotent in the light of day. Marshall consciously remembered the recurring nightmare about the child's scrawled cursive. He remembered the cold sweats and the terror he'd felt before waking. He remembered, too, the electric pulse of panic, after a long day—after the suspect ended up in the hospital—seeing the defendant's loopy initials scribbled at the end of each line of his confession.

Little stabs of anxiety. I've felt the same wondering whether I turned off the coffeemaker in the morning. I always turn off the coffeemaker.

Marshall recalled those memories in order to face them, deconstruct them, and reveal their silly powerlessness. He smiled, thinking about his Great Aunt Gracie, who consistently talked of her dreams. Aunt Gracie's dreams—in Aunt Gracie's opinion, at least— were prophetic. They were always near water and often yielded lottery numbers.

Is it a woman thing? A Black-woman thing? A generational thing? Wonder what Veronica would have to say.

Marshall's dreams had stopped as soon as he had told Veronica he was planning to transfer out of Homicide. He reasoned the nightmares had been simple manifestations of stress. Once he'd put an end date on his career as a murder detective, his hypothesis proved true. The nightmares had ceased.

◈

It didn't take long for Marshall to hear his name called. He swore to tell the truth and sat down in the witness chair.

Kirk delivered a bright, "Good morning" before asking Marshall to outline his ten-year police career for the court.

As Kirk walked toward the prosecutor's table to get his notes, Marshall got a clear view of the defense table. Behind Royals and his attorneys sat a couple, somewhat older than himself, holding hands. *They've got to be his parents.*

He watched as Clarice lifted her eyes. The woman looked first at the judge and then at the prosecutor. Marshall sensed warmth from his suspect's mother, and the feeling continued to emanate from her, even when her eyes found his. He read her half-smile as rueful.

How could this kid so callously break his mother's heart?

"Sergeant Marshall." Kirk resumed his questioning. "Do you recall the day you first met the defendant?"

"Yes, sir. I do."

"Tell us about that."

"Officer O'Donnell brought the suspect to the Homicide Division after he stopped him, as he was running away from a gunshot homicide."

"Objection, Your Honor." Hampton stood up.

Marshall saw—and heard—Aaron Hampton as if for the first

time. His voice was full, low, and distinctive. *If it isn't James Earl Jones.*

The judge frowned and looked at Kirk. "Sustained."

"Let me rephrase, please, Your Honor," Kirk said. "Sergeant Marshall, where did you first meet the defendant?"

"In the homicide office."

"And who brought him to you?"

"The arresting officer, O'Donnell."

"And what time would you say it was?"

"I'm not sure. I'd have documented it in my report. It seemed like it was getting to be lunchtime."

"Why do you say that?"

"Because I had just eaten, and I had arranged to get something for the sus—the defend—um, for Mr. Royals there."

"Something to eat, you mean?"

"Yes. I did not want a hungry suspect. I noted on my report the time he ate."

"So, you provided him with lunch?"

"I got him a sandwich and a Coke, yes, while Detective Pershing continued to process him for evidence."

"And so, the defendant ate this sandwich and drank this Coke?"

"Part of it, yes. He ate part of the sandwich and drank part of the Coke."

"At what point did he vomit?"

"After he ate. After we began questioning him."

"And to what do you attribute the vomiting?"

Hampton stood again. "Objection. Does it matter what the sergeant thinks—or thought—about why my client got sick?"

The judge stared at Hampton for a moment. "Well, it might matter, actually, yes, as it may have bearing on the sergeant's assessment of his health later on. The witness may answer."

"Your Honor," Hampton said, "this is in direct opposition to your ruling last week, when the sergeant's partner wanted to speculate as to why my client got sick."

"It is a different ruling, yes. For a different witness—the one who took his alleged confession," the judge said. "Your objection has been noted, Mr. Hampton." She gestured for Marshall to answer.

"Why do I think he vomited?" Marshall asked Kirk.

"Yes. What did you attribute it to?"

"At the time, I thought, 'He's losing his lunch because he's scared. He's in way over his head and he knows it,'" Marshall said, looking in the defendant's direction. He saw the boy looking down, doodling or drawing on a legal pad. It was an old defense trick he recognized—it keeps the accused's hand busy, in order to help him appear nonplussed by the testimony.

"So," Kirk continued, "custodial suspects have gotten sick before and during questioning?"

"Yes, sir. Not every day, but often enough."

"And is there any correlation, in your experience, between a suspect getting sick—vomiting, I mean—and a suspect's guilt?"

"Objection, Your Honor," Hampton interjected. "Correlation does not equal causation, and correlations about other suspects are irrelevant to my client's case."

"You are correct, Mr. Hampton," the judge said, "but this isn't offered as proof of your client's guilt. We aren't trying his case today, remember? We're gathering the totality of the circumstances—the degree to which your client may have been impaired, and how the detectives might reasonably have perceived that potential impairment—while they were having him waive his rights to counsel. I will allow the question insofar as it relates to Sergeant Marshall's experience."

The judge looked at the witness, prompting him to answer.

"In my experience, the answer is yes, there's a correlation. Each time a suspect has vomited in my interrogation room, he's ended up confessing, and those confessions have stood up in cases where they went to trial."

"Are you saying, Sergeant Marshall, you've never had a confession thrown out on the basis of coercion?"

"On any basis. I've not had any confession that I have personally received from any suspect excluded from evidence, sir." Marshall sat back in the witness chair.

Feels good to say it out loud.

Looking toward the defense table, Marshall observed Hampton scribbling something on a legal pad, which he passed to his client, who smiled when he saw it.

You think you'll be the first? Marshall silently challenged the defense attorney. *Bring it.*

◈

After a short break, Detective Marshall's testimony turned to Jason Royals' custodial right to counsel and his right to avoid self-incrimination. Kirk started by asking about whether the defendant had received a Miranda warning.

"Yes, sir," Marshall said. "As soon as he was brought in, I validated that he had been advised of his rights upon arrest. I asked him if he understood them, and he affirmed." Marshall looked again at the defendant, who looked up from his notes as if he were waiting for more to write.

"Thank you, Sergeant. Now, let's get past this vomiting episode, past the defendant getting cleaned up and asking about an attorney, and let me ask you: What did you and Detective Pershing do next?"

"We prepared to drive the—Mr. Royals—back to the scene to see if he could recover the murder weapon for us."

"You took him back to look for the gun?"

"Yes, sir."

"Did you stop on the way back to the scene?"

"Yes—we did—but when I say we took him back to the scene, we took him to the woods between the motel and where he was caught running, and not to the motel room itself."

"Why the woods?"

"Because the evidence technicians had thoroughly searched the motel premises and the surrounding five blocks, including dumpsters—except for those woods."

"Thank you, Detective. On your way back to the…" Kirk paused for a moment. "On your way to the site where you looked for the gun, where did you stop?"

"We stopped at the … it's not a … I don't recall the name of the place but it was a convenience store."

"And why did you stop there?"

"I wanted to pick up a snack to settle Mr. Royals' stomach, and again, to make sure he wasn't hungry."

"You bought the defendant a snack?"

"Yes, I bought the defendant some peanut butter crackers and a Diet Coke." Marshall looked again at the defense table where Jason was scribbling intently on his notepad.

"And do you recall about what time you stopped?"

"It would have been around one thirty or so that afternoon."

"How do you know, Sergeant?"

"Because Pershing radioed in at one forty p.m., when we reached the—the *site* where we believed Mr. Royals had discarded the gun. It couldn't have taken more than ten minutes to get from the store to that site."

Kirk walked to the prosecution table where he plucked a printed piece of paper from the top of a stack. Before presenting it to the witness, he showed it to the defense team, who turned to the same page in their files.

"Can you tell me what this is?" Kirk asked Marshall.

"Yes, sir. It's the dispatch record showing the time Pershing radioed in, at one forty-two p.m."

The soft rip of paper being torn from a legal pad emanated from the defense table. Wrinkling his forehead in serious determination, Jason Royals passed the paper to Katrina.

Kirk threw an admonishing glance toward Jason, then turned to Marshall, and said, "Thank you, Sergeant. Your Honor, I'm finished with this witness for now, reserving the right to recall him if need be."

"Thank you, Mr. Kirk. All of us could use something to eat about now," she declared, "and I have some other matters, besides lunch, which need my attention. We'll resume at two thirty this afternoon."

Marshall exited the witness box and shook hands with the prosecutor. As Kirk chatted, Marshall looked over the prosecutor's shoulder and became distracted by Jason's interactions with his parents. The defendant was showing the short, slight man—presumably his father—a paperback that looked familiar. He caught a glimpse of the title. It was Sun Tzu's *The Art of War*.

CHAPTER 55

Power, Authority, and Experience

At five before three in the afternoon, the judge apologized for bumping into counsel's appointed time. Marshall was reminded of his oath and took to the witness chair again.

"Mr. Hampton, you're on," Judge Drake said.

"Thank you, Your Honor. Sergeant, let's go back to when you met my client for the very first time. You didn't see the suspect while he was being paraded past the victim's husband at the murder scene?"

Marshall's eyes grew wide. Kirk wasn't as fast as he could have been, but the witness's face prompted him soon enough.

"Objection, Your Honor. Assumes facts not yet—"

"I've got you, Mr. Kirk," Hampton said, waving a piece of paper.

The judge interrupted him, shaking her head. "Mr. Hampton, I'll remind you now. Our other pretrial hearing is set for the week after next." Turning to the witness, she asked, "Sergeant, did you see the defendant at the crime scene?"

"No, Your Honor."

"Were you present at the scene when the defendant was…" the judge cleared her throat, "well, when the arresting officer took him over to the motel?"

"Yes, I was there, but I was inside the room where the shooting happened, Your Honor, when Officer O'Donnell and Mr. Royals returned." Marshall looked at Jason.

"Returned?" Hampton retorted, incredulous. "So, you know for a fact my client had been at the motel sometime before Officer O'Donnell brought him there?"

"Objection, Your Honor." Kirk was on his feet again. "He knows what the witness meant. He's splitting semantic hairs."

The judge interceded, "Would you like to rephrase, Sergeant?"

"I was inside the room when O'Donnell brought the suspect, the defendant, to the motel."

Hampton was unfazed. "And what time was that?"

"I'd have to refer to my narration, or to dispatch records, but I'd say ten thirty a.m."

"Okay, let's fast forward to lunchtime," Hampton said, standing so as to block the witness's view of the defendant.

"Would you say, Sergeant, your stomach is a pretty good indicator of when it's lunchtime?"

Marshall laughed. "Between my stomach and the clock, I know when it's lunchtime."

"You can set your clock by your stomach?"

"No, sir. I wouldn't go that far."

"Fair enough. What I'm getting at is this: After lunch, and after you and your partner took my fifteen-year-old client out into the woods, after you had my suspect in police custody until dusk, your reliable stomach didn't tell you it was dinnertime?"

Kirk was indignant. "Objection, your—"

The judge held up her hand. "I want to hear this."

"Could you please repeat the question, sir?" Marshall addressed the defense attorney directly.

"Did your stomach alarm go off later in the evening, while my fifteen-year-old, hypoglycemic client was confessing to you?"

"No, sir, not at that time." Marshall's answer was calm and cool.

"And what time would that be, Sergeant?"

"I'd have to look at the confession, sir, in order to remember."

"Okay. Let me have you take a look at this," Hampton said, walking toward the defense table. After showing Kirk the confession form, and providing the judge with the exhibit number, he brought it to Marshall. "Will you please read the beginning time on the confession sheet?"

"Five-o-nine p.m."

"And now read the end time, please."

"Seven thirty-six p.m."

"Did my hypoglycemic client have anything to eat during that approximate two-and-a-half-hour window?" Hampton asked.

"No."

"And you were aware of his medical condition?"

Marshall frowned. "Medical condition?" He shook his head. "He told me earlier in the day that he occasionally got low blood sugar, if you call that a medical condition."

Hampton was unfazed. "You asked him about his medical history while you had him in custody?"

"It came up when he asked me to buy him a Diet Coke instead of a Coke at the convenience store."

"And you previously said you gave my client this convenience store snack about one thirty in the afternoon."

"Correct."

"And how much of that snack did he eat, Sergeant?"

"About half of it."

"Would you say that's about three of those little peanut butter crackers?"

"Sounds about right."

"All right. Is it your testimony, Sergeant Marshall, that despite knowing my client suffered from hypoglycemia, and despite his vomiting up the little bit of lunch that he had eaten—is it your testimony you provided him only three peanut butter crackers for the rest of the time he was in your custody?"

"That is probably correct."

"*Probably*, Sergeant?"

"I don't recall offering him anything else, but I might have."

Hampton walked back to the defense table and picked up a document, showing it to Kirk and then to the court. "Is this your narrative report, Sergeant Marshall?"

"Yes."

"Would you please look over it and see if you provided my client with any food at any time after one thirty p.m.?"

"I did not notate it, no, sir."

"How about after the alleged confession? Did you arrange for him to eat afterwards?"

"I arranged for him to be transported to a juvenile facility," Marshall answered.

"So, he wasn't your problem anymore after you got what you wanted?"

Kirk jumped up. "Objection!"

"Sustained," the judge said, in a matter-of-fact, inscrutable manner.

"What was my client's general demeanor, when you were extracting his confession?"

"He was tired; he cried, off and on."

"Did he seem confused as to what was happening?"

"Confused? No."

"So, then, he was alert? Sharp?"

"He was tired."

"Did you tell my client he could go home after he initialed each line of the confession?"

"Objection," Kirk intoned.

"I'll allow it," the judge said. "We may be in adult court but we are still dealing with a juvenile defendant. Answer the question, Sergeant."

"It is common police practice to—"

"Yes or no," Hampton's interruption boomed. "Did you or did you not tell my client he could go home after he completed his paperwork with you?"

All eyes in the room turned toward Marshall. "Yes, I—"

"Thank you, Sergeant." Hampton looked down at his list of questions. "Did that paperwork include his Miranda waiver?"

"Yes, but—"

"Thank you, Sergeant." Hampton referred to his notes again. "Did you bring up my client's parents during this time, between five p.m. and seven thirty p.m.?"

"I don't recall, but it's possible."

"Okay, Sergeant. Fair enough. Do you recall talking to my client about Christian forgiveness?"

Marshall opened his mouth to speak but paused, pressing his lips together. He looked down before answering. "That's possible, too."

"Isn't it true, Sergeant, that you talked about both Christian forgiveness and my client's parents during the time period in which you took his *alleged confession?*"

"It's not uncommon for—"

"Yes or no, Sergeant?"

"Yes."

Jason didn't look up from his writing pad, although his pen had stopped.

"Now, let's go back a little bit, please, and let me ask you about what happened when my client first walked into your office, when you said you had my client *processed* by Detective Pershing. What did you mean by *processed?*"

"We took his shoes in order to cast his footprints, and we tested his hands for gunpowder residue."

Hampton nodded, as if he were digesting new information. He raised his eyebrows, ostensibly impressed. "Tell me, Sergeant Marshall, did my client show traces of gunpowder residue?"

"Objection, Your—"

"Your Honor." Hampton interrupted Kirk. "We contend the lack of useful evidence resulting from these processes may have amplified Sergeant Marshall's sense of urgency in obtaining a confession. They had nothing else. They had to get a confession. My question goes to Sergeant Marshall's *motivation* as part of the totality of the circumstances leading up to the confession."

The courtroom went silent. Every reporter in the room hustled to get down every word of Hampton's explanation. Marshall looked at the judge.

"I see your point, Mr. Hampton," she began, "and it has been noted for the record. But I'm more interested in the subjective condition of the defendant, and I'm going to sustain the objection again. We will hear about the gunpowder residue—or lack thereof—at trial, I promise."

Setting his notes aside, Hampton went in a different direction. "Sergeant, how tall are you?"

"I'm six feet, four inches."

"Rather tall."

Marshall nodded. "Sure. Yes."

"A good ten inches or a foot taller than my client was, at the time of his arrest."

"I'll take your word for it, sir."

"And what is your weight?"

"Two hundred."

"Would it surprise you to know, even now, my client weighs sixty-five pounds less than you do?"

"No, sir."

"Would it surprise you to know, on the day of his arrest, he was a full eighty pounds lighter than you?"

"No, sir. It would not," Marshall said, looking at Jason.

"And your partner, Detective Pershing, he's taller and weighs more than my client, too, right?"

"Yes."

"And you both are well-educated adult men, correct?"

"Well, he and I both have our bachelor's degrees."

"A whole lot more than a tenth-grade education, right?"

"Sure. I mean, yes."

"So, while you were interrogating my client, while you and your partner had him out in the woods, would you say you were aware of the differentials in height, weight, and education between you and my client?"

"Yes, obviously."

"*Obviously*," Hampton repeated the word to no one in particular, yet to everyone in the courtroom. "And was it *obvious*, Sergeant, there was a clear difference in power, authority, and experience with the criminal justice system?"

"Objection." Kirk stayed seated.

Judge Drake nodded. "You can take them one at a time, Sergeant. Power, authority, and…"

"Experience, Your Honor." The witness filled in the blank. "Experience in the criminal justice system." Marshall turned to address Hampton. "We saw that he had no criminal record in Beau Rêve, but we also knew several gang members who attended the defendant's high school, so it was reasonable to believe that he might have a connection to those gang members—the College Lifers."

"The College Lifers. Did you ask my client whether he was mixed up in this group?"

"Yes, I did."

"And what did he say?"

"He denied being involved."

"Isn't it true, Sergeant Marshall, that my client told you he'd never even heard of the College Lifers?"

"Yes. He said he hadn't heard of them, but—"

"He said he hadn't heard of them," Hampton repeated, cutting off Marshall.

"Hold on, counselor," Judge Drake said. "I'd like to hear the rest of what Sergeant Marshall has to say."

Marshall spoke. "I was going to say that we didn't believe him."

"Oh?" Hampton once again donned his look of false surprise. "What was it about my then five-foot-four, one-hundred-twenty-pound client, which led you to believe he wasn't telling the truth?"

"Most of the people we deal with don't tell the truth, sir. And the gang members are getting younger and younger, and their crimes are getting worse and worse."

"To clarify, Sergeant, we're talking about gang members in general, and not my client in particular, correct?"

"That remains to be seen, sir."

The courtroom stirred in reaction to Marshall's jab.

"It remains to be seen? Am I to understand you have your own doubts about my client's guilt, Sergeant?"

Marshall was stunned. He looked to Kirk, but Kirk didn't object.

He said, "Mr. Hampton, I stand by the evidence my partner and I have brought to this court."

"You're referring to the alleged confession you...*obtained* from my client, aren't you? And not any physical evidence relating to Mrs. Patterson's murder?"

"Objection." Kirk stood up. "Your Honor has already made a ruling about the time and place to discuss other evidence, and it's not during this pre-trial hearing."

"Well, yes, Mr. Kirk," Judge Drake said. "But that was before your client opened the door in his testimony. The witness may answer."

"I stand by the written confession I obtained from your client."

"Are you conceding there wasn't any physical evidence tying my client to your murder case?"

"There was the witness identification," Marshall said.

"That's not physical evidence, is it?"

"No, sir."

"In fact, we are disputing it in a subsequent hearing," Hampton intoned.

"Is there a question there, Your Honor?" Kirk interjected.

"I'll withdraw my last comment," Hampton said. "But let me ask you, Sergeant, did you ever express an opinion about the manner in which Officer O'Donnell obtained the witness identification of my client?"

"Objection, Your Honor. As Mr. Hampton already said, we're set to have an entirely separate hearing on the witness identification issue."

"I'm sorry, Mr. Kirk. Again, the door has been opened. Please answer the question, Sergeant."

Kirk tried again. "Then I object on the grounds it's irrelevant."

Hampton wrinkled his brow. "It's irrelevant whether this experienced homicide Sergeant expressed a concern about the witness ID?"

"Overruled," the judge said.

Marshall paused before answering. "Yes, I have an opinion."

"Well, please tell us about your opinion of the witness ID process, Sergeant."

"I had concerns about the witness ID." Marshall looked at Kirk, who was shaking his head.

"You were concerned the ID was improperly obtained?" Hampton asked.

"Yes." Marshall saw that Jason had stopped scribbling. The boy looked directly at him, glaring with contempt. The courtroom went dead silent.

Hampton nodded, taking advantage of the quiet moment. Then, in a softer voice, he asked, "Did this complete lack of physical evidence, coupled with your concerns about the witness ID, pressure you toward obtaining a confession from my client?"

"Did it pressure me? I wouldn't use that word, no."

"Did it highlight the urgency of getting a confession from my client?"

"Only if your cli—"

"Yes or no, Sergeant."

Marshall avoided looking the defense attorney in the eye. "It *highlighted* the need to gather additional evidence, yes."

"Including a confession?"

"Only if it was forthcoming, and it was."

"After he was in police custody for more than nine hours?"

Marshall thought for a minute. "Yes."

"One trip to the woods and three little crackers later?"

Marshall sighed. "Yes."

"Thank you." Hampton flipped some pages on his legal pad. "During those nine hours, how many times did you permit my client to try to reach his parents?"

"How many times?" Marshall asked.

"Did you at any time permit my client to try to reach his parents?"

"Yes. I provided him my cell phone."

"Before the fateful trip to the woods, right?"

"Your Honor…" Kirk started to stand but the judge waved him to sit down.

"When did you permit the defendant to use your phone?" she asked Marshall.

"Before lunch, Your Honor."

Hampton jumped back in. "Did he reach them?"

"No."

"Did you permit him to try again?"

"I…on the way to the—"

"Yes or no, please," Hampton interjected. "During the nine hours you held my young client, did you give him more than one opportunity to call his parents?"

"No."

"Thank you, Sergeant." Hampton turned to a different page in his notes. "Now let's get back to discussing the *need* as you called it, the *need* to obtain more evidence in order to connect my client to your murder case. Let's talk about when you and Detective Pershing took him to the…not the crime scene…but the woods nearby. The *site*, someone called it."

"The investigation site."

"And we are talking about the woods, right?"

"Yes."

"Why did you two take my fifteen-year-old client to the woods?"

"It was the wooded area between the motel where the homicide occurred and the spot where he was caught running away from the scene."

"Oh. So, you know for a fact my client was running away from the scene, and not just running across the street, when he was stopped?"

"I misspoke. The woods were between the motel and where your client was caught running, period."

"You and your partner, two adult policemen, took my client out to the woods?"

"We are adults, yes," Marshall said.

Hampton laughed. "Yes. And you're also authority figures, right?"

"Yes, sir."

"Did you or your partner have your hands on my client at any time during your little outing to the woods?"

"Yes. We guided him."

"As you were guiding my client, did you knock the wind out of him?"

Marshall did not answer. All eyes were on him.

"Sergeant?" the judge asked, alarmed. "Did you strike the defendant?"

"No, ma'am. I did not strike him in the sense of intentionally hitting him. There was a point…he was walking and he looked like he was going to lose his footing. I may have stuck my arm out to keep him from falling."

"Did your arm come into contact with his abdomen?" Hampton asked, prompting Marshall to turn away from the judge.

"Yes."

"Did it knock the wind out of him?"

"I don't know. He did stop walking."

"Did he bend over?"

"Yes."

"So, as your arm contacted my client's abdomen, and he stopped walking and bent over, is it possible my client construed your…your… *sticking out your arm*," Hampton asked, "as you striking him?"

"Not in my mind, no."

"I'm not asking about your mind," Hampton said. "Is it possible he could have perceived your action as a direct hit?"

"Objection, Your Honor," Kirk said. "Calls for speculation."

"Sustained."

"Your Honor," Hampton intoned. "I take exception. When police are interrogating a suspect they have in custody, they have to be mindful of the effects of their own strength, their own physical power and authority over that suspect. The differential in power is essential to establishing the defendant's subjective point of view."

"Your exception is noted. The objection is still sustained. Move on, please."

Hampton's attention returned to the witness. "You say my client lost his footing."

"Yes."

"Was he disoriented?"

"No, sir."

"Why would my client lose his footing?"

"The ground, you know, the woods. The ground is…" Marshall looked up as if to locate a word. "Uneven."

"I'm going to direct you to our defense exhibit number nine." Hampton held up the piece of paper and showed it to opposing counsel. "The state has stipulated to these documents. They're my client's medical records from the evening of the day of his arrest. I'd direct you to page four of the—"

Kirk objected. "The witness cannot attest to anything from the hospital. He wasn't present when the defendant went in."

"I'm not asking him to do that, Your Honor," Hampton said.

"Overruled, pending your question, Mr. Hampton."

"If you'll turn to page four," Hampton picked up where he left off, "you'll see two images of a human body there, front and back, representative of my client's condition upon entering the hospital. Would you please look at the abdomen on the frontal drawing, and the notes connected to it?"

Marshall found the diagram.

"See where the nurse has marked 'contusions' on the front, left side of my client's abdomen?"

"Yes."

"Is it possible those bruises could have come from the contact that your arm made with my client's abdomen in the woods?"

Marshall's mouth dropped. He looked at the judge, who nodded at him to go ahead and answer. Marshall took a moment before he began speaking. "Anything's possible," he said. "But I would be very sur—"

"Thank you, Sergeant. Now, if I may direct your attention to the right side of the head on the frontal drawing, depicting my client's face."

Marshall looked down, nodding.

"Could that laceration and bruise have come from my client's foray into the woods with you and your partner?"

"It was a scrape!" Marshall exclaimed.

"Is that a yes or a no?"

Marshall looked at the judge. "My partner accidentally flung a branch into the suspect's face."

"So, it's a yes," Hampton said.

Marshall conceded the point. "Yes."

"Where were you in relation to your partner when he did this?"

"He didn't…" Marshall shook his head. "He was a few steps ahead of me. I wasn't aware the suspect got—that he was—that the branch hit him, until he screamed."

"Until who screamed?"

"Your client."

"So, you really can't say whether your partner intentionally aimed to fling this branch at my client's face or not, can you?"

"I don't believe—"

"Yes or no. Do you know whether your partner meant to injure my client?"

"My partner said—"

"Your partner said? You and your partner talked about this injury?"

Kirk was quick this time. "Hearsay, Your Honor."

"Not when it's a statement against their interest, it isn't," Hampton shot back.

"Overruled. The witness will answer defense counsel's questions."

"When did you and your partner discuss my client's injury?" Hampton asked.

"When your allegations of police brutality aired on the news."

The courtroom hummed in reaction to Marshall's response.

Hampton digested the answer, walking toward the defense table. "Police brutality," he said, turning around, "is a pretty serious charge to allege against any police officer, is it not?"

"For me, it is. Yes, sir."

"Okay. So, at some point, you heard or saw news that my client had been hurt in police custody, right?"

"Yes."

"And at that point, the press had been reporting charges of police misconduct, right?"

"Yes."

"And at some point after, you conferred with your partner,

Detective Pershing, about my client's injury, correct?"

"Correct."

"Why?" Hampton laid out the question, simply, in a manner that begged for an equally simple answer.

"Why what?" Marshall asked.

"Why did you confer with your partner about my client's injury?"

"To review the facts surrounding the injury."

"Review?"

"Yes."

"Didn't you say, a few minutes ago, you were trailing a few steps behind your partner in the woods with my client, so you didn't see exactly what happened until my client screamed?"

Marshall sighed. "Yes."

"So, when you and Detective Pershing talked about it after the news came out, it was less a review of the facts than an original exploration of what really happened out there?"

"You could say that. Yes."

"I am saying that, Sergeant. What I'm asking is this: were you worried your partner intentionally hurt my client?"

"I cannot speak to his motivations."

"I'm not asking you about his motivations. I'm asking whether you conferred with your partner because you were worried there might be something to my client's allegations of police misconduct."

"I wanted to confirm," Marshall said, "there was nothing to worry about."

"You wanted to confirm that there was no misconduct, is that accurate?"

"Yes."

"Because you thought your partner might have committed misconduct?"

"Objection! Asked and answered, Your Honor!" Kirk was animated. "How many different ways is he going to ask this question?"

"Your objection is sustained, Mr. Kirk. Mr. Hampton, how much more do you have for this witness?"

"Actually, I'm finished, Your Honor."

"Mr. Kirk?" she asked.

"No redirect at this time."

"We'll take the nurse and your child endocrinologist tomorrow, Mr. Hampton. Any chance we can wrap this up then?"

"Probably, Your Honor. Don't forget my expert on false confessions," Hampton said.

"Okay, that makes three witnesses. Let's go ahead and schedule briefs for the end of next week then. Does that work for both of you gentlemen?"

The lawyers flipped through their calendars.

"I'm in trial next week, Your Honor," Kirk said.

"Fancy that, counselor. I am too. How about if I give you until the following Monday for briefs?"

The lawyers agreed.

"At that time, make sure you're ready to call your witnesses for the motion to exclude the eyewitness identification. I've got the hearing scheduled for the same Monday. Let's make it Monday afternoon. Two o'clock."

CHAPTER 65

The Lindbergh Baby

Back in his cell after the first set of hearings, Jason felt relieved. Seeing his lawyer in action in the confession hearings had given him a charge of hope.

The courtroom, Jason realized, was Hampton's natural habitat. Detective Pershing had looked like a nervous turtle by comparison, and Sergeant Marshall—well, Marshall was no match for a civil rights attorney of Hampton's caliber. Marshall had bitten hard on Hampton's bait, and Jason enjoyed watching the detective squirm on the stand.

The tables have turned.

Jason thought for a minute about the actual table in the interrogation room; the handcuffs; the vomit; the weak, teary-eyed confession of the unhinged, young boy he'd once been. The defense table in a court of law evened the playing field—at least it did for defendants who actually had the money or family connections to get to that table. Instead of Jason answering police officers' questions, they now had to answer *his* questions, through Aaron J. Hampton.

Now that's power. Real power.

Jason silently recalled the litany of his future plans:

> *Get out of here.*
> *Get back to school.*
> *Make good grades.*
> *Graduate.*
> *Get into a top-tier state college.*
> *Make good grades.*
> *Graduate.*
> *Apply to…*

There would be a lot of steps—especially if he wanted to study the law. Seeing Hampton in action in court, though, made him believe in his future again.

Hopping down from his bunk, Jason retrieved the *How to Draw Animals* book his mom had sent him. Putting pencil to composition book, he took his time with the turtle, Detective Pershing. The fish, aka Sergeant Marshall, he drew quickly—followed by a sharp-pointed hook through the animal's upper lip.

Farther down on the page he drew a medical cross, like the one on the hospital logo from St. Mary's, where Jillian worked.

Jillian had gone to bat for him in court, along with Officer Howard, the older, white police officer who ended up driving him to the hospital.

"I could see immediately something was amiss medically," Howard had said in court. Jason allowed the words to roll around in his head. He decided to write them in his journal.

"He was not alert and aware that evening at all—not like he is today," Howard testified. The police officer had made eye contact with Jason from the witness stand, nodding. "Your client was obviously out of it. Completely confused, and that was before he lost consciousness," the uniformed man added, directly contradicting what Marshall had said the day before.

Jason grinned when he remembered the prosecutor's reaction. You could practically see steam coming out of his ears, just like the cartoons in his dad's old *Mad Magazine* collection. Jason wanted to remember those days, wanted to write them down, but didn't want to put too much detail in his composition book because he knew it wasn't private.

He drew a *Mad Magazine* version of Assistant State Attorney Fred Kirk, complete with the steam coming out of his ears.

"You see, son," Jason's lawyer had whispered after the interchange. "There are people in this world who'll do what is right, no matter what team they're on."

One good cop out of four. All right. I'll give you that, Hamp.

Jason winced a little bit remembering the endocrinologist's testimony. *Hypoglycemic twilight. Temporary psychosis.*

Jason started to write the word but stopped after "psych."

He found his dictionary, hoping the word "brain" would have an illustration. It didn't, so he ad-libbed a doodle of the organ, the best he could.

Then he flipped to the birds' section of his animal-drawings book, and tried to remember what it was he and Octavius had seen back when they were out on the basketball court together.

Cow egret? No, too small.

Great egret? Maybe.

Louisiana blue heron? No, I believe it was a great egret. Like the one I saw when…

Jason's eye shifted to the illustration of the humongous wood stork, which seized his imagination. He copied the rough outlines of the creature in flight. He drew the clichéd knapsack around its beak, but stopped short of penciling in the clichéd baby.

Instead, he wrote the name "Lindbergh," in his best script, onto the hanging pouch. *I hope I spelled it right.*

The "stork," he mused, had landed in the form of Dr. Mark Redvine, the expert witness on false confessions. Redvine had spoken about the effects of physical strain, coercion, and psychological duress. He discussed the Central Park Five case in New York, where five separate suspects confessed to the brutal gang rape of a female jogger but were later cleared by DNA evidence. He also talked about the Lindbergh baby and how two hundred different people had confessed to the infamous kidnapping and murder in 1932.

Jason embellished the letters as a calligrapher might.

Whether or not he had completely lost his mind, whether or not he could have slipped out of reality like the endocrinologist suggested—those questions became irrelevant given Redvine's testimony. Jason felt vindicated.

It happens to other people. More than we know. I'm not the only one.

Fortunately, a legal cure existed for false confessions. He'd put the other matter—hypoglycemic psychosis—on the back burner. *I don't know if I ever want to talk about psychosis.*

Jason preferred to take the moment to digest the "relative success," as Hampton had called it, which they had experienced with the first set of pretrial hearings. Hampton said he was confident the judge would exclude the confession, even though she would not announce her ruling until after the second set of hearings, the ones about the witness identification. Meanwhile, Jason would spend another week in jail.

Please, he prayed to a God he wasn't sure he believed in. *Let it be my last.*

CHAPTER 57

Adrenaline

Judge Drake took her place on the bench. "This afternoon we will hear defendant Royals' motion to suppress state's evidence related to suspect identification. Defense has made a prima facie case in support of excluding the identification. Mr. Kirk, the burden of proving this evidence *should* be included at trial now rests with you. Are you ready for your first witness?"

"Yes, we are. The state calls Officer Craig O'Donnell."

The stocky, pinkish man in blue moved to the witness chair with all the ease of a rhinoceros. While bulletproof vests always added bulk to an officer's physique, O'Donnell's muscled arms hung away from his body, straining the fabric at the biceps. Then again, there wasn't a portion of his uniform that didn't appear ready to burst at the seams. O'Donnell's prominent forehead was abutted by bushy blond eyebrows—the largest features on a head decidedly too tiny for its body.

Jason recalled his original impression of the man. *Steroids.* Years before, he'd learned about their effects from an *Afterschool Special* on TV.

O'Donnell raised his pink, muscle-bound arm and swore to tell the truth.

Judge Drake signaled for Kirk to begin. O'Donnell was the state's first witness on the suspect identification issue.

"It'll be hard for O'Donnell to salvage this," Katrina had written on Jason's legal pad. He took a deep breath, hoping she was right, steeling himself in case she was wrong.

"Good afternoon, Officer O'Donnell," Kirk said.

"Afternoon." The uniformed officer was curt but clear.

"Officer, how long have you been with the Beau Rêve Police Department?"

"Twelve years," he said, adding, "I'm a patrol officer."

"What area of the city do you patrol?"

"East Beau Rêve, along U.S. 1 all the way up to downtown."

"Ah, yes. U.S. 1. Would you tell the court, please, what street that is, here in Beau Rêve?"

"Broward Highway." O'Donnell squinted at Kirk, as if the answer should be obvious to everyone.

"Perfect. Do you recall the day you stopped the defendant on Broward Highway?"

"Yes, sir," O'Donnell said.

"That would have been Sunday morning, April 29, 2001?"

"Yes, sir, Mr. Kirk, if you're getting the date from my arrest report."

"I am." Kirk held up the piece of paper, proffering it to the court and to his opponent. "Do you also remember why you stopped the defendant that day?"

"Yes, sir. I do. I saw the suspect running across Broward Highway while I was responding to a dispatch about a gunshot homicide."

"To be clear, the defendant, Jason Royals, was running?"

"Yes. In the opposite direction from the scene. He stopped and stood in the median for a moment before running fast across the southbound lane. He was running, and he matched the description of the gunman who fled the Vacation Station Inn."

Jason's blood ran cold. He was determined not to appear scared, however. He slowly worked on his sketch of a flamingo, the only pink creature he could think of. He kept his head down while the questioning continued.

"You were on your way to the scene when you spotted the defendant?" Kirk asked.

"I was surveying the area *around* the crime scene."

"And you are talking about the location surrounding where Mrs. Betty Patterson was allegedly murdered?"

"Yes, sir."

"You mentioned a description?" Kirk asked.

"Yes, sir. Dispatch had issued a BOLO, um, "be on the lookout," for a Black male in tan pants."

"And did you see a Black male in tan pants?"

"Yes. The defendant." O'Donnell pointed at Jason.

"What happened next, Officer?"

"I motioned for the defendant to come to the parking lot on the corner of Broward and College. Which he did."

"And then what happened?"

"I began to question him about his whereabouts. He said he was looking for a job, which I thought was strange, because it was Sunday. He then asked me if something happened at the motel, the Vacation Station Inn."

"What did you do then?"

"I moved to apprehend the defendant, given his knowledge about the crime scene."

"Objection." Hampton stood up. "Officer O'Donnell said my client mentioned the Vacation Station Inn. Mentioning a motel does not equal having knowledge about a crime scene."

Judge Drake raised her eyebrows. "I'm going to sustain that. Officer O'Donnell, would you like to rephrase your answer?"

"Yes." O'Donnell pursed his lips, in the manner of a man trying not to roll his eyes. "When the suspect mentioned the name of the motel where the crime had just occurred, I moved to apprehend him."

"And when you apprehended him," Kirk asked, "what happened?"

"He tried to run."

"Hence the resisting-arrest charge?"

"Yes. Resisting arrest with violence. I had to wrestle him down."

"Were you able to subdue the defendant?"

"Yes."

"And then what happened?"

"I read him his rights, I put him in the back of my patrol vehicle, and I began filling out my arrest report." O'Donnell's face was expressionless.

"What happened next?"

"I transported the suspect to my lieutenant, who was working the scene."

"To be clear, Officer, your lieutenant was working the gunshot homicide scene at the Vacation Station Inn?"

"Yes."

"When you took the defendant to the motel, where did you park?"

"It was a pretty busy place by then. I parked down towards the end of the motel, the part farthest from College Boulevard."

"Did you remove the defendant from your car?"

"Yes, sir, I did. I took him to my lieutenant, who was parked closer to College."

"And can you describe what happened?"

"It was my understanding, from the commotion, that the victim's husband made a positive ID of the defendant at the scene."

"Objection. Hearsay." Hampton stood up.

"Sustained." Judge Drake looked at Kirk as Hampton took his seat.

Kirk tried again. "Let me ask you this, Officer. What did you see or hear as you walked toward your lieutenant with the defendant."

"There was another officer, who had been standing closer to the victim's husband, and I heard him say something to the effect of, 'We've got our man.'"

Hampton started to stand up but then thought better of it.

Judge Drake wrinkled her forehead. "Do you have an objection, Mr. Hampton?"

"No, ma'am," he said.

Kirk spoke to the witness. "Thank you, Officer O'Donnell. Your Honor, I'm finished with this witness for now, but I reserve the right to recall him."

"All right. Mr. O'Donnell, if you could stay for a bit longer, please, I'd like to keep going and see if we can't get this done today," the judge said.

Hampton rose to his feet once more, legal pad in hand. "May it please the court, I'd like to begin my cross examination of Officer O'Donnell."

CHAPTER 58

The Crossing

"Go ahead, Mr. Hampton." Judge Drake signaled Hampton to begin questioning Officer O'Donnell.

Hampton stood at the defense table, taking in the scene. Katrina and Jason tilted their eyes up toward the lawyer—the warrior—who took in a determined breath as he appraised his adversary in the witness box.

"Good afternoon, Officer O'Donnell."

"Good afternoon."

"Officer, you say you've been a patrol officer for twelve years now?"

"Yes, sir."

"Did you ever want to be a detective or anything?"

"No, sir. That's not for me." O'Donnell's brusque indifference yielded into a slight smirk as he added, "I'd rather be on the streets than working a desk."

The minor dig generated a rustle in the courtroom. Hampton ignored it. He asked, "How about field training—is that for you?"

The witness said flatly, "I have served as Field Training Officer in the past."

"When?"

"In 1998 and 1999."

"You were an FTO for about two years, then?"

"No, sir. For about fourteen months."

"Why did you discontinue your work as an FTO, sir?"

O'Donnell squirmed in his seat, looking toward the prosecution table. Kirk stared at him, frowning.

"I received a complaint from one of my subordinates," O'Donnell said.

"What was the nature of the complaint?"

"She did not appreciate my management style."

"Your management style?" Hampton's tone was incredulous.

"Objection, Your Honor. Relevance," Kirk interjected.

"Goes to credibility, judge," Hampton said.

"Overruled."

Hampton began again. "Isn't it true that your subordinate lodged a sexual harassment complaint against you?"

"It was unsubstantiated."

"That's not what I asked you, Officer. Did a subordinate file a sexual harassment complaint against you?"

"Yes."

"And that's a little different from taking issue with your management style, isn't it?"

"If you say so."

Hampton stared at O'Donnell, allowing his answer to hang in the air a moment.

"Officer, I'd like to take you back to when you first responded to the homicide call at the Vacation Station Inn. What route did you take to get there from downtown?"

"As I said before, I drove south down Broward Highway, then turned left at College, going east."

"Thank you. At this time, Your Honor, I'd like to introduce a graphic depiction of the corner of Broward and College, to which the state has stipulated."

"Go ahead," the judge said.

Katrina set up the tripod with the schematic and handed Hampton the pointer. Hampton looked at the street map and turned it upside down, with "south" appearing at the top of the drawing.

"Officer O'Donnell, you say you made a left turn off Broward onto College when you were first dispatched?" Hampton moved the pointer along in a fashion to indicate the left turn.

"Yes, sir. That's correct."

"Then it's okay with you if we orient the map this way, with 'north' on the bottom, so we can share your perspective of making a left to go east."

O'Donnell was nodding, attentive. "Fine with me."

"So, as you traveled south on Broward, and made a left on

College," Hampton asked slowly, as he drew a dotted red line on the board to represent O'Donnell's path, "were your lights and sirens on?"

"Yes, sir," O'Donnell said.

"Why?"

"Why?" The squinty sneer returned to the policeman's face.

"Yes. What are the reasons for turning on lights and sirens when you've been dispatched to a crime scene?"

O'Donnell's incredulity at the simple question came off as disdainful. "To bypass traffic, for starters."

"Okay, to bypass traffic. Any other reason to have lights flashing and sirens blaring?" Hampton held his palms upward at O'Donnell.

"Yeah," O'Donnell huffed. "It tends to send the bad guys running." He tilted his forehead in Jason's direction.

Jason did not flinch. Hampton and Katrina had prepared him well. They had hurled much viler insults at him to get him ready for the hearing, their most challenging day in the courtroom yet. While mild electrical panic flitted through his veins, Jason channeled it to his hands, under the table, grasping a pen. His eyes—resolute—were on Hampton.

"*Bad guys.*" Hampton repeated O'Donnell's words, one at a time, as if trying them on. "I see. Let me ask you, Officer O'Donnell, on the hierarchy of all the possible offenses a *bad guy* could commit, how do shootings rank?"

"How do they *rank*?" O'Donnell's forehead wrinkled, contorted in confusion.

"Yes. In comparison to other crimes—how urgent is a radio call about a shooting?"

"*Very* urgent."

"Is anything *more* urgent—in your estimation as a veteran patrol officer?"

"More urgent than an armed killer on the loose? No. Unless one of our own has been shot."

"A fellow officer, you mean?"

"Yes."

"So, what happens when you get a call as...*urgent*...as the call to the Vacation Station?"

"What happens? Well, if I get a homicide call and there's a gunman at large, unless I'm tied up transporting a suspect, I'm going to stop what I'm doing and get over there."

"Is it fair to say a fair amount of adrenaline kicks in, Officer, when you get a gun homicide call?"

"You bet, counselor. Adrenaline is part of a cop's day-to-day life."

"Unlike the lives of people who sit behind desks?"

Before Kirk could get the objection out of his mouth, O'Donnell said, "You got that right."

A rumble rolled through the courtroom, punctuated by a loud cackle from the back—from another uniformed officer. Heads turned. Spectators hissed their outrage in sharp whispers.

The judge slammed her gavel on the dais.

"If there are any more outbursts in my courtroom, those responsible will be forcibly removed, and will face jail for contempt of court." Judge Drake glared at the policeman in the back row. "You have been warned." Frowning at Hampton, she said, "Now, counselor, I expect you to stay on topic."

"Yes, Your Honor." Hampton nodded his submissiveness and turned back to the witness. "Officer, would you have stopped any Black person you saw in the vicinity of Mrs. Patterson's murder?"

Kirk did not object, but O'Donnell didn't take the bait, either. "It depends," the witness replied.

"On?"

"On if said *Black person* matched the description of the suspect."

"So, when you stopped my client, you were only doing what any good police officer would do?"

"That's right."

"Do you remember what my client was wearing?"

"I remember he matched the radio description."

"Blue golf shirt, tucked in?"

"I don't recall."

"You don't recall which? A description of a golf shirt on the radio? Or whether my client was wearing one?"

"Neither."

"What *do* you recall?"

"Something about tan pants."

"*Something* about tan pants?" Hampton lifted his hand in the air as if to summon the mystery. "Size twenty-eight waist?" Soft chuckles reverberated throughout the courtroom as the judge rolled her eyes.

"Your Honor." Kirk stood as he groaned. "Counselor is badgering my witness."

"Sustained. Counselor, please don't try my patience. Move on."

Hampton moved on. "What did you do, Officer, when you stopped this particular Black male?" He extended his arm toward Jason.

"I questioned him. He tried to run away from me, and I stopped him. Then I cuffed him."

"Hold on—let's go back to the part where you questioned my client. Did you ask him where he was going?"

"Yes."

"Do you recall what he said?"

"He said he was job hunting."

"Was he dressed for job hunting?"

"I don't recall."

"You noticed his khaki pants, though?"

"They were tan."

"Khaki, tan—Your Honor, will this court take judicial notice that the terms can be synonymous?"

"For this limited purpose, yes. The court recognizes the synonyms. I trust you have a point, Mr. Hampton?"

"Yes, Your Honor. We're getting there." Hampton faced O'Donnell again. "What was it about my client, that morning, that caused you to stop him?"

"As I said, he matched the description."

"Okay. Let's talk about the description, then. So far—and you'll correct me if I'm wrong, please—from what you've said, we know that the suspect was Black, was male, and was wearing tan pants."

"Correct."

"What else?"

"What do you mean?"

"Well, maybe you could tell *me*, in your capacity as a law enforcement officer. When you answer a call and take down the description of a potential suspect, what kinds of questions do you ask?"

"I ask the victim or the witness to describe the suspect."

"In what terms?" Hampton rolled his hands in the air, in a tell-me-more gesture.

"I ask if they could tell the race of the suspect, confirm the sex of the suspect. I ask if they can describe what the suspect was wearing."

"Anything else?" The lawyer knew the witness was going to make him work for his answers.

"Like what?"

"Do you generally ask about the height and weight of the suspect?"

"Sure."

"How about the age of the suspect?"

"Yes. That, too."

"So, when you were dispatched on the morning of April 29, 2001, to a gunshot homicide, what other descriptors were mentioned besides Black, male, tan pants?" Hampton counted the traits on three fingers, which he then held in the air.

O'Donnell was silent for a moment but then answered, "I don't recall."

"Officer, what is it that you don't recall, exactly? You don't recall the rest of the dispatch description, or you don't recall whether there was more to that description?"

"Neither."

"You don't recall an age range for the suspect?"

"No, sir."

"You don't recall height, weight, build?"

"No—"

Kirk stood up. "Objection. Asked and answered, Your Honor."

"I agree, Mr. Kirk. Mr. Hampton, we get it. Move on."

"Was there anything else about my client—besides being Black and the, you know, the pants—was there anything else about him that prompted you to stop him?" Hampton asked.

"No, sir. Wait. Yes, sir. The fact that he was running in a direction opposite from the Vacation Station."

"Remind us *where* this running occurred again?"

"He ran across Broward Highway."

Hampton used a green marker to note Jason's path, then asked the witness, "That's generally a busy street, isn't it?"

"Less on a Sunday, but yes. It's a four-lane highway, divided by a median. That's where the suspect was standing when I first saw him—on the median."

Hampton stood motionless for a moment. Then he turned to Jason to verify this tidbit of information. He mouthed the words, "The median?"

Jason replied with a nod.

"Excuse me, Your Honor," Hampton said. "I need a moment to confer with my client, please."

"Take fifteen minutes, Mr. Hampton." The judge took off her glasses and pinched the top of her nose. "Let's all take a fifteen-minute break, if it suits the parties."

"Yes, ma'am, Your Honor. Thank you," Hampton said.

O'Donnell's burly shoulders dropped as he flopped back in his chair, in the manner of someone who suddenly realized he was going to be stuck at the courthouse for the rest of the afternoon. He looked at the prosecutor, who said, "No objections, Your Honor."

"Thank you, Gentlemen. You may leave your exhibit in place if you like, Mr. Hampton."

❖

"Hello, again, Officer O'Donnell," Hampton said as the proceedings resumed.

The policeman nodded his acknowledgement.

"Before the break, Officer, we talked about where and when you spotted my client for the very first time, right?"

"That's right."

"And you said something about him standing in the median on Broward Highway, right?"

"That's what I said, yes."

"So, this business about running away from the scene, when exactly are you saying *that* happened?"

"I'm not just *saying* it happened," O'Donnell protested. "It did happen. When I came back around, your client was running."

"When you came back around?" Hampton pretended the information was new to him. He pretended he didn't know that O'Donnell had seen Jason twice before he stopped him, or that he had turned his squad car around to pursue him.

O'Donnell nodded as he said, "Yes." Drawing with his finger in the air, he said, "I saw him in the median about here, as I was making the turn. Something told me to turn around, and when I got back to him he was running across the southbound part of Broward Highway." He traced his path in the air and then lowered his hand.

"Which direction was my client headed?" Hampton pointed to the schematic.

"What do you mean?" O'Donnell, flustered, held out both hands in a shrug.

"North, south, east, west?"

"I suppose it was west," the witness replied, annoyed. "At any rate, it was in the exact *opposite* direction from my crime scene."

"The *opposite* direction?" Hampton repeated the witness's words, as was his habit, to clarify.

"Yes."

"What if he'd been running south instead of west?"

"What?" O'Donnell's impatience was unmistakable. "He was running *west*."

"I understand he was indeed—at that moment, Officer. But let's say, for argument's sake, he was running south. Would you still say he was running *away* from the crime scene you were trying to get to?"

"Well, yeah. Yes. I imagine I would."

"When you say you saw him running *away* from your scene," Hampton asked, extending one arm, "do you mean that he wasn't running toward it?"

"Obviously." O'Donnell's pink face grew pinker and his bushy, blond brows knitted slightly. "He surely was not running toward the crime scene."

"Is it accurate to say, then, that my client was running in a direction that would not lead him to the murder scene?"

"That's what I've been saying."

"No, sir, Officer. What you've been saying is that he *ran away* from the scene, right?"

Kirk stood. "Objection. Counsel is splitting hairs, Your Honor."

"Overruled," Judge Drake said.

Hampton resumed. "When you first saw my client standing in the median on Broward Highway," the lawyer asked the witness, pointing to an imaginary median in an imaginary street, "do you know exactly where he was coming *from*?"

"He ran across the street from the median when I came back. He was traveling east to west."

"That's not what I asked you, Officer. Help me understand—when you saw him for the very first time, standing in the median, while he was standing there, was he moving in any direction?"

"You're asking me if he was moving while he was standing still?" O'Donnell's voice pitched upward, incredulous, as soft tittering sprinkled the courtroom.

"That's what I'm asking."

"Okay, well, no." O'Donnell crossed his arms and slammed back in his chair. He pointed his forehead at Jason. "He was only *standing* while he was standing."

O'Donnell's sarcasm reminded Jason of their first encounter; it triggered memories of the derision dripping from the officer's query that day: *Where are* you *going?* This time, though, Jason let the electric panic flow down through his body, through his feet, into the floor. The witness's disdain didn't scare him—not in the courtroom. Despite the reverberating whispers they generated, O'Donnell's words steeled Jason. Eighteen months earlier, on a Sunday morning, he'd been a scared little boy. But in the courtroom, with Hampton fighting for him and with his parents behind him, he relished the fight. It was the police department's turn to feel what it was like to not be believed—to be taken down, if only verbally.

"So how could you know, Officer O'Donnell, what my client was doing before you spotted him standing in the median?" Hampton's voice grew louder. "How could you possibly know?"

"I made an inference."

"Ah, an inference. Is an inference the same as a fact?"

"No, but—"

"Might you just as easily have assumed," Hampton interjected, "that my client had been walking—or even running, let's say running—south to north or north to south, before deciding to cross Broward Highway at that spot?"

"It's possible, sure."

"But you really didn't know, Officer, at that moment when you were driving to that scene, that moment he's standing in the median," Hampton stretched an arm toward Jason, "you didn't know where my client had been just prior to that, did you?"

"No."

"Thank you, Officer. Now, since you didn't know where my client had been prior to your spotting him, you can't possibly know why he ended up running, can you?"

"Why he was running away from the police?"

"No. Not *away* from anyone. Not *away* from anywhere. You just said you didn't know where he'd been before, right?"

"Right."

"Or why he ran across that section of highway, right?"

"Right. I inferenced it, but I did not know. Half my job is inferencing."

"Understandable. Let me ask you this, Officer. Could you just as well have *inferred* my client was rushing across Broward to beat the traffic?"

"Sure, why not?" O'Donnell was deflated.

"Thank you. Now let's get to what happened after you stopped him."

"All right," the witness said, with a breath that acknowledged Hampton was not about to let up.

Jason leaned over the table to tend to his fake doodling, and to hide his grin.

"Let's move from the place where you stopped my client— arrested my client," Hampton began. "The corner of... Where were you?"

"College and Broward," O'Donnell replied.

"How did you stop him?"

"I motioned for him to wait for me to pull my car into the parking lot."

"And did he stop?"

"Yes."

"In your experience, Officer O'Donnell, do most murder suspects fleeing from their crime scenes follow the directions of the police?"

Kirk jumped up. "Objection. Speculation."

Hampton countered. "I'm asking about his experience, Your Honor."

"Overruled," the judge said. "The witness may answer."

"I don't have enough experience with murder suspects to know the answer to your question," O'Donnell said.

"Really?" Hampton's surprise showed on his face. "Not in twelve years of service?"

"Objection," Kirk said. "Asked and answered."

"Sustained. Move on, Mr. Hampton," Judge Drake said.

Hampton raised his eyebrows. "Hmm," he said, walking back to the table to pick up another document. "Did you bother to check my client's alibi before, during, or after you arrested him?"

"I had probable cause to arrest your client, sir."

"That's not what I asked. Did you check out his story about going to meet a friend to apply for a job?"

"I had probab—"

"Your Honor," Hampton said.

The judge asked Officer O'Donnell, "Did you do anything to verify or disprove the defendant's alibi, Officer?"

"No, ma'am," O'Donnell said.

"Thank, you," Hampton said. "Let me ask you this, Officer. The police department had multiple squad cars heading down Broward and turning on College to get to the scene of the crime, correct?"

"Two or three. Yes."

"So you all had a pretty visible presence in the area as you were responding to the call, right?"

"Right."

"Officer, wouldn't you say that anyone in the area during that time would have noticed the police cars all heading to the motel?"

"Well, your client—"

"It's a yes or no question, Officer. Wouldn't anyone in the area have observed the police heading to the crime scene?"

O'Donnell pursed his lips together before answering. "Yes. That's certainly possible."

"Thank you, Officer. Okay, let's move forward in time. You've now gotten my client into your squad car. Was he handcuffed?"

"Yes."

"And you had already issued your Miranda warning, correct?"

"That's correct."

"Then what?"

"Then…" He paused as if to recall. "I took a moment to document the arrest."

"Is that standard procedure?"

"It's *my* standard procedure. The only way to get the paperwork done is to do it right then, right after an arrest."

"And the department encourages this?"

"Oh, yes. Absolutely."

"And I assume you called it in?"

"Yes, sir. Of course. I called it in to dispatch, and they patched me to my lieutenant, who was at the murder scene."

"This would be your patrol lieutenant, right, not a detective lieutenant you're referring to, right?"

"That's right."

"And did your lieutenant issue any orders?"

"Yes, he did."

"And what were they?"

"He told me to bring the suspect to him at the scene in case the detectives wanted to question him there."

Hampton's expression of surprise at O'Donnell's answer looked so genuine that Jason couldn't tell whether his lawyer was acting, or not. The young defendant channeled his urge to shout back at the witness—as he had throughout both hearings—through his penned hand and onto the legal pad in front of him.

Question, hell! No one questioned me at the motel. He was doing the walk of shame with me. Like I was some runaway dog he caught.

"You took my client to the scene for *questioning*?" Hampton asked.

"Yes, sir."

"So, you drove my client, in your police vehicle, to the Vacation Station Motel?"

"Well, yeah. I believe they call it the Vacation Station *Inn*, though. It's basically a motel."

Hampton stood erect. "It is indeed, Officer, and you're right." Hampton held out his arms in a pose of momentary surrender.

"Objection, Your Honor," Kirk said. "Where's the question?"

"Counselor?" Judge Drake looked at Hampton.

"I beg your pardon, Your Honor, counselor." Hampton turned to glance at his opponent and gave him a quick, deferential bow. Facing the judge again, Hampton asked, "If it please the court, Your Honor, could I have my assistant bring forth our exhibit number...well, I don't know the number. It's the schematic of the Vacation Station Inn."

Katrina rose and looked at the judge, who nodded and beckoned affirmatively.

"Let's give counsel a moment to state the exhibit number for the record," Judge Drake said.

"Twelve, Your Honor." Katrina read the exhibit number aloud and then she rested the schematic on the tripod, over the one denoting the intersection.

"Alright, Officer O'Donnell," Hampton said, elongated pointer in hand. "You pulled into the motel in your squad car, right?"

"Yes."

"And where is my client at this time?"

"Your client?"

Hampton looked at the witness with widened eyes, waiting for a response.

O'Donnell replied, "He was in the back seat."

"Behind the cage?"

"Well, yeah."

"Okay. If you could please take a look at this board, here, for the court, Officer. Tell us, where did you park when you drove in?"

"Down there," O'Donnell said, pointing, "right around room nine or ten."

"Here?" Hampton tapped the board with his pointer.

"Give or take a room, that'd be correct."

"So, you might have parked in front of room nine, or ten, or eleven. Is that fair to say?"

"To the best of my recollection, yes."

"To the best of your recollection," Hampton shot back, "were you past room seven?"

"Yes. As I recollect."

"Do you recall, Officer, which room the victim's body was in?"

"No, sir, I don't recall."

"Do you recall knowing whether you drove past the victim's room before parking?"

"I believe I did, yes."

"How do you believe you knew you drove past the victim's room?"

"Because other cars were parked along the rooms, there," O'Donnell said, pointing toward the middle of the display board. "I went down toward the end where no one else was parked."

"Thank you, Officer. Now, after you parked, what did you do?"

"I escorted the suspect to my lieutenant."

"You escorted my client to the lieutenant?" Hampton asked.

Kirk stood up. "Objection, Your Honor, asked and—"

"Sustained."

Hampton nodded to the judge and pivoted, as if he were going to look over his shoulder at Kirk. Instead, Hampton stopped himself and dropped his chin for a second. Looking up at O'Donnell, he asked, "*As* you were escorting my client, was he handcuffed?"

"Yes, he was."

"Hands behind his back?"

"Yes, sir." O'Donnell's voice betrayed an undertone of pride.

"And while you escorted him—well, first off, let me ask—you started escorting him around *here*, correct?" Hampton circled rooms nine, ten, and eleven with his pointer.

"That's where I parked and got him out of the car."

"You didn't keep him in the car—didn't call your lieutenant to come to the car?"

"No." O'Donnell was irritated at having to repeat the obvious.

"Where was your lieutenant at this time, Officer O'Donnell?" Hampton asked.

"He was over by the office," the witness said, pointing.

"Way down here?" Hampton used the stick again.

"Yes."

"So, when you say you *escorted* my client, in handcuffs, down along this entire row of motel rooms," Hampton asked, tracing the path with the pointer, "which side were *you* on and which side was *he* on?" He laid the stick across the bottom of the easel.

"Which side?" O'Donnell's bushy eyebrows narrowed as he squinted his confusion at the lawyer.

"Yes. Did you *escort* my client on your left or on your right to see your lieutenant?"

O'Donnell suppressed a smug grin. "We weren't exactly side by side."

"How, exactly, *were* you?" Hampton's voice was quiet, but sharp.

"He was basically in front of me." O'Donnell held out his hands, as if guiding an imaginary suspect.

"Were you touching my client as you...strolled along?"

"Objec—"

"Sustained," the judge said, before Kirk could get the entire word out.

Hampton's eyes stayed on the witness. "Were you touching my client at this time?"

"Well, I had one hand firmly on his shoulder," O'Donnell said, holding one hand higher, "and the other hand on his handcuffs." The officer's lower hand balled into a fist.

"So, you were frog-marching him?"

"Excuse me?" O'Donnell's blond eyebrows knitted again.

"Frog-marching. It's a figure of speech. Basically, what you were doing was a perp walk there at the motel, right?" Hampton kept his eyes on the witness as Jason sat back in his chair at the defense table, exhaling.

O'Donnell delivered his carefully chosen words through clenched teeth. "I *escorted* the suspect down to my lieutenant."

"Did your lieutenant specifically ask you to do that?"

"To bring him to the scene? Yes."

"No, Officer. That's not what I'm asking." Hampton lowered his head slightly, eyes fixed on O'Donnell, as he proposed the question with more vigor. "Did your lieutenant," he began, as aggression amplified his voice, "ask you to *parade* my client past everyone at the scene, including the victim's husband?"

O'Donnell glanced toward the prosecutor, but Hampton moved his stance in order to block the officer's view.

"Let me rephrase that," Hampton offered, before an objection could be articulated. "Did your lieutenant specifically ask you to walk my client from your car to this office area where he was waiting?"

"I don't recall."

"You don't recall." Hampton's echo smacked of incredulity. He nodded at the witness, grinning. "So, you might have *escorted* my client in such a manner voluntarily?"

"I don't recall."

"But you do recall, don't you, marching my client down the sidewalk here, right?" Hampton held his hand toward the display board.

"Yes, I do." O'Donnell lifted his chin in defiance of the attorney in front of him.

"Right past the victim's husband?" Hampton accused.

"I don't recall."

"Oh, I see. *Because*," Hampton said, wielding the words as if flashing a sword, "if you *had* known the victim's husband was standing there as you paraded past him with my client in handcuffs, you would have nullified his alleged witness identification of your suspect?"

"But I didn't know." O'Donnell's response was quick and matter-of-fact.

Hampton grinned broadly at the witness. "So you say. Let's assume Mr. Patterson had been there," Hampton reached one hand back toward the Patterson family's area of the courtroom. "Let's assume he's a potential witness and he's standing there. Wouldn't it have been highly suggestive if he saw," Hampton's voice boomed, "*my client* riding in the back of the police car, and then marching in front of a uniformed police officer—*handcuffed*—would you say that's suggestive, Officer O'Donnell?"

"It depends."

Hampton raised his eyebrows. "On what?"

"On if a potential witness was actually there. I had no way of knowing."

"You had no way...you mean to tell me Officer, when you walked my client past a number of people at the scene, you couldn't tell the difference between people who were police officers and those who weren't?"

"I don't recall."

"Thank you, Officer. Your Honor, I have no further questions for this witness at this time."

"Redirect, Your Honor?" Kirk asked.

"Well, we could finish it this evening, or start again tomorrow," the judge said. "It's your choice, depending on how much time you need."

"Thank you." Kirk stood up to address the witness. "This won't take long. Officer O'Donnell, did you know before you arrived on the scene that the victim's husband was still there?"

"Objection, Your Honor, relevance," Hampton said.

The judge tilted her head at Hampton, befuddled, given the defense attorney's last line of questioning. "Explain why you think it's irrelevant, please," the judge said.

"In our view, it doesn't matter whether Officer O'Donnell knew a potential witness was at the scene or not. The officer had a constitutional *duty* to avoid violating my client's Fourth Amendment due process rights. Even if he didn't know, he should have known, or he should have taken steps to find out, before irrevocably tainting any future identification procedures."

The judge looked at Hampton and then let her eyes trail upward for an instant as she consulted her own understanding of the law. "Mr. Kirk?"

"The witness is testifying that, to the best of his knowledge, he did not know. He doesn't have a constitutional duty to be clairvoyant."

"Your Honor," Hampton began, "may I address that point?"

"You may."

"The witness had no memory of notifying his lieutenant when he arrived at the scene, and he neglected the opportunity to wait with my client in the squad car for further instructions. He testified he had seen numerous people at the scene, numerous cars, because he drove past them to park. It was reasonably foreseeable that there might be a witness at the scene. The witness's own testimony establishes he disregarded his duty to protect my client's rights when he decided to do his little perp walk in front of everyone there."

"Watch your tone, Mr. Hampton." The judge frowned. "Did you mention this *duty* in your brief?"

"Yes, ma'am."

"Okay, that's a legal question that I will consider," she said. "But I think we can keep your legal question held separately from this witness's testimony. As we keep that question open, I'm going to ask for a provisional answer. Mr. Kirk, please ask your question of this witness."

"Officer O'Donnell," Kirk asked, "were you aware, when you walked the suspect down the sidewalk at the motel, that witnesses were present?"

"No, sir. I was not."

"Thank you, Your Honor. The state has nothing further for this witness."

"The witness may be excused," Judge Drake said.

O'Donnell, eyes fixed on the courtroom doors, climbed down from the witness stand, and stormed out.

Hampton turned to face Katrina and Jason, who were both smiling. Standing up, Jason pushed a yellow legal pad past Katrina to Hampton. In huge block letters filled in with ballpoint hatch marks were two simple words: "YOU ROCK."

CHAPTER 59

The Principal

"All rise." The courtroom shuffled as Judge Drake entered.

"In the matter of State v. Royals, we are hearing the state's second witness pertaining to witness identification. Are you ready, Mr. Kirk?"

"Yes, ma'am."

An older, gray-haired man was sworn in. Gerald Patterson stated his name for the record, swore to tell the truth, and took his place on the stand.

"Mr. Patterson," Kirk began.

"Good morning, sir," the witness replied.

"Morning," the prosecutor said. "Mr. Patterson, first of all, please allow me to relay my condolences to you and your family, on the loss of your wife." Kirk motioned behind him, to three people sitting behind the state's table. "Would you please state your wife's name for the record, Mr. Patterson?"

"Elizabeth Grace Smith Patterson. She always went by Betty."

"Thank you, sir. Now, would you please tell the court where you were going when you stopped to check into the Vacation Station Inn?"

The witness nodded toward the people in the pew. "Betty and I were traveling to see our daughter and son-in-law in Fort Lauderdale."

"And where were you traveling from?"

"Our home in Fitzgerald, Georgia."

"And you decided to stop at the Vacation Station Inn?"

"Yes. We knew we'd have to make the trip in two legs, but by the time we reached Beau Rêve, it was getting dark. We left town later than we'd planned." A wistful expression moved over Patterson's face, and the widower looked down.

"Yes, sir, I'm sorry we didn't cover that. What was your occupation at the time of Mrs. Patterson's...death?"

"I was Principal of Jimmy Carter High School. I'm retired now."

"And your school had an event that Saturday before you left Fitzgerald?"

"Yes, sir. I dropped by the car wash one of our organizations had hosted."

"And what was your wife's occupation, sir?"

"She was a homemaker, mother to our daughter, Emily, and she volunteered for Meals on Wheels and for our church."

"Thank you, sir. I'm going to ask you now to tell the court about what time you checked in at Vacation Station."

Hampton looked up from his files at the defense table but did not object to the prosecutor's question. Instead, he looked at the witness and waited for him to answer.

"It was around eight o'clock." The witness turned and looked at the judge when he spoke.

"Any particular reason you chose this motel?" Kirk asked.

"It was closest to the interstate and had a few restaurants close by."

"Thank you, Mr. Patterson. Now, I'm going to fast-forward you to the morning of your wife's murder. I know this is difficult, but tell me about the next morning, Sunday morning, when you two woke up. Would you please tell us about that morning?"

"I woke up first," Mr. Patterson said. "I made some coffee for the both of us. Betty usually sleeps—" he stopped himself midsentence. "I generally would get up before she did."

"About what time did you get up that morning, sir?"

"About seven forty-five."

"What happened next?"

"I made the coffee and got into the shower. I got dressed quietly so Betty could sleep. And then I went to go get a newspaper from the machine outside the office. I locked the door that time, when she was sleeping."

"Did you come back with the newspaper?"

"Yes."

"And then what happened, Mr. Patterson?"

"Betty sat up and had a cup of coffee with me, and we spent some time reading the newspaper before she got into the shower."

"And while she was in the shower, what were you doing?"

"Packing."

"And after she finished her shower?"

"She got dressed. We talked about where to get breakfast and some better coffee. We talked about calling our daughter to let her know about when we'd be arriving." Mr. Patterson lifted his chin toward the gallery, toward his daughter.

"So, you decided to call your daughter? To call Emily?" Kirk motioned behind him to indicate Emily Patterson.

"Betty said she'd call her." He looked down, again, forlorn. "She told me to load up my bag and check out. She was going to finish getting ready to go, and call Emily." Mr. Patterson watched from the witness chair as his daughter bowed her head.

"And then what happened?"

"I loaded up my bag in the car, and I walked down to the office with the motel key."

"And then what, while you were in the office?"

"I turned in the key and I had a talk with the motel clerk about how loud the air conditioning had been the night before."

"Okay, you talked about the air conditioning. How long did your conversation with him last?"

"Not three minutes. I was still talking to the clerk when we both heard it."

"Heard what, Mr. Patterson? What did you both hear?"

"The gunshot," he said. "It sounded like a firecracker, but then I saw the look on the clerk's face. He picked up the phone—I guess he was calling the police. I walked out of the office to see if I could see anything and—"

Kirk held up his hand to slow the witness down. "When you first heard it, did you know it was a gunshot?"

"I was afraid it was, yes." His voice pitched higher. "I wanted to get Betty and get on out of there."

"And what did you see after you left the motel office?"

"The exact moment I walked out of the office?"

"Yes, sir."

"Nothing. I went around the corner before I saw—"

"The corner of the motel office?" Kirk interjected.

"Yes, sir."

"And what did you see after you rounded the corner?" Kirk asked.

"I saw a man running toward the other end of the motel, then taking off."

"Were you able to describe this man to the police when they arrived?"

"Yes, sir. He was a Black man, wearing tan pants."

"Thank you, Mr. Patterson. Did you see the same man later in the morning?"

Mr. Patterson nodded. "I saw the man the police caught, the one they brought back to the motel. He was wearing tan pants."

Kirk walked back to his table, picked up a document, and showed it to the defense. He made sure the court reporter recorded the exhibit number and then handed it to the witness. "Do you remember, Mr. Patterson, talking to Sergeant Marshall about forty-eight hours after Mrs. Patterson's murder?"

"Yes, I do."

"Will you please tell the court what you are holding in your hands?"

"It's my statement to Sergeant Marshall."

"Objection." Hampton rose from his seat. "The state says Mr. Patterson saw my client at the scene. The witness identification at issue is the identification allegedly occurring at the motel, which throws into question the value of the identification process done days later down at the police station."

"Your Honor," Kirk said. "I am only refreshing the witness's memory as to what he told Sergeant Marshall during the course of the homicide investigation."

"May I?" The judge looked at the witness, holding her hand out to receive the document. She read the highlighted portion and handed it back. "Mr. Hampton, I'm going to let this in."

Kirk addressed the witness. "Please read the highlighted portion of your statement to Sergeant Marshall."

The witness cleared his throat. "I believe suspect Jason Royals is the same man who ran around the back of the motel after the gun was fired."

"Thank you, sir. Tell me, did Sergeant Marshall have you identify the defendant from a photo spread?"

"Yes, sir, he did."

"And you identified the defendant?"

"Yes, I believe I did."

"The state tenders the witness, Your Honor. We reserve the right to recall this witness."

"Thank you. If it's all right with you gentlemen, I'm going to adjourn this hearing until after lunch. What do you say we meet back here at two p.m.?"

"Fine with me, Your Honor," Hampton said.

"Me, too," Kirk replied.

Jason watched as Hampton and Katrina gathered their belongings. They would have lunch in one of the conference rooms down the hall, while Jason returned to the holding area for yet another prisoner meal.

◈

The proceedings resumed after lunch, with Hampton ready to take a turn with the murder victim's husband.

"Good afternoon, Mr. Patterson." Hampton's voice was distinctive but not booming.

"Good afternoon, sir." Mr. Patterson sat tall in the witness chair, pulling his suit jacket down a little behind him. At the defense table, Jason tugged at his suit jacket, too, sitting on his coattails to prevent his suit collar from creeping up.

Hampton turned his body to shift the witness's attention to the defense table. "My client, the Royals family, and I express our deepest condolences on the loss of your wife."

Mr. Patterson's eyes widened, taking in the vision of Jason's parents who were sitting behind their son. He brought his eyes back to Hampton, slowly, and then, as if suddenly remembering his manners, he added, "Thank you."

"Will you please bear with me as we go over the events of the morning Mrs. Patterson was murdered?" Hampton asked.

"Well, of course. Yes." A tone of accommodation chimed in the witness's voice.

"Thank you. You've told the court that you and your wife arrived at the motel, the Vacation Station, about eight o'clock on Saturday night."

"Yes."

"And you described your morning routine and said you went to check out while your wife called your daughter." Hampton turned his body in deference to Emily Patterson, who was again sitting behind Kirk's table.

"That's right," Mr. Patterson said.

"You turn in your key, talk about the air condi—"

"Objection, Your Honor. Is Mr. Hampton going to go over every point of the witness's testimony from this morning, or is he actually going to ask a question here?"

"Mr. Hampton, please economize the court's time to the best of your ability," the judge said.

"Yes, ma'am, Your Honor." Hampton looked at the witness. "Mr. Patterson, I'm sorry to have to do it this way, but it looks like we're going to have to cut to the chase. There's no easing into it."

The witness nodded, waiting for Hampton to continue.

"Between the time you heard the gunshot," Hampton began, "and the time you ran out of the motel office to see what you could see, how much time elapsed between those two events?"

"No time at all. Once I saw the clerk's facial expression, and I knew it was a gunshot, I felt compelled to go out and see what was happening, right away."

"And at what point, sir, did you see anything after coming out of the motel office?"

"I saw something—someone—run down to the end, then cut around toward the back."

"Thank you. Excuse me a moment, sir. I apologize. Your Honor, I believe I'm going to...the defense would like to use Exhibit 12 again, to which the state has stipulated. It's the schematic of the Vacation Station Inn."

"The state has no objections." Kirk did not look up from his notes.

"Go ahead, counselor," Judge Drake told Hampton. She watched as Hampton's law clerk set up the tripod easel and the large display board, partially blocking the witness's view of Jason. The motel was shaped like a block-letter L, with the short arm of the L, the motel office, facing College Boulevard. Katrina handed a collapsible pointer to Hampton.

"So, Mr. Patterson, you were rounding this corner," Hampton said, indicating the motel's office, "and you've testified you didn't see anything at this point."

"Not at that point, no sir."

"Okay. I'm going to trace my pointer here, from the office toward your motel room, and you tell me—"

"Objection. Foundation," Kirk intoned.

"I'm sorry, Your Honor, forgive me." Hampton turned to the witness. "Mr. Patterson, do you remember what your room number was?"

"Seven."

"And as you left the office, where were you heading?"

"Toward room seven."

"So, as I trace my pointer along the path you took—after you heard what you felt sure had been a gunshot—will you please tell me at what point you saw something?"

The witness nodded as Hampton began to move his pointer.

"Hold on, counselor," the judge said and then turned to the witness. "Sir, I'm going to need you to verbalize *yes* or *no* for the record."

"Ready, Mr. Patterson?" Hampton asked.

"Yes."

Hampton moved the pointer from the office door to the first corner that led toward the Pattersons' room. "Was it here you saw someone?"

"No."

Hampton then moved the pointer around the rear of the office, toward the first room in a straight row of twelve numbered rooms. "How about here?"

"That's about right, yes." Gerald narrowed his eyes, wrinkling his forehead as he looked at the map of the motel grounds.

"Your Honor, we're going to mark this with a Post-it Note."

"No objections," Kirk said.

"Okay, Mr. Patterson, and this is very important. This is room seven." Hampton tapped the numeral on the poster with his pointer. "And this is room one," he tapped again, "where you first saw... Well, what exactly did you see, sir?"

"I saw a man running away, around the end of the motel building, down there." Gerald pointed to the opposite end of the display board.

"When you first saw the man, who was running away—try to picture exactly where he was when you spotted him. What room was the man closest to when you first saw him?"

"The last one. Room twelve."

"So, when you reached room one..." Hampton said, tapping his pointer on room one on the schematic. "The man you saw running away was way down here at room twelve?" He tapped his pointer at the other room.

Mr. Patterson nodded. The judge looked at him, eyebrows raised until he verbalized his answer. "Yes."

"And to be clear," Hampton said, "it was the man's back you saw as he was running away, right?"

Gerald thought for a moment. "That's right," he said.

"Can you please describe the man you witnessed running around the corner, here?" Hampton pointed to the last room in the bank of motel rooms.

"Yes. He was wearing tan pants."

"And that's all you saw?"

"Yes."

"You didn't see what color shirt he was wearing?"

"No, sir, not that I can remember now."

"The man was running pretty fast, then?"

"Yes."

"And he was pretty far away?"

"Yes, if you figure each of the twelve motel rooms were about fifteen feet wide," Gerald stopped to do the math in his head, "I'd say that's at least sixty yards away."

Hampton nodded and stepped back to look at Katrina, who was working the math out on a sheet of paper. She looked at him and gave a thumbs-up. Kirk also made a note.

"Is it fair to say, Mr. Patterson, that you caught only a *glimpse* of the running man before he was out of your sight?"

The witness looked at Hampton for a moment. "Yes, that's fair. It all happened very fast."

"Thank you, Mr. Patterson. Now, I'd like you to listen closely to my next question. You've just said you barely got a glimpse of the *back* of the man who was running away after the gunshot, right?"

The witness didn't answer right away. After finding his daughter's eyes, he turned back to Hampton and said, "Yes. That's right."

"Okay, sir, if you'll stay with me for another minute, please. From that single glimpse, at that single moment, when you were running out of the motel office, around the corner, toward room seven to get to your wife—can you say, with one-hundred-percent certainty to this court, that the man you saw running away was my client?"

The witness tried to peek around the display board but was only able to glimpse Jason's polished black church shoes.

"Here, let me…" Hampton moved the board and the tripod, leaving Mr. Patterson with an unobstructed view of Jason. His parents sat, still as two deer in the headlights, behind him.

"No, sir," the witness said. "I cannot be one hundred percent sure it was your client."

Jason's smiling, grateful eyes met the witness's.

Hampton allowed the stillness in the courtroom a moment to solidify before he spoke again. "Thank you, Mr. Patterson." He gathered his exhibits, leaving the tripod and the pointer. He leaned it in front of the defense table, still in view of the witness, and sat down. "I have no further questions of this witness at this time, Your Honor."

"Mr. Kirk?" The judge looked at the prosecutor.

"Yes, Your Honor. I'd like to redirect." Kirk addressed the witness. "Sir, you estimated that the motel rooms were fifteen feet wide. What if they were only ten feet wide?"

"Well," Gerald said, thinking. "The bed itself, the way it's situated, is going to take up at least six feet of that space. So, some motel rooms might be that small—but there'd be hardly any room between the foot of the bed and the dresser at the other end. I'm thinking those rooms had to be at least twelve feet across."

"So, that's more like forty-five yards, then, between you and the man you saw running?"

"Well, I'd say closer to fifty yards, but that's still pretty far away."

"Thank you." Kirk rifled through a couple of pages on his legal pad, pulling out a document lodged inside. "Mr. Patterson, do you recall the date of the statement you gave to Sergeant Marshall, a couple of days after Mrs. Patterson was murdered?"

"No, but I do remember talking to him soon after it happened."

"Soon after it happened? Okay, well, here we are today, a year and a half after her murder, recalling those events. Mr. Patterson, do you trust your recollection—as written on this document two days after your wife's murder—do you suppose this document is more or less accurate than your recollection here today, some eighteen months later?"

Mr. Patterson stared at the assistant state attorney for a moment before answering. "I honestly don't know."

Kirk was stunned. "You don't *know*? You don't *know* whether your memory of your wife's murder got better or worse with the passage of time?"

"No, sir. I don't rightly know." The witness was animated and a little indignant. "Small details keep coming back to me, over time. Like the fact she had her tennis shoes on. Details like that." Mr. Patterson sighed. "But it's not something I really *care* to remember."

A hush fell over the courtroom.

Kirk's shoulders dropped and he said, "I can't begin to imagine, sir. Of course, I can't. Please forgive me." Kirk then paced a little, back and forth, in front of the witness box. Suddenly, he stopped and turned to the witness. "Mr. Patterson, in general, in logical terms, would you say people's memories of an event are more accurate closer in time to the event, or much later?"

Hampton's jaw dropped, but the witness answered before he could object.

"Mr. Kirk," Patterson said, looking the prosecutor straight in the eye, "I cannot speak for other people's memories; I can only tell you I was upset at the time. I'm told I might have been in shock. I'm embarrassed to say so, but I'm told that I fainted on the day of—"

"No further questions, Your Honor," Kirk abruptly interjected, holding his hand up to signal the witness to stop talking.

The judge turned to the witness. A concerned look crossed her face. "You fainted, Mr. Patterson?"

"Yes. I'm afraid I did. I lost consciousness at the motel."

The judge raised her eyebrows and turned toward Hampton. "Anything further from you, counselor?"

"Yes, ma'am." Hampton stood up and walked toward the witness. "Mr. Patterson, do you remember when, exactly, you fainted?"

"Objection, Your Honor. Relevance," Kirk said.

"Your Honor, this may turn out to be very relevant. It's certainly relevant to the witness's state of mind at the time."

"I'll overrule. I'd like to know the answer to this question, myself."

The witness continued. "I was trying to get back to my wife. The police wouldn't let me back into the room after…well, you know." He glanced at his daughter, who did not flinch or look down.

"They were investigating the murder scene at this point," Hampton said.

"Yes. They kept sitting me down in the back of a police car. We were waiting for the chaplain to arrive."

"The police were trying…were they trying to keep you calm?"

"Yes. That's probably right. It's a bit of a blur—the whole morning."

"Thank you, Mr. Patterson." Hampton decided to stop there.

CHAPTER 60

A God of Justice

On the morning of Judge Drake's pronouncement, more people than usual filed in to watch the proceedings. The courtroom was alive with movement and chatter as the wall clock ticked from three, to four, to five minutes past eleven. It was the most important moment of Jason's young life, and the judge was running late.

Jason could not sit down.

Earlier, he'd forced down a few bites of bland prison oatmeal, without any sugar or fruit, fearing the spikes and dips of the momentous day in front of him. As the noise in the courtroom spun around him, nausea set him teetering.

Instinctively, Katrina steadied him, reached for the water pitcher, and poured him a glass.

"Little sips. Don't gulp," she whispered.

Jason nodded, foregoing the offer. Feeling his mother's hand on his shoulder, he turned to greet his parents. They didn't usually run late, either. A stern look from the bailiff was all Clarice needed to remove her hand.

It took a moment for Jason to see that his parents had brought Lucas—Jason almost didn't recognize him. An electrical shudder jolted Jason, grounding all impulses to vomit, and anchoring him on his feet.

Jason was shocked by how much his brother had changed. At thirteen, Lucas' soft boyishness had begun to harden into adolescent muscle. He hadn't thinned out as much as he had filled in. Lucas looked like a smaller version of their Uncle Mack. Jason wished he could hug his little brother.

Taking a quick inventory of the room before he turned to face the dais, Jason spotted his grandfather, Uncle Mack, Aunt Brenda, and Cousin Cam.

"Who told my whole extended family to come?" he whispered sharply to Katrina.

"Must have been your mom and dad," she said.

"What if...what if I lose? They all look ready to celebrate. They're making me nervous," he intoned. "Jesus!"

Looking at the clock again, Jason breathed slowly and deliberately, containing the impulse to run, to scream, to upturn the table in front of him, to jump out of his own skin. He'd been adamant about protecting the younger boys from seeing any aspect of his incarceration. He finally understood, all at once, his decision had been a sacrifice. He'd missed so much of their lives.

Never. Never. Never. Jason vowed to do everything in his power to prevent anyone he loved—especially Lucas or Cam—from ever going through what he was enduring.

Please, let the judge throw it all out.

The clock on the wall ticked from seven to eight minutes past nine.

Jason repeated his wish, or thought, or prayer over and over again in his mind. *Please let her throw it all out.* The notion was directed more at the judge than at God.

Keep hope alive! It was a perfectly summoned memory—in the cadence of Jesse Jackson.

How many times did the man actually say it? Keep hope—

"All rise."

Jason snapped to attention. Trembling, he searched the courtroom, eyes darting desperately, as if the marble floor, or the wooden tables, or the empty witness stand held some clue to his fate.

"Here," Katrina said, pushing her chair back and pulling Jason in front of her. As she guided the young man to stand in her spot, he bumped the table. The water in the glass sloshed wildly but did not spill, and the two traded places.

Jason felt the heat emanating from Hampton's body. As the judge situated herself, the older man put a hand on Jason's shoulder.

"No matter what happens, Jason, I'll be standing right here," Hampton whispered. "For as long as it takes."

"I'd like Mr. Royals and counselors to remain standing," the judge said, "but the rest of you, please, have a seat."

Without word or thought, the three at the defense table joined hands.

"This court has before it three motions and three responses. First is defendant's motion to exclude defendant's confession from evidence, and the state's response. Second is defendant's motion to exclude the eyewitness's identification of the defendant from evidence, and the state's response to it. Last is defendant's motion to dismiss all charges for lack of sufficient evidence, and the state's response. I am now ready to rule on the first motion.

"On the matter of the defendant's confession, this court finds the confession was obtained in a manner completely inconsistent with the defendant's Fourth and Fifth Amendment rights. This court finds not one but two violations of defendant's right to pre-trial counsel. The confession obtained by police is therefore highly suspect and unreliable, and this court will issue a written ruling to that effect. The confession is excluded from evidence."

All at once, Hampton and Katrina tightened their grips on Jason's hands. As he stood between them, they all looked at each other with bright smiles. A soft but joyous murmur erupted behind Jason. He could hear his mother whispering to his little brother.

Don't get excited yet, he told himself. *It's not over yet.*

Next, the judge faced the state's table.

"As for the eyewitness identification purported to have occurred at the scene of the murder," she said, "it too is excluded from evidence. The eyewitness has stated, before this court, that he cannot say, with any certainty, the defendant is the man he saw on the day his wife was murdered." The judge's eyes fell on Gerald Patterson. "Furthermore, given the suggestive and frankly unacceptable circumstances by which the defendant was presented to the witness, this court rules that the circumstances leading to the earlier, alleged identification violated his Fourth Amendment right to due process of law. Therefore, any and *all* statements of Mr. Patterson's identification of the defendant are hereby held suppressed and will be excluded from evidence in the state's case against Mr. Royals."

"Is that good, Daddy?" The child's soft voice was Cam's. A warm, mirthful murmur filled the room.

Jason held his muscles rigid, refusing to give into the relief that began to wash over him. The most important ruling was yet to be heard.

Judge Drake waited for the excitement to subside, casting her narrow-eyed frown onto the room as it quieted.

Katrina and Hampton moved in closer, buttressing Jason for the judge's next ruling.

"As for the defendant's motion for dismissal, I have read both parties' briefs on this matter. This morning, this court has excluded two pieces of evidence. I now ask the State of Florida, is there any additional evidence, above what you have presented in your brief, upon which you would ask this defendant be held for capital murder charges?"

With the exception of Katrina, Jason, and Hampton, who stared straight ahead, everyone's attention shifted, as if in a tennis match, to the prosecutor.

Kirk stood. "Your Honor, the state maintains it had probable cause to stop and detain the defendant, his description matched the one provided from the scene to the dispatcher, and he resisted arrest. We believe the matter of his guilt should therefore be a question for a jury of his peers."

"I believe that was in your brief, counselor." The judge's voice betrayed a slight growl. "I will ask you once again: setting aside what you have already presented in court and in writing, does the state have anything else, Mr. Kirk?"

"No, ma'am."

"Thank you, counselor. Mr. Royals," the judge said, turning her attention to the defendant's table, "before I announce my ruling, for you and for the benefit of those present here today, let me make one thing clear. This court is…*alarmed* by the manner in which the evidence against you was obtained by the police. My concern deepens when I consider that you have not yet reached the age of majority. The fact that you were to be tried as an adult does not change the point that you were only fifteen years old at the time of your arrest. In my written ruling, I will strongly urge the state attorney's office and the Beau Rêve Police Department to take note of the mistakes in procedure and practice that were employed in your case, and to learn from these egregious mistakes in order to avoid making similar ones in the future."

A silent chill ricocheted around the room.

"As for my ruling," the judge continued, "this court finds that even if the state proves the scant matters that it offers against you, such proof would be, as a matter of law, insufficient to convict you of these charges beyond a reasonable doubt. For all of these reasons, I am dismissing this case. Mr. Royals, you are now free to leave."

Jason could barely breathe as he felt Hampton's strong hug. As his parents rose, he heard his mother's thankful sobbing behind him. A beat or two later, his young cousin's "Yay!" punctuated sighs of relief and restrained, nervous laughter. A titter of a child's clapping followed, and the courtroom erupted again into warm murmurs, spattered by applause. Jason, stunned, jostled from hug to hug—from his lawyers to his parents to his little brother.

It's over.

Judge Drake's ubiquitous frown melted—for an instant—into satisfaction. As she surveyed her domain, however, her narrow-eyed, judicial face reappeared. Leaning forward, she tapped her gavel three times on the dais and nodded to the bailiff.

After waiting for those who had risen in celebration to retake their seats and resume decorum, the bailiff said, "All rise." As the judge exited, the revelry recommenced.

"We hope you can both drop by the house this afternoon," Clarice said to Hampton and Katrina, as the legal team held the railing gate open for Jason. Stepping back to allow him a wide berth, the lawyers pointed the way.

Jason stepped through the gate and gave his entire family one massive hug. Then, hugging his mother tight he said, "Can we please get out of here now? I want to go home." Without waiting for an answer, he turned and walked with determination out of the courtroom. His brother, his father, his aunt, his uncle, and his cousin trailed closely behind.

◆

It was all Jason could do to zip out of the courtroom as a horde of reporters pressed forward to question Hampton about the hearing. As Jason approached the elevators, he saw his lawyer leading the gaggle to the press-staging area at the end of the hall. Stanchions and velvet ropes had been arranged for the event.

He'd already told Hampton that if they won, he didn't want to be on TV. Looking over his shoulder toward the media gaggle, he was tempted to change his mind.

Everything he ever wanted to say to the police, but couldn't risk writing in his journals in jail, came flooding back. *I never should've been here. Bastards.*

Jason's father saw him looking. "Do you want to go over there with Hamp? Do you have something you want to say?"

"What I'm thinking, Dad, they don't let you say on TV." Jason pressed the elevator call button repeatedly. "I already told Hamp no."

"You're sure?"

"Yeah. I really want to get out of here."

"I'm with you, son."

By the time his mother handed Emily Patterson the ivory envelope with Gerald Patterson's name on it, Jason was already entering the elevator with his dad and brother. As Emily turned to pass the letter to her father, Clarice slipped away toward the courtroom doors. She did not look back.

Gerald opened the envelope and read the note inside:

Dear Mr. Patterson,

Our family is praying for yours and also for justice for your beloved wife.

"Yet the LORD longs to be gracious to you;
therefore he will rise up to show you compassion.
For the LORD is a God of justice.
Blessed are all who wait for him!" Isaiah 30:18

Mr. Patterson, we await His justice with you.
– Jason, Lucas, Alvin, and Clarice Royals

Exiting the courthouse, Jason walked slightly ahead of his family and skipped quickly down the steps to the sidewalk. He gazed up at the clear, blue Florida sky. The November air was clean and crisp, but not quite cool.

Grass. Trees. Color. No chain-link fences. No barbed wire.

"We're parked over this way," his dad said, holding out his thumb and chuckling. Alvin reached out to guide him, but Jason's feet were planted in place.

"Dad, it's over!" His face beamed. Abruptly, realizing that his father seemed a little shorter than he remembered, Jason lifted his hand and, holding it flat, moved it from the top of his head toward his dad's. A broad smile crossed Jason's face.

"Yeah, well, I always figured this day was coming," Alvin said. "You've got about a quarter inch on me."

"More like an *inch*!" Lucas edged between them. He stood on his thirteen-year-old tiptoes and tried to match his brother's height. "I'm gonna be even taller than you, Jason. You wait and see."

Jason and his father laughed. Mack and family caught up to them.

"We'll see you at the house, Jay!" Mack said, slapping his nephew on the back.

His Aunt Brenda hugged him tight. "I'm proud of you, baby. Not everyone could have survived everything you just came through, with such a good attitude. You're a very brave young man."

"I had a little help," he replied. "A lot of help."

"C'mon, Brenda," Mack shouted, walking ahead of her. "You can hug on him some more at the house."

"Can I run, Daddy?" Cam was yanking Mack's hand. "Can I?"

"Wait 'til we get around the corner—stay on the sidewalk," Mack's voice faded as they walked away. "When I say...on your mark...get set..."

Jason watched them, grinning, then turned back to his dad and Lucas. "Where's Mama and Granddaddy?"

"Granddaddy and his friend, Matthew Hampton, already left. But your mama..." Alvin looked up the courthouse steps.

"There she is!" Lucas yelled, pointing as she walked toward them.

"Where'd you go?" Jason asked her.

"I went where you gentlemen aren't welcome."

"Oh." Her three men uttered the word in unison.

"C'mon, now, your grandma's waiting at the house," she said to Jason, before stopping to embrace him, firmly, one more time. "Thank the Lord."

"And Aaron J. Hampton," Alvin quipped, winking at Jason from over his mother's shoulder.

"And Aaron J. Hampton, too! Amen," Clarice replied.

Jason looked down at the white cuffs peeking out from the dark sleeves of his suit jacket. He watched his shiny dress shoes as they made their way down the sidewalk, intrigued by the light that reflected up, and then he stepped off to walk in the grass. Stopping, he allowed his family to amble ahead of him. He bent down, ran his fingers over the grass, and then pulled off his shoes and socks, so his toes could feel it too.

No green or orange prison uniforms were in sight. No correctional officer herded him, prodding him in one direction or another. The caustic, fluorescent light of jail had been removed, lifted like a glass bell jar from above his head. He jogged forward to meet his family, inhaling the smell of pure sunshine, looking up to the breadth of the sky.

"What's that?" Jason asked his mom, pointing to an eagle-like raptor making its way toward the river.

"Hard to see with the glare from the sun. Maybe an osprey." Clarice shaded her eyes with her hand. "Yes. Looks like an osprey. Did you catch what he said?"

"What? Who?" Jason wondered which "he" she meant.

"You are my beloved child, in whom I am well pleased," she said, hanging her arm around his shoulders.

Ohhh. The bird. Jason grinned as he took his mother's hand. It was tinier than he remembered.

PART THREE

*"Some say forgiveness is the key
But there isn't a hole in the lock."*

—Devin D. Coleman,
Prisoner to Poet

CHAPTER 61

Little Trips

On the way home, Clarice insisted on riding in the back with Lucas, leaving the front seat for Jason. Looking up through the windshield, he marveled at the steel beams crisscrossing above him, fascinated by the architecture of his favorite bridge.

I've crossed it a thousand times with eyes wide open. How is it I never really saw it?

Looking down, he caught a glimpse of the silver-blue mosaic below them, allowing the sun's fractured reflections to temporarily blind him. As he moved his eyes forward to the treetops on the approaching shore, Jason felt a little dizzy and a little nauseated. His discomfort subsided when they descended the bridge ramp and turned onto College.

He grimaced when he saw the Burger King and took a breath to steel himself as they passed the stand of woods near the interstate overpass. He was almost home.

As Alvin turned onto their street, Jason couldn't help but notice the neighborhood houses looked smaller than he remembered. His own home looked shabbier than the snapshot he'd held in his memory for the past year and a half. The green paint was somehow browner, the white trim, yellower. His eyes were drawn to two giant pots of bright-yellow chrysanthemums framing the artwork on the front door.

"Did you make that sign?" Jason asked Lucas.

"Yep! Like it?"

"You bet I do!"

A banner comprising several sheets of computer paper, with the perforated printer tracks still attached, stretched diagonally across the door in the style of a beauty queen's sash.

"Welcome home, Jason!" it read, in bold, rainbow magic marker.
"What's all this?"

Jason walked through his front door for the first time in over
a year and a half. The ceiling felt lower, and the room was more
brightly lit than he remembered. The living room furniture—the
old, yellow, flowered couch and chair—had been moved back against
the walls. In their place stood two large, cafeteria-sized tables,
end-to-end, with chairs all around. Red tablecloths hung on the
tables, and near the center point, someone had put a small pot of
yellow chrysanthemums. Jason flinched, trying to absorb the room's
unfamiliar configuration.

He eyed the familiar green curtains, pulled to one side of the
sliding glass doors. The same off-white sheers hung behind the green
fabric, across the length of the doors, softening his autumn afternoon
view of their back yard. The rusty swing set, one small child away
from complete collapse, eulogized his childhood.

"What would have happened if we lost in court this morning?"
Jason said, to no one in particular.

"Lost?" Jason's grandfather's voice erupted from the dining room.
"Lost? With Matt Hampton's boy arguing for you? Not possible. Not
in a million years."

Jason walked toward his grandfather and his lawyer's father, and
introductions were made. The smell of roasted turkey enveloped
them. His mouth watered. Brenda brought out bread and butter as
his mother and Mrs. Sullivan from next door worked in the kitchen.

"Your Grandpa Clarence and I go way back, Jason. I'll have you
know both you and your lawyer come from a smart bunch of fighters.
Do you know who Asa Philip Randolph was?" the elder Hampton
asked him.

Great. I just got out of jail, and it's time for a civil rights pop quiz.

"Matthew!" Clarence interrupted. "Do you think I'd let my
grandson grow up not knowing his own history? Alvin, you've got to
hear this." Clarence summoned Jason's dad.

Jason watched as his mother opened three different store-bought
pies and placed them on the sideboard, while Mr. Hampton and
Grandpa Clarence talked on about their union days.

"Well, your granddaddy and I worked with Mr. Randolph when

the Brotherhood of Sleeping Car Porters joined up with the AFL-CIO," Hampton the elder said. "And then there was the matter of our little trip to Washington back in '63."

"Little trip!" Clarence shook his head and laughed. "Tell him Jason—you know what he's talking about, right?"

"The March on Washington?" Jason replied.

"The *what*?" Alvin teased. His elbow prodded his son to remember.

"The March...The March on Washington for Jobs and...Workers?"

"Close enough, Jason, close enough." Mr. Hampton chuckled. "The March on Washington for Jobs and Freedom."

Jason smiled, and held his smile in place, even as the light in his eyes dimmed.

I went out for a job, the last time I left this house, and ended up fighting for my freedom.

He stood politely with his father, listening to the two older men.

"The March, the speech, none of it would have happened without Asa Philip Randolph, you know," Clarence said, but Jason had heard it all before. "A *lot* never would have happened without Asa Philip Randolph. He was the father of the modern civil rights movement, long before Reverend Martin Luther King became the drum major."

"Did you know your granddaddy and I were there too, Jason?" Mr. Hampton asked.

"Yes, sir. I understand Mr. Randolph put you both to work that day."

"You know it. He arranged union leave so we could ride up there and make signs," Mr. Hampton said. "Never saw so many people—so many Black people and white people—in one place at one time. What a sight—people crowded up as far as the eye could see, all the way to the Washington Monument, hanging on his every word."

"Dr. King's words, you mean," Jason said.

"Yes, indeed, Dr. King's words. 'I have a dream.' You come from activists, son. *Fighters*," Mr. Hampton said. "Don't you ever forget it."

Jason blushed and nodded. "I won't, sir."

"You give any thought to what you want to do with your life, son?" Granddaddy Clarence asked.

"Yes, sir," he replied. "I've had some time to think."

"Clarence!" His grandmother's voice rang out from her perch at the dining room table. "The boy just got home. Let him *eat*!" Jason made his way to her, excusing himself as the men continued sharing memories of their historic day. He smiled as he heard them reminisce about hearing the queen of gospel, Mahalia Jackson.

"Grandma, you know Thanksgiving isn't 'til *next* week, right?" Jason said, pointing to the feast before them.

"Oh, but I'm so *thankful*, honey. So thankful."

Jason bent to hug her.

She clasped him sharply. "Are you okay?"

"Yes, ma'am. I'm fine; I promise you."

"This is your mama's and Brenda's doing, here," she said, holding her hands in front of her. "Now get a plate and go to it. I'm going to have someone help me move to a seat in the living room."

"I've gotcha, Grandma."

"No, honey. This is your day." She squeezed his arm. "A day I will always be so thankful for." Releasing him, she raised her voice, "Ma-ack?" She lilted the name into two syllables. "Clarence, Junior? Where are you, son?"

Mack appeared at her elbow. Jason helped his uncle lift his grandmother to her walker.

Recognizing his chance for a clean getaway, Jason sneaked back through the living room and down the hall to his bedroom's closed door. His green, white, and orange nametag, a plastic bike tag he'd bought on a day trip to St. Augustine, sat a little lower on its nails than he remembered. He reached up to feel the letters, reading them with his fingers, as if curious as to what they spelled.

He opened the door to find his room the way he left it. *Did I make up my bed that day?* Maybe his mother had done it. She had definitely run the vacuum cleaner; he could see the marks in the carpet. He walked to his dresser and saw his old digital watch lying there. *Maybe wearing this would have helped me.* He thought about the timelines he and Katrina had worked on, tearing yellow sheets from legal pads, lining them up end to end on the conference room table at the jail. *Got up. Ate two bites of cereal. Left the house. Got arrested. Taken to woods.* Holding the watch in his hands, he debated whether to strap it on. *Nah.*

Jason wriggled his feet out of his dress shoes, grinding his heels together as he'd always been taught not to do. He loosened his tie.

Pulling open a drawer, he realized he wouldn't have much in his current size. He walked over to his closet and opened the bi-fold doors. Two new, long-sleeved Henley shirts hung before him, price tags still attached. A new pair of blue jeans hung next to them. He looked at the waist size and length.

Mama must have gotten these when she bought the new suit for court.

He changed into the new clothes, hanging up his jacket and pants, and threw his shirt into the empty hamper. He threw the tie on the bed and looked at it for a long moment. It stretched like a dead snake over his bedspread. He wanted to join it—to throw himself on the bed and sleep long enough to erase everything that had happened since he was last in it. Sitting at its edge, Jason's muscles felt heavy. Malaise invaded his body and fogged his mind as the adrenaline that had charged him for days evaporated.

He heard the doorbell, muffled by distance. *Probably Hamp.* Soon after, he heard a woman's voice. *Definitely not Hamp.*

"I know he'll be glad to see you, Kim." His mother's voice was drawing nearer. "I'll go get him for you."

Kim?

After all the nights and weeks and months in jail—after all the time spent staring at cinderblock walls—Jason knew he should *want* to see her.

But when he heard his mother's inevitable knock on the door, he cringed.

"Jason?" Clarice tapped on the door as she opened it. "Kim's here."

My mom knows Kim? "You've met Kim?" he asked her.

"Well, yeah. I met her the day you went missing." Clarice lifted her eyebrows, nodding. "Plus, she's called here to see about you a few times. Last time we talked, I told her we had this party planned. Hamp told us not to plan it, just in case, but your Aunt Brenda, she…"

Jason didn't hear whatever it was his mom was saying. *The girl I like has been talking to my mother? Checking on me? Without me knowing it?* He dropped his head into his hands.

"Jason?"

He looked up at his mom.

"Honey, don't you want to see your friend?"

He blew out a long sigh as he rubbed his temples. "Yeah. I guess so."

His mother gave him a worried look.

"Yes…I mean…I absolutely do want to see her. Can you give me five minutes? Tell her I'm changing or something?"

"Sure, baby. Are you okay?"

"Yeah. Just tired is all."

After his mom left, shutting the door behind her, Jason pushed himself off his bed and walked to his dresser. *A real mirror.* He smoothed his hand over his still-short hair, barbered right before his series of hearings.

I look a little better in a real mirror—but not much.

He straightened his new jeans, tugged down his Henley, took a deep breath, and went to meet Kim.

"There he is now," Alvin said, pointing at Jason as he entered the living room. The crowd of relatives around Alvin and Kim unfurled. Kim stepped forward with open arms, hugging Jason.

"What do you say we give these young people some space?" Alvin asked.

Clarice appeared with two plates, each filled with pie and cookies.

"Here you go. You two go catch up now. It's nice outside if you want to step out on the patio." Clarice handed the plates to Jason and two forks to Kim and walked over to open the sliding glass door. She pulled the sheer curtains closed again after they walked outside.

"Your mom is sweet," Kim said, as the two found seats at the outdoor table.

"Yeah, I understand you two have become great friends," Jason quipped, and then, taking in the sight of her, he smiled. "Thanks for checking on me."

"Hey, I feel like I've got to look out for Wellstein's." A twinkle lit her eye. "Even though I don't work there anymore. Gotta make sure their potential employee is okay."

"Did you ask them to keep the job open for me?"

Kim laughed, covering her mouthful of pie with her hand.

"You need something to drink?" he asked.

She shook her head, laughing with her mouth closed. "I'm good."

"You sure are."

She blushed and smiled, tilting her head downward before raising her eyes to his. "How are you? I mean for real. You look a little sad."

"Gee, thanks, I really—"

"I didn't mean it that way."

"I know," he said. "I was joking. I guess I'm too tired to be funny."

"Long day, huh?"

"Longest damn day of my life." Popping a piece of cookie into his mouth, he shook his head. "Second longest day of my life."

"I can't even get my head around what it's been like for you."

"Please, don't try. I don't want you to. I don't want anyone I...I... care about to ever know what it was like. No one should be treated like I was." He looked at the plate of food in front of him, moving around the cookies with his fingers. "Hey, how come you're home from Gainesville so early? Thanksgiving break isn't until next week, right?"

"Yeah, well, three of my five classes are cancelled next Monday and Tuesday. And I did well on my midterms so I'm blowing off the other ones."

"So...you're going to be home for a week?" he asked, his voice rising with hope.

"No," she said, looking down. "That's one of the reasons I'm here now. I..."

"There's something you don't want to tell me."

"Yeah. I drove here to see you today, but I'm flying out to Colorado tomorrow afternoon."

"Colorado? I know you spent Christmas there, but—"

"I should have told you before. But I didn't know it was going to matter."

"Told me *what*?" he asked. "Didn't know *what* was going to matter?"

"My parents moved there, to Aspen. I'm still enrolled at Florida—and I'm going to try to finish up this year down here, at UF."

Jason's puzzlement showed on his face. "The year? This is only your second year. Why would you leave Gainesville when—"

"My mom's got ALS. Lou Gehrig's disease. It's bad." Tears welled in her eyes.

Stunned, he didn't know how to reply. "Is she...?" He stopped himself. *Her mother might die?* "I'm so sorry. That sucks, Kim, it really sucks."

Kim nodded, wiping away the tears. "It's been a week," she said.

"It's been the best of weeks and the worst of weeks. A tale of two weeks. But it's all the same week. I found out about my mom on Monday. Finding out about your hearing…it made it a little better."

"I don't want to even imagine what might have happened if I lost in court." Jason looked over his shoulder toward the sliding glass door. Peering through it, he could make out the silhouette of his mother, picking up plates and cups. "Your mom, Kim. I can't believe it."

"It's degenerative, meaning it's only going to get worse. She'll lose the use of her limbs. She'll lose her ability to speak. Eventually," Kim took a deep breath, "eventually, she won't be able to breathe."

"Do the doctors know how long…?"

She shook her head. "They can't give us a timetable on it. Could be two years. Could be ten. I'll be in Colorado next week, and for Christmas, too, so I can help her. She wants me to come back to school in Gainesville in January. That's the plan, anyway, but I don't know. She's trying to be positive for my dad and me. She's gearing up for some sort of fight…but…" Kim shook her head.

Jason reached over and grabbed Kim's hand, and she melted into helpless sobs. The two sat without talking as her tears subsided and she wiped her face.

"I'm sorry," she said. "This is supposed to be a happy day for you."

"Oh my God, Kim. Don't be sorry. I'm here for you like you've been here for me. The visit, the letters…you have no idea. You've helped me, big time. Now it's my turn."

More Pie

The relief Jason felt waking up in his own bed came second only to the knowledge that he could eat all he wanted, whenever he wanted. The casseroles of Thanksgiving at Aunt Brenda's had ranged from sweet to savory, and from crisp to congealed. Tupperware containers crammed the Royals' refrigerator.

His mom smiled that morning when he told her he thought he'd have sweet potato pie for breakfast.

"It's been calling my name since I woke up," he said.

"Let me get you some milk to balance out your sugar." She slid a slice across the kitchen table. "You're a skeleton!"

"I've seen skeletons—living ones, Mama."

Eyes wide, Clarice stared at her son. "What skeletons?"

"This one guy," Jason said, "you could see his eye sockets and his cheekbones. His arms were like toothpicks. He had to be on drugs."

"What makes you think so?" Worry crept across his mother's face. She sat down with him.

"I figured he was coming down from drugs because of the way he screamed in the middle of the night. Screeching in his cell like he was going to die."

Clarice's mouth fell open. "Sweet Jesus, Jason. Did they just leave him there?"

"Naw. They came and got him, Mama. I'm sorry—I shouldn't have mentioned it. It's over now. I'm home."

His mother put on a wistful smile. "Thank the Lord. I'm so sorry this happened to you." She looked down at her hands. "I keep thinking back to when Mack and I were looking for you.... I should have—"

"No!" Jason said, his mouth full of pie. He chewed it quickly. "This isn't your fault, Mama. We all know whose fault it was."

Clarice nodded, agreeing. "Whoever shot Mrs. Patterson is to blame."

Jason's jaw dropped.

"What?" his mother asked him.

"I was gonna say the cops—it was O'Donnell's fault for arresting me and taking me down to the motel. And it was the detectives' fault for…well." Jason shook away what he was thinking. *The woods. The confession. The hospital.*

Clarice pressed her fingers to her forehead and turned her head as if to refuse the oncoming tears. As she composed herself, an involuntary whimper escaped. She cleared her throat.

"I'm glad you're here, now. My heart," her voice began to break, "is whole."

Jason squeezed his mother's hand, which gripped back fiercely.

Clarice's tears leaked through her resolve, down her cheeks. One tiny drop puddled on the table before she turned her face away again.

All Jason could do was hold her hand and let her cry the tears he could not. She would cry for both of them. And while he felt—somewhere deep in his numbness—that he was sorry to have caused it all, he couldn't summon the words to tell her.

Griefless, speechless, and tearless, Jason's mind moved to somewhere behind his body—behind and above, high enough to watch, as if it were someone *else* sitting with his mother. Somewhere in the distance, he heard his own plaintive sobs. The soft cries were recorded deep in his memory. They were faint and far away—as was Jason.

❖

"Welcome back. It was a mistake—letting you out in the first place," the correctional officer explained, nonsensically, as only dream characters can do. "We don't have the certificate. You have to wait for certification, see. And tomorrow is your birthday. You'll be an adult."

Part of Jason's mind told him that wasn't right. He was born in August; it was November—Thanksgiving—and he was home. But he could not speak. "The prosecutor has assigned you a roommate." The correctional officer pointed to someone behind Jason.

"Room service!" The voice, contemptuous and familiar, terrified him. It woke him up, every time.

In the wee-hour blackness, Jason jolted up in a cold sweat, panting through several heart-pounding seconds. That night, he'd needed fewer breaths than the night before, in order to remember he was home. *It's over.*

He was free to walk around his house at night, free to turn on the lights at his own whim, and free to eat the leftovers in the refrigerator.

I'll bet there's more pie.

Only after several mouthfuls during his solitary moment at the kitchen table, only after he'd stuffed the void that could not scream and could not cry, only then could he slow down and taste what he was eating.

Jason sighed under the glaring kitchen light. The rest of the house was dark. No one else was up. Still, he felt exposed, as if standing on a darkened, otherwise empty stage, with a single spotlight shining upon him.

He pressed the creamy sweet potato filling through his teeth, into his cheeks, and sucked it back again, savoring the weight of it on his tongue.

◈

For a couple of weeks, Jason had the house to himself during the day. His mother worked Monday through Thursday during school hours caring for her patients, including her mother, his grandmother. Even though Jason wasn't set to go back to school until after Christmas break, his mom knocked on his bedroom door each morning about seven thirty.

Unlike those other mornings, one bright, early December day she returned to knock again at nine, ten thirty, and eleven.

"Okay, I'm getting up now," was Jason's response each time.

Why should I get up? To watch the Cartoon Network again?

At noon, she rapped the door two times before barging in. "I know you don't want to sleep the day away." She flipped on the lights.

Sure, I do. Why not? Jason sat up in bed, squinting.

"Listen, Jason. You've been home for two weeks. Your dad and I wanted you to get settled at your own pace—you've been through a lot. But now I'm thinking you'd have been better off going back to school. All this sleeping is starting to worry me, honey." Clarice walked to the bed and patted his blanketed legs. "Let's get you up."

Her pats became nudges until Jason swung his feet to the floor. "I'm taking you shopping for clothes and shoes. Christmas is coming early for you."

Jason couldn't think of anything he'd rather do less.

◈

That afternoon, Jason shopped for clothes with his mother, looking on as she picked out a few shirts for his brother and his dad for Christmas.

"Does this look like something Lucas would wear?"

Jason nodded, noncommittal.

It doesn't feel like Christmas.

Once again, he sensed he was watching himself and his mother from some vantage point above. He heard the Christmas music and saw the shoppers swirling through the department store. Wreaths with oversized red bows plastered every cashier's station. Jason observed the scene in the way a child marvels at an anthill.

They are busy, those ants, rushing around gathering what they need in a pattern that makes sense to them. But it's their world—not mine.

CHAPTER 63

Christmas, Unwrapped

Christmas came and went without any particular magic. After all the trouble Jason had gone to "keeping Santa alive" for his little brother, he learned the White-bearded One had already faded from Lucas's imagination. At the foot of the tree, the old, red, felt stockings appeared once again, filled with goodies as they had been every Christmas morning of Jason's first fourteen years of life.

He smiled when he pulled out the candy and the movie gift certificates, which he knew were from his mom. His smile dimmed a little, though, when he pulled out the package of black socks.

The socks were an annual reminder from his dad. Alvin had grown up very poor, raised by his grandmother in Louisiana; to him, socks were a luxury not to be taken for granted. As Jason held the gift in his hands, his thoughts drifted back to Octavius, who was still in jail. The familiar pall of defeatism fell over Jason.

Should I go visit Octavius?

No. I can't go back there. I'm home now.

Jason looked on as his little brother, animated and carefree, dug through the presents to find a gift tagged "Lucas."

I can't go back to being like I was before, either. The way Lucas is now. I can't un-see what I've seen.

His family tittered around him—batting around jokes about stockings full of socks. They passed out presents and searched for more amid the discarded wrapping paper. As he sat on the floor in sweatpants and a T-shirt, surrounded by his family on Christmas, Jason couldn't quite grab the feeling. It lingered just short of his reach, like a familiar person who was too far away to recognize.

He stood up and looked at the tree, at the homemade ornaments with their photographs from Christmases past—bright-eyed little boys smiling in a sea of wrapping paper. The memories flooded back: the bicycles, the scooters, and the basketball goal Santa had left outside on the driveway.

The current year's presents were mostly clothes. Jason's mom and dad bought him a new watch, too—a grownup one with a face and hands and a little square for the date, the numeral "25."

"It's seven forty-five," Jason said, flopping onto the sofa, staring at his watch, still in its box.

"You boys and your digital minutes!" Clarice laughed. "We old people call it a quarter to eight."

"A quarter to eight," Jason repeated, looking at the timepiece again.

"You see why?" Clarice asked.

Jason nodded.

Alvin rose from the floor and walked over to the stereo set, where he carefully placed the Temptations' *Christmas Card* onto the turntable. Vinyl record-playing was a rare sacrament.

Alvin turned to Clarice. "Honey, you need a warm-up on your coffee?" Alvin headed to the kitchen without waiting for an answer. "I am at your service!"

Room service! Jason flinched as the words rang in his head. He squinted to block out the memory of cinderblock walls, prison bars, and the ugly refrain that followed. His muscles felt heavy and weak, as if he were being pulled downward. The upbeat tones of "Rudolph the Rednosed Reindeer" only added to his sensory distress.

He forced himself to stand up. "I'm going to go back and lie down for a few minutes." He left the room, pretending to stare at his new watch.

He didn't see the alarm on his mother's face.

❖

"I'm going to have to take him to the doctor, Alvin," Clarice told her husband the evening of Christmas day, after they'd both turned out their bedside lamps. She didn't have to explain which him she meant. "Readjusting is one thing. All-out depression is another. And there may be some infection or something I'm not seeing."

"Well, I'm glad you're on top of it, but don't go borrowing trouble, now, okay?"

"Too late, Alvin." She turned to face her husband. "He's our baby. When he's not right, *I'm* not right."

❖

Strep cultures, blood work, and more blood work revealed nothing discernibly wrong with Jason.

"It doesn't mean nothing physical is going on," Dr. Francis had explained at the follow-up visit. "But if there is, we haven't found it yet."

"What do you say about school?" Clarice asked. "He's set to go back next week."

Jason sat mute on the exam table, shoulders hunched, looking at his feet. Instead of dangling over the edge of the table, his feet comfortably touched the step below. He couldn't remember the last time he'd been to the doctor's office, but he'd been shorter, for sure—in a kid's body. A little embarrassed that his mother was commandeering the appointment, he was too fatigued to object.

"There should be enough time to rest before school starts," the doctor said, directing his comments to Jason. "If there's something viral going on, it should resolve by then. I'd say try to go back, and if you're not feeling better by then, come and see me. Let's keep a good eye on you, okay?"

"Okay," Jason said.

"Now let's talk a minute about what you've been through." Dr. Francis waited for Jason to look him in the eye before continuing. "Don't underestimate the stress of everything that has happened to you," he said, "and its effects on your body."

Jason nodded.

"I usually don't offer antidepressants to patients as young as you, but you say the word. Do you want to try them?"

Clarice's eyes misted over, but she cleared her throat and said to her son, "I can step out now if you want me to."

Jason shrugged and then shook his head. "You can stay." Turning to Dr. Francis, he said, "I don't want to be on any medications if I can help it."

"I can respect that." The doctor nodded, searching Jason's face. "But what happened to you has been affecting your body for a long time. It's no sin if you want a little chemical assistance to help reverse it."

Jason sat silent.

"You let me know if you change your mind, okay?" the doctor said.

Jason was still absorbing what he'd heard. *Stress affects the body.*

"Either way, though," Dr. Francis continued, "I would really like for you to go talk to a friend of mine. He's good with young men your age who are dealing with extraordinary circumstances. Trauma."

"A psychiatrist?" Jason asked.

"No, he's a counselor, Jason. Any one of us, given what you've been through, would want to do the same. You're young and strong and you *will* overcome this, but you deserve to not go it alone. Depression or post-traumatic stress can interfere with healing infections, you know."

"Post-traumatic stress?" Jason asked, in awe of the words. A shaft of light penetrated his gloom. *There are words for it.*

"I'd say the arrest and jail—well, let's let you and Dr. Greenspan wade through it together. He's the expert." Dr. Francis handed Jason a list of counselors, with Dr. Greenspan's name circled. "The point is we need to take care of you on all fronts. Zone defense."

The basketball analogy elicited a smile from Jason.

"Will you go see him?"

Jason nodded.

"Smart man." Dr. Francis patted him on the back. "Let's see you again in a month, sooner if you need me."

Jason took the doctor's extended hand and shook it, nodding.

"Hey, pretty soon you can drive yourself here, right?" Dr. Francis was grinning.

Jason's eyes found his feet again and he sighed. "I still gotta learn."

CHAPTER 64

Philodendrons

Jason looked around the waiting room. Dr. Greenspan had wanted to talk to his mom first and promised Jason he'd see why, soon. He rose to examine the lush, green fountain in the opposite corner of the room. Jason couldn't decide whether the plants—set in a clever scaffold along the falling water—were real or fake. He reached out to touch a cool, waxy philodendron leaf, fingering the thick vein underneath. He then pinched a tiny tip off the end to make sure.

They're real.

Startled by the sound of an opening door, he played it cool. He mentally apologized to the plant, caressing the underside of another leaf between his thumb and forefingers. He then heard his name, pronounced in some sort of northern accent. *New York?*

Clarice smiled at her son as she took a seat.

"Would you like to come in now?" Dr. Greenspan asked.

Jason nodded and followed him into the compact room. There was no desk, only a loveseat, two comfortable chairs, and a couple of end tables.

No real couch. TV therapists always have couches.

"So, you're a *counselor*?" Jason asked, opting for the loveseat.

"Yes. I got my Ph.D. at the State University of New York, Stony Brook."

New York. I knew it.

Jason's forehead wrinkled into a question. "Ph.D.? That's above a master's degree, right?"

"Exactly right. It's an academic doctorate. Medical doctors, as you probably know, have M.D.s."

"So, how does that work when you're talking about seeing

patients—I mean clients?"

"That's a very good question. Dr. Francis told me you were bright." Dr. Greenspan took a seat on one of the chairs. "Let me see if I can explain it. While I've studied how the body reacts under stress, my focus is addressing it from a cognitive point of view, instead of a medical point of view. We talk about thoughts and feelings: where they come from, why we have them, and how, hopefully, we can start to change the ones that don't work for us."

Pick out thoughts and change the bad ones? Jason's eyes grew wide with astonishment. *There's an idea.* His back straightened a bit. Then a shadow of worry crossed his face. "Did you and my mom talk about my thoughts?"

Dr. Greenspan's whole face broke into a large, warm grin. "No. We talked about her thoughts."

"And?"

"And, I can't share everything. Just like I can't share your confidences with her or anyone else. Not without your specific permission. But I know she's comfortable sharing she is concerned about you."

"She thinks I'm depressed."

"Do you think you're depressed?"

"I don't know. Isn't that why I'm here, so you can tell me?" Jason heard what he said—and how he said it—only after it came out. "I'm sorry, I didn't—"

"Don't worry about it," Dr. Greenspan said, his nasal accent emerging. He waved his hand as if to shove aside Jason's compunction. "I want you to feel comfortable talking to me, okay? I believe we can have some great conversations. And yes, if you want a diagnosis, we can talk about that, too." He reached for his clipboard and pen, which lay on the corner table next to yet another plant.

"Okay. Well, do you think I'm depressed?"

"I don't know enough to know. Tell me about your days since you've been home."

"All I want to do is sleep." Jason sank into the cushions on the loveseat.

"Why?"

"I feel tired all the time. Exhausted."

"Are you sleeping more in the daytime or the nighttime?"

"Well...both. But sometimes I get up at night while everyone's in bed."

"Are you having nightmares?"

Jason looked at Dr. Greenspan as if the therapist had read his mind. "Yeah. Awful ones."

"Would you like to tell me about them?"

"Well, mostly, I'm back in the jail and they won't let me out. They put me with the worst guy I knew of in there, a murderer, and that wakes me up."

"Wow. That would wake me up, too. Let me ask you, once you're awake, do you get up?"

"Yeah. With all the holiday food around, I usually go fill my face."

"Your body needs the calories to heal. Besides, with everyone else sleeping in the middle of the night, it's nice to have the house to yourself."

"Yeah." *Man, he really does know about this stuff.*

"Can you point to anything in particular making you tired?"

Jason inhaled and thought for a moment. "Everything," he said, his body falling with the release of his breath.

"Okay. Everything. Fair enough. Tell me, how is your family reacting to your being home?"

"They're really, really glad it's over—especially the jail part. It's like they've been holding their breath all this time. Especially my mom."

"Would you say they're relieved?"

"Yeah. They're relieved it's done—at least the criminal law part of it. There's still a civil law case to get through."

"I thought there might be. I followed it a little bit in the news. They charged you with first-degree murder, right?"

"Yeah."

"They arrested you and held you without an attorney, without your parents?"

"Yeah."

"Pretty outrageous. Unbelievable to people like me, reading the paper."

"Believe it." His reply was flat and matter-of-fact.

The therapist looked at Jason, holding his eye contact for a long series of seconds. Jason did not look away.

"They dropped the charges, right?" Dr. Greenspan asked.

"Right."

"And now you're home again?"

"Yes…"

Dr. Greenspan's eyes were kind, as he waited for Jason to continue. "I'm *at* home," Jason said.

"You're *at* home now. And you're exhausted." Dr. Greenspan's nasal voice expanded with the word *exhausted*. "And I'm betting," the counselor continued, "that things are different from the last time you lived at home."

Jason nodded and looked up, beyond the older man's shoulder, as if focusing in on the scene of himself at home with his family. "It's like I'm a different person. It's like I used to belong there, and I can almost feel it—but not quite."

"That's a pretty good description, Jason. A pretty insightful way of putting it—of what traumatic events can do to a person."

"Traumatic? Do I have post-traumatic disorder?" Jason asked, remembering Dr. Francis' words about Dr. Greenspan. "Aren't you a specialist in P…S…T…?"

"PTSD. I do have experience in post-traumatic stress. Yes."

"So, you think I've got it?"

"Well, yes," Dr. Greenspan said. "It looks like you've been having some natural human responses to what's happened to you. You've had some life-changing events. The arrest, for starters."

"For starters."

"And you were innocent—you are innocent. None of it should have happened to you."

"But it did, anyway."

"Yes, it did. And I am sorry. You didn't deserve it."

Jason exhaled. He allowed his eyes to meet Dr. Greenspan's.

"There is no getting around the fact that it's made your life harder, Jason." The counselor treaded lightly as he continued. "But I believe together, with some time, we can get you through it."

"How long is it gonna take?"

"Well, there's a saying in my business. 'It takes what it takes.' But I'd ask you to give us an hour a week for at least a couple of months," Dr. Greenspan held his hands out, palms up, "*if* you would like to work with me, that is."

"Just talking like this?"

"Basically, yeah. What do you say?"

Jason nodded. "Okay," he said. "Two months of talking. I can do that."

"Great. I want you to remember, too, that it's no sin to try medicine, if you think you might want a little boost for what's happened to your mind-body."

"My mind-body?"

"Yeah. They're kind of like computer software and computer hardware, you know?"

"I think so."

"We'll work on the software here, but if you feel like the hardware needs a boost, you let me know. It helps the software run better sometimes."

Jason nodded, smiling when Dr. Greenspan pronounced "hawdwayuh" in his New York accent. *I think I get it.* "Okay. I'll think about it. I need some time to think about that."

"Sure."

Relaxing a little, Jason picked up on something about his new friend from New York. "Can I ask you something, Dr. Greenspan?"

"Anything. Ask away."

"Are you Jewish?"

"Born and bred."

Curiosity lit up in Jason's eyes as he tried to process the new information. In his young life in Beau Rêve, Florida, he'd never met a Jewish person. His mouth opened to form another question, but he stopped himself.

Dr. Greenspan chimed in to ease the awkwardness. "How 'bout you?"

"Me? No. I'm not Jewish."

The doctor beamed at him. "Well, do you practice any religion?"

"Practice?" Jason considered the word for a moment. "Not exactly. I was raised Christian. But…well…" Jason shook his head and blurted out another question. "Can I ask you something about *your* religion?"

"Sure. I went to Hebrew School every Sunday of my life—for the first thirteen years anyway. But don't expect me to be an expert on Judaism."

"Okay. Well, in Judaism," Jason began, pronouncing the word for the first time, "people don't believe in Jesus, right?"

"Believe in?"

"Yeah. You know, that He was the Son of God and all."

"Eh," the older man said, waving his hand again. "As a Jew, I believe he lived and died. Jews view him as one of the great teachers—we call them rabbis."

"So, you don't believe he was the Son of God?" Jason asked.

"No more than you or I are sons of God. No."

"So, you don't believe in Christmas or Easter?"

"Those are holidays. I believe they exist." Dr. Greenspan's eyes twinkled a little.

Jason laughed. "You know what I mean."

"Yes, I know what you mean, and no, we don't celebrate the birth of Jesus or Easter."

Jason nodded, comprehending. Comfortable on the loveseat, he looked around the room. It seemed to have more color in it than when he first walked in. Reaching out, he touched the long leaf of a peace lily on the table next to him. "I like your plants."

"Thanks, Jason. I like them, too."

CHAPTER 65

Jay-SON

"Jay-SON! Jay-SON! Jay-SON!"

His name rang out like a war chant. It was only his second day back at school, but word got around. Jason vaguely recognized the kid who had shouted. They'd gone to elementary school together.

Trevor? Man, he grew some muscles. Kid is buff.

Jason managed a smile and a half-nod to the kids who recognized him, even if he couldn't quite place who they were.

His newfound celebrity both buoyed and drained him. Who wouldn't want to hear their name in a cheer? But after a half dozen shout-outs from students he did not remember, he felt the familiar pang of loss—the one he thought he'd left behind when he left jail.

During lunch, Jason sat next to CJ, a friend from middle school who, Jason recalled, made a habit of enjoying mealtimes.

"So, what did you eat, Jason? I mean while you were…you know."

"C'mon, man," Slim admonished CJ from across the table. "He don't want to talk about it. Leave the man alone."

Jason was trying to recall Slim's real name. *Chester? Lester?* He'd been "Slim" since at least fourth grade.

"Nah, it's alright," Jason said. "People are curious. Everything tasted like… metal. Like the inside of a can."

"Kinda like here, huh?" CJ asked, smiling as he forked in a load of green beans.

"What do you expect with your free-lunch punch card?" Slim wailed, "What you think it's gonna taste like, your mama's home cooking?"

"My mama's dead," CJ said, looking down at the tray in front of him.

Jason felt CJ's words in his gut.

"What'd you say?" Slim was on the precipice of pure cruelty.

"Leave him alone." The depth of Jason's growl surprised him. He thought of Octavius from jail, and Octavius's mother—if you could call her a mother. "You still got your dad, CJ?"

"Long story," CJ muttered, in between bites.

How could I have known CJ for so long and not known about his family?

They'd gone to the same middle school together and had begun high school together, but of course, Jason had missed the end of ninth grade, all of tenth, and half of eleventh. Jason had become a different person, with a different perspective. Everyone had gotten older, but not everyone had grown up.

Even though Jason had been forced to mature fast, even though he was cheated out of nearly two years of his life, he had something CJ and Octavius didn't have: parents he could count on. His childhood ended, but at least he'd had one.

A pang of guilt pulsed through Jason's chest.

The lunchtime exchange depleted Jason. He took a deep breath, pulled his shoulders back, and began walking to fourth-period Chemistry. *How am I ever going to concentrate on Chemistry? I just want to sleep.*

Jason found his seat a few rows back from the front of the classroom, before the initial blare of the bell assaulted him. Flinching, he looked down and braced himself for the duration of the noise. Mercifully, it didn't last long.

He and his peers pulled notebooks and pencils from their bookbags, settling in for Mr. Moretti's instruction.

"Now, if you'll pull out your homework from Chapter Nineteen, let's see who can—" The teacher was interrupted midsentence by a student who walked in late. Carleen Jones was a talented pupil, but punctuality was not in her repertoire. As she handed Mr. Moretti her tardy slip, he yanked it away from her, sighing. The girl froze in place, panic-stricken, tears welling as she hugged her books to her chest.

Moretti shook his head at her, exasperated, and pointed with a jerk for her to take her seat. A single move of the teacher's hand thrust Jason back into the day of his arrest.

Yes, you.

Images of Officer O'Donnell flashed in Jason's mind like a slideshow of his worst-lived moments: the mouthed words; the accusatory finger; the disdain in the man's face and in his voice; the hatred, laced with subtle glee; the derisive pleasure he took in stopping Jason. He felt the kick to his shins, the blow to his chest, and the weight of O'Donnell's knee on his back. He struggled for breath, coughing, spitting out the taste of the pavement at the corner of College and Broward.

Adrenaline flowed down its icy pathways to Jason's fingertips and his toes as he sputtered, trying to catch his breath. The silence spread outward from his seat, from student to student, until they all were as still as rabbits. To his horror, Jason realized that everyone, including Mr. Moretti, was staring at him.

"Are you alright, son?" Moretti asked.

Jason could only nod, slowing his breathing, clearing his throat, calming his terror.

"Want to go get some water?" the teacher asked.

Jason blew out a sigh, nodded, gathered his supplies, and shoved them back into his backpack.

Yes, I'll go get some water. He stood, pulling his backpack up over his shoulder. *And then I'm going home.*

CHAPTER 66

"That Was Torture"

The following Sunday, Jason caved in to his parents' request and returned to church. The service was tolerable. He got through communion and the prayer that followed. Next would come the Peace, when everyone would shake hands and greet one another.

Before the Peace, Pastor Junior instructed the rest of the congregation to be seated, but he asked Jason to remain standing. Jason clenched his teeth, enduring the nightmarish moment.

Predictably, Junior proceeded to turn Jason's personal tragedy—the arrest, the jail time, the trial—into a story about staying faithful. "The Lord saw him through it all, and—praise Jesus!—He's brought him back to be here with us today!"

Jason stood silent for what felt like an eternity, amidst the lulling murmurs of "amen" and "praise Jesus" and the rising voice of Pastor Junior feeding off the crowd. The sounds were familiar. Women's voices lent a soft undercurrent to the voice of the man in front, like background music to a melody Jason had heard before. Never, however, had he ever before been the object of Pastor Junior's—or anyone's—chorus.

Oh, Lord, Jason thought as he stood mute, red-hot anger rising to his cheeks. He waited patiently for Junior to finish exalting him—to a spot somewhere right underneath the biblical Job, who ranked, in turn, someplace beneath the Reverend Dr. Martin Luther King, Jr.

If you don't hurry up and finish this, man, I'm going to run out of here. Jason eyed the exit to his left, a pair of doors near the altar.

His feet resisted the impulse. He remained planted until Junior finished and for the next flourishes of "praise Jesus." Though Jason moved to sit afterwards, his family buoyed him up again, joining the entire congregation in a standing ovation. He held out for a moment before sinking down onto the pew. The rows of people around him turned to face him in a circle of emotion and clapping. One lady, a friend of his grandmother, wiped her joyful tears away with a freshly pressed handkerchief.

Jason softened a little and smiled at her. He'd grown up seeing her at church all his life.

❖

Outside in the car, as they waited for Clarice and Lucas, Jason spoke to his father. "That was torture, Dad. It was Hamp who fought for me. Jesus didn't have anything to do with it."

"Jason!" Alvin was miffed. Catching his son's eye in the rearview mirror, he said, "Don't you dare speak like that in front of your mama. She has brought you up in a community that you better believe had *everything* to do with getting you out. Same way Aaron Hampton was raised. Far be it from me to tell you what to believe, or how to live your life, but you will respect your family's church."

Jason shook his head. "How can you stand it, Daddy? Them going on and on about some magical man in the sky while Junior collects their money?"

"Magical man in the sky?" Alvin squinted at Jason in the mirror and shook his head. "That's the best you can do? You'd better think for a minute, about where you came from. You think about all those people still in jail, innocent people like your friend, whose families don't have the faintest idea how to get them out. They leave them there to rot. Think about all the people in the world who figure Black people get what they get."

"But it's not *Jesus* who's going to save them! It's educated people— people who know how to work the system and fight."

Alvin sighed. "Okay, yes." His voice became more patient as the teacher in him emerged. "But what do you suppose people like Hampton are fighting *for*?"

"I don't know. Justice. Fairness."

"All right, then. Where did we get this idea we should have fairness in the world?"

"We just *did*, Dad. You're the history teacher. Natural rights of man and all—*that's* where we got the idea. You don't need *God* to believe in *that*."

Alvin sighed. "For some people that *is* God, Jason. Our ideals. What we want to be. How we should act toward each other. The body of Christ."

"Then why don't they say so? Why do we have to pretend someone's up there looking down on us, pulling our strings? It's stupid."

Alvin whipped his head around to the back seat, eyes flashing in a manner Jason rarely saw. Instead of dressing him down, though, Alvin raised his head and said, "Here comes your mother. You better watch it, son."

The Scream Deferred

It sneaked up on Jason when he least expected it.

He was hoping to catch Brendan before pre-calculus for help on a graphing problem. Waiting outside the classroom door, it struck him.

"It" was the sight of his friend lumbering down the sidewalk with his arm around a girl—a stunningly beautiful girl. Since his return to high school, Jason had noticed countless girls, but he never spotted *her*. She was nearly as tall as Brendan, and as athletic, but softer. As Brendan strutted, she glided along with him, her silky movements shimmering in the Florida winter sun. She was the perfect complement to Brendan's lean, muscled build. Her complexion was clear iced tea to Brendan's smokier coffee. They looked so happy together, as if they had stepped out of a magazine.

Jason stared as the couple walked, facing each other, smiling, lost in their own private world. Their walk was a dance: a slow, progressive two-step, lulling Jason, mesmerizing him.

All he could think was, *Damn.*

Jason looked down as the twosome ambled closer, before they could catch him staring. They didn't notice. Their eyes remained locked on each other.

She's way outta my league. Heavy waves pounded Jason's chest. *What is my league? Do I even have a league?*

A rush of memory paralyzed him, followed by another—image upon image, fast and dizzying—unleashing an intense longing that threatened to undo him.

Kim. Her freckles. Her laugh. Her smooth, pale arms stocking the shelves at her job.

He relived the feeling, the stirring—the slight tilt terrifying him and thrilling him at once.

The tiny diamond on her nose. Her eyes. Our plans.

And then...and then...

Jason stifled a scream. He turned his body away right as Brendan and his girlfriend reached the door.

Shit. Fighting back tears, he decided to cough. And he coughed again, and again, with more violence.

"Hey, Jason. You okay?"

Brendan disentangled himself from the beauty, reaching to turn Jason around. To Jason's horror and embarrassment, Brendan's girlfriend was at his heels, also appearing concerned.

Jason doubled over, coughed another short round, and then he pulled himself together to face his friend. "Damn oak pollen," he lied, dragging his arm across his face to hide the tears. "Allergies are killing me, man. I gotta go wash up."

"Yeah, sure. Stuff is brutal," Brendan said. "You can meet Lisa later." He grabbed her hand, pulling her close again.

Jason nodded, pretending to stifle another cough. "Sorry," he managed to choke out as he hurried past them. He made a beeline to the boys' bathroom, which was—thankfully—empty.

Fuck, fuck, fuck, fuck, fuck!

The piercing, sixth-period bell obliterated Jason's long, guttural cry. The cry welled into a roar. Jason beat the open stall door with his fist first, then with his foot. The loud rattling of hollow metal on metal engulfed him and kept him punching. The noise fed his rage, and his rage fed the clatter.

"You took my life away!" His wrath crashed against the open door. "All of you!"

"Fuck you," he yelled. Each jab reverberated as the door hit the stall wall and again as his fists hit the door. "Fuck you, you pink-ass piece of shit! You Irish albino son of a bitch!"

His loud, clattering frenzy covered his yelling. "You and your fucking police car and your fucking intimidation."

It was easy to channel his hatred for the first cop. His bloodied knuckles made it palpable. His feelings about the rest of them swirled deeper in his gut: shame, defeat, outrage, fury. They churned inside of him and then erupted.

He screamed and punched, punched and screamed.

"Fuck you, Detective John Marshall! You and the whole goddamned Beau Rêve Police Department."

A hot sharpness seized his knuckles, and he stopped.

Oh, man. Jason pulled his hands to his stomach and bent over in pain. After several long, deep breaths, he clenched and unclenched them, kneading away the acute stabbing, smearing the blood.

What the hell just happened?

Jason shut himself in the stall, locked the door, and sat. He was panting. His heart thumped against his chest in a thunderous drumbeat, matching the cacophony that had just ended. He could hear his own blood pulsing.

They took my life away from me. They took being fifteen away from me. They took sixteen. Damn near got seventeen. I'll never get any of it back.

As his breathing slowed, Jason sat staring at the inside of the stall door, in a daze, for what felt like hours. But when he found his bearings and looked at his watch, he realized only a few minutes had passed.

Walking to the sink, he almost didn't recognize himself in the cheap, stainless steel plate passing itself off as a mirror. He wanted to punch it, too, to smear his reflection with blood, the way his life had been bloodied—beyond recognition.

Instead, he plunged the top of the water spigot, allowing a trickle of cool water to stream over his abrasions. The miniscule stream stopped too soon, angering him again. Leaning over the sink, he hung his head for a minute. Not knowing whether to laugh or to cry, he tapped the institutional spigot again and again, rubbing his hands until he'd washed away the blood. He shook them over the sink as he scanned the room for paper towels.

Of course, there are no paper towels. He fumed, watching as his wounds gushed red, all over again.

"Jesus Christ," he said aloud, alone in the cinderblock room. *I've got to get out of here.*

He realized he was late to class.

He hung his head, and then he laughed out loud—the thin, high-pitched cackle of a young man teetering into tears.

I'm late by two fucking years.

CHAPTER 68

"A Different Kind of Cancer"

Jason sat down on the loveseat and inhaled, looking directly at the psychologist.

Dr. Greenspan motioned for him to come out with whatever was weighing on his mind.

"I can't go back there." Jason spoke his burden into the air between them. He crossed his arms and sank back into the old, tattered cushions.

"Back where?"

"To school."

"Do you want to tell me what happened?"

Looking down, he shook his head. "I'm not sure what happened. I'm not sure what it was that set me off—but something did—and I was out of control."

"Out of control?" Dr. Greenspan wrinkled his forehead. "What do you mean?"

"I was able to keep it together until I got to the bathroom. Then I just lost it."

"You lost it," Dr. Greenspan repeated. "Tell me what you did."

"I coughed to keep myself from crying in front of my friend," Jason said, "who was with his girlfriend—drop-dead gorgeous, this girl. And I ran to the bathroom even though class was about to start. And it all just came out. I was crying and screaming and punching the door to the stall. Kicking it."

Jason held out his hands for viewing.

Dr. Greenspan's eyes widened. "Was anyone in there with you?"

"No—thank God."

"Thank God, why?"

"Because I could not have held it in even if someone else had walked in."

"What were you holding in, Jason?"

"Everything." His voice pitched upward and his body stiffened. "All of it." He leaned forward. "Everything I lost. My entire sophomore year of high school. My life. Everything they took from me."

"They who?"

"The cops. Those goddamned racist, son-of-a-bitch, incompetent cops."

"You're angry." Dr. Greenspan's tone was even, leaving room for Jason to fill in the emotion.

"Goddamn right, I'm angry!" Jason yelled, incredulous at Dr. Greenspan's remark. "I've been cheated out of almost two years of my life. I'm seventeen and I still don't know how to drive. I've never even gone out with a girl." Jason's voice broke, threatening to unravel him. Instead, he growled. "I've never had a job. I was sitting in jail while my friends were doing all of that." He held out his arm as if to point to the others.

"They're worried about their grades and which overpriced shoes they're going to buy and what movie they're going to see and I'm sitting in jail, wondering if the judge thinks I'm a criminal and if she'll put me away for good. Why shouldn't she? I fit the profile." He scoffed, "That's why they picked me up in the first place."

"You have a right to be angry."

"I know. That's what scares me."

Dr. Greenspan's forehead wrinkled again, prompting Jason to continue.

"I can't keep it in, Dr. Greenspan. It's leaking out everywhere, when I least expect it. I wanted to jump down one kid's throat at lunch the other day."

"You wanted to? Meaning, you didn't?"

"No—I didn't do anything to him, but he could tell I was pissed. He wasn't acting right, but it's not his fault I got locked up. It's not his fault—what I went through. I don't want to take it out on other people. I don't want to walk around feeling like I'm going to explode."

"What happens if you explode?"

"I lose control. Like in the bathroom. It also happened in

Chemistry class."

"What happened in Chemistry class?"

"Something my teacher did, the way he pointed his finger...it's so stupid..."

"It's not stupid. Your teacher pointed his finger and then what?"

"I freaked out. I felt like I was getting arrested all over again. That hand movement..."

"It reminded you of what happened?"

"No, it took me *back* to what happened." Jason's voice pitched upward as his breathing morphed into panting. "That cop was on me, taking me down. I was living it all over again."

Dr. Greenspan looked at Jason, giving him time to tell more.

"I had to leave the room, I was freaking out so bad."

"Tell me what you mean, Jason. What does 'freaking out' mean?"

"It was like I was there, all over again, the moment when I first got arrested. I couldn't breathe. I fake-coughed until Mr. Moretti told me to go get some water."

"Did you? Get water?"

"Yeah. Then I went and called for my mom to come get me. My Aunt Brenda ended up getting me and driving me home."

"You didn't think you could take a minute to recompose yourself? Or go see the counselor at your school?"

"Naw. She's always swamped. I could spend half the day waiting to get in there." His face fell, and his eyes betrayed bewilderment. "Man, it was sudden. Such a stupid little thing...a hand movement. And I just came undone. It was so fast. I don't want anyone to see me like that. Ever. I don't want to break down at school. I came too close."

"The hand movement, Jason. It *triggered* you. You're more perceptive than most people are; you're already able to identify what it was that set you off. You might want to do some journaling about the words, phrases, sights, sounds, smells—anything that tends to trigger that level of distress."

"Trigger is a good word, Doc, because I exploded."

Dr. Greenspan put his hands together and tilted them toward Jason in a question. "Have you thought about taking a few days off?"

"I feel like I did that already." Jason shook his head. "After they released me from jail. I tried staying home for a while—it didn't help." He stopped himself from whining, took a breath, and said, "I'm not going back. I'm not like those kids anymore."

"You feel like something has changed in you?"

"Yeah. I feel like they're all living in a fantasyland. Like they have no fucking idea what could happen to them at any minute—how the world *really* is."

"Maybe what you call 'fantasyland' is how the world *really* is for *them*, Jason. Can you leave room for the possibility that the world is both? And more?"

"I hear you. Two realities. But I can't live in *theirs* anymore."

"At least not now. I agree."

"You do?" Jason was stunned with relief.

"I do."

"What about my parents?"

"What about your parents?"

"How am I going to tell them I'm not going back to school?"

"Well, I'll help you. But let's not focus on what you *don't* want to do. Let's talk about alternatives. You've got to finish school. Your dad's a high school teacher, right?"

"Yes."

"Have you thought about going to *his* school? You could get a special assignment."

Jason shook his head. "I love my dad, Doc. I really do. But I do not want to be the teacher's kid. No way."

"Have you known any teacher's kids in your experience?"

"No. It's got to be hell, though. My dad—he's a corny dude. He probably wouldn't even realize if kids were making fun of him, or he wouldn't care, but I would. And I don't have a lot of extra patience right now."

"Point well taken. Okay. Let's shelve the idea of Dad's school for now. Do you want to talk to your parents about homeschool? Or hospital-homebound school?"

Jason turned the words over in his head. *Hospital-homebound.* He wasn't sick, exactly—or was he? Perhaps trauma counted when it came to being sick. Dr. Greenspan sounded like he could get him in.

"Maybe," Jason said. "I had a great math teacher who came to tutor me in jail. I liked doing class one-on-one. That's what hospital-homebound is, right? They come to me?"

"Yes, they do. I have a nephew in California who did it for a while—they gave him videos for math and let him go at his own pace. He even emailed in some of his work. The teacher only stopped by once a week or so."

"Is he okay now?"

"My nephew? Yes. In full remission." Dr. Greenspan smiled. "Thank you for asking."

"Remis—? Oh. Oh, my God." Jason knew what the word meant. One of his mom's patients had been in remission from colon cancer, until she wasn't, and the disease killed her. He thought about Kim's mom, and her ongoing fight, too. "How old is your nephew now?"

"He's twenty-two. Finishing college at UC Davis. He wants to be an oncologist."

"A cancer doctor?"

"Exactly right." Dr. Greenspan beamed at Jason, pleased. "He's got a long way to go, but the experience of having leukemia changed him. He's clear about what he wants to do with his life."

Jason nodded. "I get it. You don't want for anyone else to have to go through what you did. You want to make the world better."

"Sounds like you want to make the world better, too."

"Yeah. I do. But not for cancer patients."

Dr. Greenspan turned up his chin. "In a way, what you're talking about is a different kind of cancer."

"Yeah—and our whole country still has it."

Dr. Greenspan nodded, urging Jason to go on.

"I've got some ideas, but I don't want to talk about them yet. So, I guess you can get into college if you go through hospital-homebound school?"

"Yep. It's one possibility. Or, you might be ready to go ahead and take some college classes. Ever heard of dual enrollment? Where you finish high school and take college classes at the same time?"

"They have that?" Jason looked surprised.

"They have that." Dr. Greenspan's face lit up in a broad grin. "Tell you what...let's get your parents in here and talk about all of these possibilities. It may be that you work on your classes at home for the rest of the year, then take a dual-enrollment path next year. Then there's always the GED as a last resort. There are lots of ways to finish high school, Jason, if you're sure you can't go back."

"I can't. I just can't. And I can't tell my parents that I can't."

"You'd rather tell them you have a stomach virus?" Dr. Greenspan reached for his calendar.

"How did—? Did my mom mention my stomach when she called?"

The psychologist nodded. "She's pretty worried about you."

"Yeah—the thought of having to go back to school made me want to—"

Jason stopped himself, remembering the episode in the police station, remembering the embarrassing mess he'd made. He bristled for a minute at the memory of how the white officer had made fun of him. *"Trouble with his tummy."*

There's a trigger, right there.

Sighing, Jason sank into the well-worn loveseat. "I've always had stomach problems. Ever since I was a little kid."

Grapefruit

Jason placed his cereal bowl in the sink just as his father came in through the kitchen door, carrying his harvest. As Alvin set the fresh-picked grapefruits on the counter, one tumbled onto the linoleum. Ignoring it, he plucked the leaves and stems from the citrus in front of him.

"Your mother is not going to like the idea," Alvin said to his son, "not one little bit."

"I know. I didn't expect *you* to like it either." Jason rescued the stray fruit from its roll across the floor.

"Oh, I don't. I'd rather you stay in school. But you're not dropping out, per se. It sounds like you have a plan for finishing and going to college, right?" Alvin gathered the leaves and took them to the compost can.

"Right." Jason hung his head. "I just can't go back, Dad. I'm way too...*different* now."

Alvin nodded, without looking up. He piled the grapefruits in a large bowl, leaving one out and then rinsing it.

"I hear you, son." He motioned for Jason to join him at the table. "I've seen young men like you disappear from my classroom. It happens a lot on that side of the river. More often than I care to count. The difference is, you've got your mama and me. You've got your grandparents, your aunt, your uncle. You've got a whole lot of people who are not going to let you fall—"

Jason opened his mouth to speak, but Alvin held up his hand to stop him.

"Let me finish. I know you're not always going to need us like this, but we're here for you." He reached over and touched his son on the shoulder.

Jason relished the weight of his dad's hand, the feeling of his father being supportive. It wasn't mushy or demonstrative—it never would be—but it was enough.

As his father thrust his thumb through the skin of the Pink Marsh, Jason regarded him through new eyes.

The man sitting at the table with him was more than the nerdy history teacher who stopped boys in the street, admonishing them to pull up their pants. His father linked him to a long chain of men who grew up in the struggle, and who felt it in ways Jason never would. Justice, freedom—they were values men of Jason's father's generation did not take for granted.

Jason knew younger Black men couldn't, either.

"Dad?" Jason was surprised the question was finally occurring to him. "How come you never told us about when you got stopped by the police?"

"I did."

"No, I don't mean the hotdog time. Or the shopping time. Or the what-are-you-doing-here times. We know about those. I'm talking about the driving time. When you were in college."

Silence filled the kitchen for a moment before Alvin nodded. "It wasn't anything like what happened to you, son. But it did scare the bejesus out of me."

"Bejesus?" Jason laughed.

"You haven't heard that expression?"

Jason shook his head, still grinning. "Bejesus." He tried out the word, tasting it. "Be—"

"Alright now." Alvin's voice was serious, but his smile gave him away. "You want to hear about it or not?"

"Yes, sir."

Alvin pursed his lips and shook his head, handing a section of fruit to his son, who tugged off the white veins before biting into it. Jason slurped as he bit, wiping the juice off his face with his hand. His father passed him a napkin.

"It was only a traffic stop. But I was terrified," Alvin started. "I was on a two-lane road in Picayune, Mississippi. On my way to New Orleans to see your great-grandmother. Long before you were born. Not long before she was gone. Anyhow, I'm on this two-lane road in rural Mississippi—"

"What year was this?"

"About 1979. May I continue?"

"Yes, sir. I'm sorry."

"We were on a little, tiny road—in the backwoods, in the South, in 1979—the sheriff's deputy and I. He was right behind me in a no-passing zone, and I could tell he wanted to pull around. So, there I was, minding the speed limit, looking out for the white line to break up, so he could go ahead and pass me." Alvin bit off a section of citrus, savoring tart pulp before wiping the juice off his hands and resuming his story.

"Now keep in mind, no one else was on the road for miles. We were out in the middle of nowhere. I'm thinking to myself, do I have a brake light out? Didn't I renew my tag? I knew for sure I wasn't speeding. After sweating it out for a few more miles, I finally get the broken white line. And I slow down, thinking he would come around me."

Alvin stacked the loose peels in a pile in front of him.

"Big mistake," he told Jason. "Big, big mistake. That deputy flipped on his lights and his siren so fast—just as soon as my foot touched the brake."

"Why?"

"Good question. I sure didn't know at the time—but I pulled over anyway. I was shaking like a leaf when he stormed out of his car and started coming toward me. The way he was walking, I could tell he was steaming."

"Why was he so pissed off?" Jason asked.

"Why was he so *upset?*" Alvin rarely passed up an opportunity to correct his children. "See if you can guess."

"He was white?"

Alvin laughed. "No. I mean, yes, he was white, but that's not why. Anyway, he was a large guy with red hair. Built kind of like your Uncle Mack. Large enough to be scary. He was kind of muscular, but much older than I was, and a little of out of shape, like he played ball at one time, when he was younger.

"So, he says to me, loudly, 'Boy!' He called me…" Alvin shook his head, casting his eyes downward. "The thing you've got to remember about Black people in my generation is that we had to fight back against feeling humiliated. We didn't earn the shame ascribed to us; it was never ours to begin with, but it was there all the same. The shame of being something allegedly less than white."

Jason looked at his dad before speaking, remembering old conversations from years before. "I thought you said all that changed when people like Muhammad Ali and Kwame Ture came around."

"Very good. You *have* been listening all these years. You're right—those men taught us Black pride, yes. They taught us not to let the white man define us. But that doesn't mean that white people ever got the memo. It doesn't mean that white men in power—like that sheriff's deputy in Mississippi—weren't going to enforce that shame, regardless. That was his job, as far as I could see. He was out to remind me of the caste system in America—and my place in it."

Jason's eyes widened. Caste system in America? He knew what a caste was, but his teachers always used it describe other countries' undemocratic systems—and never in reference to the United States. As Jason recalled the humiliation of having been thrown into the back of a police car, his father's words made instant sense.

Jason shared another part of the burden with his dad, too. Trying to transcend the anger felt like a never-ending battle. He stayed silent, watching as his father divided the last two sections of fruit.

Alvin's voice grew quiet. "Rural Mississippi." Grief eclipsed his face. "Who knew that 1979 rural Mississippi would be no match for Satsuma County, Florida, in 2001?" After a moment, he looked up to resume his story. "Where was I? Oh, yes. 'Boy,' this deputy says to me, 'you know why I stopped you?'

"Now that seemed to me like a trick question. No matter how I answered, I figured he was going to be mad at me. I didn't know what I was dealing with. If something were to happen to me out there, the only ones who would have ever known were the cows." Alvin's laugh fell flat.

Jason sat back in his seat, horrified. Pine trees and pine straw flashed before his eyes—memories of the day of his arrest, his own exposure to terror.

"Anyway," Alvin continued, "I had to answer him. So, I say to him, this big, redheaded, freckle-faced deputy, 'I'm sorry, sir.'

"I apologized right off the bat, deferential as I could be, and not in any smart-off way, either. And as demeaning as it was, I apologized a second time. I still had no idea what it was I did, or whether I had done anything at all. So, I waited for him to tell me."

Alvin stopped talking.

"Well?" Jason demanded. "Did he?"

"No. He asked me for my license and registration. I gave them to him, and he went back to his car. I could see in my rearview mirror he was making a call on his radio. Had to be the longest ten minutes of my life."

Jason's pulse quickened. He thought about Officer O'Donnell, about sitting captive in the back seat of the patrol car, bruised and bloodied, heart pounding, waiting for the man in the front to finish filling out paperwork. He thought about how each excruciating minute felt like an hour. He thought about how he was at the complete mercy of the white officer on the other side of the cage.

Jason's voice cracked when he asked, "What happened then?"

"Nothing like what happened to you, Jason. Nothing like it." Alvin's tone softened. "He came back carrying something that looked like a citation tablet, and I thought, oh, Lord, he's going to give me a ticket. But then he stopped to look at the back of my car. 'Son?' he asked me. We had progressed from *boy* to *son*, I guess."

Jason winced.

"'Son, you a college student?' the deputy asked me.

"'Yes, sir,' I said, still trying to be respectful. 'Morehouse College,' I said. He kind of raised his eyebrows, as if I'd given him the right answer, and then he asked me, 'Morehouse? They got football there?'

"He seemed like he was relaxing a little, but I wasn't taking any chances: 'Yes, sir,' I said again. And then what he did next could've knocked me over with a feather." Alvin looked down at the grapefruit peels in front of him, remembering.

"What?" Jason heard the scream in his voice, and then he lowered it. "What did he do next?"

"He says to me, 'Tell you what,' this big, white, redheaded policeman says to me, 'even though you're not an LSU Tiger like you should be down here,' he was starting to sound friendly, joking around, he said, 'I'm going to let you off on a warning.'"

Jason raised his eyebrows. "He let you off?"

"Yes, he did." Alvin looked at the wall as if watching the scene on a movie screen. "But just when I started to breathe again and started to feel relieved, just when I said, 'Thank you, sir,' he got serious all over again. At least I thought he was serious. To this day, I'm not sure."

"Why? What did he say?"

"He told me the minimum speed on that road was forty. I said, 'Yes, sir,' holding my breath again. And then—and I'll never forget this—he told me to wait and let him go ahead of me. So, I did."

Jason gasped as his eyes lit up in revelation. "He wanted to get in front of you! He stopped you because you were driving too slow!"

"Too slowly," Alvin corrected his son. "Yes. Apparently, I made him put his foot on the brake and he didn't like it. The police are like that, you know—impatient. You've probably seen them turn on their blue lights in the intersection just to get around everyone."

Jason's mouth fell open.

"I got lucky, Jason. In the end, this big, white, deep-dyed Southern deputy turned out to be basically human. It was all about the circumstances—right officer, right time, right place." Alvin shook his head. "Plus, I had a Morehouse Maroon Tigers bumper sticker on the back of my old clunker. Can you imagine? And all my *respect.*" Alvin spat the words. "Yes, sir. Yes, sir. Yes, sir." His face dropped the third time he said it.

Jason could count on one hand the times he'd seen beyond his father's well-maintained veneer. That morning, his dad's practiced positivity had worn thin, and the strain showed on his face. It happened the first time his father visited him in jail and again on nine-eleven. There, at the kitchen table, the burden emerged once more.

"Whoa," Jason said quietly. "Did that cop even have probable cause to pull you over?"

"I doubt it. Even now, I don't really know. Maybe you should ask Mr. Hampton about it sometime. But I'll tell you, I'm certain your lawyer would refer to him as an *officer.* Not a cop."

"Yes, sir."

Alvin bristled at his son's response, but then he gave him a half-smile. "Now you're sounding like I did, back then."

"Gets old, doesn't it?" Jason asked. "All the deference. All the respect."

"As old as time, Jason." Alvin sat for a little while, absently rearranging the grapefruit peels. When he spoke again, he said, "It's constant gardening."

"Grapefruit?"

"No!" Alvin laughed. "Well, yes, they also take some tending to. But I was talking about justice. Equality. It doesn't just happen. You have to keep fighting for it. Always."

"It shouldn't be that way, Dad. That...*officer* never should have stopped you."

"There's no *should* about it, Jason. In this world, people are either part of the problem, or part of the solution. There's no middle ground. If you decide to be part of the solution, you've got to know, in one way or the other, and for the rest of your life, you will be fighting."

Jason opened his mouth to speak, but he thought better of it. He hung his head thinking, *"Yes, sir."*

The younger man got up, brought the compost can to the edge of the table, and scooped in their rinds.

CHAPTER 70

"Chop wood. Carry water."

Jason adjusted easily to one aspect of being out of school. He'd learned in jail to study independently: read, digest, write, and read some more.

Chop wood, carry water. He remembered Dr. Greenspan's words—and his explanation. They were Zen Buddhist shorthand for "Focus on the work in front of you, and do the best, next thing."

Chop wood. Carry water.

Read history. Do math. Math was trickier than his other subjects and much less self-explanatory.

Read history. Wait for math tutor.

Read books. Coach at the Y.

Jason read Ralph Ellison, Derrick Bell, and Toni Morrison. He had to set aside *The Bluest Eye*, though. Donald "Harry" Varken from the jail—and what the man had done to his own little niece—haunted Jason.

May he rot in hell. How could anyone hurt an innocent child?

Jason memorialized Varken's niece, whose name he did not know, every time he thought of her uncle. *Wherever you are now, little girl, you didn't deserve it.* He wasn't sure he believed in a literal heaven, but he pictured a rosy-cheeked, blond, little white girl there anyway, swinging on a tire swing, happy.

He realized Varken's victim was about the same age as the boys he coached at the YMCA. Jason relished his time herding the young basketball players, the Teal Cats. They helped him forget himself, and they reminded him to laugh.

"Like this, Coach Jason? Like this?" Xavier was the funniest of all with his sporadic, un-rhythmic dribbling.

Jason's face lit up with memories of himself at age nine, a hapless dribbler. He went over to the child. "Let me show you, Xavier. See, you've got to give a bounce for every step you take. Bounce, step, bounce, step. You try it."

The boy muttered the sequence under his breath, finding his own awkward rhythm.

"Who's the best, Coach?" Little Rodney asked, clamoring for attention.

"You know the answer," Jason said, eyes never leaving Xavier.

"Yeah, yeah, yeah." Rodney rolled his eyes. "It doesn't matter. We're a team."

◈

The only chance Jason had to interact with kids his own age was an occasional evening pickup game, once the parents had collected their grade-school children. He hadn't seen or talked to Brendan since the day outside of their math classroom.

I'll call him one of these days, Jason thought, shaking his head as if to shake away the memory of the school bathroom, his bloody knuckles, and his dim reflection in the steel plate that passed for a mirror.

Not today, though. Not yet.

◈

Sometimes, the thought of…everything still made Jason want to scream.

"It's normal," Dr. Greenspan had told him. "But I promise you, that feeling is going to shrink as you get on with your life. Imagine it fading into to the background, like a dream. When you feel it, take a few deep breaths. Feel it come on; take the time to hear what it is saying to you. Breathe through it, and watch it drift away. Then power forward to the best, next thing."

Jason inhaled as he considered the best, next thing. Classwork. Coaching.

"You can tell that awful feeling to shut up, you know. Anytime you want," Doc had told him.

"Devil, get thee behind me," Jason had said.

"What?" Dr. Greenspan asked, laughing. "I haven't heard that one, but I like it."

"I've heard it all my life, Doc. Pretty sure it's a church-lady thing."

"Devil, get thee behind me. Perfect."

◈

Breathe in. Breathe out.

Chop wood. Carry water.

Check mirrors. Start car.

At least Jason was beginning to learn to drive. "When do I get out of the parking lot, Dad?"

"How about next Saturday morning?" his father had answered.

"That's what you said *last* Saturday."

Alvin then launched into his a-car-is-a-deadly-weapon speech.

Oh, Lord. Here we go again.

"Jason." The lecture continued. "You, of all people, should know it only takes a split second for a tragedy to occur."

Breathe in. Back out.

◈

Life had changed in a heartbeat for Jason on the day of his arrest. Everything changed again on September 11, and then again when Kim left school and went to Colorado to be with her mom. He hadn't seen Kim since the night of his release, right before Thanksgiving, 2002.

Her mom died the following January.

After Kim moved, he wrote to her at least every other week. They spent a lot of time on the phone, too, during her mother's last few weeks.

"I'm here for you, Diamond Girl."

"I know it. Thank God for you, Enno."

Jason ached to see her, but he pushed the sadness away, which made him think of Jay-Z, who let his music do his weeping.

Don't open that floodgate, Jason told himself. *I get it, Jay-Z. If I let one tear fall, I just might drown.*

After her mom died, Kim planned to remain in Colorado to help her dad. Maybe when things settled down a bit, he'd take them up on their invitation to come visit.

Our timing's bound to be right, one of these days.

❖

In the meantime, Jason held steady—even as the world flipped itself upside down once more on March 20, 2003. President George W. Bush had declared war on Iraq.

Jason didn't watch the TV coverage of Operation Desert Storm— it was way too real to him. He knew he'd have to register for the draft in five months—yet one more fact of his bitter reality that made him want to scream.

Giving up nearly two years of my life wasn't enough?
Breathe in. Breathe out.
Chop wood. Carry water.
Read books. Do math.
At least I'll graduate on time.

Thanks to his dad, Jason was on track to get his diploma in May 2004. Alvin had insisted that he continue through hospital homebound for his English and advanced mathematics classes, but he completed most of his other credits independently, through Florida Virtual School. College brochures filled the Royals family mailbox. The outcome of the civil trial might have an impact on whether he'd go to a private university or a public one.

Eyes on the prize, he thought without wincing, resuming the mantra of his fifteen-year-old self. *The little things add up to the big things.*

CHAPTER 71

"A Junkie? Really?"

Detective Sergeant John Marshall looked at the message on his desk. It was from Pershing. His old partner must have called while Marshall was in Orlando retrieving an armed-robbery fugitive. Marshall had garnered some good publicity, smiling in the newspaper photo as he brought back the cuffed suspect to stand trial.

He was still biding his time in the Fugitives and Warrants division, waiting to transfer full time to the Police Athletic League. The question was when to do it. Part of him wanted to make sure no further allegations would emerge regarding the events of the day he had spent with Jason Royals. The other part wanted to speed up the process, before the suit settled, before PAL had a chance to reject Marshall's application—but he knew they could always reject him later.

He stopped himself from reliving the afternoon in the woods.

It couldn't have been me that bruised him. Could it? He was such a little lightweight.

The review board had sided with Marshall. The board had cleared Pershing as well.

No matter how much he dreaded returning Pershing's call, he needed to get it done. Never mind that the two hadn't spoken for months—since before he had betrayed his homicide partner from the witness stand.

Damn defense attorney.

His ex-partner answered the phone on the first ring.

"Pershing?" Marshall said.

"Hey, buddy. I was wondering when you were going to call me back."

"Oh, I figure I've owed you a phone call for a long time, man. And," Marshall sighed before continuing, "I also owe you an apology, for what I said on the stand during the Royals hearings."

Pershing was quiet for a minute, and then he said, "I wasn't going to bring it up, Sergeant." An awkward silence engulfed them.

They both started speaking again at the same time, and Marshall stopped.

"You first," Pershing insisted.

"Okay. Well...I'm sorry. I need you to know I never doubted you. I know you wouldn't hurt a suspect intentionally—I know this about you, Rick. It's the way the phrasing came out, the way the attorney had me cornered. I should have had more presence of mind, man. I should've gone to bat for you better than I did."

"I appreciate hearing that. I do. But we're square, John. Don't give it another thought. We've all been there with defense attorneys."

"Yeah, well, we have now. Pretty sure Aaron Hampton was my first."

Pershing chuckled. "Hampton. Yeah, well, you got burned by the best." Pershing was quiet for a moment before saying, "Hey, did you hear about O'Donnell?"

"Yeah. Good riddance. I hear his past came back to haunt him— some citizen complaints. Minor disciplines add up. He was smart to resign—lucky he didn't lose his pension."

"Isn't it amazing how bad police can fall through the cracks—for years?"

"It's the old-boy network. Still alive and kicking."

"I agree. I agree. Just don't lump me in with those old boys, all right, Sarge?"

"Nah. You're good police, Rick. I'm thankful the review board could see it, too. They can see the difference between us and... ahem...O'Donnell."

"I guess you heard the federal judge dropped us from the suit," Pershing said.

"Well, yeah, as private individuals, anyway. As long as the department is facing trial, though, I'm going to feel like I am, too," Marshall said.

"I feel you. It might help you to know your old LT says not to worry. He's seen a lot of these cases. He says it's all on the city now.

But I didn't call you to talk about all that crap."

"Okay…"

"Actually, I take it back. It's sort of related to the crap at hand."

Marshall chuckled. "What's up?"

"You remember the victim, Betty Patterson?"

"Sure."

"Vice found her wallet in a trap house two nights ago. They busted it up when an undercover encountered a woman—an addict—who tried to trade her three-month-old baby for smack."

"Jesus." Marshall closed his eyes for a moment before asking, "How's the baby?"

"Okay, as far as I know. Department of Children and Families has her. Her mama's in jail."

"Thank God," Marshall said. *God keep that child. Probably born addicted.*

"Anyway, we found some prints, and something else. You're not going to believe—"

"What?"

"The gun. We're still waiting on ballistics, but it's a nine."

"You think it's the murder weapon? What about prints on the gun?"

"We ran 'em. They're a match for the prints on the wallet. It turns out we've already got the guy on a possession charge." Pershing paused and then added, "Heroin."

Marshall's jaw dropped. "A *junkie* murdered Betty Patterson?"

"We're still waiting on ballistics, like I say, but yeah. Looks that way."

"Since when do junkies do gang-style robbery-murders?" Marshall wondered aloud.

"I said the exact same thing. Weird, isn't it?"

"Very weird. I mean it could've been a straight-up robbery-homicide. He could've been speed-balling. But would he have the mental wherewithal to execute a woman in cold blood?"

"You're starting to sound like a defense attorney, Sergeant."

Marshall let out a sigh. "Yeah."

"But, hey, we can only go where the evidence takes us, right?"

Marshall frowned, thinking about the guys in Vice, picturing the underworld of guns and narcotics and three-month-old babies in drug houses. "Where was this house, anyway?"

"Less than a mile away from the motel. Smack dab in the middle of the College Lifers' territory. It's at the edge of an older neighborhood—they said it was boarded up, grass growing high. Neighbors have been calling for months. You know the drill—people coming and going all hours of the day and night. The BRPD finally shut it down."

"Just in time to save a baby," Marshall said.

"Save a baby. Solve a murder. Pretty good day for Vice."

"And the journalists can't report it because they can't break Vice's cover."

"Chapter one-nineteen, Florida statutes. Vice won't be returning any media phone calls. And the reporters are not going to hear anything from anyone else in the department. But the news will break once the ballistics report comes back. And we can guess how Royals' lawyer is going to spin it."

"Yeah." Marshall thought for a beat and then said, "Because now we supposedly have the real murderer. It argues for Royals' innocence. I'll need to give Ziggy a heads up."

"Yep. I'll be calling my guy, too. We should let the lawyers deal with the city on this."

"I agree. Hey, Pershing?"

"Yeah?"

"What's the junkie's name? The one whose prints—"

"Demarius Williams."

"If I'm in town when you get around to talking to him, you mind if I tag along?"

"You got it. I'll give you a ring when I get it set up."

"Thanks, man." John Marshall hung up the phone.

A junkie? Really?

CHAPTER 72

Color of Law

Jason sat in Hampton's office during one of his biweekly visits. He was there to check in and to talk about the civil lawsuit. Two months after Jason's release from jail, Hampton had filed a Section 1983 Claim, which said people who were acting under the color of law—that is, people who represented the government—had violated Jason's civil rights. The civil lawsuit, unlike the criminal case, would be heard in federal court.

"Color of law, huh?" Jason repeated the new legal phrase he'd learned. "More like 'law of color,' if you ask me."

"Hmph. I like that," Hampton said. "I think I'm going to steal it, if you don't mind."

"Go ahead. The law of color is still running us."

"Until we enforce the Constitution."

"Yes, sir." Jason absorbed Hampton's confidence and admired his certainty. "Hey, Hamp?"

Hampton tilted his chin upward, ready to listen.

"Speaking of the Constitution, when do I get to tell those cops how their stupidity screwed up my life?"

Hampton raised his eyebrows and tapped the air with his index finger before speaking. "The important question is," Hampton spoke slowly, "what evidence can we produce to show the damages they've caused you? We're in the process of gathering that evidence."

"So, I don't get to tell them what they've done to me?"

"Not exactly. But here's what you can do. When you have some spare time at home, write a letter to the police officers—all of them, each of them. Use as much venom and bile as you want, because these letters won't ever be sent. You bring them in to me and we'll go through them, to make sure we've covered our bases as to damages. I want to know every way this affected you—in jail, since jail, in school, out of school—everything. Write it for yourself and for me, and we'll make sure they know, but we'll do it in a manner befitting the dignity of the aggrieved party at law."

Aggrieved. That's one word I don't have to look up. I'm living it.

During his visits, Hampton encouraged Jason to read the court documents from the civil lawsuit. "Pleadings," they were called: The Complaint. Request for Discovery. Response to City's Motion to Dismiss. Notice of Deposition.

Hampton was doing everything he could to avoid a trial in their civil lawsuit. The attorney wasn't afraid of the courtroom, he told Jason—quite the opposite, as Jason saw with his own eyes during the criminal, pre-trial hearings. A good settlement, however, would save attorneys' fees all around, and Hampton explained that the last thing the Beau Rêve police department wanted was years more publicity on a police brutality case.

The law, Jason had learned, always seemed to move at a snail's pace—even without a full-blown trial.

Hampton had warned Jason about counting his chickens before they hatched, but he also told him he needed to consider what he wanted in life—with or without a nice settlement.

Jason had given some thought to opening a retail sports business with his Uncle Mack, and, of course, he wanted to pay his parents and grandparents back for what they spent defending him. He also thought about buying a house, if he were to win, and about how far his new house might be from the various state universities to which he'd applied.

Mostly, he thought about empowering himself with an education no one could ever take away from him. His dad was right: the most important kind of enfranchisement is the kind that happens in your mind, even if it did mean four years of college and three more years of law school. He planned to do everything he could to protect younger kids from ever having to go through what he did—his little brother, his little cousin, his little basketball players—every boy he knew.

Every Black one, anyway.

Yeah, I know about the color of law. It's white. Until otherwise enforced.

Bubbling Up

Over dinner at home with Veronica, Marshall shared the news about the arrest in the Patterson case. The leftover pot roast tasted as good as the original meal. He loved when it was her turn to cook, and he loved it even more when she cooked enough to make leftovers.

"So, you're telling me," she said, setting down her fork, "what looked like a gang jump-in turned out to be a junkie, out of his mind, coming down?"

"It appears so. But who knows what those gang vermin are capable of?" Marshall's arms rose and fell in an I-give-up gesture. "Williams probably spends half his life high on heroin. It wouldn't be too hard to pin something like this on a junkie."

"Hmph."

"It'd be a nice stab at the police, too, with this civil suit still out there. Now that the police can supposedly solve the murder, Royals gets exonerated."

She wrinkled her forehead. "You think the College Lifers read the papers?"

"They at least watch TV. I wouldn't put anything past them."

"Is it possible Royals is part of it? Could he be planning to kick back part of the lawsuit settlement to the Lifers?"

He raised his eyebrows, considering the possibility for the first time. "Nah." He shook his head. "I wouldn't give them too much credit." His shoulders fell. "But, then again, I don't know. I obviously don't know very much about a lot of things, anymore."

"John," she whispered, reaching across the table to take his hand. "You know you didn't do anything wrong."

"There's a judge who'd disagree with you."

She narrowed her eyes, resolute. "The circumstances were extraordinary. It's not your fault. You saved Royals' life, remember?"

He nodded.

"You heard the confession expert. Lots of people confess to crimes they didn't commit. All the time. *Without* coercion."

Marshall stared into his iced tea as if it held the secrets of the universe. After a moment, he looked back at her. "Did I ever tell you," he asked, swishing his bread around in the au jus on his plate, "about Yoda?"

"Yoda?" she chuckled. "The green guy from *Star Wars*?"

"One and the same. Yes."

She laughed. "What on God's green earth are you talking about?"

"I'm talking about Jason Royals' correspondence with his little girlfriend while he was in jail. Kirk showed it to me. The girl drew him a valentine with Yoda on it."

Veronica wrinkled her nose in question, holding up her hands. "And?"

"And…what kinds of kids draw Yoda valentines?"

"So, you're saying that gangbangers don't send valentines?"

"When you put it like that…yeah. That's exactly what I'm saying." He shook his head. "But I really don't know what they do. When I was in school, I was busy at ball practice or mowing lawns or washing cars at my dad's lot. I didn't have time to get into trouble."

"You were fortunate, John." Veronica bit her lip and then said, "I went to school with a lot of poor kids. No one was there to teach them how to play ball or wash cars. They never learned how to take one step at a time on anything…they only saw what other people had and were angry at being have-nots."

"Sounds like my *clientele*," he said, sighing. He rose from the table, gathering the dishes.

"Hey—don't underestimate the effects of being poor," she said, following him to the sink with their tea glasses. "I mean dirt poor. I mean the kind of poor where you can't fix anything in your house. You can't fix your car, if you even *have* a car. And if you do have one, and you manage to fix it, you can't afford insurance. Not that any of it matters because you can't even afford to renew your tag, anyway."

She dumped the glasses into the sink as if to punctuate the point. "I'm talking about the washing-machine's-broken-but-you're-out-of-gas-and-money-so-you-can't-get-to-the-laundromat kind of poor," she said. "And you're praying the electricity and water stay on so you can hand-wash your underwear."

"Ooh," he said, wincing again as he let the water run hot. "I can't imagine."

She looked at him, nodding. She'd let out little bits and pieces of her childhood over time, but he knew he hadn't heard the half of it—not yet.

"But you turned out okay," he said.

"Did I?" Veronica stared at him. "I'm not poor anymore. But last time I checked, I'm still Black."

Marshall looked at her. "Me, too. And this junkie. And this kid suing the department."

"And," Veronica nodded, "a disproportionate number of your *clientele*, as you so lovingly call them."

"Yes."

"Yeah, well, my granddaddy taught me to work within the system to make lasting change," she said. "But sometimes I think we might need something more...*direct*. Less apologetic. We need to stop giving a damn about what the white world thinks. Make waves. Tell the ugly truth. The civil rights movement left a lot of unfinished business...the racism never went away. Look at the 2000 elections."

"I remember."

"Twenty-thousand ballots up in Jacksonville, John. From Black neighborhoods. Thrown out."

"I know, Vee. Wasn't that long ago." He sponged down the table.

"We think we've come so far, but it's still out there, you know? It's like I can feel something bubbling up." She joined him at the sink. "I feel like the kids—not all kids, but a lot of young Black men, especially—they can sense it. It's in the air."

He plunged his hands into the hot, soapy water and scrubbed one of the plates. "I just hate being part of anything that makes me look like I'm on the wrong side of history." He brought the dish up and examined it, running his fingers over its surface, before handing it to her.

"Baby, we work for a system so drenched in racism it's hard to even see it." She rinsed the plate, then turned to face him. "It's built in, John. You know that. It's in most of our neighborhoods—the redlining, the white flight. The green flight, and you know I'm not talking about trees. So, our Black neighborhoods are naturally going to be magnets for the police. I'm not excusing criminal behavior—I'm just saying it raises the odds of things going wrong.

"But, you've got to remember, you made the call that saved that kid's life—gang member or not. And now you're going to go save other kids' lives in ways you can't yet imagine."

Marshall scrubbed the other plate, without meeting her eyes, and gave it to her to rinse.

CHAPTER 74

Avalanche

It's a weird time to go running.

He had wanted to get up earlier. Jason was alone in the house, and he was mad at himself because the clear, bright summer morning was melting into noon.

Willing himself to the sofa, sneakers in hand, he vowed to do his run before eating breakfast—or, rather, lunch.

In jail for eighteen months, and what do I do when I'm finally free? Sleep.

Disgusted, Jason shoved one foot into an unyielding, still-tied shoe. *Pathetic. Truly pathetic.* He pulled the shoe off and set it on his lap to undo the lace.

He heard Dr. Greenspan's words in his head: "Baby steps. Start small, and build up from there."

Chop wood. He put on and tied shoe number one. *Carry water.* He reached for the other. Shoes tied and ready to go, he was looking for his keys when the phone rang.

"Turn on the TV, Jason." His mother was a little breathless on the other end of the line. "Right away, honey. Turn it on now."

"Why?" Jason walked over and switched it on, waiting for the image to appear.

"Channel 3," she said.

"Wh—?"

The "crime" graphic popped up on the TV—a spinning police light. He backed up a little to see it better.

"And again, we have breaking news this hour. The Beau Rêve Police Department has arrested a new suspect in the 2001 murder of a Georgia tourist."

"They caught him?" Jason's voice went high. *Holy shit.*

"Shh. Listen."

"Fifty-eight-year-old Betty Patterson was shot dead at the Vacation Station Inn on April 29, 2001," the anchorman said.

Tell me something I don't *know.*

"Police arrested fifteen-year-old Jason Royals near the scene, but prosecutors could not make their case against the juvenile defendant, and all charges were dismissed."

The juvenile defendant? Sheesh.

"Now, police say twenty-four-year-old Demarius Lee Williams…"

Those were the last words Jason heard. His eyes were glued to a mug shot of the suspect on the screen.

"Mama! It's Skeleton Man!"

"What? What are you—?"

"Don't you remember? I told you about him!"

"You told me about a skeleton man?"

"I told you about the guy on drugs in the jail. Remember? How they had to carry him out in the middle of the night because he was screaming?"

"The man who was detoxing. Yes. I—Jason, is that him on TV?"

"Yeah! I could never forget *his* face. He was in the jail at the same time I was. I can't believe he's the killer, Mama. I can't believe they had him for all this time and—"

"I know, baby. Shh. Listen."

For a moment, Jason stopped breathing. He backed up some more and sat down on the couch. *Skeleton Man. They think it was Skeleton Man?* He listened closely to the news story.

"Police say they've had Williams in custody for several months, but he's spent most of that time in the hospital for drug abuse and related medical issues. After Williams was sent back to jail last month, he allegedly confessed to another inmate.

"Today, police refused to answer any specific questions about their investigation into Williams' involvement in the motel murder. Tomorrow morning, they will hold a press conference. Eyewitness News will be on hand live."

"I can't believe it, Mama." Jason's heart was pounding. "I mean *I* know I didn't do it, but I never thought they'd get the real killer. They screwed up the case so badly." He was too agitated to sit. He got up and started pacing.

They had him since at least last September. And I still had to go through all those hearings in court?

His mother was saying something, but Jason didn't hear what. He was pacing faster, veins throbbing at his temples. Jason grabbed a pillow and squeezed it, and then he started hitting the couch with it.

"Jason, are you there? Are you all right?"

"I'm here." He threw the pillow across the room, knocking a framed photo off the end table. It clattered to the floor.

Shit.

"Should we call Hamp?" she asked him.

Jason walked over to the toppled photo. The glass had shattered. He started picking up the pieces, piling them onto the bare photograph, setting it all on the table. Two plump, little-boy faces stared back up at him through the wreckage, smiling.

"Hamp could help us find out if this is for real or not," Clarice explained.

Oh, no, don't tell me this is not for real. Do not tell me that. This has to be for real. It's gotta be. "I'll call him right now," Jason said.

"I'm happy to do it, sweetheart, if you like. I know you've been through so—"

"I got it, Mama." His tone was curt but he wanted to hear about the arrest from Hampton. *How could this not be for real? Or if it is, how do I know the police didn't violate Skeleton Man's rights, too?*

"Okay, sweetie. Call me back as soon as you know anything."

"Will do." He hung up the phone and walked toward the kitchen to get the broom and dustpan. He didn't get two steps away before the phone rang again.

"Jason, it's Katrina. Did you hear the—"

"Yeah! Is it true, Katrina?"

"Yeah, we believe the confession is real, Jason. Hamp is getting ready for a hearing, but he wanted me to call you to let you know we're trying to get a handle on what happened. The police have found a gun in a house where Williams used to shoot up. We want to see the ballistics report."

"How long will it take to get it?"

"Good question. I don't know, but we've got a connection down at the state attorney's office. We hope he can tell us what's what."

"It would be nice if it were true, huh?"

"Yes, it would. On so many levels. Are you going to be around for a while? Can I call you back?"

"I'll be back in ten minutes," he said. "I was getting ready to go run before I found out about this. Now I feel like I could run a hundred miles!"

"I bet." Katrina laughed. "When you get back, sit tight and I'll call you as soon as I can."

"Will do."

"And Jason?"

"Yes ma'am?"

"When you go on your run, stay away from Broward Highway."

Jason snorted. "Yeah, right, Broward Highway. Like I'm going to run there."

When her meaning dawned on him, he relaxed into a chuckle but then stiffened as nausea swirled upward to his chest.

The two said goodbye, and Jason hung up the phone and took a few deep breaths. In a flash, he was back on the pavement in the parking lot on Broward Highway, watching the traffic and the sky twirl around him.

Breathe in. Breathe out.

The room's spin began to slow.

Like getting off a merry-go-round.

CHAPTER 75

Splash

On a late-July day in 2007, Jason stood on his back patio, behind the home he'd bought the year before. He heeded Hampton's advice and bought a simple, three-bedroom house in a family-oriented neighborhood, instead of going hog wild like many clients do, mistaking substantial legal settlements for outrageous lottery winnings.

The police had arrested their second suspect in the Patterson murder in 2003, but it took another year to settle Jason's civil suit. In the fall of 2004, he began college at "The Brick," the local students' name for Beau Rêve Community College. Jason figured it would be a low-key way to complete his first two years, giving him time to figure out how to best invest his settlement.

After repaying his family for the cost of his criminal defense, he bought and renovated a building for the sporting goods store he and his Uncle Mack would then operate together, while taking a couple of business courses at The Brick. Once the store opened, he bought the house. He transferred from BRCC to a state university to finish college, which was an hour's commute each way from his new home. Jason treated college like a job—leaving home early and working steadily around his classes, from eight a.m. to six p.m. three days a week.

His days at both school and work were long and exhausting, but he was investing in his education—and in his future.

"You'll never regret the hard work you do while you're young," his dad always told him.

Smiling, he watched his relatives enjoying his back yard. He still couldn't believe the slice of suburbia—complete with a nice little in-ground pool—belonged to him. The sight of Lucas sneaking a beer jolted him from his reverie.

"You'd better not let Mama catch you drinking," Jason said, approaching his brother.

Lucas drained the beer bottle. "You're not going to *tell* her, are you?"

"As long as I don't see you drink any more of them, and as long as you don't get behind the wheel, then yeah, we're good." He took the bottle away from the teenager and dropped it in the recycling bin.

Lucas's shoulders slumped and Jason shook his head, suppressing a grin. He thought for a moment about Lucas's more typical childhood, the high school years minus the incarceration.

As he approached his twenty-second birthday, Jason realized he was too young to settle down. Buying the house had put his life on fast forward—and he wrestled with the urge to rewind.

The pressure was beginning to fissure around the edges of his life, particularly in his relationship with Nikki, an extraordinarily beautiful girl he'd met at The Brick. The first time Lucas met her, he was equally enamored.

"Damn, Jason. Nikki could be Beyoncé's twin!"

After Jason and Nikki passed the six-month mark in their relationship, he began getting questions from his family about whether they planned to get engaged. Even though he'd never had a girlfriend in high school, he found the nature of adult dating relationships got serious, fast.

Nikki insisted she wasn't in any hurry to get officially engaged. Hurrying wasn't in her nature. She was running late, as usual, to Jason's cookout. Nikki was sure about where she wanted to get married, though, when the time came. She wanted a church wedding. On that point she would not budge. It was an issue about which his mother tried to have a say, earlier that day, when the subject of Nikki came up.

Why couldn't I just keep my mouth shut? I shouldn't have mentioned to Mama that I don't ever want to get married in a church. I'm years away from all that anyway. He grabbed a beer from the cooler and popped off the bottlecap. *I shouldn't have said all that stuff about not believing in God.*

Oh, Lord, here she comes. She is not going to let this go.

Cold water splashed across the patio from the pool. It soaked Jason's entire side as he lifted the ice-cold beer bottle to his lips. Worse, his mother was drenched. His twelve-year-old cousin, the offending splasher, surfaced and swam farther away from the patio where the adults were standing.

"Cam, you'd better watch where you are jumping!" Clarice warned her nephew. Do you hear me?"

Cam kept swimming away from Clarice and Jason, pretending not to hear.

"Cam! Stop splashing the grownups with your cannonballs, son! We don't *do* that!" Clarice's voice had escalated—a rarity for her. Jason knew his mother's frustration was with him, and not with the child in the pool.

"Cam? Did you hear your Auntie Clarice, son?" It was Uncle Mack's deep baritone.

Jason grinned. *Uh-oh, the kid is in trouble now—even though he did me a favor. Literally threw cold water on a conversation I do not want to have. What is it with these women?*

Jason walked over to the picnic table, grabbed some towels, and turned around to find his mother one step behind him.

"You don't get away that easily, Jason. We're not finished with our conversation from earlier."

"You mean the one about church weddings…and me being mad at a God I might not even believe in?" He handed her a towel.

Clarice dried her neck and arms and dabbed at her face. Her damp hair glistened in the sun. Waterlogged, she appeared smaller than usual, younger even. Jason caught a fleeting glimpse of his mother as—simply—a woman. He saw her, for a brief second, as someone he might have known from school, or as a customer walking into his store; he perceived her as the woman she was, maybe, before she became his mother.

"God can take your anger, son," she said. "But I have never heard you doubt the faith you were brought up in."

"Brought up in? Aw, come on, Mama, give me a break, will you? Even though you took us to church, and you taught us the ways of the Lord," Jason said, pronouncing "the ways of the Lord" in a mock-resonant preacher voice, arms outstretched, beer in hand.

"Lower your voice," Clarice bit back in a sharp whisper. She tugged him by the arm, leading him away from the picnic table where her own seventy-four-year-old mother sat. "What's come over you?" Clarice asked her son. "I've never seen you like this."

"Please, Mama. Let me have my agnostic thoughts, like you always let Daddy have his." Jason watched his mother's mouth fall open in stunned silence.

"Auntie Clarice," said a voice coming from behind her. Exasperated, she turned around. Her face softened when she saw the contrition on her nephew's face. "I'm sorry I splashed you and Cousin Jason," Cam said.

"I appreciate your apology, Cam." Clarice sighed. "You are forgiven. Watch better next time, okay?"

"Yes, ma'am," the boy replied. "I love your pool, Jason!" he yelled as he ran back to the pool and jumped in, ramrod straight—feet first, a splash-minimizing choice. Jason and his mother both laughed at the boy's antics.

"Hasn't been long since you were his age," Clarice said to her son. "You're all grown up now."

Jason began to respond, but Clarice raised her pointer finger to signal she wasn't finished. "I brought you into this world, so will you please do me the courtesy of hearing what I have to say to you, adult to adult?"

"Mama," Jason began, shaking his head.

Clarice took her son's cheeks in her hands, stilling his face. She had to stand on her tiptoes to reach him.

"Look here," she said. She fixed her eyes upwards, onto his, as she fiddled with his collar. "What kind of mother would I be, if I didn't tell you that my faith has helped me through some mighty difficult times? It helped me through that awful business from six years ago. And here you are, standing with me, in your beautiful backyard on this beautiful day and—well, I don't understand how you can't see God's hand in it."

To Jason, the mention of "that awful business" felt like a punch to the gut. At a loss for words, he looked over his mother's shoulder. His Grandpa Clarence was walking toward him with a metal cane. He was recovering well from his knee surgery.

"Clarice, I need to borrow your older son here, before your husband goes and burns down the neighborhood with the grill,"

Grandpa Clarence said, eyes twinkling.

Darned if the old man ain't coming to my rescue. Thank you, Grandpa.

"I'm done with him—for the moment," Clarice told her father, while looking at her son.

"Alvin," Grandpa yelled across the yard to his son-in-law, "just 'cause you went to school in Atlanta doesn't mean you have to re-enact Sherman's fire!"

CHAPTER 76

"Or What?"

Sunday mornings were among the rare times when both Jason and Mack were away from the store. It didn't open until one, and the help could unlock the doors and handle the business until Mack arrived. The men agreed—after Mack insisted—Jason would have Sundays off while school was in session.

"You need time to get your ducks in a row before classes get underway again on Mondays," Mack had said. "Your real job right now is college, Jason. Put your hours there first. We got it now to where the store practically runs itself, anyway."

"What about you? Don't you need a whole Sunday off, too?" Jason asked.

"I get Saturdays and Mondays and that's plenty. And it's slow enough on Sunday afternoons I can bring Cam in with me and give Brenda a break."

Some Sunday mornings, Mack joined his parents and his sister at church, as he had done all his life. But at least once a month—not before ten o'clock out of respect for the neighbors—the two men could be found in Jason's driveway shooting hoops.

"Oh, by the way," Mack said, dribbling before he sank a practice shot. "You know you got your mama worried about your eternal soul."

Jason laughed. "How 'bout you, Uncle Mack? You worried?"

"About your soul?" He grinned, bouncing a pass to Jason. "Hell, no. I'm more worried about your self-esteem, you know, because I'm about to kick your ass again."

Jason smiled as he launched his shot and then cursed as it bounced off the rim.

Mack caught the ball and shot it back to Jason. "You're in

basketball hell, anyway, son. Not even Jesus can help you."

"You done?"

"Let's see what you got."

Jason bounced the ball where he stood, aimed to shoot, reconsidered, and bounced again. Focusing, he shot the ball in a perfect arc to and through the basket—no backboard, no rim, all net. He smiled, satisfied. "We gonna play today, old man, or what?"

"Who you calling old man?" Mack smiled, ball in hand. "You were born older than I'll ever be." He passed fast and hard to Jason, and the two squared off, ball thumping and shoes shuffling amid periodic victory yells.

It was the one feature Jason missed from jail: the pure distraction of basketball, the total physical immersion that made him forget, if for only a little while, the reality of his life. He'd had a taste of it as a kid at the Y, all those years ago. He wondered if Xavier, Rodney, or any of the others he'd coached had stuck with it. Jason had never experienced the sheer joy of the game, the hard-driving push of it, until he was in jail. Mack, the one relative who didn't pressure him, brought it back to him on their Sunday mornings.

The older, stockier man headed toward the ice bucket in Jason's open garage, signaling he needed a break. "So, what'd you say to your poor sweet mama to torture her so, Jay?" He threw Jason a Gatorade and set out two lawn chairs.

Jason sat down next to his uncle. "I told her I was an agnostic."

"What the hell does that mean?"

"Agnostic? It means I believe in *something*, maybe like God, but I don't know exactly what. Not fairy tales. Not Santa Claus."

"Oh, Lord."

"Yeah, well…yeah. She looked at me like I had two heads. And then I got the same reaction from Nikki. She wanted me to go meet with her preacher about premarital counseling and…"

"And…?"

"And what?"

"Well, are you gonna go with her? You are getting engaged, right?"

Jason took a long swig of his Gatorade.

"Oh, Lord, Jason. You been dating this girl going on a year. You getting married? Or what?"

"Or what. Sheesh, Mack. I'm only twenty-two."

"Shit," Mack said quietly. "You dumped her?"

"More like she dumped me. She was patient at first. 'I'm on your time, Jason,' she'd say. Until she wasn't, and then she wanted an answer right then. Was I going to meet with her preacher or not? Am I a Christian man or am I not? Were we going to settle down together and raise our kids in Bethany Baptist, or not?" Jason drained the rest of his drink.

"Kids? She was talking kids?"

"Yeah. I mean, *future* kids. One day. But not with *her*. Not now."

"Is it something you can patch up? Or is she really gone?"

"I don't want to patch it up. I need the space, Uncle Mack. I spent a year and a half in jail for something I didn't do, then spent all the time since then on automatic pilot, doing what I'm *supposed* to do." Jason sighed. "Now all of a sudden, I've got a house, and a business—don't get me wrong, I'm thankful—but I'm not ready to have the rest of my life carved out for me. I don't know *what* I believe, and I'm tired of people telling me what I should or should not think."

"Then you definitely not ready for marriage, Jay, 'cause wives are real good at wanting to do your thinking for you."

Jason grinned. "You should know," he said, and then his grin dropped into a serious frown. "It's all I can do to deal with Mama right now." He leaned forward, elbows on his knees. Lacing his fingers together, Jason looked at his feet. "I'm not doing this to hurt her, but I don't know if I buy all the Jesus stuff. No one knows for sure what happens when you die. Why can't people be honest and say so?"

"Hmph." Mack grunted, and he grunted again before he spoke. "It's scary for people, Jason. Your mother is imagining a heaven without you in it."

"Why? Because I don't want to say her magic words to be in her Christian club?" Jason sat up. "What kind of God," he asked, animated, "if there is a God, keeps people out of heaven, if there is a heaven, on a trick question?

"Well," Jason continued, bellowing in a deep, grandiose God-voice, "'well, I gave you Jesus two thousand years ago when there was no electricity and no camcorders and people swear they saw him after he was dead, so that should be good enough for you.'" Jason scoffed, "What kind of God would expect such blind acceptance? Why would

He give us brains and still actually expect that?"

"Good questions," Mack answered, pursing out his lower lip. "But I'm the wrong person to ask."

"You believe in God, Uncle Mack?"

"Yeah, basically. It's not something I think about the way you do, Jason. God made me to throw balls and sell sporting goods. All I want is to live like a decent person and enjoy my life. Enjoy my *family*. Maybe there'll be something wonderful after it's over. What do I lose if I'm wrong and death is the end? I'll be too dead to care then."

"Well, what you just said makes more sense than anything I've ever heard in church," Jason said.

"The Gospel according to Saint Mack."

Jason laughed. "Hedge your bets on Jesus because there's nothing to lose?"

"Something along those lines," Mack said. "And in my second chapter there is a high commandment: Thou shalt not hurt thy sweet mother."

"I won't. As long as she leaves me alone about it."

"Well you don't expect me to tell her that, do you?"

"You're no Mack truck, Mack. You're a big chicken."

"When it comes to the women in my family, you bet your sweet ass I'm a chicken."

Jason erupted in a belly laugh that shook his whole body. Before he could compose himself, his uncle rose to leave.

"I gotta get my chicken-butt to your store," Mack said. "My boss is a real hard-ass. And an agnostic, too, so I hear."

Jason shook his head and kept laughing. Then, from his chair, he picked up the basketball and threw it at his uncle's backside as he walked away.

"Ow!" Mack yelled, feigning pain. "What'd I tell you? You gotta watch those damn agnostics every *minute*."

CHAPTER 77

The Prize

SPORTS-TOPIA.

Jason never tired of seeing the giant letters on the front of his store, or the massive solar array he had installed on the roof. None of it was cheap, but he wanted something he could be proud of every time he drove up. He even mailed a photograph of it to Kim in Aspen.

"Way to go, Enno!" she'd responded in an email. "Looks like you finally landed a paying job!"

Six years and four months after the Wellstein's job debacle, he had no trouble laughing at her joke. Maybe next summer, after he graduated, he'd take her up on her invitation to visit Colorado.

A man's got to keep his options open.

Jason parked away from the entrance as usual, leaving room for his customers. He and Mack were considering opening their second store in Beau Rêve, perhaps after he started law school. The sales numbers had been excellent over Labor Day weekend. Between back-to-school shoppers and preseason NFL enthusiasts, it was one of their highest-grossing weekends. When he drove up on that September, Tuesday morning, however, the business was quiet.

"Don't you have class today?" Mack said, as Jason came through the door. "Doc Ock and I have it covered. You don't need to be here."

"I know," Jason said. He waved to Octavius, who was hanging football jerseys on the rear wall of the store. "My morning class got canceled. I don't have to be in Gainesville until later this afternoon, but I'm going to grab my test-prep book and drive over there soon, anyway. I left it in the office."

Jason headed toward the back.

"How's it look, boss?" Octavius asked. He was hanging teal-and-black Jacksonville Jaguars jerseys. Number "28" was their most popular seller.

"They're not *all* Fred Taylor, are they?" Jason asked, joking.

"Naw," Octavius said, grinning.

"Let's put an extra-large away for Lucas for Christmas."

"Did he get his college applications done yet?"

"Not yet, but he's got a little time."

Octavius nodded. "You comin' up to the Jags game on Sunday?"

"You and Luc might have to go without me this time, O. I've got to make sure I survive this test."

"You're smart, Jay. Plus, Mr. Hampton been prepping you. You're gonna do fine."

"Thanks, man." Jason walked through the open door into the workroom. He shuffled through some spreadsheets he'd left next to the desktop computer. Underneath the papers, he found what he was looking for: his workbook of sample questions for the Law School Admissions Test. Practicing a few logic problems with Hampton had churned the gears in his brain.

◈

"You're learning to think like a lawyer," Hampton told him. "It's different from the way most people think," Hampton said. "You can't let your assumptions get in the way of the evidence right in front of you."

◈

Jason picked up the book, but before leaving, he couldn't resist taking another peek at his store. He walked up the carpeted steps leading to the tinted windows, which sat high on the back wall. Octavius moved in and out of Jason's field of vision, while Mack was greeting a man who had just walked in.

Mack and the customer struck up a conversation Jason could see but not hear. Jason watched as Mack glanced back toward the office door, and then upward to the windows, as if he knew Jason was there looking down at him. Next, Mack walked the customer to the football area. Jason deduced from where they stopped the man was shopping for shin guards. Leaving the customer there, Jason's uncle sped to the office as fast as he could walk without running.

"You okay, Jason?" Mack said, closing the door behind him.

"Yeah. Why wouldn't I be?"

Mack climbed up next to him on the steps. "You don't recognize him?"

Staring at the top of the customer's head, Jason said, "Kind of hard to see his face from this angle."

"Here's a hint: Police Athletic League."

It dawned on Jason who it was. "No way." He rapped his knuckles on the window casing, startling Octavius, who looked up.

Detective Sergeant John Marshall was shopping for shin guards in Sports-topia.

"He's on my turf now." Jason clenched his fists and started descending the stairs.

Mack grabbed his forearm. "Wait just a minute. You're not going down there."

"The hell I'm not." Jason tore free of his uncle's grasp.

Mack ducked underneath him and shifted, popping up between Jason and the office door. "You're gonna have to get through me first, son."

"You need to move out of my way, Uncle Mack. I've got some things I need to say to that man."

"What are you going to say to him that $2.1 million hasn't said already?"

Jason backed up a bit, pointing to the other side of the door. "Damn it, Mack. That man ruined my life."

"So? What? You're going to go beat up on him now?"

Jason sighed. "You know me better than that."

"Do I? You look like you're ready to knock him out with one punch."

Jason sneered, "Yeah, that's me." He shook his head. "Me and my thug ways, you know."

"Ain't gonna do you no good to go out there and start something, Jason. You've won it. You've got to let it go. Not for him, but for you."

"You don't know what he took from me, Uncle Mack. You have no idea."

"Oh, I have no idea?" Mack said, his face contorted in pain. "First of all, let's get one thing straight. It wasn't only about you." Mack's voice began to crack with emotion. He lowered it to an urgent whisper, pointing his finger in anger. "It damn near broke your mama and daddy—don't you forget."

Jason sighed and lowered his eyes. After a moment, he looked at his uncle again and nodded.

"Second of all, and you better listen, because I'm only going to say this once. Everybody knows what happened to you was wrong, Jason, but you can't go back in time. You can't." Mack pointed to his knee, the one he busted years before on the field. "I can't go back, either. Neither can Octavius, and God knows he deserved better. No one gets to go backwards. None of us."

Jason hung his head.

"And you wouldn't want to, even if you could," Mack said.

Jason thought for a minute. Wouldn't he, though? If he could go back in time, wouldn't he change everything? For starters, he wouldn't have talked to the police—any of them. He wouldn't have tried to cooperate. He would have called their bluff and demanded an attorney. Maybe, if he'd done those different things, that horrendous day six years before would not have happened.

Then again, in their town, with those cops, he probably would have sat in jail, anyway. Or different things might have happened. People screw up; innocent people get hurt. People still get hurt even when it's no one's fault—like Kim's mom. He'd never know what might have been.

Time only moves in one direction.

"Now," Mack said. "I'm going to walk out there and ring up this detective, so Octavius doesn't foul up the damn cash register again. He still needs a little help ringing up customers, you hear?"

Jason couldn't help but laugh. "Yes, sir. He sure does."

"So, are you going to come out with me, quietly, and walk calmly out the front door? Or will you please stay back here until Detective Sergeant Thug-catcher leaves?"

"I'll hang back a few minutes." Jason grinned. "Thug-catcher, huh? TC for short."

"The man has no idea the trouble I saved him. No idea."

Jason couldn't keep from chuckling. "Go on, Uncle Mack." *And while you do, I'm going to watch.*

Jason traversed the steps again. He observed as his uncle met Octavius and John Marshall at the checkout counter. Looking down at the book in his hands, Jason hugged it to his chest and exhaled. He let go of the emotion he'd been holding onto and looked at the facts right in front of him: The store was his business. He'd made the Beau Rêve Police Department pay for their mistakes, and he was going to dedicate his life to keeping police officers like John Marshall in line. Moving forward was what mattered.

He walked down the steps, book in hand, opened the door, and exited his office. He strolled through his store and over to his cash register, where the detective who had once tried to break him was handing his uncle a credit card.

Keep on paying, he thought, as he stopped at the counter to get a look at Marshall's face. He was tempted to engage the man. He wondered whether, if he stood there long enough, Marshall would recognize him.

"Bye, Jason!" Octavius said, oblivious to the fact that Mack was holding his breath.

John Marshall looked up, his eyes shifting from Octavius to Jason.

Jason watched the detective's face as puzzlement sharpened into recognition. The detective's eyes met his.

"If I don't see you before your test," Octavius said, "good luck."

Jason held his gaze on the detective for a beat longer, and then he looked at his friend. "Thanks, man. I appreciate it," he said, and he walked out of the store.

The crisp breeze was unusual for early September. He'd heard on the radio that a cool front was keeping Tropical Storm Gabrielle well off the coast of Florida. Jason looked up, seeing not a cloud in the sky.

From the corner of his vision, a blur of black caught his eye. As he turned to look, he could see the raptor was clutching a large fish, it claws piercing flesh as it flew toward a giant nest at the top of a nearby pine. Jason looked around him, realizing the bird must have flown from Mirror Creek, a tributary of the mighty St. Johns. Between two black wings, a flash of white appeared.

Is that a bald eagle? With the sun in his eyes, it was hard for Jason to be certain.

As awestruck as a little boy, he squinted, hoping to catch another glimpse of the creature's white crown. He tracked the bird as it delivered its prize to its babies, marveling at the thought of it reaching down to pluck its prey from the dark waters. Jason smiled the satisfied smile of a twenty-two-year-old man with a purpose. Holding his shoulders back, walking to his car, he felt a little taller.

He remembered the blessing his mother gave him—her own version of the bible verse—recited a thousand times over the course of his childhood. Upon seeing the magnificent bird, recalling it was as effortless as breathing.

"You are my beloved child," he said aloud, "in whom I am well pleased."

Just because I'm agnostic, he thought, glancing toward the sky, *doesn't mean I have no soul.*

THE END.

ACKNOWLEDGEMENTS

Seen would not have been possible without the support and guidance of numerous individuals, starting with my husband, Tad, without whom, nothing. To Buddy, Maia and Carter, thank you for sharing your mother with the people of Beau Rêve.

Thank you, John Boles, for your years of tutelage, patience, and encouragement, and most of all, for your editing skills. To Judith Erwin, Jason wouldn't be here without you. Over years of writers' workshops, I benefitted from interacting with innumerable classmates, whom I now thank. Special thanks to Keith Gockenbach and Michael Heubeck.

John Meeks, your insights, suggestions and help were invaluable, as is your friendship. Devin Coleman, with every conversation, you continue to amaze me. Thank you for all you've taught me. Thank you, Tim Gilmore, for your professor's perspective, your comma-crisis interventions, and your friendship. Thank you also for birthing the JaxbyJax Literary Festival, which continues to blaze the trail for local literary pioneers.

To my friend and constant cheerleader, Jim Minion, I can't wait until it's my turn to read yours. Damon Jameson, your perspective as a former police officer in Jacksonville helped me tremendously, and I'm thankful for our friendship. Melissa Morgan and Karen Sadler, a girl couldn't ask for better besties.

Very special thanks to Valarie Esguerra, for your unique spiritual validation of Jason's story. You nailed it.

To Jacksonville attorney Gray Thomas, thank you for generously sharing your essential expertise in criminal law, civil rights, and courtroom practice. Any mistakes in law or procedure are the fault of the writer, and not her legal adviser.

To artist and activist extraordinaire, Hope McMath, thank you for bringing your formidable talent to the cover of *Seen*, and for the exquisite vision you hold for our community.

Thank you, Darlyn Kuhn, book polisher and publishing midwife, for telling me when the book was ready to go, and to Brad Kuhn, whose wizardry made it happen. Brad and Darlyn, your creativity, faith, and work on behalf of Jax by Jax is a gift to our community and its writers.

Finally, Seen is a work of fiction inspired by true events in Jacksonville, Florida. Our city boasts a criminal defense bar whose members step up without hesitation to make justice happen, especially for our children.

May God continue to bless you and your clients in your important and honorable work.

ABOUT THE AUTHOR

Julie G. Delegal is a freelance journalist and author living in Jacksonville, Florida. Through her writing in Folio Weekly, Jacksonville Magazine, Florida Politics Online and other media, Julie has developed a reputation as an advocate for education and social justice. She is also "editor emeritus" at Delegal & Poindexter, P.A., for which she has written and edited for more than 25 years. She is the mother of three adult children.

Made in the USA
Columbia, SC
16 September 2021